Patrol to the Golden Horn

ALEXANDER
FULLERTON
PATROL TO THE
GOLDEN HORN

CANELO

First published in the United Kingdom in 1978 by Michael Joseph Limited

This edition published in the United Kingdom in 2019 by

Canelo Digital Publishing Limited
57 Shepherds Lane
Beaconsfield, Bucks HP9 2DU
United Kingdom

A CIP catalogue record for this book is available from the British Library.

Print ISBN 978 1 78863 410 6
Ebook ISBN 978 1 91159 152 8

Look for more great books at www.canelo.co

Printed and bound in Great Britain by Clays Ltd, Elcograf S.p.A.

Publisher's Note

This book includes some views and language on nationality and ethnicity that were common at the time in which it is set. The publisher has retained this terminology in order to preserve the integrity of the text.

Prologue

Mist curtained the exit from the straits, adding to the dawn a milky thickness that clung to the black water and allowed only sporadic glimpses of the land's outlines against a lightening sky, and the raiding ships came out through it like ghosts, grey-steel engines of destruction thrusting westward into the Aegean. The four destroyers which had escorted the big ships from Constantinople across the Marmara and through the winding, mine-sown Dardanelles were already invisible in the dark to starboard; Admiral von Rebeur-Paschwitz had detached them a few minutes ago, at five-thirty a.m., when by dead reckoning *Goeben*'s navigating officer had known that Cape Helles was abeam. The destroyers would sweep to the westward of Cape Helles now, and then if they drew a blank they'd turn and re-enter the straits while the more powerful ships pressed on in search of targets for their guns.

Goeben, battlecruiser, 23,000 tons and with a main armament of ten eleven-inch, led the four-funnelled cruiser *Breslau*. Both ships were closed-up at action stations, expecting at any moment to run into the British destroyer patrol which was known to haunt the approaches to the straits; and since any seaman knew that you could see over fog and under it but no distance through it, lookouts were stationed down on *Goeben*'s foc's'l and in the spotting positions on both mastheads. Seventy men manned each of the battle-cruiser's five twin-gunned turrets, and the guns were ready loaded.

Goeben's wake curved as she swung to port, leading her consort round to a south-westerly course which was designed to take them clear around certain barriers of mines that the British had laid for the precise purpose of interrupting such a raid as this. Before the attack on Mudros which was the main target of the sortie, those British patrol ships had to be found and eliminated.

'Our course is south sixty west, sir.'

'Thank you, captain.' Von Rebeur-Paschwitz's intention was to sweep south-west for about ten miles and then, if the patrol hadn't been encountered either by himself or by his destroyers west of Cape Helles, he'd turn north and search for them off the coast of Imbros, where in any case there'd be other prey for his guns, perhaps inside Cape Kephalo and certainly in Kusu Bay. He walked out to the wing of the battlecruiser's bridge and gazed astern, watched *Breslau* tucking herself neatly into the bigger ship's wake after the swing to port. Light was increasing now but the mist still trailed over them like a blanket: it was a blessing, an unhoped-for bonus to their chances of success by prolonging the element of surprise, but he knew that at any moment it could begin to lift and dissipate. His force was at this moment seven miles west of Kum Kale and five miles due north of Mavro Island; there was a British lookout station on Mavro, and the longer this course was held the closer *Goeben* would be getting to those British eyes. But the temptation to turn away and cut the corner had to be resisted, because of the risk of finding himself in mined water. The admiral wished, almost desperately, that his intelligence reports of the British minefields could have been more precise.

Nine minutes past six: he'd gone into shelter from the wind, leaning over the covered chart-table in the forefront of the bridge, to light his first cigar of the day.

He'd just emerged from under the canvas hood when he heard a shout from the young sailor who was manning the telephone from the foc'sl lookout: 'Mine, port bow!'

'Hard a-starboard—'

Goeben shuddered to the explosion. Black water leapt, cascaded across the bridge, a heavy stinking rain. Echoes of the crash still lingered ringingly; the captain was calling for reports from below. The bridge revolution indicators showed the admiral that his flagship hadn't slackened speed; nor had her course varied by as much as one degree. And reports were coming up from the compartments: damage was so slight that it could be ignored. The impact had been abreast the for'ard turret and thus against the eleven-inch-thick main armoured belt.

Von Rebeur-Paschwitz realised suddenly that he had a lit cigar between his fingers and that he'd been forgetting to smoke it. There was an inch-long cylinder of grey ash on the end of it. He drew pleasurably on the fragrance of the Havana leaf, enjoying simultaneously this proof of his flagship's contempt for British mines. Expelling smoke as her captain came to report to him on the inconsequential extent of the damage below decks, he remarked to him that Messrs Blohm and Voss of Hamburg certainly knew how to build ships.

Ten minutes later course was altered to due west, and after another ten minutes – at six thirty-two a.m., by which time it was considered that they'd come right around the perimeter of the mined area – to north, towards Imbros. Mist still shrouded them. It was like – he heard the navigator remark to the torpedo lieutenant – steaming through potato soup. Luck, von Rebeur-Paschwitz appreciated, was certainly on his side, and he decided to make the most of it while it lasted. Aerial reconnaissance twenty-four hours earlier had shown that two British monitors were lying at anchor in Kusu Bay: he ordered *Breslau* to push on ahead at her best speed in order to block any possibility of their escape.

Breslau's best speed was about twenty-two knots; *Goeben*'s only twenty. Both ships had been capable of better than twenty-seven when they'd entered service in 1912, but four years holed up at Constantinople without dry-dock or dockyard facilities had taken a natural effect.

At seven a.m. *Goeben* was five miles from the south coast of Imbros, roughly eight miles south-west of Cape Kephalo, and after a brief consultation over the chart the admiral ordered a four-point turn to starboard in order to skirt the island's south-east corner on a track that he reckoned would be well to the westward of the mine barriers. This north-east course was held until seven thirty-two, at which point the battlecruiser hauled round to port, to a northerly course that would take her exactly two miles off Cape Kephalo.

The mist was rising, at last. And the period of secrecy and silence was in any case about to be shattered by the thunder of the German guns. There was a wireless signal station on Kephalo, and it was to be *Goeberi*'s first target for destruction: a warm-up, a chance for the gunners to get their eyes in. As the great ship steamed up towards the point her five turrets swung smoothly under electric power and under directions passed from two armoured control-towers amidships. In the spacious turrets – there were no divisions inside, between the individual guns – men grinned at each other, delighted at this prospect, finally, of action.

'Fire!'

One gun in each of the five turrets had fired, recoiled. Five other guns were ready for the second salvo. Reload projectiles and charges came up on the hoists between the pairs of guns and were presented to the breeches on rocking trays: the charges were in brass cylinders and in two halves, each half weighing 140 lb. Fumes wreathed acrid from the breeches: projectiles and charges rushed in, impelled by wooden rammers with spring-coil heads. Breeches slamming shut... 'Fire!' The second salvo was right for line, but short. Range had to be adjusted: and as Cape Kephalo was almost abeam now it would be opening, increasing, from now on. There was a rate instrument in each turret, and also a rangefinder, all of them connecting to one central transmitting station.

'Fire!'

Over...

'Fire!'

Flame, black smoke, flying masonry and rock and earth...

'Check, check, check!'

The gunnery lieutenant reported to the bridge by telephone, 'Target destroyed, sir.'

'Very well.'

It had been easy: much too easy for anyone to expect congratulations. Two miles, 4,000 yards, was really point-blank range. And having whetted her appetite

Goeben now altered two points to port in order to run up past Kusu Bay.

Breslau, pushing on northwards to carry out the admiral's orders, had sighted a British destroyer. This was *Lizard*, and when the German sighted her she was about six miles to the nor'ard. *Breslau* gave chase, but *Lizard's* better speed enabled her to stay clear of the more heavily gunned ship; she was waiting to be joined by the other patrolling destroyer, *Tigress*, who had been some miles to the west and was now hurrying back to join her.

The monitors in Kusu Bay, *Lord Raglan* and *M.28*, were shortening-in their cables and trying to raise steam; but their anchors never left the ground. *Goeben*, appearing out of still poor visibility around Grafton Point, began immediately to deluge them in a rain of highly accurate gunfire from which there was no possibility of escape. By eight a.m., both monitors were sunk. It had been easy, unopposed, like target practice, and everything so far had gone exactly to plan. The only slight worry was that the explosion of that mine had upset *Goeben's* compass; if the fault couldn't be rectified it might be necessary, von Rebeur-Paschwitz thought, to order *Breslau* to take the lead as guide. Meanwhile he ordered a reversal of course, in order to steam back and around the south of the island and thence westward for Mudros. At Mudros there'd be bigger prizes: bigger opposition too. Not that there'd been *any* here; and he had the satisfaction of knowing he'd left nothing afloat here that could bar his eventual line of retreat to the Dardanelles. By twenty minutes after eight *Goeben* was leading *Breslau* southward past the still smoking ruins of Cape Kephalo.

Then over that smoke-haze appeared a flight of British aircraft: bombers, from the Imbros airfield. *Goeben*'s 24-pounder AA guns swung their barrels skyward: and *Breslau*, to clear the flagship's range, swung out wide to port. Too wide: at eight thirty-one, by which time the first flight of bombers had dropped their loads into the sea and turned back for more, *Breslau* struck a mine.

She was under helm at the time, and the explosion was right aft: her steering was smashed, and so was the starboard turbine. With no operative rudder and with only one screw she was unmanoeuvrable. Von Rebeur-Paschwitz had no option but to order *Goeben*'s captain to take the damaged ship in tow. *Breslau* had in fact steamed into the western edge of the mine barriers: and *Goeben*, closing in to take up a towing position ahead of her, was now running into exactly the same hazard. While the cruiser's sailors worked frantically to range her cable on the foc'sl and prepare for the tow, and just as a second flight of bombers came racketing overhead – *Breslau*, lying stopped, took a direct hit in this attack – *Goeben* also hit a mine.

Suddenly the picture had changed entirely. There was a steady succession of attacks from aircraft: both ships were in clear Mediterranean water in which the dark shapes of mines could be seen all around them: and *Tigress* and *Lizard*, were racing southward in the hope of a chance to use torpedoes. All the lighter guns in the German ships were blazing away at the persistent, mosquito-like bombers. *Goeben* was trying to pick her way between the mines: *Breslau*, unable to control her steering, hit another four in the five minutes after nine a.m. She was already listing to port: after the fourth eruption, the death-blow, she swung upright, lifted her bows high in the air and slipped swiftly stern-first to the bottom.

Admiral von Rebeur-Paschwitz abandoned all thoughts of an attack on Mudros. He had to accept now that he'd be doing well to get his ship back into the Dardanelles. He ordered a south-westerly course, then south, and finally north-east, in order to skirt around the mines; and *Goeben* was on that final north-east leg, very close to where she'd been when she'd hit the first one, when the third exploded against her quarter.

There was some extensive internal flooding, and she'd taken up a fifteen-degree list to port. Aircraft were still chasing and attacking, and the bombing continued even after she'd entered the Straits. Behind her the Aegean Sea was a furiously-buzzing hornet's nest: and there was a lively awareness that the Germans wouldn't lose a minute in making good the damage to their battlecruiser and that what had been attempted once might very well be tried again. However safe *Goeben* might feel herself to be in her heavily defended Turkish hideout, she would now – somehow – have to be eliminated.

Chapter 1

'Steady as you go!'

'Steady, sir… South twenty-six east, sir!'

CPO Perry had flung the wheel back the other way; its brass-capped spokes flashed sunlight as they thudded through his palms and *Terrapin* steadied on her course across Kusu Bay, cleaving blue water under a cloudless sky. The bay mirrored a whitish crescent of beach framed in crumbly-looking rock; higher up on the island, patchy green slopes broken by rock outcrops rose to support the canopy of Mediterranean sky. There were more strikingly beautiful islands in the Aegean than Imbros – Nick had had his first sight of some of them during the fast passage from Malta – but even this, to his home-waters' eye, was fairly stunning.

Truman, the destroyer's captain, glanced again at his coxswain. 'Steer two degrees to starboard. Stop both engines.'

One island they'd passed within sight of had been Skyros; and on Skyros Sub-Lieutenant Rupert Brooke of Hood Battalion in the Royal Naval Division lay buried, his grave heaped with the island's pink-veined marble. Brooke's close friends had piled it over him – so Sarah had said, and Sarah knew everything about Rupert Brooke.

Nick hoped that some opportunity might arise for him to visit Skyros.

Why? Because Sarah was so emotional on that subject? And he, Nick Everard, even more so over Sarah?

It was a shocking thing. Of *course* it was. Objectively, one knew that – and at the same time thrilled, thinking of her. You could lose yourself in a dreamworld filled with pictures, echoes of her voice. And worry, too – the puzzle – her actions since, and that she'd said *nothing*... As a passenger – he'd been sent out to assume command of *Leveret*, a five-year-old destroyer employed mainly as a despatch vessel between Mudros and Salonika – on passage, with nothing to do except sit and stand around, there'd been too much time for that kind of self-indulgence. He knew he'd surrendered to the temptation far too much, and he pulled himself back into the present and the sunlight now – to Cruickshank, the navigating lieutenant, at the binnacle and watching the transverse bearing as *Terrapin* slid up, with very little way on her now, towards her anchor berth; and to Truman, keenly aware – you could see it in his self-conscious manner – of the light cruiser two cables' lengths on his port beam, and the fact that *Terrapin* would be under close surveillance from that crowded quarterdeck. Truman was a stuffy, humourless lieutenant-commander. All the way from Plymouth he hadn't opened a single conversation, so far as Nick could recall, that hadn't borne directly on some Service matter.

A submarine lay alongside the cruiser, and a haze of smoke over her stern showed that she was charging her batteries. That would be E.57, presumably, the boat Jake Cameron was to join – in a hurry, which was the reason for *Terrapin* having been diverted here instead of going straight to Mudros, her original destination. Cameron was a passenger too, but he'd only joined in Malta. He was an immensely burly young RNR lieutenant – about Nick's age, but twice his weight. He was at the back of the bridge now, his wide frame squeezed into the corner between rail and flag-locker.

Cruickshank – bony, intent, crouched mantis-like at the binnacle – murmured, 'Five degrees to go, sir.'

'Stand by!' Truman had a rather plummy voice. Harriman, his first lieutenant, was at the bridge's front rail; he'd raised one stubby arm above his head, and Granger, down on the foc's'l with the cable party, waved acknowledgement. A languid wave: 'lounge-lizard Larry' was what the other officers called *Terrapin's* dark-eyed sub-lieutenant. They were a good crowd; better, Nick thought, than Truman deserved. Cruickshank called, 'Bearing on *now*!'

'Let go!'

Harriman dropped that arm. On the foc's'l a hammer swung to knock the Blake slip off the starboard cable and send its anchor splashing, plunging into clear-blue sea. As the cable roared away and then slowed its initial rush until you could hear the separate *clank* as each link banged out through the hawse, Nick did some elementary mental arithmetic: eight fathoms of water, and three eights were twenty-four, so—

Truman had made the same calculation. He told Harriman, 'Veer to two shackles, and secure.'

Two shackles added up to twenty-five fathoms, and three times the depth of water was minimal for safe mooring. In this flat calm the minimum was as safe as houses.

Terrapin floated like a model ship in a bed of blue-tinted glass; the air was motionless, smelling faintly of the nearby island. Such picture-book stillness: it seemed incongruous to come to such a place for any warlike purpose. But Nick reminded himself, as he pulled the strap of borrowed binoculars over his head and slung them on the binnacle, that climate and scenery had nothing at all to do with it. Three years ago, when he – and the rest of Jellicoe's Grand Fleet – had been dying of boredom in the frozen wilderness of Scapa Flow, on sun-kissed beaches only ten miles east of this island a million men had died.

Near enough a million – counting Turks as well.

Cruickshank told Truman, 'Signalling from *Harwich*, sir.'

Harwich was the light cruiser, now on their quarter. Four-funnelled, *Bristol* class, with two six-inch and ten four-inch guns. Where would she have been, Nick wondered, a couple of months ago, when *Goeben* had come crashing out of the Dardanelles and caught everyone with their trousers down? He was looking over towards the cruiser and seeing that there were two submarines alongside, not just the one he'd seen before. *Harwich* was lying bow-on and you could see them both, one each side of her; the rumble of diesels from that battery-charging was a deep mutter across the quiet bay.

From a wing of the cruiser's bridge, a light was still winking its dots and dashes. Truman bent to the engine-room voicepipe.

'Finished with main engines. Remain at immediate notice.'

'Aye aye, sir… Shall we be fuelling, sir?'

That had been the voice of Mr Wilberforce, the commissioned engineer. And Truman evidently resented being asked a question he couldn't yet answer. It was a surprise that he'd been told to anchor; he'd brought Cameron to join his submarine, and the natural thing would have been to stop for long enough to drop him off and then push on to Mudros. He answered testily into the voicepipe, 'At present, Chief, I have not the slightest idea.' Now glancing round, he found Nick watching him, and raised his hooped, bushy eyebrows, his lips twisting in a smile inviting sympathy for the patience one had to exercise, tolerating unnecessary questions: one commanding officer to another... And Nick's facial muscles had gone wooden. He hadn't found himself exactly seeking Truman's company, during the passage out from England; he thought the man was an idiot, and one of his own failings of which he'd always been aware was an inability to hide such feelings. Awkward, particularly when dealing with officers senior to oneself; and this personal Achilles' heel of his was likely to prove even more of a handicap, he thought, now that the war looked like ending pretty soon... *Terrapin*'s leading signalman saved him from the battle to contort his features into some sort of smirk; the signalman was presenting his pad to Truman.

'Signal from *Harwich*, sir.'

'Indeed.' Truman took the pad casually, glanced down frowning at the message. His frown deepened: 'Bless my soul!' He'd looked up, at Nick, with those thick brows raised again: now he was re-reading the signal. He told the killick, 'Acknowledge, and VMT... Everard, you and I are invited to luncheon over there. Eh?'

Nick shared the man's surprise. He didn't think he knew anyone in the cruiser; or that anyone aboard her knew of his, Nick Everard's, presence aboard *Terrapin*: of his existence, even. And the signalled invitation, to which the reply 'VMT', standing for 'very many thanks', was already being stuttered in rapid flashes from the back end of the bridge, would have come from *Harwich's* captain. Truman had called to Jake Cameron, the submariner, 'They're sending a boat for you and us at twelve-thirty, Cameron.'

'Aye aye, sir. Thank you.' Cameron nodded – cheerful, enthusiastic. He'd been in a submarine that was refitting in the Malta dockyard, and they'd needed him here urgently to join another – E.57, which presumably was one of the pair alongside the cruiser.

Harriman reported to Truman, 'Cable's secured, sir, at two shackles. May I pipe hands to dinner?' Truman began to waffle – about not knowing yet what was happening, how long they'd be here… Nick checked the time, on his American wrist-watch. It was still a novelty; and it had been a present from his now famous uncle – Hugh Everard had become a rear-admiral after Jutland, but he was now a vice-admiral and *Sir* Hugh… Wrist-watches had been almost unobtainable earlier in the war; officers destined for the trenches and other forms of active service had advertised for them, as well as for revolvers and field-glasses, in the 'Personal' columns of *The Times*. Nick had been a midshipman then: it was just a few years ago, but it felt like a whole lifetime. To Sarah he must have been just a little boy in a sailor-suit.

How did she think of him *now*?

Back to earth again: or rather, to *Terrapin's* bridge, where Truman had consented to his ship's company being piped to dinner and Harriman – thickset, monosyllabic – had passed the order to Trimble, the bosun's mate. Cruickshank, Nick saw, was taking a set of anchor bearings, noting the figures in his navigator's notebook; and Harriman was telling PO Hart, the chief buffer, to rig the port quarterdeck gangway. It still felt odd, to be a passenger, to see and hear the business of the ship being conducted all around one and just stand idly by: it wasn't at all a comfortable feeling.

The killick signalman reported to Truman, 'Your message passed to *Harwich*, sir.' A West Countryman, in voice and craggy features extraordinarily like another signalman, one named Garret with whom Nick had shared, at Jutland, certain rather hair-raising experiences; having survived them and returned, more by luck than good judgement, to the Tyne, he'd got himself and Garret into hot water by sending him off on a leave to which he had not been entitled. There'd been a stew over letting him have an advance of pay, too. The thing was – not that one had been able to explain it at the time – they'd found themselves home, and alive, when there'd been every reason for them to have stayed out there in the North Sea with six thousand others, dead... And Garret had been a newly-married man, longing for the feel of his wife in his arms again: it had seemed *right* to send him off to her, and unlikely in the circumstances that anyone would give a damn.

One lived, and learned!

From Nick's angle, it hadn't been a case of a swollen head, of his achievement in bringing the ship home in its shattered state having left him cocky. It had been a weird feeling, in those early days of June 1916: as if that sort of rubbish didn't count now, as if the experience of battle had taken one out clear of the morass of petty restrictions and red-tape that he'd often fallen foul of. And in the two years since then he'd observed what had seemed to be similar reactions in other men, after action. Survivors of sunk ships, for instance, hauled half-drowned over a destroyer's side, recovering into surprise at being alive and immediately emptying their pockets, throwing away money and papers and small possessions... He'd known how they'd felt.

After Jutland his uncle Hugh had suggested drily, 'Feeling your oats somewhat, Nick? That it?'

'No, sir, I—'

'Don't do anything so damn silly again, boy. You've a *chance* now. For heaven's sake make use of it!'

Before Jutland, Nick had not been reckoned to have any sort of chance. He'd been a failure, a sub-lieutenant 'under report' in a dreadnought's gunroom; and if there was such a place as hell, a Scapa Flow battleship's gunroom must surely come pretty close to it. Had done, anyway, in those days.

Uncle Hugh's star, of course, had risen even more dramatically than his nephew's. At Jutland as a post-captain he'd commanded the super-dreadnought *Nile* and earned promotion to flag rank; and now more recently his successful cruiser action resulting in the destruction of the *Gottingen* had won him the second promotion and a 'K'.

Nick joined the RNR submariner, Cameron, at the after end of the bridge. 'Which of those sinister-looking craft is yours?'

Jake Cameron pointed. 'Starboard side there. Other boat's French.' He rubbed his large hands together. 'Find out what all the flap's about presently, with luck!'

Obviously it was some kind of flap. *Terrapin* wouldn't have been diverted without good reason. En route from Devonport to Mudros she'd called at Malta for fuel and – hopefully – a day or two of shoregoing for her ship's company; but she'd only been alongside the oiler in Sliema Creek about ten minutes when a signal came informing Truman that he was required to sail again forthwith, taking one passenger to Mudros. One additional passenger, they'd meant. Later, when the ship had been well into the Aegean, another signal had changed the destination to Imbros. But alongside the oiler in Malta they'd been expecting some important personage to arrive on board – a general, or a politician – and what had turned up had been this outsize but otherwise very ordinary RNR lieutenant.

He and Nick had found they had a friend in common – Tim Rogerson, who'd helped to ram the old submarine C.3 and her cargo of high-explosive into the viaduct at Zeebrugge, to the considerable inconvenience of the Germans, at the same time as Nick in his 'oily-wad' destroyer *Bravo* had been playing Aunt Sally to Hun artillery inside the mole... It was like something one might have done, lived through, in an earlier age, not just six months ago. But the 'Zeeb' raid had taken place on St George's Day of this year, 1918, and it was only October now; and another odd impression was that one felt as if it had been experienced by some other person, not by oneself but by someone who up to that time had occupied one's skin.

Punctured skin. He'd been knocked about a bit, in *Bravo*, and spent nine weeks afterwards in hospitals and another month convalescing at Mullbergh, his father's enormous, gloomy house in Yorkshire. Sarah, his father's young wife, ran Mullbergh as a recuperative centre for wounded officers, and it had seemed natural enough that he should go there. But given that decision to make again now — if he were back in Miss Keyser's private hospital in Grosvenor Gardens and Sarah in that funny little green hat had been asking 'Sister Agnes', 'Let me have him now? Let me fatten him up at Mullbergh, for a few weeks?' — given that situation again now, would one let it happen?

Well, it had seemed like an obvious move. And he didn't think — hard to turn the mind back, but he was fairly sure of this — he didn't think he'd ever regarded Sarah, up to that time, as anything more than a close, warm friend who happened also to be much nearer his own age than his father's, and yet his father's wife, and beautiful, and kind, and — well, nothing else. Not then.

He'd have given anything to know now, this minute, what she was thinking, feeling. When she'd written, she'd managed to say absolutely nothing; but almost immediately after he'd left Mullbergh she'd gone down to London to meet his father, who'd been sent home on an unexpected leave from France. Sarah had spent the ten days of it with him in some Mayfair house lent to them by friends. It had been an astonishing thing for her to have done: incredible, in the context of that miserable marriage. And in the letter when she'd told him, there'd been no explanation, no kind of comment. Nick had begun to think of her as suffering from remorse, as being *less* happy because of him, because of what they'd — well, become to each other; and thinking of her in that state it felt as if he, just like his father, had – oh, *fed on* her… It was an agony to think of it in that way: he shut his eyes, certain that if he could have been with her now to put his arms round her, reassure her… He asked himself, *Reassure her of what? Of my feelings for her? What use can they be to her?*

It was simply that he couldn't help them. And that despite the misgivings and a kind of loneliness he'd never experienced before, constantly thrusting through the worry and concern was a sense of excitement and happiness that was like being half-drunk.

Muffled piping from below decks broke into the jumble of his thoughts. The squeal of the pipe was followed by Trimble's roar of 'Ha-a-ands to dinner!'

Cameron levered his bulk off the bridge rail.

'I'm going down to see my gear's packed.' He jerked a thumb towards the cruiser. 'You're coming over too, did I hear?'

'Apparently.' Nick stared across bright water at *Harwich* and the submarine alongside her. He hadn't the least idea how or why he'd been honoured with this invitation.

–

The boat, with its three passengers in the sternsheets, sheered away from *Terrapin's* gangway and headed for the cruiser. Truman had told Harriman, 'Get the ship cleaned up. If there's any news I'll give it to you by signal; otherwise assume we're here for the night. After tea you can pipe hands to bathe and non-swimmers to instruction.'

It was extraordinary how many non-swimmers there were in the Navy, and how many of them tried to shirk instruction.

Cameron, beside Nick in the boat's stern, was examining E.57 as they chugged down *Harwich's* starboard side. She was just like any other submarine, Nick thought – a dirty, stinking tube, not in any sense a ship; he'd never understood submariners' fascination with their wretched craft. Now, as the boat curved round the big ship's stern, E.57 was out of sight and Cameron was studying the French one. Equally nasty… The boat's coxswain, nosing her up towards the gangway on the cruiser's port quarter, was slewing in too fast, and he'd put his engine astern too late: the boat thumped against the platform, bowman and sternsheetman struggling to fend off with their boathooks. From the quarterdeck up above their heads Nick heard the order, 'Pipe!' Truman glanced briefly at the somewhat chagrined coxswain.

'Devil's the matter with you, Markham?'

Then he was climbing the gangway into that squeal of piping. The custom stemmed from days of sail when captains, admirals and other dignitaries had been hoisted aboard in a boatswain's chair slung from a yardarm whip. Nick, hanging back to give Truman all the limelight, thought it must have been embarrassing for the gouty old men, to be dumped like sacks of spuds on their ships' decks… As the second wail of the pipes died away he went quickly up the scrubbed oak steps and over the cruiser's sides: saluting, finding himself on the edge of a group of officers, and having a quick first impression of a lot of gold-peaked caps; then, sorting wheat from chaff, he realised that actually there were only two of those: one was on the head of a small, pink-faced commander who was pumping Truman's hand, and the other—

Reaper!

Commander Reaper: who, as a staff officer on Roger Keyes's planning team at Dover before the Zeebrugge Raid, had sent Nick on a crackpot cross-channel raid in a coastal motor boat... Narrow head: deepset eyes: his expression was one of mild amusement as he stared back at Nick's obvious surprise.

'Didn't I say we'd meet again, Everard?'

'You did indeed, sir.' Shaking his hand. Astonished: and pleased: but also puzzled... 'Did you know I was a passenger in *Terrapin*?'

Reaper nodded. 'From our exchange of signals with Mudros when we needed to divert you to this place.' He cocked an eyebrow. 'Last time we met, or thereabouts, I had the pleasant duty of telling you that you were getting a DSC. You've done better since, I hear.'

'Thanks to you, I think, sir.'

He'd won a DSO, at Zeebrugge – in a single hour when eleven other men had won VCs. But it could only have been on Reaper's recommendation that Nick had got his first command – *Bravo* – and taken her on that wild excursion... He saw a tall, rather benign-looking lieutenant-commander come hurrying on to the quarterdeck: he was looking from one face to another. 'Cameron?' Over Nick's head: 'Are you Jake Cameron?' Reaper, answering Nick's last remark, waved a hand dismissively: 'Nonsense. But I can tell you I'm extremely glad you've fallen into my hands again. You're exactly what the doctor ordered!'

'But I'm on my way to Mudros—'

'You *were* on your way to Mudros. I've arranged to borrow you, for this operation. In point of fact, Everard, you're the answer to my prayers.' The other commander, the little tubby one, was in the act of joining them, interrupting Reaper: but he broke off again, seeing the newcomer, the tall man who was latching on to Cameron: 'Ah, Wishart — wondered where the deuce you'd—'

'Frightfully sorry.' Wishart had quite a belly on him, for a man still under thirty. Reaper introduced Nick and the little commander: he was the executive officer of this cruiser, *Harwich*, and his name was Gillman. 'Heard a great deal about you, Everard. And you're Hugh Everard's nephew, I'm told. Delighted...' Rambling on, with a sort of boyish enthusiasm, as they shook hands: 'Never met your uncle, unfortunately... But what a corker, eh? I mean, dishing the *Gottingen*, eh?' Nick would have liked to listen only to Reaper, pump him, find out what he was being 'borrowed' for; but he was surrounded, getting bits and pieces of about three conversations at once, and having to respond politely to Gillman's affability. He heard Wishart addressing Cameron just behind him... '*Just* in time, I may say. My navigator's John Treat — know him? Well, he went and exploded his appendix, and I had to leave him behind in Mudros. Furious, of course, to be missing this show...'

What show? And how could what was obviously a submarine operation concern him, Nick Everard?

Reaper tapped the tall man, Wishart, on his shoulder. 'Want you to meet Everard.'

'Why, of course!'

Wishart turned away from Jake Cameron, to shake Nick's hand. 'Very glad we'll have you with us. We'll try to see you're not *too* uncomfortable — but mind you, with two other passengers as well—'

'He doesn't know anything about it yet.' Reaper told Nick, 'Lieutenant-Commander Wishart is captain of E.57. You'll be sailing in her tomorrow.' He glanced over his shoulder: 'But come on down now. We're lunching with Captain Usherwood. We'll see you later, Wishart.'

Gillman and Truman had gone ahead.

'I'm taking passage somewhere in E.57?'

He could think of nothing he'd like less. The very thought of going inside a submarine sickened him. Reaper said, 'A bit more than just taking passage. You'll be going through the Dardanelles and into the Marmara, in order to sink or at any rate immobilise *Goeben*.' He glanced sideways at Nick, just very briefly, as he led the way in through the port-side screen door. 'All right?'

One could hardly have given a quick affirmative to *that* question…

Going through the Dardanelles would mean running the gauntlet of just about every submarine hazard that existed. And submarine hazards, one might reasonably feel, were things best reserved for the enjoyment of submariners. He certainly couldn't see how or why Reaper wanted to involve *him* in it.

Reaper had stopped at the top of a steel ladder that led down to the cruiser's main deck. Truman and Commander Gillman were still on it, going down. Reaper seemed to guess Nick's thoughts; he told him, 'This is not at all a straightforward submarine operation, you see. *Goeben* is at Constantinople – inside the Golden Horn, well protected from torpedoes. So she has either to be winkled out – induced to put to sea so that our friend Wishart, or the French boat which will also be in the

Marmara, can sink her – or alternatively, blown up where she's lying.'

'Oh…' A chink of daylight. 'A landing party?'

The narrow head and its gold-peaked cap nodded.

'You'll have an explosives chap with you. But he's incredibly green. I need someone with him who's got a bit of savvy and can keep his head in an emergency. As you did once when you stole a trawler for me, eh?'

'A trawler's crew, sir.'

'Quite. You did the job we wanted done.'

A pause: Reaper peering down the ladder… It was difficult to believe in this business yet. It had been sprung too suddenly and unexpectedly. Nick sought escape in levity.

'So, for "trawler" read "battlecruiser", sir?'

Reaper didn't smile. He said gruffly as he started down the ladder, 'You won't have to steal her, Everard. Just destroy her.'

–

The brow down to E.57's casing was a ribbed plank with the unusual embellishment of a rope handrail. Wishart flipped it contemptuously as he preceded Jake Cameron down the steep incline. 'Guest-night stuff. They don't realise we develop sticky feet.' He stopped on the casing and a sailor in paint-stained overalls, emerging from the submarine's fore hatch, edged past him with a bucket in each hand.

'What's that lot and where's it going, Finn?'

'Spud peelings, sir. Goin' inboard, gash-bin.' The torpedoman grinned. 'Less the Frogs'd like it, d'ye reckon, sir?' He went up the brow chuckling to himself: stocky, fresh-faced, in his early twenties. Wishart told Jake, 'We've got a damn good bunch, you'll find… Come on down.'

Into the fore hatch, grabbing its upper rim and slinging themselves in feet-first on to a ladder that slanted down into the torpedo stowage compartment. Further for'ard, in the narrowing bow, were the two bow torpedo tubes; reloads for them were in here, one each side of the compartment. Behind the fish to starboard was the for'ard heads; opposite it, the officers' cooking stove. Lockers filled other ship's-side spaces, and any other gap not taken up with machinery and working gear had been crammed with crates, boxes, sacks of stores.

In the centre of the for'ard bulkhead was the big, brass hand-wheel that controlled the shutter-gear, hull doors protecting the firing ends of the tubes; about twenty pairs of socks hung on its gleaming rim and spokes. Wishart frowned at it, and a leading seaman – a large man with a smooth face and thick brown hair – told him apologetically, 'Won't let us 'ang no dhobey topsides, sir, not in workin' hours. Sailin' tomorrer, makes it awkward.'

'Who says you can't?'

The killick shrugged. 'Inboard, sir.'

'I'll have a word with someone.' Wishart told Jake, 'Leading Seaman Morton is second cox'n… Lieutenant Cameron's joined as navigator, Morton.' He asked him, 'Cox'n on board, is he?'

'Gone to dinner inboard, sir. Shall I fetch 'im?'

'Heavens, no.' He moved towards the bulkhead doorway. 'Let's have a chat, pilot, while there's some quiet. Then lunch in the wardroom inboard. Two o'clock there's a briefing session in Captain Usherwood's day cabin – you'd better join us.' He went through into the control room. Jake had come from one of the older E-class boats, and this was a much more recent version, but the variations in her internal layout were small and it was all familiar. The smells and sounds were familiar too: like the creaking underwater noises as she rubbed herself against the cruiser's side, and the oily smell that was part of a homey sort of warmth.

'Ah-hah!'

A small man – a lieutenant RN – looking up from paperwork spread around on the pull-out wardroom table and one of the bunks. Wishart nodded to him.

'As you say, Number One – ah-hah. Here's the johnny we've been waiting for.'

E.57's first lieutenant was small, sharp-faced; he had crinkly yellow hair, freckles and a belligerent expression. He stared at Jake like a hangman weighing up a customer for the noose.

'H'm. Have to take ten or twelve gallons out of the buoyancy tank.'

To compensate for Jake's extra weight, he meant. Wishart introduced them: 'Cameron – Hobday.' They shook hands. Hobday was like some kind of dog – a bull-terrier, Jake thought, shaking a hand that felt like the knuckle-end of a wheel-spanner. Wishart suggested, 'Let's have a welcome-aboard glass of gin – d'you think?'

'One excuse is as good as another.' Hobday's sentences came in short, clipped bursts, like sudden rattles of small-arms fire. He'd crossed the compartment to open one of the lockers above the chart table: Jake saw gin, bitters, glasses. He took the enamel jug from Hobday: 'I'll get that.'

'Good man.' Hobday began dripping Angostura carefully into three glasses, and Jake went for'ard into the TSC to fill the jug from a tap in the heads. A man his size could just squeeze into the tiny cabinet, when he needed to; now, he just reached in to the tap. Wishart asked him when he came back into the control room, 'Know what sort of a lark we're engaged on, do you?'

'No. I'm hoping you're about to tell me. Say when?'

'When. Sit down, old lad. You're at home now.'

Home from home... He sat facing them across the pull-out table. This corner of the control room had a curtain that could be drawn around it, and it constituted the wardroom. Two bunks were fixed against the curve of the pressure-hull, with drawers and this table under the after one; below the other was a third bunk, which was itself a sort of drawer that could be pulled out when it was wanted or shoved in out of sight. This one was the third hand's – Jake's. Its disadvantage was that when it was out it blocked the gangway, and you had to get used to being walked over.

He added water to his own gin. Plenty of it, knowing that later on today he'd have to check over all the charts they'd be likely to need, and the confidential books, signal equipment, compasses – everything in the navigator's department... Wishart raised his glass: 'Welcome aboard, old lad.' He put the glass down again. 'The point of all this, in a nutshell, is we've got to nobble the battlecruiser *Goeben*, alias *Yavuz*.'

Jake let that sink in. He nodded. 'So we're going through the Dardanelles.'

'That will certainly be the first step.'

Hobday murmured, 'No small step either.'

Wishart swirled the faintly pink liquid around his glass. A stoker came from aft, glanced curiously at Jake, passed on for'ard. Hobday called after him, 'There'll be no dinner left for you, Peel, if you don't run for it!' He told Jake, 'Stoker Peel. Twister, they call him.' Wishart admitted, 'We can't expect the welcome mat to be out for us, certainly. What we know is that the Turks've put in new nets and minefields, and more guns on the beach than they had before, plus – so we're told – hydrophone listening gear and fixed shore torpedo tubes. Also, their patrols have depth-charges now, which of course one didn't have to contend with in '15.' He sipped gin. 'We'll simply – well, deal with interruptions as they arise, that's all.'

For two years, Jake reflected, no submarine had attempted the passage of the Dardanelles. With the abandoning of the landing operations, there'd been no need for it. Then after *Goeben*'s recent sortie they'd sent E.14 up after her. Saxton White's boat. She'd been Boyle's, in the earlier campaign, and Boyle had won himself a VC in her. From this last excursion, White and that veteran submarine had not returned.

Jake said thoughtfully, 'It must be considered fairly important that we should have another go at it?'

'Yes.' Wishart nodded. 'You'll hear all the background this afternoon. From that chap Reaper. He's running the show – he seems to be some sort of specialist in planning unorthodox operations – and he'll be going along in *Terrapin* to act as a command and communications base, in the Gulf of Xeros so as to shorten the wireless range.'

'But surely we shan't be – well, advertising our presence in the Marmara?'

'Quite right.' Wishart looked approvingly at his navigator. 'We shall not. Not a peep – unless *Goeben* provides us with a target or – God forbid – gets past us, westbound… No, it's more for the benefit of the French. *Louve* – that's the Frog submarine on the other side, and it means "She-wolf", not some picture gallery as my uneducated first lieutenant chose to imagine – *Louve* is taking two evil-looking civilians to land somewhere or other and do heaven knows what. Political. This whole business is tied up with persuading the Turks to chuck their hands in, by the way. Reaper'll be explaining all that.' He shook his head. 'These chaps they're putting ashore look more like carpet-salesmen than politicians.'

Hobday agreed. 'Either of 'em 'd sell you his sister for the price of a pipe of opium, if you asked him.' He snorted. 'Personally I wouldn't.'

'Wouldn't what?'

'Touch either of their sisters with a barge-pole.'

Jake asked Wishart, 'Does anyone know where *Goeben* is exactly?'

'At the Horn. *In* it.'

'Above the bridge, where we can't get at her?'

'Two answers to that. One, she may not remain in cover. From the purely naval point of view, that's a worry: she may try to break out again. Our chaps have reason to think it's on the cards, in fact. And from our point of view – this boat's, I mean – let's hope she does, so long as we're in position to have a crack at her.' He added, 'But they're nervy about it, up at Mudros. When she last popped out, they were caught very badly on the hop.'

'We heard there'd been a stink.'

'Did you hear the admiral commanding the Aegean had been sent home?' Jake shook his head. Wishart told him, 'You probably know we've two old battleships based at Mudros. *Lord Nelson* and *Agamemnon*. Well, the admiral wanted to visit Salonika, and his own yacht was temporarily out of action, so the old idiot took *Lord Nelson* away with him. As good as sending the Hun an invitation to come out and make hay... Mind you, *I'd* have sent him home just so as not to have to see him dribble. Perfectly awful – chin running with slobber... But as I was saying—'

'What about Saxton White?'

'What about him?'

'He went into the straits after *Goeben*, didn't he, almost on her heels?'

'Yes.' Wishart was silent for a moment. 'But – oh, I don't think it can help us much to talk about White, you know.'

Hobday backed Jake up. 'If we had some notion of what happened to him, surely—'

'You know, as I do, Number One, that E.14 was lost and that Saxton White is almost certainly dead.'

'Yes,' Hobday persisted, 'but until he went up, nobody had gone in there since – well, 1915, when we were doing it all the time. And as you've said, sir, the nets and mine-fields, and the shore batteries and so on will all have been changed, and—'

Wishart peered into his glass, frowning slightly. 'There's a new minefield between Kum Kale and Cape Helles. We know that because we saw them laying it.'

'If we could work out what White—'

'He got through the Narrows and close to Nagara. That's where *Goeben* had run aground. She hit a mine, you know, she had some minor flooding… She was stuck there, and bombs our 'planes dropped on her every day for about a week just bounced off her. During that week they were getting a boat fit to go up and torpedo her, and the only one available and within reach was Saxton White's. But by the time he went into the straits they'd refloated her and she'd gone. We *think* he then turned about and started back. But we don't know anything for certain, except they sank him. And just speculating, as everyone's been doing *ad nauseam* ever since, doesn't do anyone a shred of good. Saxton had bad luck at some point, that's all.'

Hobday waited to be sure that that was all his captain had to say. Then he argued, 'If they turned back from halfway up the straits, perhaps that was the worst thing about it. I mean, if the Turks had detected them on their way up, and then they turned sixteen points and gave the swine another shot at 'em—'

'Number One.' Wishart's easy manner was wearing thin. 'Either I've been failing to express myself clearly, or you're being particularly obtuse. The point I have been trying to make is that in my view it would be more helpful *not* to dwell on what might or might not have happened to E.14. All right?'

Hobday blinked at him. He looked puzzled.

'I beg your pardon, sir. I—'

'Where'd we got to… About *Goeben* being out of reach unless they shift her – and the French taking those odd characters with them…' He told Jake, 'We've our own landing party. Actually, we'll be transferring them to the French boat, and the Frogs'll do that part of it.

31

But we're taking a chap called Robins — an RNVR two-and-a-half. I gather he works for the Foreign Office in some way. He talks French and Turkish and thinks rather well of himself — perhaps not the ideal passenger... I may be wrong, of course... The second man's a young Red Marine — Burtenshaw. Supposed to be an explosives expert and I believe he talks German. And finally this lad Everard, who seems to be Commander Reaper's afterthought.' Wishart asked Jake, 'What's he like?' 'Very decent.' Cameron nodded. 'Despite numerous medals — and having that uncle who's the admiral—'

'And a baronet for a father?'

Jake showed his surprise. 'I didn't know that.'

'Baronet, MFH, currently a brigadier in France. And this chap here is heir to the title and some huge estate in Yorkshire. If you spent several days in his company and didn't know it—'

'Not a hint.'

'Well...' Wishart glanced round the cramped compartment. 'Be a bit stretched, to make room for three extra bodies. Still, it won't be for long.' He pushed his chair back. 'We'd better go up while there's still some food left.'

—

Commander Reaper glanced round the table. Nick Everard was on his left, and the French submarine captain between Nick and the RNVR lieutenant- commander, Robins. Burtenshaw, the Marine — he looked like a rugger player, and probably not long out of his public school, and very much under Robins's thumb — was at the bottom of the table, while Jake Cameron, Aubrey Wishart and *Terrapin*'s captain, Truman, occupied its other side.

Hobday had asked to be excused. He had a lot to do, and Wishart could brief him on any points that were new.

Reaper murmured, 'Smoke if you care to.'

'*Quoi?*'

He had to repeat it in French, to *Louve's* captain. It was an embarrassing thing to have to do, because he'd just noticed, with a flicker of those deepset eyes in his bony, very English face, that Lemarie was already sucking a black cheroot. Odd, Nick thought, that he hadn't noticed its stink before. The Frenchman was short, muscled, swarthy, in his early thirties, and he wore the three narrow stripes of a *lieutenant de vaisseau* on his epaulettes. Hard brown eyes... A tough customer, Nick thought; might be a Corsican. Getting the translation from Reaper he raised his thick eyebrows, shot a glance at the cheroot in his fingers, and stuck it in his mouth with a kind of snort as he looked back at Reaper... Reaper leant forward, and clasped his hands on the table in front of him.

'My object in calling this meeting is to make sure we all have a grasp of the strategic background to the operation, the reasons for embarking on it and the absolute necessity of completing it successfully. Most of you already know your own sides of it; this is a matter of understanding the background from a common standpoint and, so to speak, in the round.' He glanced down the table. 'It's also, of course, for the information of those officers who have only just joined us.'

Robins muttered a rapid French translation into Lemarie's hairy left ear. Reaper paused now and then to give him time to catch up; and sometimes Robins paused, ignoring bits he didn't think worth translating.

'I'll begin with a reminder as to how *Goeben* came to be where she is.'

He embarked on a résumé of the scandal in 1914 when *Goeben*, one of Germany's newer battlecruisers, had been allowed to escape into the Dardanelles, to then neutral and undecided Turkey, instead of being brought to action and sunk. Rear-Admiral Troubridge, the cruiser admiral, had been court martialled for it; but there was a body of opinion in the Service which reckoned that Troubridge's superior officer, 'Arky-Barky' Milne, should have been held responsible. Nick's uncle, Hugh Everard, had no doubt of it; and Jackie Fisher had said that *he'd* have had Milne shot. Though in fact – quoting Hugh Everard – there might not be many senior officers whom Fisher would *not* have had shot, at one time or another... But the messy business of *Goeben's* escape was old-hat now – except to Troubridge, who'd been acquitted of all charges but still hadn't been given another job afloat. Not a happy situation, for a descendant of the Troubridge who'd fought at Nelson's side.

Reaper, luckily, didn't take the story back as far as Nelson.

'There's little doubt now that *Goeben's* arrival at Constantinople was a major factor in Turkey's decision to enter the war against us.'

Robins snapped, without looking at anyone in particular, 'I'm sure we've all accepted *that* premise.'

Everyone except Burtenshaw glanced at him in surprise. Robins had very little chin, and the mouth above it was small, turned down at the corners. Dark hair, oiled, was swept back from a high swell of forehead. Probably very brainy, Nick thought, but also waspish,

34

self-opinionated. He wondered why Reaper didn't pull him up. But the commander only continued in his even, quiet tone. 'The point I wish to make is that *Goeben* lying at the Horn now is still a factor in Turkey's *continuance* in the war. There are positive indications that the Turks would like to arrange an armistice. As you know, Damascus fell several weeks ago to Colonel Lawrence's Arabs; and now the Fifth Cavalry Division under General Allenby is advancing rapidly on Aleppo. More than halfway there, in fact... At the same time, we and our allies have changed the shape of things in France. So there's an end in sight, at last; and if we can push the Turks into surrendering, it should come more quickly.'

In July there had been the second Marne battle. Ludendorf's great offensive, aimed at snatching victory before the American armies could be trained and brought in to tip the scales, had been stopped, the initiative seized from him. Then in August an offensive by British, Canadian and Australian troops had been launched east of Amiens, in such secrecy that not even the War Cabinet had known it was being planned. Secrecy had paid off in the shape of 16,000 prisoners on the first day. And in September the Americans had been blooded when Pershing's 1st Army had struck at Mihiel and scored a knock-out; the momentum of victory was increasing now with American weight behind it.

Robins had just interrupted again.

'There are other *very* good reasons, of far-reaching political consequence, which suggest we should reach the Bosphorus with as little delay as possible.'

This time Reaper looked at him. His tone was mild enough, to start with.

'I've always found it easier to make one point at a time. Would you bear with me, meanwhile?'

The small mouth had compressed itself like that of an offended governess. He began thinly, 'As a representative of HM Foreign Office I should rather think it was *my*—'

'Foreign Office be damned!'

The lieutenant-commander looked shocked: as if he hadn't expected Reaper to be capable of anger. Reaper told him, speaking quietly again now, 'The only White-hall authority identifiable to us here as your employer, Robins, is the Board of Admiralty. The Board's authority is vested in the Commander-in-Chief, who has seen fit to place you under my orders. I must ask you not to interrupt again.'

Lieutenant Burtenshaw, RMLI, was plainly embarrassed. He'd turned sideways, pink-faced, fiddling with a pencil, blinking into sunshine that streamed in through a scuttle.

Reaper cleared his throat.

'There are *several* reasons why it is necessary to eliminate *Goeben* as a fighting unit. The most obvious one to us here is the possibility of her breaking out of the straits again, as she did recently. The Hun might well try it. He's losing the war, he knows he is, and he might well prefer offensive action to simply waiting for the end... Last time *Goeben* came out, remember, was just after the Turks had lost Jerusalem, and it's considered that Admiral von Rebeur-Paschwitz was trying something dramatic to bolster the Turk morale. So far as we know, Paschwitz is still flying his flag in her – and Turk morale's right down the drain! Megiddo... Damascus... and very soon Aleppo...' He nodded. 'She may well come out again.

If she did, what might be her objectives? We see three probables. One: break through into the Adriatic and link up with the Austrians. Two: inflict as much damage as she can on our supply routes and then dodge back into the Dardanelles or to Smyrna. Three: attack our bases at Mudros and Salonika – through which of course we're supplying the push against Bulgaria – or even Port Said and Alexandria.'

He was silent for a moment. Then he looked up again. 'I ought to mention that they've had time to get her back into fighting trim. You probably know she hit some mines during her last outing. Air reconnaissance suggests she's repaired and fit for sea.'

Truman asked, in his fruity voice, 'Is she definitely inside the Golden Horn, sir?'

'Yes. As recently as yesterday she was moored above the Galata bridge.'

Lieutenant de vaisseau Lemarie had a silver pocket-watch in his palm; he was staring down at it and making tut-tutting noises. He muttered in French now to Robins. Robins told Reaper, in a tone that suggested he'd rather have nothing at all to do with him, 'The *lieutenant* has to leave us now. He has matters to attend to before he sails.'

'Of course.' Reaper stood up, and the others followed suit. 'I wish you – we all do – a very successful voyage and a safe return… Naturally, we'll be on deck to see you off.'

Jake Cameron wondered how the Frenchman might be feeling about this jaunt. Everyone in the cabin knew roughly what sort of odds were to be expected – and they certainly weren't good ones. But a French submariner should be even more acutely aware of them. Since

Dardanelles operations had begun, back in '14, there'd been dozens of successful British patrols in the Marmara, at a price of four E-class boats lost; but in the same period five French submarines had entered the straits and not one of them had come out again. Jake had been discussing it during luncheon, with Hobday and Wishart, and the names of the French boats ran through his mind now as he saw his new CO go round the end of the table to shake Lemarie's hand. *Saphir... Marietta... Joule... Turquoise...*

The fifth: he was stumped for it. And suddenly it seemed like the blackest omen that he couldn't name her... As if by not doing so he was putting *Louve* in that fifth place?

When the door closed behind the Frenchman, Reaper waved them back to their chairs.

'I've referred already to the fact that we know Turkey wants peace-talks. Now I'll tell you – in confidence – what puts it quite beyond doubt.' He glanced round at their faces. 'In the Mesopotamian campaign that came to grief at Kut – after one of the bravest defences, I may say, in the history of British arms – General Townsend and a Colonel Newcombe were among the thousands taken prisoner. Two-thirds of the other-rank prisoners have died since in Turkish hands – but that's digressing... What I'm telling you is that the Turks have let General Townsend and Newcombe out – shipped them out so they can help with armistice negotiations outside Turkey.'

Robins raised his head, stared contemptuously at Burtenshaw. Reaper went on, 'Fact is, Turkey's still at war with us *only* because of the German presence – General Liman von Sanders's troops, and *Goeben*. The troops are in poor shape and bad heart; ninety per cent of the

Hun strength lies in *Goeben*'s guns. They call her *Yavuz* – in full *Yavus Sultan Selim*, meaning "Sultan Selim the Terrible". And her crew wear fezes, and she flies the Turkish ensign. So far as we're concerned they can wear top-hats and fly last week's washing – she's still *Goeben*, and she's manned by Huns... And she's more than just a symbol of German power – the Turks know perfectly well her guns could knock Constantinople flat, so she's *effective* power too. And you're beginning to understand, I hope, why we rather badly need to sink her...' He shook his head. 'That's not all, though. You're aware, of course, that the Russian Black Sea Fleet mutinied in February. Also that the Germans and the Bolsheviks signed what they call the Treaty of Brest-Litovsk in March – since when the Bolshies have started calling themselves 'communists' and murdered their royal family, and we've occupied Archangel to keep the Germans from getting there through Finland, and so forth... As far as the Black Sea's concerned, though, it's thought in London that there's some danger of the Huns taking over those Russian ships and using them against us. Quite a powerful fleet, it might be – and led, no doubt, by our friend von Paschwitz in *Goeben*... And we can eliminate this threat in two stages. First by action against *Goeben* as we now intend; and in the longer term by establishing ourselves at the Horn and controlling the – well, for the time being let's just say the Bosphorus. This we cannot do until we have a Turkish surrender, so that we can move the Fleet through the Dardanelles – and before we can do that, we have to deal with *Goeben*.'

He sat back, and his eyes flickered from face to face.

'I've explained all this in order that you should understand and accept one simple conclusion. That to destroy *Goeben* is worth any effort, hazard or cost. Quite literally – *any*.'

Chapter 2

On the cruiser's upper deck her ship's company were being fallen out from evening Quarters and mustered along her starboard side, ready to cheer E.57 off to patrol. This time yesterday they'd given a similar send-off to *Louve*.

Hobday shook Commander Gillman's hand. He'd only come up from the submarine to say goodbye to him: just as Aubrey Wishart would at this moment be saying goodbye to Captain Usherwood, down in the cuddy.

'Most grateful for your hospitality and help, sir.'

'Not a bit of it.' The small, rotund commander beamed. 'Just knock that damned Hun for six, now!'

From E.57's fore casing, Jake Cameron watched Hobday come down the sloping plank. He'd given Jake until sailing-time – *now* – to know the name of every man on board. Twenty-four hours he'd had, to memorise nearly thirty names, as well as attending to all the small preparations, checking of chart-corrections, and so on. He'd been up most of the night, sorting out the charts and CBs.

The coxswain, Chief Petty Officer Crabb, was waiting for Hobday by the open fore hatch. Crabb was a grizzled, veteran submariner. Roman nose, cleft chin, voice like a dog's growl.

'Hydroplanes, diving rudders and steering gear tested in 'and and in electric, sir. Diving gauges open. All 'ands on board, all gear below secured for sea, sir.'

'Thank you, cox'n.' That had been the first of a long litany of reports which the first lieutenant had now to receive. 'Stations for leaving harbour, please.'

'Aye aye, sir.' Crabb yelled the order down into the hatch as Morton, the big, soft-faced second coxswain, came ambling aft with a meaty hand resting on the jumping-wire.

'Casing secured for sea, sir.'

The second coxswain, under Jake as casing officer, was responsible for ropes and wires and for the casing itself, this steel deck that was full of holes so that when the boat dived all spaces outside the pressure-hull filled with water. It was just staging, something to walk on. The bridge superstructure was the same; in the centre of it the conning tower was a vertical tube with a ladder through it connecting from the control-room hatch to an upper hatch in the bridge deck, but the surrounding framework supporting that deck was free-flood, like a colander... Hobday told the leading seaman, 'Single up, and stand by the brow.' He looked past Morton at Jake. 'I want you to come through the boat with me, Cameron.'

He slid down the ladder into the torpedo stowage compartment; Jake and CPO Crabb rattled down behind him.

'Shut fore 'atch!'

'Anderson!'

CPO Rinkpole, the torpedo gunner's mate, had snapped the name over his shoulder, and Anderson, a dark-haired, very tall torpedoman, came aft from the tube space. Rinkpole jerked his bald head towards the hatch; Anderson reported to Hobday as he moved towards it, 'WRT's full, bow shutters open, sir.' From a few rungs up the ladder he reached up and dragged the hatch shut over his head. It wasn't only a matter of shutting and clipping it; there was a strongback to be bolted on inside it. Rinkpole told Hobday, 'Torpedo circuits tested, spare torpedoes lashed, sir.'

Forty-ish: not *entirely* bald… Rinkpole had been at sea for a quarter of a century and in submarines since the Navy had first recognised their existence. His torpedoes, Hobday had said, were his babies; if they hadn't been seventeen feet long he might have taken them to bed with him. Cole, the second LTO – electrical rating – was waiting to make his report: 'Bells, 'ooters an' Aldis tested an' workin', sir.' Cole's nickname was 'Blackie'; but it was uncertain whether it derived from his surname or from the thick mass of beard out of which his eyes seemed to glint like some animal's from a bush.

'Thank you, Cole.' It was already twice as cluttered in here as it had been yesterday. While they'd been alongside the cruiser the offwatch crewmen had been accommodated in her messdecks, but now hammocks and kitbags as well as extra stores, sacks of fresh vegetables, and so on, had been embarked. By the time the torpedomen's hammocks were slung in this compartment the only way to reach the tube space would be on all-fours.

Following Hobday aft, Jake saw Burtenshaw, the German-speaking explosives expert, perched on a chair in the control room; he had an open book on his knees and he was stooped over it, oblivious of the activity around him. No sign of his lord and master, Robins. But Everard was standing in the middle of the control room, staring up through the hatch at the bright circle of sky. As if, Jake thought, he was storing up a memory of it against the time when he wouldn't be seeing it much. Everard asked Hobday, 'Shall I be in anyone's way if I go up into the bridge?'

'Skipper'd like you to, I'm sure.' Hobday saw the gunlayer waiting to report. He cocked an eyebrow at Jake, who murmured, 'Roost'. A short, strong-looking man, with a broad face and wide-spaced eyes; according to Hobday, Roost had been a blacksmith's apprentice until 1914.

'Gun greased over, bore clear, gun secured, sir. Grenades, rifles, pistols and Lewis gun ready, sir.'

'Thank you, Layer.'

'Stowed 'is gear in the magazine too, sir.' Roost had nodded towards Burtenshaw. The Marine's gear was a large rucksack packed with demolition charges. Hobday nodded, moving aft through the control room. The signalman – Jake named him, *sotto voce* – reported, 'Challenges ready, sir.' Hobday nodded. 'Thank you, Ellery.' But they wouldn't be needing recognition signals. The destroyer patrol between this island and the straits would have been warned that they'd be passing; just as they'd have been warned yesterday to expect the Frenchman. And *Louve* should have got through by now, she'd be in the Marmara. If she wasn't, Jake thought, she'd – well, she *had* to be… He focused on the leading telegraphist, 'Professor' Weatherspoon, who behind his thick glasses and diffident manner looked fed up.

'Wireless and hydrophones correct, sir. But…' He shook his close-cropped, narrow head; the size of his ears and the high dome of skull made it look even narrower than it was. 'Well, I dunno, sir–I mean, there's me gear to be got at, maintenance an'—'

Hobday had caught on to the reason for his gloom.

'Only be for a day or two. And if we find it doesn't work, we'll change it. Meanwhile, when you have to get in there, he'll have to make way for you.'

'He' was the other passenger – Robins. They'd given him the little 'silent cabinet', the wireless office, to doss down in. It wouldn't give him room to stretch his legs out fully, but it would keep him out of the way and at the same time pander to his ego by making him think he'd been given a sort of minuscule cabin.

Jake, after a couple of gins and five minutes of Robins's conversation in the cruiser's wardroom last night, had said privately to Wishart, 'I'd put bloody bars on it if I were you.' On the silent cabinet, he'd meant... Hobday asked Weatherspoon, 'Is Lieutenant-Commander Robins on board?'

'No, sir. But 'is gear's all over the—'

'He's with your captain.' Burtenshaw took his nose out of his book. 'At least, he *was*.' He'd resumed his reading; Jake, peering over his shoulder, saw that the book was a rather battered copy of Tolstoy's *The Kingdom of God and Other Essays*. Strange reading, he thought, for an explosives expert. He followed Hobday aft. Finn, the man who'd joked about feeding spud-peelings to Frenchmen, was waiting near the control room's after bulkhead.

'Beam WRTs are full, sir.'

'Thank you, Finn.'

WRT stood for water-round-torpedoes. Each tube had to be filled with water around the fish inside it before

45

it could be fired, and water was blown up by air pressure from the tube's own tank.

Chief Engineroom Artificer Grumman came lumbering for'ard to meet Hobday in the beam torpedo compartment. This was exactly amidships, halfway along the submarine's 180-foot length. Grumman was built like a prize-fighter; but he was an easygoing, kindly man. 'Engines ready, sir. No bothers.'

'Good. We'll be on our way pretty soon now, Chief.' Hobday squeezed past Grumman and went on aft, over the platform that bridged the pair of tubes. It was less easy for Jake and Grumman to pass each other. At the doorway ERA McVeigh, the 'outside' artificer – his responsibility was all the primary machinery outside the engine-room – glanced at Jake cautiously, as at a stranger whom he, McVeigh, would view with distrust until he had reason to change his attitude. McVeigh had a wild, uncouth appearance: his ginger beard was ragged, as if rats fed on it.

'Telegraphs tested, sir. Steering gear and Janney lubricated. Air on the whistle, sir.'

'Very good.'

Moving into the engine-room, they were met by the stoker PO. He had a wad of oily cotton-waste in his hand, and he was wiping his chin with it. A Yorkshireman, short-legged and thickset, with a way of talking without any noticeable movement of the lips. Jake tried to adopt a similar technique as he murmured, 'PO Leech.'

'Comp tanks as per your orders, sir. Engine-room gear secured. External kingstons open.'

The amount of water in each compensation tank was decided after elaborate calculations concerning the boat's trim. Stores, fuel, fresh water, lubricating oil, extra personnel or gear – each change affecting the boat's weight in the water and balance fore-and-aft had to be taken into account. If you got the sums wrong and left her too heavy, when Wishart dived her she'd go down like a stone; if she was too light, she wouldn't get under at all. It would be just as bad too heavy or light at one end. Trim was one of Hobday's responsibilities.

In the motor-room Leading Seaman Dixon, the senior electrical rating, made his report. Dixon was short and fat: he was reputed – Hobday's story – to have been seen with seventeen boiled potatoes on one plate of mutton stew. He reported now, with the copper switchgear of the main switchboard shining like dull gold behind his overalled, egg-like shape, 'Main motors ready, sir. Motor bilges dry. Ventilator caps on, sluices 'alf closed.'

Hobday nodded. 'And the box is nicely up, eh.'

By 'box' he meant the battery – in fact four of them, each of fifty-five cells, each cell half the height of a man. The battery tanks were under the deck of the control room, and the cells stood in them on wooden gratings. They'd be getting a top-up charge this evening before the submarine dived for her run-in towards the straits and the Turkish minefield.

The *first* Turk minefield. Pretty well the whole way through there'd be mines.

Lindsay, one of the boat's two leading stokers, reported that the bilges were pumped out and dry and that the capstan had been tested. They went on aft, passing the humped casings over the actual motors and moving between banks of auxiliary machinery into the next compartment. Compressors, circulating pumps, pump motors. On each side, large handwheels to the kingstons of main ballast tanks – number 7 to starboard here, number 8 on the other side. Kingstons were large valves for opening or shutting flood-holes in the bottoms of the tanks; they were open now, as PO Leech had just reported, but the water stayed out because air pressure in the tanks kept it out. When the vents in the tops of the tanks were opened, though, the air would be released and the sea would rush up to fill the tanks and dive the submarine.

A mass of pipes continued on both sides and overhead: trim line, LP air-line, brass handwheels on the connections from the air-line to the tanks… Stores and gear filled any empty spaces. Some of the crew messed in here; the long mess table was slung up on chains under the deckhead, and could be let down when it was needed. Hobday stopped at the last bulkhead before the stern compartment, the after ends, and peered through. At the far end on the centre-line was the rear door of the stern tube. Emergency hand-steering gear was in the starboard after corner; and hand-operating gear for the after hydroplanes. Most of the off-watch crewmen slept in the after ends. A stoker sorting spanners glanced round from his crouched position beside a tool locker; Jake murmured, 'Stoker Peel'. He knew that 'Twister' Peel's diving-stations job was to watch the packing of the shaft bearings and help with the stern tube. Another man – a torpedoman – was squatting, writing in a notebook – diary, perhaps – writing slowly and laboriously, licking the pencil-lead between words. His name was – *oh, damn it all…*

He'd stood up. He was the after endsman and he had a report to make. He had a name too, but—

'After WRT full, sir.'

'Good.' Hobday cocked an eyebrow at Jake: and the name was on the tip of his tongue, but… Then the torpedoman reached out, hooking his hands over bunches of piping, exercising his muscles by swinging to and fro like a monkey in a cage: there were tattoos all over his arms. Tattoos triggered memory.

'Smith.'

'Cap'n comin' aboard, sir!'

Agnew, the Boy Telegraphist. Crabb must have sent him with the message. Sharp-faced like a weasel: pale: sixteen years old.

'Thank you, Agnew.' Hobday started for'ard, squeezing past individuals and through groups of men, to the control room, and up the ladder into the conning tower with its thick glass ports, up again into the bridge and the brilliant sunshine. Jake, arriving close behind him, saw CPO Crabb at the wheel with the portable magnetic compass in its bracket in front of him. The signalman, Ellery, was at the after end of the bridge with his Aldis lamp ready, its cable trailing down through the hatch. Everard was back there too. Jake climbed over and down to the catwalk and for'ard along the casing; Wishart was halfway down the brow and Robins, strutting in front of him, looking irritatingly self-important. Jake checked that Morton had singled up the hemp breasts so that casting off would be quick and simple, and that the cruiser's first lieutenant had had a topping-lift rigged, with steadying lines to the end of the gangway, ready to haul it clear. He heard Hobday call down the bridge voicepipe, 'Stand by telegraphs and main motors. Group down.' Only the electric motors could be used for

49

harbour manoeuvring, because the gas engines couldn't be put astern. Robins arrived on the casing, and Jake allowed him a perfunctory salute. Wishart got a proper one.

'All set, pilot?'

'Top line, sir.'

Hobday saluted the captain as he arrived in the bridge.

'Ready for sea, sir.'

'Splendid.' His easy manner made it seem like a personal favour he was acknowledging. 'Let go everything, then – as the bishop proposed to the actress.' He saw Nick Everard, and nodded to him. 'All right there? Looking forward to it?'

'Well...'

'Let go for'ard! Let go aft!'

The brow swung off the casing, and the ropes fell away from the submarine's bow and stern; they went snaking, wriggling up into the cruiser's waist. Jake took his stance up for'ard, where the casing narrowed and the hydroplanes stood out like fins, and Morton and the other hands of the casing party fell in on his left. He heard Wishart's voice back there on the bridge: 'Starboard ten, cox'n', and then, muffled by the voice-pipe as he put his face down to it, 'Slow ahead starboard.' A touch of motor and a little port rudder, to swing her stern out... 'Stop starboard. Midships. Slow astern together.' Above them, on the cruiser's quarterdeck, Commander Gillman bawled, 'Three cheers for HM Submarine E.57! Hip, hip...'

—

Reaper, on *Terrapin*'s bridge and with binoculars at his eyes, heard the waves of cheering and saw a layer of white rising and falling above the heads of the men on *Harwich's* decks as they waved their caps. Shifting the aim of his glasses he saw that the submarine had stopped her motors; you could tell, although she still had stern way on, by the fact that the white surge which her screws had flung up as she went astern had begun to melt, the blue surface to mend itself around her. She was swinging slowly, bringing her bow round towards Grafton Point.

She was moving ahead again now. There was a smoke-haze above her after casing, and a powerful churning of the sea astern; the racket of her diesel engines reached his ears. And *Terrapin* could push on too. Reaper had wanted to see both the submarines on their way before he left Imbros himself, but now Truman could take his ship down south-westward to the main fleet base, Mudros, to refuel, and come back this way tomorrow and on into the Gulf of Xeros. At the eastern end of it, off the north shore of the Gallipoli peninsula, they'd be within a few miles of the Marmara, across the peninsula's thin neck.

He looked round at Truman.

'Whenever you're ready, then.'

The cable was already shortened in; all that was necessary was to pull the hook out of the sand and wind it up. Truman climbed ponderously on to the step that surrounded the binnacle; he told Harriman, 'Weigh.'

'Weigh anchor!'

Granger's 'Aye aye' floated up to them; the cable began to clank home as the capstan dragged it dripping from the sea. Two men with a hose angled down over the ship's side were cleaning the chain off as it rose. Truman looked round for his signalman.

'Mayne – make to E.57, *Au revoir. Best of luck.*'

51

He glanced at Reaper for approval, but the commander was busy with his binoculars. Harriman, observing Granger's signals from the foc'sl, reported, 'Cable's up and down, sir.'

'Very good.' The lamp was clacking away, and from the submarine's bridge a light winked acknowledgement of each word. At the same time, E.57 was piping *Harwich*, she'd backed away clear of her during the cheering interlude, and now as she went ahead she was saluting the senior ship. Presently she'd pass *Terrapin* at a distance of about half a cable, a hundred yards or so. The signalman, pushing his Aldis lamp back into its bracket on the side of the bridge, reported, 'Message passed, sir.' But now a light was flashing again from the submarine: flashing 'A's, the calling-up sign. Mayne snatched up the lamp again. Reaper, joining Truman on the binnacle step, took off his cap and began to wave it: Wishart and his first lieutenant – one tall and bulky, the other slight and short – were easily identifiable as they waved back. Further aft, another less distinguishable figure waved: Reaper put his glasses up again, and saw that it was Nick Everard. He waved again: and had to stop, lower his arm and stand to attention when he heard the pipe and saw Wishart at the salute. He hadn't known that Wishart was junior to Truman in seniority as a lieutenant-commander. Now *Terrapin* was returning the compliment... Just as it all ended, Granger hailed from the foc'sl, 'Clear anchor!'

He hadn't reported it aweigh. Presumably the clarity of the water made it visible from the surface at the same time as it broke out of the seabed.

'Half ahead together. Starboard fifteen.'

'Starboard fifteen, sir.' The telegraphs clanged as the bridge messenger slammed their handles over. 'Both telegraphs at half ahead, sir.'

'Fifteen o' starboard wheel on, sir!'

'One-four-oh revolutions.'

Leading Signalman Mayne reported, 'From E.57, sir: *Why not meet us at the Horn?*'

Reaper smiled. He heard Truman ordering, 'Midships. Steer north ten west.'

Round the top of the island, then south. About sixty miles to go; then a hundred miles back and into the gulf. Flat calm, bags of speed and time in hand... Truman suggested quietly, 'Rather early in the day for cheers, was it not?'

Reaper knew what he meant. You cheered ships into harbour sometimes after successful operations, but not usually when they set out. It had been Gillman's suggestion, though, and Captain Usherwood had agreed to it. Reaper said, 'It's the devil of a job they're taking on, you know.'

'The straits?'

'Yes.' He settled the glasses at his eyes again. 'And what's in 'em.' He shrugged. 'We've nothing to go on, that's the snag of it. It's blind man's buff.' He nodded towards the submarine. 'As all of them know full well.'

E.57 was some way off now, with her diesels pushing her along at about six knots and the sea washing streaky-white over the bulges of her saddle-tanks, spreading in a broad, lacy track astern. She had a solitary, vulnerable look about her; he thought perhaps submarines always did have, at times such as this and to outsiders watching them, but it was disturbing to realise that tonight, when

53

this ship would be safe and comfortable alongside an oiler in Mudros harbour, that one there would be groping blind through minefields, scraping under nets… He murmured, still with his eyes on her, '*Louve* must have got through to the Marmara all right.'

Truman asked him in a tone that could almost have held reproof, 'Do you have positive information on that score, sir?'

Truman wasn't his sort of man, and Reaper wasn't looking forward to the social side of life in *Terrapin*. The fellow had too keen a sense of his own importance. Reaper told him, 'No. But when the Turks sink a submarine they always make a song and dance about it. They'd have told the world, by now.'

Chapter 3

There was a scattering of white on the surface, a light breeze on the bow as the submarine ploughed southeast-ward now, one diesel charging and the other driving her towards the spot where she'd dive for the run-in to the straits. Off to port, that distant haze of land was Cape Helles with the heights of Karethia and Achi Baba further back, vague as mist against the sky; where the land faded was the gap they'd soon be steering for and entering, and to the right of that were the ridges of hills on the nearer, Asiatic coast, ridges that slid down to the Plain of Troy.

Much closer – 3,000 yards on the starboard bow – was Mavro Island. They'd come in a wide circle around the British minefields.

Hobday lowered his glasses as Wishart heaved himself out of the hatch and joined him. E.57 was just about in the position to dive. A few minutes ago Jake Cameron had been up here taking bearings; then the signalman, Ellery, had come up to unship the portable compass. Steering was from the control room now, with the bridge wheel disconnected. Wishart said, 'No loafing, this time. You can do it. Wait one minute, then pull the plug and we'll see how long it takes.'

He'd spoken quietly so the lookout wouldn't hear it and be ready for it. After a spell of inaction even the best ship's company needed to be sharpened up a bit. Wishart went below again; when Hobday dived her, he'd be watching points down there.

The bridge was nothing but a platform now. Before they'd checked the trim with a slow-time, carefully-controlled dive off Kephalo, the canvas screens had been unlashed from the bridge rails, the wires unrove and the stanchions unshipped, all of it carried below and stowed for'ard in the tube space. The wireless mast and its aerial and the ensign staff had been removed too. Then the engines had been stopped, and she'd wallowed, losing way, and Wishart had flooded her down by filling one pair of main ballast tanks at a time, so that she'd eased her way into the sea as gingerly as a flapper dithering off a beach. But this time, with only numbers 3 and 4 main ballast not already full of water, she'd make her plunge in seconds; and she wouldn't be coming to the surface again – please God – until she was through the straits and in the Marmara.

That one minute had passed. Hobday glanced round at the lookout – Rowbottom, a torpedoman. Placid, heavy-boned, slow-moving. He'd better not move slowly *now*… He was gazing out over the beam, eastwards towards the loom of land, blinking patiently into his binoculars. Hobday stooped, putting his mouth close above the voicepipe, and shouted, 'Dive, dive, dive!'

Turning his head, he glimpsed Rowbottom more or less in mid-air as the man seemed to take off, flash across several feet of bridge, and fall into the open hatch. In the same space of time Hobday had shut the voicepipe cock and leapt into the hatch on top of him. His thumb stabbed at the button of the hooter: the engine noise had died and he heard the vents in the tops of the main ballast crash open and a roar of escaping air as the sea rushed up into numbers 3 and 4. A rain of spray was falling as he dragged the lid down over his head; then he was forcing the clips on, engaging the links and pushing the levers over, using both hands to do it. He climbed down through the lower hatch into the control room, and Ellery shut and clipped that lower one as soon as he was off the ladder.

No sign of Wishart. He heard Cameron tell the coxswain, 'Forty feet', and Crabb, on the after 'planes, repeated the order. Cameron told his first lieutenant, 'Captain said I was to catch a trim at forty. He's gone aft.'

Giving them all a bit of practice, and having a bit of a snoop around meanwhile. Jake Cameron, glancing round as the hands settled into their places, met Nick Everard's eyes: just a pair of eyes and part of a face glimpsed through a lot of general movement. He was back watching the trim now. Crabb reported, 'Forty feet, sir. Touch 'eavy aft, sir.'

'Yes.' He did nothing to compensate for it, though. Being at forty feet instead of twenty made the boat heavier; when they came back to periscope depth again she'd be in trim. Also, her fore-and-aft balance would have been thrown out by Wishart having gone aft. One man's weight could make a surprising amount of difference when it moved more than a few feet. Hobday muttered in Jake's ear, 'Main vents'. Jake glanced at the panel: he snapped, 'Shut main vents!' and McVeigh's hands moved fast up the row of steel levers, slamming them back into line; the thuds of closing tank-tops ran like drumbeats down the boat's length. It was a crime to leave main vents open once the boat was dived, and many first lieutenants would have made a fuss about it. Jake nodded to him. 'Thanks.'

Wishart was back, though. 'Hundred and fifty feet. You carry on, pilot.'

'Hundred and fifty, cox'n.'

CPO Crabb and Leading Seaman Morton angled their 'planes to take her down. Jake said over his shoulder, 'Pump on the buoyancy tank.' ERA Knight opened the tank's suction and vent, and McVeigh started the pump motor. The buoyancy tank was a small one amidships, useful for minor adjustments to the boat's weight because it had no fore-and-aft movement. The trim had to be adjusted now because as she went deeper her hull would be compressed by the pressure of the sea; she'd thus displace a smaller volume of water and, in accordance with the principle of Archimedes, become heavier.

'Hundred and fifty feet, sir.'

'Very good.' Trim seemed about right; he had the tank shut off. He saw Burtenshaw leaning in the doorway of the silent cabinet; the dreaded Robins was presumably inside it. Nick Everard was on a chair pushed hard back against the wardroom bunks; he looked like a prisoner, Jake thought – trapped, and alert for a chance to make a break for it.

Hum of the motors. Warm, oily atmosphere. It would get a damn sight warmer before they reached the Marmara. Wishart cocked an eyebrow at his first lieutenant: 'Check for leaks while we're deep, Number One?' He told the helmsman, 'Port ten.'

'Port ten, sir.' Roost, the gunlayer, was helmsman at diving stations. He spun the wheel, and Wishart added, 'Steer oh-five-oh.'

That was the course to enter the Dardanelles – which about a million years ago had been a river and was no wider than a decent-sized one now.

Steering by gyro. The gyro wheel itself was inside a steel-mesh casing right against the steering pedestal. If Roost stuck his elbows out as he pushed the helm around he'd crack one on the conning-tower ladder and the other on the corner of the auxiliary switch-board. If you had a cat in an E-class submarine you wouldn't swing it round.

Having rudder on affected the boat's trim, and Morton had put some dive on the fore 'planes to counteract the bow's tendency to rise. Now Roost was easing the wheel off.

'Course oh-five-oh, sir.'

Wishart said, 'When the first lieutenant's finished his inspection we'll go to watch diving. What's our distance to the Kum Kale mines, pilot?'

'Six point one miles, sir.' He'd laid the tracks off on the chart and he had the courses and distances in his head.

'Three hours, then.'

A slow approach would conserve the battery's power – which was essential, with forty-five miles of straits ahead of them. It wasn't only a question of the distance to be covered under water; there'd almost certainly be some tricky bits on the way through – nets to break through, for instance – and to get out of difficult situations you needed, usually, at least spasms of full power on the motors. You had to save up, as it were, for the times when there'd be no option but to use the batteries to their limit.

Hobday had been right for'ard; now he passed through again on his way aft. He told Wishart, as he squeezed between Knight and Ellery, 'Dry as a bone so far.'

Morton murmured out of the corner of his mouth to Crabb, 'More 'n *I* am.' Sweat was running down his big, smooth face. 'Lover-boy Mort', they called him; something to do with a girl in Gibraltar, Hobday had said. Might she not have minded his tendency to stream with sweat? Only the 4th ERA, Bradshaw, was his equal at it, and *his* name to his friends was 'Polecat'. A wiry, very hairy man. He was at the port after end of the control room; his responsibilities at diving stations were number 3 external vent, the port ballast pump and the port mainline flooding valve.

E.57 had a complement of twenty-nine officers and men, and at diving stations fifteen of them had jobs here in the control room.

Hobday had been through to the after ends. He'd finished his tour now and he was coming back, coming from motor-room to engine-room. In the space between those two compartments, Stoker PO Leech was squatting between the engine clutches, paring his nails with a pusser's dirk. He edged sideways to let the first lieutenant pass.

'Shaft gland on the port side's seeping a bit, Spo.'

The Yorkshireman's left eyebrow twitched. 'Sweatin', more 'n seepin', sir.'

'I hope you're right.'

'Old chum o' mine, that port gland, sir.'

'Mind you look after it, then. And be sure Peel checks the bilges every watch.'

'Aye, sir.' Hobday went through to Wishart. 'No leaks, sir.'

'Heaven be praised.' Wishart told Jake, 'Bring her up to twenty feet.'

'Twenty feet, sir.'

The 'planesmen swung their brass handwheels round – big as bicycle wheels, brightly-polished brass – and watched the dials that showed the angles of their hydroplanes and the boat's depth, and the tube of the spirit-level that showed her angle in the water. Now, as she rose towards the surface, Jake had to put back into the buoyancy tank as much water as he'd pumped out on her way down. And Wishart wasn't intending to make it easy for him; as she was slowing and levelling to periscope depth, he told Hobday, 'Fall out diving stations, Number One.'

'Which watch, cox'n?'

Crabb growled, 'First part o' port, sir.'

'First part of port watch, watch diving!'

Now instead of fifteen men in the control room, there'd be only four – plus the officers in the for'ard part of it, where they messed. Two 'planesmen, one helmsman, and one duty ERA would be all the watchkeepers on duty; of the others, some would be going for'ard and rather more than that going aft. The trim would be completely thrown out.

Jake told McVeigh, 'Stand by the trim-line.'

The for'ard trim tank held a ton-and-a-half of water, the stern one a ton. They were connected by a water-pipe called the trim-line and also by an air-pipe with a vent-and-blow cock on it, here in the control room. By putting the cock this way or that, you could blow water from one end of the boat to the other, to compensate for crew movements. It was a quick and simple system, and by the time the change-round was completed Jake had her back in trim.

Hobday nodded. 'Not bad.'

Jake looked down at him. 'I'm a clever bloke.'

'Just as well to be told. Nobody'd ever guess it.' Hobday joined Wishart and the passengers. Robins had emerged from the cabinet. Lewis, the gun trainer who acted as wardroom messman, was drawing the blue curtain which converted that corner of the compartment into what passed for a wardroom; he asked Wishart, 'Tea, sir?'

'*What* a good idea.'

Robins said, 'I was under the impression we'd *had* tea.'

Lewis told him, 'That were stand-easy tea, sir. Sardines with *this* lot.'

'Lord, but we're pampered...' Wishart winked at Burtenshaw. He'd brought the chart over, and he was spreading it on the pull-out table. 'Show you fellows our route and whatnot, so you'll understand what's going on... Here – this is where we've just dived. This line's the track we're following to approach the straits. We had to start some way out, you see, or they'd spot us from the shore and be expecting us – and that we *don't* want... The distance to run in is just about six miles. That's to the shaded area here, right across the entrance – the one enemy minefield we know about for certain. So at this spot here, in about three hours, we'll go deep and slip under it.'

Burtenshaw asked hesitantly, 'How do we know when we reach that point?'

'We'll be taking fixes – periscope bearings of the headlands – during the approach. We also have a check on the distance run, from log readings.' He jerked a thumb. 'The log's what makes that ticking all the time.'

It was quite loud, when you stopped to listen to it. Behind it was the low hum of the motors driving the submarine north-eastward at slow speed, and a thinner, whining whisper that came from the flywheel of the gyro compass.

Wishart explained to Robins, 'By the time we're under the mines and inside the straits it'll be coming up for sunset. The straits aren't what you'd call wide – in fact they're darned narrow in some places – so we won't use the periscopes more than we have to, when we're in there. Not even in the dark. But we can when it's really necessary, and land-shapes should be visible against the stars. That's why we decided to make this passage at night and on a night without a moon.' He paused, rubbing his jaw; then he went on, 'As far as possible, though, we'll stay deep. Several reasons. There'll be obstructions – nets, obviously – and they all start on the surface – buoyed, mostly. Lower down, depending on the kind of net and how they've laid it, we can either pass under its foot or break right through it. Same with mines – they tend to be nearer the surface than the seabed. That's a *bit* of an oversimplification, because the practice nowadays is to moor the beastly things in lines at varying depths.' He shook his head. 'Very unsporting chap, the Turk. Not that it'll do him any good so far as *we're* concerned.'

Robins glanced up at him.

'Why not?'

Wishart turned a chair around, and sat down. 'Because – not that I'd want to boast, you understand – because I know my job, and I've an able and experienced crew, and this is a lucky ship.'

'What an experience to have.' There was a glowing smile on Burtenshaw's youthful, games-player's face. 'It's magnificent. Absolutely.'

Nick was looking at him as if he thought he had a screw loose. But Wishart patted him on the back. 'Extra rations for that kind of talk. But I'm afraid you may be disappointed if you're expecting thrills. Best way to pass the next eight hours'd be to get your head down and sleep through it.'

'Eight hours?'

'Something of that sort.' Wishart looked at Nick. 'I was going to explain – reasons for staying deep rather than going through at periscope depth – the main one is the peculiar tidal picture in the straits. Nasmith was the chap who first rumbled it – you know, Nasmith VC? Well, he buzzed up and down the Dardanelles as if he owned them, once he got the hang of it. What he discovered was that near the surface you've got a tide from the Marmara into the Mediterranean – against us, in fact – of about one-and-a-half, two knots. If you have to knock those two knots off our dived speed you'd be adding forty per cent to the time it'd take us to get right through – and then the battery wouldn't last out. That's one of the problems they faced in those days – before Nasmith found that lower down, at say seventy or a hundred feet, there's a tide running at about three knots *into* the Marmara. *With* us.'

He paused, listening, as Jake ordered quietly, 'Raise the for'ard periscope.' They heard the slight *thump* as the ERA of the watch pushed the control lever to 'up', and the hiss of the hydraulic ram as oil-pressure sent the long brass tube sliding upward. Another soft thud as the ERA stopped it, and then a click as Jake jerked its handles down.

Wishart went on, 'Surface water going one way, bottom water going in the opposite direction. That'd be odd enough. But it's more complicated than even that, in some places… One theory is that about halfway down, somewhere around the bottleneck there, the whole body of water in the straits does a sudden corkscrew twist – water from the bottom rises on one side, and surface-water slides down on the other. Bit awkward if you get caught in it – as one or two boats have, in the past. But – well, knowing it can happen, and being ready for it – that's half the battle. If you find we're suddenly blowing and flooding tanks and generally pumping around in what may seem a rather disorganised manner, don't let it worry you – it won't be anything we can't cope with. Eh?'

Robins murmured, 'One might well *hope*—'

'Or for that matter if we bump into a net. It's not unusual. If we get snarled up, we unsnarl ourselves. Been done before, lots of times.'

Able Seaman Lewis pushed in through the curtain, using his elbows to part it. He was carrying a tin tray with mugs of tea on it. Jake, at the periscope, addressed the helmsman: 'Anderson – stand by to take down some bearings.' Hobday called out, 'Hang on there.' He grabbed the chart in one hand and a mug in the other, and went over to the chart table. Jake said, from the periscope, 'I'll have some tea here, Lewis, while you're at it.'

'Aye aye, sir.' The messman was putting the other mugs on the table, and Robins was staring disdainfully at his dirty hands and black fingernails. He was still staring at them when Lewis pushed his fist into an old toffee-tin and brought out a handful of sugar lumps. He began to thumb

65

them one at a time into the lieutenant-commander's mug: 'Say when, sir...'

'One hundred feet.'

Wishart snapped up the handles of the periscope – the for'ard one, the big one with the sixfold magnification in its lenses – and McVeigh depressed the lever that sent it hissing down into its well. Wishart had just taken a new set of bearings – edges of land, and hilltops – to get a last fix on the chart before E.57 went in under the mines. At the chart table, Jake had marked the position on the chart and taken a reading of the log.

'Hundred feet, sir.' CPO Crabb spun the wheel of the after 'planes, and Morton put some dive on his. Key men had taken over the controls, although the rest of the hands hadn't been closed up at diving stations. No need for it, yet.

Robins was in the wireless cabinet. He'd said he was going to take Wishart's advice and sleep right through. Nick Everard and Burtenshaw were lying on Wishart's and Hobday's bunks, Nick with his eyes shut and Burtenshaw reading Tolstoy. Hobday watched the needles in the depth-gauges slowing down as the boat approached her ordered depth and the 'planesmen levelled her off.

'Stop the pump.'

McVeigh pushed the switch with the toe of his plimsoll. It was warm in the control room: quiet, comfortable, well-lit. Easy to drop off to sleep if you'd no special reason to stay awake. The quietest tone of voice was enough for orders and reports; if you spoke loudly you'd be heard at the far ends of the submarine.

'Hundred feet, sir.'

'Very good.' Wishart had to turn sideways to edge round the ladder; looking over Roost's shoulder he checked the ship's head by gyro. The course was 084 degrees, to run in between Cape Helles and Kum Kale.

'I'll sing out if I need you, pilot.'

'Sir.' Jake crossed from the chart table to the wardroom corner. The curtains were drawn back now, open. He sat down in the armchair, and Burtenshaw asked him if he wanted to stretch out.

Jake shook his head. 'I've my own bunk, anyway. This drawer thing here. Pulls out when it's wanted.'

'Oh yes, of course…' The Marine nodded. 'Er – mind if I ask you something?'

'I'll tell you when you've asked it.'

'Oh… Well, how did you come to be RNR, as opposed to RN or RNVR?'

'Merchant Navy. I was a cadet when the war started. Went to sea as a snotty – in a trawler based at Immingham. Then I sort of wheedled my way into submarines.'

'Will you go back to the Merchant Navy?'

'Lord knows.' Jake shrugged his heavy shoulders. The future and his place in it worried him; he didn't want to talk about it. Bad enough spending so many hours *thinking* about it – at night, even nights when you really needed sleep but you woke and it came into your mind and wouldn't go away. He asked Burtenshaw, not really giving a damn for the answer, 'What about you?'

The Marine laughed. 'Honestly haven't a notion, old chap.'

'You're not on a regular commission then.'

'Me?' He was tracing patterns in a glisten of conden- sation that was already forming on the white-enamelled deckhead above his bunk. 'Well, I was at Harrow, you see, and – how shall I put it – I unilaterally terminated my scholastic career?'

'French leave?'

'Almost. And the Royal Marines seemed as good a choice as any, so I trotted down to Deal – the depot there, you know? – and joined up, in the ranks.'

'Did you, by George!'

'Spur of the moment, really. Just sort of happened.'

'Did your people mind?'

'Ah. Well, my father took it quite well, really. And now since I've been commissioned even my mother—'

'What does your father do?'

'Surgeon. Cuts up people who can afford his stupendous fees.' Burtenshaw's chuckle faded. 'He's in France now – disguised as a colonel, cutting up people who can't… Anyway, my life in the ranks didn't last long. When they found I had the rudiments of an education they told me it was my duty to accept responsibility, all that rot.'

'What about the explosives part of it?'

'Chemistry was about the only thing I was any use at, at school. And at Deal before the Zeebrugge raid there was a chap called Brock – son of the man who started the firework factory, d'you know? – and he's a *real* expert. I mean he *was*. He was killed on the mole… Anyway, I got tied up with some of his experimental stuff, bombs and things. I applied to go on the raid in his crowd, actually, but—'

'Wouldn't take you?'

Nick, who'd known Brock at Dover, had his eyes open, listening. He heard Burtenshaw answer, '*Everyone* wanted to go on the raid, you know. For every man that went, there were fifty wanted to.'

That was true enough. And the blockships' passage crews, mostly stokers, had been so determined to get into the action that they'd stowed away, hiding until the assault was launched. He heard Cameron ask the Marine, 'D'you really think you'll be able to blow up *Goeben*?'

'I've – well, not much of an idea about it, really. I mean, what I'm supposed to do. I've got this stuff with me, of course, but how or when or where – well, don't ask me, because I don't know *anything*.'

Silence… Nick turned his head, saw Jake Cameron looking puzzled. Then Burtenshaw's hand showed, pointing towards the wireless cabinet. 'Do what I'm told, that's all. *When* I'm told.' He leant right over the edge of the bunk and spoke in a whisper, but impersonating Robins: 'Fewer people know anything about it, the better for us all, Burtenshaw…' He'd pulled back into the bunk. 'Truly, I'm simply to do what I'm told when the time comes.'

'But if—' Jake waved in Robins's direction '—if he went adrift, and you're left in the dark – surely—'

'Three of us now, thank heaven. I mean we've got this—'

A *clang* from the bow: from somewhere outside the hull.

'Stop both motors!'

Now a scraping noise. Jake Cameron had half risen in his chair, then sat back again and let his breath out. Burtenshaw was up on an elbow, pink-faced, goggling. Nick was on his back with his eyes open and staring at the deckhead. He hadn't otherwise moved although he could feel cold sweat all over his skin and his gut was tight. ERA Knight had jumped to the telegraphs to pass Wishart's order to the motor-room, and now the sound of the motors died away. But the scraping was continuous, from somewhere on the port side for'ard. Abrasive on the mind, *inside* it. Nick told himself, *Take it easy: they know their business, and this is only the first minute, we've a whole night to get through*.

He hadn't expected it to start this soon. He was getting his imagination and his nerves in hand now, hoping nobody had seen any outward sign of the sudden shock he'd felt.

'Starboard fifteen.'

'Starboard fifteen, sir.' Roost pushed the wheel around. He didn't look as if he thought anything out of the ordinary was happening. The wheel's polished brass glinted as it revolved; he'd checked it now. Morton, the second coxswain, reported an obstruction on the fore 'planes.

'Can't 'ardly shift 'em, sir.'

'It's an ill wind…' Wishart added, 'Midships. Slow astern together.'

'Slow astern together, sir.'

Calm, quiet… Voices so relaxed there was something almost artificial about them. Hobday asked Wishart over his shoulder, 'What ill wind, sir?'

'Tells us where it is, old lad… Stop port. Starboard ten.'

'Starboard ten, sir.'

ERA Knight, still acting as telegraphman, reported the port motor stopped. Burtenshaw whispered to Jake, 'What's going on?'

'For'ard hydroplanes have been fouled by something. Wire. So we're sort of backing off it.'

'Mine-wire?'

'Likely as not.'

A reverberating *twang*: still echoing: weird... Morton whispered, 'Bye-bye, dearie.'

'Stop starboard. Midships.'

Stopping the boat and then putting her astern – and with helm on, at that – had thrown out the depth-keeping. The jammed fore 'planes hadn't been able to help, either. The gauges showed a hundred and eight feet, and the submarine was still sinking slowly deeper. Hobday, trying to cope with the trim, not only spoke in the suddenly fashionable calm, quiet manner, but his movements were slower too. Normally he was an unusually brisk, jerky sort of man.

'Both motors stopped, sir.'

'Helm's amidships.'

'Port five. Slow ahead together. Knight, find someone else to work the telegraphs – you'll be cooking the breakfast, next.'

'Sir.' The ERA went to the bulkhead doorway. 'Pass the word for Davie Agnew!'

'Both motors slow ahead, sir.'

'Five o' port wheel—'

'Midships. Ship's head?'

Hobday said in a murmur to the 'planesmen, 'Get her up again now.' With the motors driving her ahead again, they'd be able to. The motors' hum was audible again: that, and men's small movements, quiet voices, and the steady ticking of the log. ERA Knight's voice in a whisper to someone near him, 'I'm right 'andy with a fryin'-pan, you'd be surprised, mate.' Nick lay still with his eyes on the sweating, painted steel above him, and tried to visualise

71

what was outside it, the dark enclosing water and taut wires growing in it like graceful stems with the flower-heads of destruction, death, swaying to the tide. He heard Wishart tell the helmsman to steer 090 degrees.

Hobday asked him, 'Shut watertight doors, sir?'

He'd put the question casually, and for a moment, Nick didn't think anything about it. Then he caught its import: Hobday was suggesting shutting the compartments off from each other so that mine damage wouldn't necessarily flood the whole submarine at once.

'Course oh-nine-oh, sir.'

'Very good... No, not yet, Number One.'

There must be pros and cons, Nick realised, and Wishart would have turned them over in his mind before he gave that answer. Perhaps communications and morale considerations versus that damage-control advantage. If one could work up a positive interest in the technical aspects of what was happening it might help, he thought. Jake Cameron had been over at the chart table; he came back now and told Nick and Burtenshaw, 'Chances of actually hitting one are pretty small, you know.' Nick wondered if Cameron believed it, or if he himself might be whistling in the dark. Agnew, the Boy Telegraphist, had obviously been fast asleep; he'd just come into the compartment blinking, stifling yawns, pale as a ghost. ERA Knight jerked his head towards the telegraphs and Agnew moved quickly to that port after corner. Jake told Burtenshaw, speaking very quietly, 'That ERA – Knight, his name is – he's from Newcastle, but his father's bought up some big London garage, and when the war ends Knight there takes over as the boss.'

He and the ERA had chatted last evening, while he'd been busy on chart corrections and Knight had been doing some job in the control room. Jake told the Marine, 'I warned him I'd be along for free gas.'

'Motor of your own, have you?'

'*I* wasn't at Harrow, my lad!' He didn't say it as if it mattered to him. He glanced up at Nick, and winked.

Clang...

'Stop together.'

The order had come quick as lightning, but not with any sense of alarm detectable in its tone. Now, on the port side, there was a noise like sawing. Not as far for'ard as the first lot had been. It was probably because it was closer, Nick told himself, that it sounded so much louder.

'Starboard twenty.'

Aiming, of course, to swing her to port around the wire, throwing her afterpart clear to prevent the mine-wire fouling the after hydroplane. Agnew reported, looking more surprised than sleepy now, 'Both motors stopped, sir.' Nick warned himself that this was only the first field of them, and that in the forty-five miles between this end of the straits and the Marmara there were bound to be plenty more. One might as well settle the mind to it, come to terms with it as an unpleasant interlude that had somehow to be lived through. But how might that be done? Surface actions and, in particular, destroyer actions were fast, brief, noisy and exciting enough to be – by and large – quite enjoyable. Utterly different. The scraping was still moving aft: a harsh, very unpleasant noise. Very close, too. He craned out of his bunk, to get a sight of the nearer of the two depth-gauges: a hundred and twelve feet: a hundred and thirteen... The submarine was not only scraping her side along the cable, she was also sliding down it. He realised that with her screws stopped, without any forward motion through the water, the hydroplanes could have no effect on depth-keeping. But perhaps that didn't matter much: since the mine would be at the top end of the wire, to slide down in the opposite direction wasn't such a bad idea. The thought made him smile: he was hardly aware of it, but he'd happened to meet Jake Cameron's glance and Cameron grinned back at him. Because the scraping noise had stopped? It *had*... But it might start again at any moment, he told himself, wanting to be ready for it if it did.

He wondered where the wire was now. And where others might be. One had no idea at all how thickly the Turks might have sown this minefield. Heaven knew, one had planted enough of them oneself: in the Channel, in the Dover days, those quick mine-laying sorties to the Belgian coast, always so damn glad when the last mine had slid off the destroyer's stern so that she was no longer a vulnerable floating bomb... Wishart blew his nose. Then he said calmly, pushing the hand, kerchief back into a pocket of his shabby grey-flannel trousers, 'Midships. Port ten. Slow ahead starboard.' He was using the screw that was on the side away from where the wire had been, and starboard rudder to counter the turning effect of using only one motor. Just to get past the infernal — Nick screwed up his eyes for about a second – *bloody* thing...

'Slow ahead both. Ship's head now, Roost?'

'Oh-five-seven, sir.' He left the port wheel on, to bring her round to starboard, which was the way they had to go. Agnew had reached up to swing the telegraph handles round. They were well above his head, on that after bulkhead, and it was difficult for him because he was so short. Hobday ordered quietly, 'Hundred feet, second.'

'Aye, sir.' Morton increased the up-angle on his 'planes. He was soaking wet by this time and he had his eyes slitted to keep the sweat from running into them. CPO Crabb glanced sideways at him, and sniffed; he muttered, 'Gawd…'

'Steer oh-nine-oh.'

Playing safe, Nick guessed, visualising the picture on the chart and trying to occupy his own mind by reading Wishart's. Going farther out to starboard as one passed through the entrance into the widening bay wouldn't make much odds, but getting too far the other way, towards Cape Helles, could spell trouble. Once this kind of zigzagging around started, so that one's position was uncertain, and on top of that not knowing much about what the tidal stream might be doing at any particular depth, it would be reasonable enough to allow some extra margin of sea-room. Roost reported, 'Course oh-nine-oh, sir.' Morton whispered sideways at the coxswain, 'What d'*you* let out – rose-water?' It occurred to Nick that if this was a sample of what might be expected all through the straits, except that there'd be much narrower places and other forms of defences, one could almost say there wasn't a hope in ten thousand of getting through: he was trying to find a way of arguing against that, when they caught the wire.

The submarine jolted hard: an arresting jerk that sent men staggering, stopped her and listed her sharply to starboard. Men were grabbing at things near them for support: Nick, with one hand hooked over piping on the deckhead and the other clutching the edge of his bunk, heard Wishart order, 'Stop together!' Then, as Agnew reached to the brass handles of the telegraphs, the mine-wire sprang off the starboard hydroplane: you could feel the jump of it, the sudden powerful wrench, the quivery spasm of release. Wishart, glancing towards Agnew again and opening his mouth, hadn't had time to speak when the wire snapped back just as violently against the submarine's starboard side – here, amidships. Faces, eyes turned that way: it would be the saddle-tank, outside the pressure hull, that the wire had clanged against and where it was now scraping and creaking. She'd angled over to port, and now she swung back to starboard, a list towards the wire as it bent itself around her and exerted some kind of twisting force. Then the mine on the end of the cable crashed into the side of the bridge above their heads.

Echoes dinned through the boat: through men's eardrums, skulls…

Extraordinarily, there'd been no explosion.

Jake Cameron, finding Everard and Burtenshaw both staring at him, realised he'd been holding his breath. He let it out – slowly, not wanting it to be obvious. The vice which had clamped on his guts a few seconds ago was easing its grip. He crossed to the chart table, picked up a pencil that could do with sharpening and read the code letters on it: HB… Thinking about those two goofing at him like that, the thought of having let them see how badly he'd had the wind up in the last minute or two was about as disturbing as anything that was happening around them.

E.57 rocked back, settled on an even keel. The wire scraped jerkily along the starboard tanks.

'Port twenty. Slow ahead port.'

Wishart had his handkerchief in his hand, holding it ready as if he was about to sneeze. The urge to do so must have left him; he was pushing it back into his pocket.

'Twenty o' port wheel on, sir.' Roost was calm, expressionless. Agnew reported in a slightly breathless tone, 'Port – port motor goin' slow ahead, sir.'

'You're doing well, young Agnew.'

The boy grinned self-consciously. Aware of several other friendly glances, he turned slightly pink. No scraping noise, suddenly. They waited, thinking – or carefully *not* thinking – about the wire and the thing it held moored to the seabed and the protuberance of the starboard after hydroplane, whether the boat would be swinging fast enough to clear it.

Wishart gave it time. Finally he murmured – as if it didn't matter terribly – 'Lost it, I do believe.' Crabb grated, without taking his eyes off the dial in front of him, 'The 'un mines go bang when you 'it 'em. That must've been one of ours.'

Everybody laughed. Wishart said, 'When we get back, cox'n, I'll buy you a drink.' He looked at Hobday. 'Let's get down a bit before we hit a live one. Hundred and fifty feet.'

–

Hobday had the watch, and Burtenshaw still occupied his bunk. Reading the Tolstoy essays now. Wishart had turned in too; he was flat out and his eyes were shut, but Nick didn't think he was asleep. Probably only discouraging conversation. Nick was in the armchair, playing a game of patience with a pack of cards that Cameron had offered him. Cameron was on the other side of the table, facing him, writing letters or *a* letter: he wrote with his head bent low over the pad, so that all Nick saw was the top of his broad, dark head.

He'd found he had no urge to sleep, and that lying horizontal, wide awake, while other men were up and working within sight and earshot, imposed the irritating feeling of being an invalid of some sort. Which of course he had been, not so long ago – and might the difficulty he'd had in accepting that status be the cause of *this* restlessness?

There could be other, contributory causes. Sarah: not knowing why she'd rushed down to London like that, to spend time with his father – whom, God knew, she had reason enough to loathe. Could it have been anything else *but* remorse? And might she, through remorse, hate *him* now?

He was holding a seven of hearts, staring at it as if it had some great significance. He put it down, and brought the game back into focus… But being a passenger was irksome anyway: it had been in *Terrapin* and it was the same here in the submarine. He told himself, as he put a red queen on a black king, that giving way to the irritation was a weakness: that he should make himself relax and accept the unpalatable truth that ships and operations could be run quite well without his help!

Leveret – this new appointment – was another irritation. All right, so he'd be at sea – when the old tub wasn't laid up with boiler trouble or other ailments – and it *was* a command. But in that Mudros flotilla an old *Laforey*-class destroyer would be the runt of the litter, the ship that got all the dullest jobs… The game hadn't come out. He began to collect the cards, to start again. He could hear the sporadic scratching noise that Cameron's pen made as he wrote his love-letter – or whatever it was. Love-letters on the brain, he thought… Through wanting one so badly, and getting only those two matter-of-fact, stepmotherly notes from her. He'd been at Queenstown in Ireland when they'd reached him, working on Admiral Sir Lewis Bayly's staff at the liaison- and training-base for the new American convoy-escort flotillas. Sarah's letters had been brief, *polite* acknowledgements of his own long, impassioned ones. He'd been puzzled; but also he'd been hard-worked up there, and busy in any spare time composing letters and pulling strings in efforts to get back to sea; there'd been little time for worrying or working things out. And now, holding the pack of cards in his clenched left hand, he stared at Jake Cameron's bowed head and saw Sarah in his mind's eye: ghostlike, vague and enigmatic, because in the weeks since he'd left home waters and heard nothing more from her she'd become the centre of almost constant speculation and anxiety – as well as—

One baulked at the word. But *all right*… He fanned the whole pack in his two hands. All right: love.

She's my stepmother, for God almighty's sake!

Cameron had raised his head: they were staring at each other across the table.

'All right?'

'What?' Coming to earth… 'Oh yes, fine, thanks.' He shrugged. 'Not very good at just sitting about, though.'

'You won't have to, for long, will you.' Jake blotted a page of his letter and turned it over. 'Only a few days, then you'll be having a run ashore in Turkey. All harems and 'Araq, so they say.'

Quiet, and warm. Since her brush with the mines, E.57 had been paddling along in perfect peace for about an hour-and-a-half. Against the background hum of her motors and the noise the log made – all of which disappeared if you didn't think about it or listen for it – one heard only the small movements of the helmsman and the two 'planesmen, a quiet order occasionally from Hobday, or some sound as the duty ERA shifted his position. Routine – homely… Jake went on with the letter to his mother.

> Having had no excitements I really have nothing very interesting to say. The climate of course is wonderful although we have had some colder days and the nights are beginning to feel quite chilly. Mind you, by English standards you'd still think it was quite summery!

All she wanted was a few pages with her son's handwriting all over them. And the security – no, she didn't only *want* that, she *needed* it – to know he was alive and likely to remain so.

> You needn't worry for two seconds about me, you know. The War is nearly over and in no time at all I shall be walking up the path and knocking on the door. In fact I have been thinking quite a bit about what I shall do when the time comes to leave the Navy. Apply to the old Line, I suppose; but then there may be rather a lot of chaps like me and not nearly enough berths for us all.

Now why had he written that? To test her reaction?

If he did apply, the Line would surely – he hoped – welcome him back. He'd become one of their cadets at the beginning of 1914; and his father Ewan Cameron had put in a lifetime's service with them. A tragically foreshortened lifetime; it had ended in the Atlantic two years ago, when the ship of which he'd been Master had been blown almost in half by a U-boat's torpedo and gone down in seconds. Jake had been allowed a fortnight's compassionate leave – two weeks in which to comfort an elderly, brokenhearted woman who even at the end of that leave, when Jake had had to return to his submarine flotilla at Blyth, hadn't learnt to believe in what had happened. The finality had been too much for her to accept as real; her emotional struggles had seemed to Jake rather like those of someone trying to condition their mind to accept the limitlessness of space, and finding the concept too elusive to be held on to. And at the same time, through the bewilderment, reality would strike in intermittently, bringing with it such an infinity of pain that it could only be described as torment. In trying to comfort her in that degree of agony, he'd been able to subdue his own quite powerful sense of loss; and after the fortnight's leave a submarine patrol in the German Bight had felt like a rest-cure. He'd felt guilty, for enjoying the relief of it.

Even now, although most of the time she *seemed* to have her feet back on the ground – as much as she ever had, anyway – wasn't she still half believing the old man would come home one day? Jake was fairly certain of it. The doubt, for him, was whether he should continue in a sea career; whether he shouldn't find himself some kind of job ashore so as to stay close to her.

I hope you are looking after yourself properly
and seeing plenty of your friends. I am quite
sure it won't be long before I am home with
you, but until then you must try to…

'Captain, sir.' Hobday. Wishart opened his eyes and
turned his head on the pillow. 'According to DR, sir, we
should be in the middle.'

'Right.' Aubrey Wishart swung himself off the bunk,
and slid down. Old flannels with frayed turn-ups, and a
cricket shirt that must once have been white but was now
yellowish with age. Tennis shoes. On patrol, nobody cared
about uniform. Hobday, wearing his reefer jacket, was the
only one who would have been recognisable to an outsider
as a commissioned officer; and the rest of his turn-out was
a pair of tweed trousers and a white shirt with no collar.
Jake had an open shirt over a string vest; his trousers were
blue serge from his cadet days.

He'd put the writing-pad away and crossed over to the
chart table. Wishart joined him there.

By dead reckoning – DR, meaning an unchecked position estimated only from the courses steered and distances
on each course by log – the submarine would now be
five miles inside the straits and just about in the middle
of Aren Kioi bay. It was the broadest stretch of water
in the whole length of the Dardanelles: pear-shaped, it
narrowed up towards the bottleneck. If they were where
they thought they should be, there'd be two miles of water
on each beam.

Wishart glanced round the control room. Chief ERA
Grumman had propped his bulk against the panel of vents
and blows, Finn was on the fore 'planes and Anderson on
the after ones. Ellery, the signalman, was helmsman.

'How long since the others got their heads down?'

Hobday looked at the clock. 'Hour-and-a-half, sir.'

'Damn it, they'll be getting bed-sores... Let's have the cox'n and second cox'n on the 'planes... You happy there, Chief?'

Grumman nodded, with that slow smile of his. 'Right as rain, sir, thank you.'

Hobday told Finn, 'Fore 'planes amidships. Go and shake the cox'n and second cox'n. Then go aft, and if there's a stoker awake I want him for the telegraphs. If there isn't, shake one.'

'Aye aye, sir.' When Finn moved away, Jake slid into his seat. Wishart nodded. 'Splendid. Bring her up, Number One. One hundred feet, to start with.'

'Hundred feet, sir...'

When she paused there, and while he made adjustments to the trim, the 'planesmen changed round.

'Fifty feet.'

The needle resumed its steady circling. CPO Crabb's eyes were like knife-holes in his leathery skin as he recovered gradually from a short, deep sleep. Morton was yawning, slumped damply on his stool.

'Stop flooding. Ease that rise, second.'

'Flood-valve shut, sir.'

Morton reduced the angle of rise on his 'planes. The boat was levelling at fifty feet. No scrapes so far. Higher up, there might easily be nets.

'Close up the hydrophones.'

Might be a patrol boat as well, of course, Nick realised. Just as well to listen for them before you pushed a periscope up under their noses. Hobday said over his shoulder, 'Burrage – shake the leading tel. Cameron –

shake Lieutenant-Commander Robins, ask him to move out of the cabinet.'

The hydrophone listening gear was in the wireless cabinet. Wishart murmured as Jake went to its half-sized doorway, 'Forty feet, Number One.'

'Forty feet, sir.'

Sounds of Robins questioning the need to move; and Cameron's low-toned explanation. Leading Telegraphist Weatherspoon appeared, blinking owlishly through his thick-lensed glasses. Wishart told him, 'Listen all round for propeller noises, leading tel.'

He'd nodded; now he was in the cabinet, muttering to himself at the disorder in there. Robins was asking Jake what was happening and how far they'd come; Jake explained that they were coming up to get a fix, and led him to the chart. Robins was wearing uniform trousers and a shirt without a collar. Burrage was back at the telegraphs. Hobday, behind the 'planesmen, stood with his feet apart and hands on his hips: bouncy, alert, the look of a bantam cock... 'Forty feet, sir.'

'Very good.'

Waiting for Weatherspoon's report on the presence or absence of surface craft. And he appeared now in the doorway of the silent cabinet, headphones flattening his big ears against his high-domed head. 'Nothing moving up top, sir.'

'Good. But stay there now. Twenty feet, Number One.'

'Twenty feet, sir.'

The 'planesmen worked as a team, with Crabb putting the angle on her and Morton concentrating on the actual depth. The submarine rose slowly in a carefully-controlled ascent. If she came up too fast and overshot, broke surface, she'd be certain to be spotted from the shore. If that happened, by the time she reached the Narrows they'd not only be floodlit but also swarming with patrol boats.

They might be, anyway. Twenty-seven feet. Twenty-six.

'Stop port. Full field starboard motor.'

Clink of the telegraphs: then Stoker Burrage's report, 'Port motor stopped, full—'

'Raise the after periscope.'

Nick, watching the processes of coming up to periscope depth, ignored Robins as he came over and eased himself into the chair that Jake Cameron had been using. Robins was rubbing his face and breathing hard, as if being turned out of the cabinet had imposed discomfort which he was stoically enduring. The periscope hissed upward. One could imagine the dark surface, glassy and reflecting starlight, and the periscope- top suddenly pushing up through it, a single eye peering into enemy territory. Wishart had cut the boat's speed to the bare minimum that would permit control of depth-keeping, one screw just idling; he'd done it so as to reduce the size of the feather, broken water where the periscope sliced the surface. Twenty-two feet: twenty-one. The top lens would be out of water now.

'Twenty feet, sir.'

The after periscope was the little one – unifocal, with only one-and-a-half times magnification. It was the attack periscope, for use at close quarters, its small-diameter top less easy to spot than the full-size one.

Wishart had swept round quickly. Now he stepped back, pushed the handles up, folding them so that the bottom end of the periscope would fit into the well, the deep tubular cavity in the control-room deck, that housed it when it was lowered.

'Down. Up for'ard periscope.'

Grumman pushed one steel lever back and pulled the other forward. Arctic oil under pressure hit one end of one ram and the other end of the second. The periscope wires, attached to the rams, ran hissing through their sheaves. Wishart had moved to the periscope: 'Depth?'

'Twenty, sir.'

He'd done a complete circle in low power. Now his right hand twisted the handle round, switching in the sixfold magnification. He circled again more slowly, his left arm draped over that spread handle. 'Stand by for some bearings, pilot.'

'Ready, sir.'

He got bearings of the land-edges of the entrance they'd come through, a summit to the north which could only be Achi Baba, and a cleft in the land-mass north-eastward. This last one, Jake pointed out, must be the line of the straits, their future course to clear Kephez Point. Wishart had sent the big periscope down and joined him at the chart table as he put the bearings on. 'This one as our course, sir – oh-three-eight?'

'Looks good enough to me.' Wishart gave that to Hobday as the course to steer. The boat was just levelling out at forty feet. Jake checked the run ahead of them: 'Good for the next eight miles.'

'Perhaps.' He might have been thinking that a great deal could happen before they'd got that far. You didn't want to be pessimistic about it, but it could be a mistake to count chickens, too. As far as Kephez the chart showed no sounding of less than thirty-five fathoms, but after the point it got shallower; and in that area two years ago there'd been a minefield and a net barrage as well. It was reasonable to guess there'd be something of that sort there now.

He moved back into the centre of the control room. 'Slow ahead together. Hundred and fifty feet.'

'Hundred and fifty, sir.'

The telegraphs clanked over. Burrage intoned, 'Both motors slow ahead, sir.'

Nosing down…

Chapter 4

Something had fastened on to Hobday's shoulder and was rocking it to and fro. He opened his eyes, focused muzzily on Jake Cameron's ill-shaven face. Jake told him, 'Coming up to Kephez. Wakey wakey.'

He'd just shaken Wishart. And he'd sent a hand for'ard for Crabb and the second coxswain. As E.57 moved into the narrow end of the pear and the land closed in on her track, it was time for key men to stand-to again.

Jake had explained the situation to Nick Everard and the Marine, Burtenshaw, who'd been up and about while Wishart and Hobday slept. Nick left the chart now, moved back to the ward-room corner as Wishart, humming some unidentifiable dirge, sloped across and let the chart table take his weight.

'How far have we come since the last fix, pilot?'

'Depending on tide, the five miles you reckoned on, sir.' Jake added, 'I've marked the DR.' He moved back into the centre, to watch the trim until Hobday had pulled himself together. With men shifting around, even just a few of them, there were adjustments to be made.

Wishart was studying the chart. E.57 was in something like thirty to thirty-five fathoms of water. Say, two hundred feet of it. Depth-gauges showed a hundred and fifty, at the moment. All right on the face of it: but if she was as much as five hundred yards to starboard of the track she was supposed to be on, the seabed ahead might shelve quite steeply upwards.

Hobday took over the trim. McVeigh, the ginger-bearded Glaswegian artificer, had relieved ERA Bradshaw. Young Agnew, leaning against the bulkhead under the telegraphs, might recently have crept out from under a wet stone. CPO Crabb slid in behind the after 'planes, displacing Able Seaman Smith, the tattoo'd torpedoman, without even looking at him. Leading Seaman Morton came shuffling zombie-like to the fore 'planes and tapped Louis Lewis, the wardroom messman and gun trainer, sharply on the crown of his scruffy head. He muttered, '*Got* it.'

Lewis scowled at him. 'Why'nt yer get a bloody 'ammer, make a job of it?' Morton grunted as he took his place, 'Will do, next time.'

'Hundred feet, Number One.'

'Hundred feet, sir.' Hobday had got the fore-and-aft trim right; now he'd have to adjust her overall weight as she changed depth. Wishart went back to look at the chart again, and Jake moved over to give him room.

'*Like* to get a new fix... But if we can get by the point without showing any periscope—' Wishart tapped Kephez with the points of the dividers '—and well into Sari Siglar here...' He'd paused. Jake knew he was thinking aloud and didn't want anyone else's comments. But he glanced sideways at him now. 'Might as well get your head down, pilot. With any luck this'll be plain sailing.'

Robins was back in the wireless hutch. Burtenshaw had flaked out in the pull-out lower bunk that was supposed to be the navigator's.

'One hundred feet, sir.'

'Very good.' Wishart sat down in the armchair, and opened Burtenshaw's volume of essays. Jake smoothed out the surface of Hobday's bunk, and climbed up on it. He lay back and shut his eyes, thinking of the bulge of Kephez Point out there – *up* there, half a mile to starboard. He could as good as see it: and the black, still water, and Turk eyes watching the surface for movement, perhaps Turk ears listening through headphones... The risks were there: so were the chances, the random rations of good luck and bad... Anyway, if the dead reckoning was more or less reliable they'd have a run of about three miles now past Kephez Point and into Sari Siglar bay, where Wishart intended to poke the stick up for another fix. From that new departure, they'd set a course through the Narrows.

He heard a kind of snort. Wishart muttered, 'Actually *read* this stuff?'

Jake turned his head, and Wishart realised – or thought – he'd woken him.

'Sorry, pilot – didn't mean to—'

'He does indeed. Fairly revels in it.'

'Extraordinary. Seems such a *normal* sort of chap.' Jake craned over the edge of the bunk and looked down at Burtenshaw. Wishart evidently thought *he* was asleep too; but he'd opened his eyes, and seeing Jake looking down at him – and Everard too, who'd twisted round in his chair – he winked. Wishart was frowning as he leafed on through Tolstoy. Lying back again, Jake thought of the half-written letter in his drawer, and of that line *You needn't worry for two seconds about me, you know...* Not strictly honest, perhaps. An outsider might well have had doubts about the survival prospects of anyone in these circumstances. But when it

was oneself in the middle of it, one didn't feel it to be so...
He wondered, drifting out of actual thinking into a vague
area between consciousness and sleep, whether when she
read that line of assurance she'd believe it, or whether she
lived in fear of losing him as well... He ought to write
to her more often. Someone else had just told him that:
he accepted it, murmuring assent, becoming aware only
gradually of the emerging noise, voices sharpening, and
the movement – rocking, shaking... But there were hours
yet, at least two hours on this course before—

'Stop together! Diving stations!'

He was out of his bunk and passing that order for'ard,
calling the hands, helping Burtenshaw to get the lower
bunk shoved in out of the way, and now he was back in his
own place at the chart table and Wishart had just ordered,
'Slow astern together!' Reality was displacing sleep and
reactions that so far had been automatic, unthinking, and
there were noises from the bow – external noises, scraping
and a sort of steady grinding like metal being screwed up
tight.

He heard Wishart say, 'We're in some kind of net.'

'Stern's sinking, sir. 'Planes aren't—'

'Wire round 'em, sir.' Morton was putting his whole
weight on the wheel. Hobday said, 'Leave it, for the
moment.'

'Stop starboard. *Half* astern port. Port twenty.'

The rush of men to their stations was finished now.
Jake saw some were in the condition he'd been in half a
minute ago: newly wakened, barely understanding what
was happening. Nobody was stupid enough to ask. Roost
said, 'Twenty o' port wheel on, sir', and Agnew reported,
'Port motor half astern, sir, starboard motor—'

'*Full* astern port.'

'She ain't answering, sir.' Crabb had the after 'planes tilted to their full extent, but they were having no effect. Held by her snout in the net, the boat had no way on, and her angle in the water was increasing steadily as her stern sank lower all the time. The racing screw wasn't shifting anything.

'Stop port.' Wishart shook his head. 'Damn thing.' He sounded disappointed but in no way anxious. 'Have to try t'other way. Starboard twenty.' He glanced at the bubble and told Hobday, 'Get some out aft.'

'I'm pumping on "Z", sir.' Hobday's tone was mild too. He'd just about emptied the after trim tank, and now he had the pump sucking on the after internal main ballast, 'Z'.

'Twenty o' starboard wheel on, sir.'

'Half astern starboard.'

He was trying to prise his way out of the mesh by twisting the submarine away from it. He'd tried backing straight out, but the net had clung to her. Jake, watching from his position by the chart table, could feel no movement other than the vibration of the screw. The net still held her, and one motor at a time with the batteries grouped down wasn't enough to tear her free. Meanwhile, the net's surface buoys would be dancing about like fishermen's floats, and if any Turks were even half awake in their lookout posts on Kephez Point they'd be whistling up the patrols by now.

Some nets were mined, and the mines' detonators controlled electrically from the shore.

'Stop starboard. Midships the wheel. Group up.'

The two pairs of batteries could be connected either in parallel or in series. Grouping down gave 110 volts, grouping up 220. On the main switchboards now – one on each side of the motor-room – Dixon and Rowbottom would be snatching out the rows of huge copper switches, each switch throwing a blue crackle of electric spark as it broke, then banging over the grouper switch and slamming the others shut again.

'Both motors stopped, sir, grouper up!'

'Wheel's amidships, sir.'

Hobday's yellow hair was standing on end: he had a habit of rubbing his head with both hands in moments of anxiety. He said, 'Stop the pump, shut "Z" suction and inboard vent.' He'd about checked the stern's tendency to sink. He glanced round, with a grimace that looked like a smile, as Wishart ordered, 'Full astern together!'

'Full astern together, sir...' Agnew, up on his toes for a bit of extra height, flung the brass handles round; the hum of the motors rose to a scream as the hands on the switchgear wound out the fields and the screws span fast in their own churned water. The submarine trembled, quivered, dragging at the net; if she broke free suddenly Hobday would have to flood that stern tank quickly through its kingston to stop her shooting up stern-first.

But she was *not* coming free.

'Stop both.'

A few more minutes of full power might have drained the battery flat. Without power, the only thing a submarine could do would be to surface. Then she'd be blown to pieces by the shore guns. Jake swivelled round, leant with his forearms on the chart and began to study the coastline of the straits and the names of mountains and rivers. *Mustchiof Tepe. Aski Fanar Bumu. Codja Flamur Tepe.* Remarkable, to think that Robins could speak it. He wondered what size of wire the net was made of and how wide its mesh might be. Big enough for E.57's bow to have thrust right in and for the folds of net then to have wrapped themselves round the hydroplanes. *Yapildak Chai.*

Wishart said, 'Have to enlarge the hole. How much in "A", "B" and "Z", Number One?'

'Less in "Z" now, sir, but otherwise all about half full.'

Jake saw that Burtenshaw was looking keenly interested but not alarmed. That was good, suggesting that the Marine saw no alarm in any of the submariners' faces. Nick Everard had resumed occupation of Hobday's bunk: he was on his back, eyes open and staring at the deckhead. Those three tanks – the ones Wishart had asked about – were all internal main ballast, and each of them held about five tons of water when it was full. Jake had often thought about being caught in submerged nets but this was the first time he'd actually experienced it. He'd guessed it wouldn't be a very comfortable sensation, and he knew now that he'd guessed correctly. *Chai* seemed to mean 'river'. Wishart had told his passengers, *If we get snarled up, we unsnarl ourselves...* Burtenshaw must have believed him; he was bolt upright in the armchair with his eyes darting this way and that, watching the unsnarling process demonstrated. He'd just jerked sideways as a drop of condensation falling from the deckhead made a direct hit on his ear. Wishart ordered, 'Stand by "A", "B" and "Z" kingstons.'

The order was being passed for'ard to the torpedo stowage compartment for 'A', back to the after ends for 'Z'. 'B' kingston's operating wheel was here in the control room, and Burtenshaw was having to move to let Lewis get at it.

'Full ahead together!'

The boat surged against the net. Grinding and scraping as the note of the motors rose. You felt the tremble in her steel, through all her hull and fittings. She was a live thing, straining muscle, a trapped animal struggling for life.

'Stop both. Stand by those three kingstons. Full astern both!'

Power coming on again. Hobday wearing that odd grin, gritting his teeth in anguish at the draining away of his battery's strength. Wishart snapped, 'Open "A", "B" and "Z" kingstons!'

Adding, as the sea rushed in to fill the tanks, about eight tons to her weight. Flinging herself astern, she was dragging at the net and at the same time – now, suddenly, dropping like a dead weight, plummeting stern-first, falling...

It was a question of how strong a net could be. Whether it could stand the extra weight and still hold her, even now.

Jake's fists were side by side on the chart and he was holding his breath as he stared at their white knuckles. Then he was listening to something like machine-gun fire, from outside the hull, as wire strands parted. Bursting, snapping steel-wire rope: he'd let his breath out, and it was difficult not to cheer.

She'd torn free but she was still going down.

'Stop together!'

'Blow "A", "B" and "Z" main ballast!'

McVeigh pushed those three vent-and-blow cocks to 'blow' and wrenched open the master valve. '"A", "B" an' "Z" blowin', sir!'

'Group down. Slow ahead together.'

The gauges showed that she was still sinking, passing a hundred and fifty; she was slowing her descent but still going down and it was a bow-down angle now. Crabb said, 'Gone 'eavy for'ard, sir.' He'd glanced at Morton; the second coxswain reported, 'Fore 'planes ain't movin' proper, sir. Reckon there's wire still round 'em.'

Wishart was behind him. 'Do they move at all?'

'Yessir. But – not the full travel, sir. And – *stiff*… Seems there could be – like weight there, sort of.'

'Stop blowing "B" and "Z".'

McVeigh shut them off. He said, '"A"'s out too, sir.'

'Stop blowing "A"…' The boat was hanging in a bow-down position at a hundred and seventy feet. Hobday asked Wishart, 'May I put a puff in No. 1 main ballast, sir?'

'What's the state of the for'ard comp?'

'Only half full, sir. Three-fifty gallons.'

'Pump that out first.'

'Aye aye, sir.' Morton still couldn't move the fore 'planes except in a very limited arc and with great effort. Hobday got a pump sucking on No. 1 compensating tank. Wishart observed conversationally, 'Most likely there's a section of net hanging on the bow.'

'Unless it's the 'planes themselves, sir – if we've wrenched 'em out of kimber, bent the—'

'There's weight for'ard too, though.' Wishart hesitated for another second; then he turned away, moving decisively as if he'd got it all worked out now. 'Starboard fifteen. Stop port.'

Jake thought, *Turning back?*

He saw Nick Everard looking equally surprised. Nick had swung over on to his side and up on one elbow: like Burtenshaw, he seemed to be trying to follow and understand the various manoeuvres.

Roost and Agnew had repeated the helm and motor orders. Wishart explained, 'We can't carry on up-straits with the fore 'planes stuck and a load of wire up for'ard. Out of the question.'

He was right, of course, Jake thought. But to turn back—

'And we can't get rid of it without surfacing.' Wishart was addressing Hobday. 'Have to cut it off with hacksaws. Nothing much else we *can* do, is there... Pilot, what's the reciprocal of our former course?'

Thirty-eight plus one-eighty: Jake told him, 'Two-one-eight, sir.'

'Steer two-one-eight, Roost.'

'Two-one-eight, sir.'

CPO Crabb reported, 'Bubble's shiftin' for'ard, sir.' What he was telling them was that the angle was coming off her, that she was responding to the suction on the for'ard comp tank. Hobday told Morton, 'Leave your fore 'planes alone now with that rise on... All right, cox'n?'

'Aye aye, sir.'

Using the 'planes might damage them – the axle or the glands – or tighten the wire around them. The after hydroplanes could manage on their own, in Crabb's experienced hands. Older classes of submarine, the C-class and ones before that, had no for'ard 'planes at all. 'Course two-one-eight, sir.'

'Very good. Slow ahead together… Number One – we'll go back a couple of miles, get into the wider part so we'll have some chance of not being spotted. Then we'll surface – trimmed right down – and get rid of that rubbish that's slung on us.'

Hobday said quickly, 'That'll be *my* job, sir!'

Leading Seaman Morton glanced round. Sweat was running in small streams down into his open collar. 'Beg pardon, sir. Casing work oughter be second cox'n's lot.'

'And the casing officer's.' Jake wasn't letting Hobday push him out of this. Work on the upper deck was the third hand's responsibility – and, as Morton had pointed out, the second coxswain's. He asked Wishart, 'May I take charge of it, sir?'

Wishart nodded. 'Need you on the trim anyway, Number One. *And* you'll have your work cut out. I want the top hatch and the bow out of water and damn little else.' He pointed at Jake: 'You'll have just one minute on the surface. *One.* That means ten seconds to get from the hatch to the fore 'planes, forty to do the job, ten more to get back. Hatch open – sixty seconds – hatch shut – *dive.*'

He added, 'Unless of course you find you can do it more quickly.'

Leading Seaman Morton looked thoughtful. Jake had an uncomfortable feeling that Wishart would stick precisely to his time-table. He looked across at Hobday. 'If you'd really *like* the job—'

Everybody chuckled. CPO Crabb suggested to Morton, 'Take a cake o' soap up while you're at it?'

'Stand by to surface!'

The reports came in: vents shut, LP air-line open to the main ballast tanks. High-pressure air was used to blow with, but it had to pass through reducers and the low-pressure line to reach the tanks.

Hobday had worked out a way to surface with not only the bridge-hatch out of water but also the for'ard end of the casing – the actual bow and the fore 'planes – which were well below the casing level. He reckoned he needed a bow-up angle of twelve degrees, so he was going to blow the for'ard pair of tanks until he'd got her to that angle, then puff water out of the next pair to them – three and four – to give her the buoyancy to stay up there.

They'd been up to twenty feet a few minutes ago, for a look round through the big periscope. Wishart had muttered, 'Search-lights, damn it...' Watching him as he swung around, Jake had seen a sudden brilliance that had made his eyes glow like a cat's as a searchlight beam swept past, flooding its harsh glare down the tube and through the lenses: then it had swung on by, leaving Wishart with his head back, blinking, momentarily blinded. He muttered, 'Have to chance 'em, that's all.' He snapped the handles up. 'Fifty feet, Number One. Pilot – you and Morton ready?'

Jake said yes, they were. He found the passengers – not Robins, who'd retired to the cabinet again – watching him. Burtenshaw, as it happened, had offered to go up with them and lend a hand. The offer had been refused, of course. For half a dozen reasons it had been a silly suggestion to have made; either he'd made it recognising that, or he was more stupid than he looked.

Wishart was giving them their final instructions. 'I'll open the hatch and get out first. You, then Morton, jump out, go straight over the front of the bridge and pull yourselves along the jumping-wire to the bow. The gun will be awash and there'll be four or five feet of water over the casing at this end, but the foremost thirty feet or so'll be sticking out and the 'planes should be well clear. Once you're there you'll have just over half a minute. Understood?'

The control room was a hot, stuffy, yellowish-lit cavern full of men with tense, sweat-damp faces. The depth-gauges showed fifty feet. Jake and the second coxswain had hacksaws, wire-cutters, cold chisels and hammers slung from their webbing belts. Apart from the webbing, they wore only shorts, swimming collars and engineers' gloves.

Hobday reported, 'Ready to surface.' Wishart gestured towards the lower hatch and Ellery unclipped it, pushed it up, the clang of its opening echoing in the hollow steel tube of the conning tower. Wishart told Jake and Morton, 'If I blow this whistle, you two drop whatever you're doing and run like riggers for the bridge. Straight into the hatch. Understand?' They nodded. He added, 'Take no notice of the searchlights. We're a long way out and our silhouette won't be any bigger than a couple of floating barrels.'

'Aye aye, sir.' He heard Burtenshaw say rather shyly, 'Good luck.' Jake winked at him. *You needn't worry for two seconds about me, you know...* He hadn't reckoned on searchlights. Then he thought, *We're the lucky ones. We don't have to sit and wait. Months – years... Compared to what she has to go through, my life's roses.*

'Let's have that twelve-degree angle, Number One.'

'Blow one and two main ballast!'

Wild-eyed – scrappy ginger beard bristling – oil-stained – lips drawn back over narrow, yellowish teeth: a first-rate man, was McVeigh, but if he'd walked into a Glasgow 'pub looking as he looked now the bar would have been evacuated in seconds... Air roaring: she'd already begun to tilt. Men were holding on, using anything solid to hang on to as the deck angled. Four degrees on the bubble: five...

Take no notice of the searchlights... The thing was, would the searchlights take notice of *them*?

Eight degrees. Nine... Wishart had one foot on the bottom rung of the ladder. Ten degrees. Depth-gauge needle circling faster now; one motor was driving her slowly ahead, and the angle of the boat was planing her upwards.

'Stop port.'

'Stop port, sir!'

Hobday glanced round at his captain. 'Eleven degrees, sir.'

'Surface!'

'Blow three and four!'

McVeigh wrenched the blows open, and the increased rush of air was deafening. Wishart climbed quite slowly up the ladder into the tower. Jake started up behind him, keeping his head well back so as not to get heeled in the eye, and using the sides of the ladder, not the rungs, as handholds. He'd had his knuckles crushed more than once, on submarines' ladders. He heard Hobday shout through the noise from down where Morton was crowding up behind him, 'Stop blowing three and four!' The conning tower smelt of wet metal and old boots.

Wishart was taking the first clip off the top hatch; he called down, 'Open the centre deadlight, pilot!'

The ports in the conning tower had lids – deadlights – that screwed down over them. Jake set to work on the one in the middle, which faced exactly for'ard. He loosened the brass butterfly nut and banged the clip off with the heel of his hand, and the cover dropped clear on its hinge. From below, Hobday shouted, 'Twenty feet… eighteen…'

'Sing out when your port's clear, Cameron.'

'Aye aye, sir.' When this glass broke surface the top hatch would be well out. Surfacing as slowly as this and with so little positive buoyancy, it would be crazy to cut it too fine, in case something went wrong and she slipped back. If you went under with a hatch open and a man in the hatch – well… Hobday's voice came thinly, 'Twelve – eleven—'

The glass port in front of his face became suddenly alive with heaving frothing sea.

'Port's awash, sir!'

He heard Wishart push off the last clip and throw the hatch crashing back: air whooshed up through the tower like gas out of a bottle of beer. He was climbing, flinging himself up and out into the sloshing, seething bridge, the sea only a matter of a few feet away from him and boiling from the submarine's emergence, sluicing round and breaking, splashing over, surging powerfully around the bridge: he jumped for the wire that ran from the periscope standards to the bow, launching himself over the front of the bridge into black water frothed with swirling white. Sea heaved around the gun: he stood on its breech for a moment, shifting his grip on the wire, then swung himself for'ard, hand over hand; a few yards more and then he had his feet on the sloping, submerged casing. The wire's abrasive exterior – designed for cutting nets – ripped at his soaked wash-leather gloves as he dragged himself along it. Light – searchlight – a flash of it as it passed: well, it *had* passed. Morton close behind him, gasping and grunting. There were sharp edges to the gratings and he wished he'd worn plimsolls. The surface was quieter now, settling as the submarine settled too. The jumping-wire sloped right down to her sharp nose. Jake lay flat, clinging to flood-holes, peering down at the port hydroplane — horizontal, a dark ear-shaped thing with the gleam of starlight on its wet steel surface. No sign of any net or wire. He was straining his eyes to make sure there was nothing round it where its axle passed into the hull-gland; he heard Morton bellow, 'Over 'ere, sir!'

He scrambled over. Glimpsing, without looking straight at them, half a dozen wavering searchlights on the southern, Asiatic coast. Small-looking though, far off, farther than he knew they were. Morton slid over the side, right down on to the 'plane itself, and Jake hung over the casing's edge above him. Light swept over them: its brilliance hardened, lit everything: then it had passed, arcing across the sea, and Morton shouted, 'Like a lot o' bloody knittin'!' Jake could see only his hunched back: there wasn't room for two down there, and they were both big men. He heard Morton's hacksaw rasping at wire-rope, and called down unnecessarily, 'Room for me to help down there?'

'No, sir, not—' His voice rose: 'She's *away*, sir!'

He heard a clang. Then Morton's face, a pale blob in the dark, turning up towards him: 'Lost me bloody saw!'

'Here!' Hanging down half over the side, he caught a groping hand and pushed his own saw into it. The light's beam washed over them again. It crossed the bow, swept on thirty yards, paused. It was sweeping back again. Jake thought, *Oh God, now we're in for it!* Morton was sawing again – shouting – *singing*! The light picked them up briefly, and swung on. Glancing back, Jake saw it hover on the bridge, move on, stop again: he guessed they'd been spotted. Morton was standing, clinging to the side with one hand and heaving up a bight of wire in the other: 'Work 'er for'ard as I clear 'er, sir?' Dragging the bight with him, Jake crawled to the submarine's sharp bow. Straddling the bull-ring, he got the wire over his shoulder and began lunging and jerking at it, shifting it for'ard inch by inch. Morton would be working the mesh outward, he imagined, over the hydroplane's outboard curve. And – incredibly – Morton *was* singing! Gustily, panting the words out, a sea-song about a sailor and a tart: '*Saying take this my darlin' for the damage I have done, If it be a daughter or if it be a son…*' Gaining wire still, but too slowly, too damn slow by half. Light behind him, all around him: he wondered why Wishart hadn't blown his whistle. Morton shouted, 'Keep your weight on 'er, sir, she's partin', she's near…' Near *something*.

The light had left them again. It came from the northern shore and he knew he mustn't look that way, that he'd be blinded if it turned on him… Nothing coming in now, the wire felt solid: Morton's saw scraping and gasping spasms of that raucous song: '*If it – be a son – send the bastard – off to sea!*' Light fixed on them, holding them: a hoarse ripping sound like canvas tearing and from the north a crack of gunfire. Another shell scrunched over and the light still held them: Jake thought they were in the intersection of two beams. He was throwing his whole weight against the wire's resistance: a cross-piece, part of its mesh still intact, gave him a handhold. He was cursing, screaming at it. The sea leapt in a tall spout twenty yards off the bow, and another shell hurtled overhead. They were shooting faster now. Morton yelled, 'Stand from under, let 'er go!' Jake dropped his shoulder and twisted round, let the wire slide away, got his right leg up and out of it so the wire wouldn't be tempted to take his foot with it. It was an enormous weight of net. The light's dazzle was beaming from right ahead now; Wishart must have turned the submarine bow-on to it, so as to present a smaller target to the Turkish gunners. Morton's voice screeched suddenly, 'I'll *murder* you, you bloody 'orror!' Jake was where he'd been before, leaning out above him, trying to see what was happening. He heard clattering as Morton's dark bulk shifted and he strained at the wire: then a long, metallic slither and Morton's voice in its normal, deeper tone, 'Well, well, fancy *that*...' They'd been in darkness for several seconds, with no shooting, but as the second coxswain stood up on the hydroplane the light came back, blinding, savage. Jake yelled downwards, 'Is it clear?'

'All gone, sir!'

Two or three shells whirred over and one burst short, exploding as it struck the water. Stinking vapour-reek: metal racketed off the bridge and whistled off into the dark. One puncture in the hull and they'd be done for. A lot of gunfire, yellow-red flashes on the shoreline. Morton was clambering up: he assisted him, shouted, 'Back now – quick!' The light helped: you could see the jumping-wire and the gun. Another burst, with bits of shell screaming over and something clanging against the casing – aft, he thought. Morton had reached the bridge. Another yard – Jake swung off from a foothold on the gun – and he'd be there himself. Gunfire noisier now: Wishart bawled, 'Down below – *down!*' Brilliant light: Wishart's idea of helping someone into the bridge was to tear an arm or two out of its socket. Jake didn't pause to thank him. A shell came scrunching over; he landed in the hatch on top of Morton and then Wishart came down on top of him like five tons of pig-iron, only harder. The klaxon roared, shattering his eardrums; cursing, he let go of the ladder and fell about ten rungs before Morton's bulk cushioned his fall and allowed him to catch hold again, cracking one elbow and a kneecap; the hatch had slammed shut up there, and Wishart called down, 'Fifty feet!' Jake told Hobday as he landed in the control room, 'Fifty feet. The 'planes are clear. Morton did it all.' McVeigh had opened the vents of those four main ballast tanks, and Hobday was flooding the for'ard compensating tank which he'd emptied because of the weight of the net on their bow. Jake saw the depth-gauge needle passing fifteen – sixteen – eighteen feet: safe from the Turk gunners now. He noticed McVeigh staring at him interestedly; looking down at what seemed to be the target of the scrutiny he found a mess of blood running from lacerations on that shoulder. He hadn't felt the net doing that to it. Morton was crouching in a pool of water with his head between his knees. Wishart came slowly down the ladder. He said, 'Lucky they're such rotten shots.'

–

Lewis had produced more tea. Hobday had the watch, and was sipping his with an eye on the depth-gauge and the trim. Wishart and Jake had theirs up on the bunks, while Robins, Everard and Burtenshaw sat at the pullout table. Leading Telegraphist Weatherspoon was in the silent cabinet, keeping a listening watch on the hydrophones. Two patrol boats – small, high-speed launches of some kind, Weatherspoon had guessed – had gone down-straits half an hour ago; they'd passed close and then the sound of their screws had faded southwestward. A hopeful sign, possibly. If they'd come down as a result of E.57's fracas on the surface, the fact they'd continued in that direction suggested that the Turks thought they'd been shooting at a submarine on her way *out* of the straits... It was wishful thinking, perhaps; but the way those boats were going was the way they would have gone if that had been the enemy's belief. They'd have gone to sit over the minefield off Kum Kale – to wait for the bang and for bodies to float up.

Robins said, 'Midnight... And if my memory is accurate, we started under the minefield at seven-thirty. Four-and-a-half hours ago?'

Jake blinked at the gleaming paintwork on the pipes overhead.

'Right.' And they'd dived three hours before that.

'It was supposed to be an eight-hour passage from one end of the straits to the other, and we've used up four and a half. Are we anything like halfway through yet?'

'No.' Wishart had his eyes shut, but he was only resting. '*Nothing* like.'

'So it will take considerably longer than eight hours?'

'Reasonable conjecture.' He turned his head, and asked Robins mildly, 'Want to get out and walk?'

Hobday reported from the chart table, where he'd just checked the log reading, 'That's three-quarters of a mile, sir.'

'Good. Come round to oh-four-oh, please.'

Robins sipped his tea, made a face, put the mug down. He went on with his nagging.

'And we have now to start all over again, make a new attempt at getting through that net?'

Wishart shrugged. 'At getting past it, yes.'

'Might it not have been simpler, having torn a hole in it, to carry on through the hole?'

'Not with the torn-off section of it dangling from our 'planes, no.'

Nick, looking across the table at Robins's ratty little face, was surprised at Wishart's patience with him. But Robins wasn't letting go quite yet.

'Have we any reason to imagine it will be any easier this time than it was before?'

'Some.' Wishart nodded at the deckhead. 'Mind you, it's all a toss-up. One backs one's hunches, that's about the size of it.'

The helmsman reported quietly, 'Course oh-four-oh, sir,' Hobday came over and put his cup down on the table. 'Stay at this depth, sir?'

'Yes. I think we said one-and-a-half miles, pilot – that right?'

Jake Cameron, with his face buried in a pillow, mumbled yes, it was… They'd headed north, to get over towards the European shore. Wishart had reckoned that since the greater concentration of searchlights seemed to be on that coast, it was likely that any clear channel would be on that side too. So he'd decided to move over to that side and to take her down to a hundred and fifty feet when they came opposite Kephez. When they'd hit the net they'd been in the middle of the straits and at a hundred feet; if the thing extended right across and went down as deep as a hundred and fifty it would have to be fairly gargantuan. Perhaps it was. But the northern shore was steep-to, with thirty fathoms or more right up close to the beach, and that was an advantage for the submarine.

They needed an unimpeded passage from here on. The battery had already taken a beating, in the efforts to break out of the net; and as Robins had just been so kind as to point out, they weren't even halfway through yet.

Nick saw Robins returning from a visit to the chart table; his lips were pursed.

'It seems extraordinary that as the crow flies Imbros is no more than fifteen miles from our present unenviable position.'

He sat down. Burtenshaw looked embarrassed. In Robins's presence he usually did. Nick thought Wishart was going to ignore the comment; but Robins was beginning, perhaps, to get under even *his* skin. Apart from the irritation-value of the carping, it happened that Wishart's eyes had been shut, and for all Robins knew he might have been asleep; if he had been, the crime of waking him with another of his silly criticisms would have been fairly unforgivable. But the eyes opened, and the head turned slowly.

'One: we are not crows. At least, *I'm* not… Two: our "unenviable" position is in the waterway through which we are bound to pass before we can deposit *you*, Robins, in the Marmara – and this I am as impatient to accomplish as you are yourself.'

Nick laughed. Robins shot him a glance of contempt. Then he muttered waspishly, 'The French seem to have found it easy enough.'

'Have we any way of knowing that?'

Robins shrugged. Wishart added, 'I hope you're right. Up till now the French haven't had much luck in these waters.' Nick could tell from his tone of voice that he was trying to keep things on an even keel. Because you couldn't afford quarrels in a submarine, because there wasn't room for them? On that basis, he realised he shouldn't have laughed just now. He was going to have to work with Robins, when the time came for the landing. Wishart said, 'Talking of *Louve*, though – the two civilians in her are politicals, aren't they. Wouldn't it have been simpler for the three of you to have formed one party?'

'Had the French proposed it – yes.' Robins shook his head. 'In fact it's on account of *their* ambitions that I have to – to go about things in my own way. Counteract – no, to *balance*—'

'Aren't we and the French on the same side any more?'

'A somewhat naive question, Wishart. The Eastern Mediterranean is – politically – a French sphere of influence. But we can hardly neglect our own—'

'Hydrophone effect, sir!'

'Diving Stations!' Robins had to move fast or Wishart would have flattened him. Jake, in a sort of flying-trapeze act, brought up hard against the chart table as Hobday repeated the order and the short, sharp rush swept through the compartments. Wishart was asking Weatherspoon about that HE – propeller noise.

'Astern an' like before, sir.'

'Two of 'em again?'

'Could be. Bit confused, sir.'

Ears like soup-plates, clamped against his skull by the head-set. His eyes were open but not focusing or seeing anything; his operative sensors were those great ears of his. 'Seems about steady, sir. Go over the top of us, I reckon.'

Wishart glanced round. The hands were closed up now, at their stations.

'Hundred and fifty feet.'

'Hundred and fifty, sir.' Brass wheels spun, reflecting yellow light. Wishart gestured upwards and told Hobday, 'When he's gone over I'll have a shot at following him. We'll stay deep to get the tide's help, but it'll take both motors half ahead.'

Hobday met his captain's stare. It was a kind of challenge, inviting him to comment on the state of the battery. But if you could trail an enemy through his own defences it might save a lot more amps, in the long run, than it consumed.

CPO Crabb grated, 'Hundred an' fifty feet, sir.'

'Very good.' Hobday busied himself with adjustments to the trim. Wishart crossed over to the cabinet; Weatherspoon pointed a finger upwards, nodded. He was saying, *Here it comes...* And suddenly everyone could hear the rhythmic churning of the Turk's propellers: faint at first, rapidly growing louder... Weatherspoon said, ''nother astern of 'im, sir. Same pair as before.'

The pair that had gone down-straits earlier. Drawn blank, coming back up here to hunt? Wishart didn't question the leading telegraphist's judgement; different ships' propellers made their own individual sound- patterns, and an experienced operator could usually recognise screws he'd heard before.

'Half ahead together.'

Agnew repeated the order as he reached up to the telegraphs. In the motor-room Dixon and Rowbottom would be winding down on the rheostats, taking resistance out of the armature fields to allow the motors to speed up. Weatherspoon scowled, shook his head. 'Lost 'em, sir.'

'Stop together.'

If you made much row yourself, you couldn't hear the enemy's noise. Hobday told McVeigh, 'Stop the pump.' Weatherspoon's eyes blinked at Wishart as the hum of machinery died away. 'Close to the bow, starboard. P'haps green five, sir.' He jerked his chin upwards towards the deckhead. 'Other lad's comin' over now.'

'Steer oh-four-five. Slow ahead together.' Wishart went to the chart table. They could all hear the second Turk boat now. Jake pointed at the latest DR position. If it was accurate they were already in the narrow section created by a bulge of coastline that had Kephez Point as its northern tip. Wishart muttered, more to himself than to Jake, 'Even if we stick close to him we could still run into deep ones.'

Mines, he meant. It would be safe enough to follow an enemy on or near the surface, but at this depth it was anybody's guess. But they needed the depth so as to get the benefit of the deep tidal stream. The flatter the battery got, the more important that current was.

There could easily be a deep minefield on this side. It would make sense − Turk-type sense − to have one here. A net − the one E.57 had hit − on the other side where the inshore stretch was shallower, and deep layers of mines over here. So if the patrol boats were worth following at all, it would be better to do so at periscope depth.

It was a gamble, though. You had to stake thirty lives on it. Possibly much, much more than thirty, when you thought of the operation and the likely results of its success or failure. And the difference between that success or failure you could reckon, in a situation such as this, in inches.

'Come up to fifty feet, Number One.'

'Fifty feet, sir.'

'After that, twenty. But easy does it.'

Up by stages, so as not to risk the loss of control that could send her floundering to the surface. It was in this section that the straits had been known to go mad, turn upside down. Another point worth bearing in mind was that on each side here the shore guns would be less than a mile away.

At fifty feet, Hobday had the trim adjusted, and Wishart stopped the motors. Weatherspoon could still hear the second of the two patrol boats, and it was still right ahead.

'Slow ahead together. Twenty feet.'

Half a mile to starboard was where they'd tangled in the net. And three miles ahead was Chanak, the Narrows, the *real* bottleneck.

–

'Down periscope.'

The small after periscope hissed down, and McVeigh eased the lever over gently to avoid the thud that always came with a more sudden check. Wishart had taken a few quick bearings; now he joined his navigator at the chart table to see what sense could be made of them.

If any. It was pitch dark up there, and with the coast inside spitting-distance he'd had to work quickly for risk of the feather being spotted.

Jake suggested, 'If the left-hand edge was *this*: and the tower could be this fort or whatever it is at Kilid Bahr?' Wishart agreed. 'Well, the last one would've been Kephez Point, and that fits well enough. Puts us *here*.'

Right in the Narrows. Between the points of Chanak and Kilid Bahr.

'Did it look like that, sir?'

Wishart shrugged. 'Looked like the inside of a pig's bladder, old lad.' Jake suggested, 'If we take this as our position, we ought to come round to about—' he moved his parallel-ruler across to the compass rose '—three-five-oh?'

Wishart glanced round at Hobday. 'Alter course to three-five-oh, Number One.' He added, 'Gently. Five degrees of wheel.'

The less helm you used, the less effect it would have on the trim. There was land with Turkish gun batteries on it less than a thousand yards on one side and as little as five hundred on the other. It wasn't a place for mucking about in. Wishart glanced round to see what his passengers were doing. Robins seemed to be asleep, in Hobday's bunk, and Burtenshaw was on Wishart's, reading that book of his. Everard was sitting on a chair pushed back against the bunks. Wishart asked him, 'Like to see where we are?'

'Thank you.' Nick got up. He'd been wishing he could have had a look at the chart, but he hadn't liked to move, for fear of getting in the submariners' way.

'Cameron'll show you.'

Weatherspoon called sharply, 'Surface vessel closin' on us from astern, sir!'

Nick hesitated: then he sat down again. Jake Cameron smiled, spread his hands in a that's-the-way-it-goes gesture. Wishart was at the doorway of the cabinet and Weatherspoon told him, 'Comin' fast, sir, *very*—'

'Sixty feet!'

Now you could hear the screws: high revs, much faster than the others had been. Like being on a railway line with an express train rushing at you. Morton reported from the fore 'planes, 'She don't answer, sir!'

'Open "A" kingston, half ahead together!'

Lewis dived like a goalkeeper for the bulkhead doorway, to get at the kingston's handwheel in the next compartment, but Anderson was there ahead of him. The submarine's bow dipped sharply, and the speeding motors bit, drove her down. The propeller-noise rose to a crescendo, right on top of them.

'Shut "A" kingston!'

She was diving fast now, accelerating away from those screws that must have passed perilously close to her up-angled stern. The Turk had gone over now. Jake thought, keeping his face expressionless, *Near squeak...* Wishart had slowed the motors and Hobday was getting a pump to work on 'A'. There'd be pressure in that tank now, so the pump should have an easy job of it. Needles still belting round the gauges. Sixty – sixty-five feet: he'd looked away from the gauges for a moment, and glancing back again he saw she was approaching eighty.

'Stop together – half astern together!'

She hit the seabed with a jolting crash that sent every-body flying. The lights went out. Nick, sprawled on the deck, heard men and objects falling everywhere. The gyro alarm-bell was an ear-splitting shriek, almost drowning Wishart's shouted order for the motors to be stopped. Jake Cameron was struggling across the compartment, aiming for the auxiliary switchboard, to shut that hideous noise off by breaking the main gyro switch. Bodies all over the place – men trying to sort themselves out, find out where they were. Wishart yelled, pitching his voice up to beat that hell, 'Emergency lights!' Jake reached the board and found the gyro switch and pulled it out. The racket stopped. Then by chance his hand touched another switch that was hanging loose and must have been thrown out by the impact. He wasn't certain he was doing the right thing – electrics weren't his strongest suit – but he took a chance and made the switch, and the lights immediately glowed up everywhere – not the emergency circuits but the main ones. A hand that had been groping close to his own turned out to be Hobday's. As first lieutenant he did know all about the boat's electrical systems, and he'd been trying to locate the switch that Jake had come across by chance.

Wishart said, 'Well done. Now give me a magnetic course, pilot.' For the time being, the gyro would be out of action. Wishart was as calm as a vicar at a garden party. Calmer – than some vicars. Dixon; the leading electrician, had come for'ard from the motor-room. 'Both motors stopped, sir.' Small round eyes in his moon-face were checking items on the auxiliary board. McVeigh reported, 'Still pumpin' on "A" tank, sir.' Everyone seemed to be back in their normal places. Hobday told Agnew, 'Ask PO Leech to check the bilges. All compartments check for leaks and report.' He looked at Dixon. 'Better have a sight of the battery tanks.'

If any cells had been cracked there'd be an acid spillage. Then any sea-water that might be in the tank already or that got into it later would create chlorine gas.

Reports were arriving to the effect that no leaks had been detected. The coxswain murmured, 'She's light enough, sir.' He'd seen a faint stirring of the needle on his gauge. There was a depth-gauge in front of each of the two 'planesmen. Hobday told McVeigh, 'Stop the pump.'

'Check the bow shutters, Number One.' Wishart, moving over to consult with his navigator at the chart table, asked Nick Everard, 'Are you all right?'

Nick was on his chair again. He indicated the bunk above him, where Burtenshaw was nursing bruises to various parts of his anatomy. 'Soldier took a bit of a high-dive.' Burtenshaw had been catapulted out of his bunk, and it was sheer luck he hadn't landed on top of Nick. Robins had managed to hold on, somehow. Burtenshaw told Wishart, 'I'm all right, sir, thank you.'

'Good.' Wishart leant on the table beside Jake. 'Well?'

'Our former course is north fourteen-and-a-half west, by magnetic, sir. But that last fix—'

'We must be here.' Wishart's finger tapped the chart. 'Somewhere near that nine-fathom sounding. So we're through the narrowest part already. The last bearing of that bunch must have been the high ground behind Kephez, not the point itself.'

Jake nodded. 'So now we need to steer – well, north thirty-five west, or—'

'That'll do.' Wishart turned away. 'Your gear in order, Weatherspoon?'

'Still 'earing 'im, sir. North-west – very faint now, an'—'

Dixon told Hobday, 'Dampish in the tank, but—'.

'Any smell?'

The fat man wrinkled his nose. 'Always a bit of a niff, sir. Can't say it's no worse 'n what—'

'Tell Cole to wash through with soda. You'd better get back on the motors, yourself.'

'Aye aye, sir… I – do think it's all right, sir, in—' Wishart cut in: 'Dixon – *I* thought we were in forty fathoms…' He asked Roost, 'Ship's head now?'

–

Cole was with Rowbottom on the main switchboard, freeing Dixon to work on the gyro. Jake had been tinkering at it with him; he came back now to join the others at the wardroom table. Passing Hobday, who was leaning against the ladder and humming to himself as he watched the trim, he offered, 'Like me to take over for a spell?'

Hobday's otherwise sharp nose had a round end to it, like a knob. Gleaming with sweat on it, it was more noticeable. He shook his head. 'I'll tell you when I do.' Wishart was saying, 'Mistake to take too much for granted, but it looks as if they must have reckoned we were on our way out of the straits when we popped up. Otherwise there'd be hunting craft now like fleas on a dog's back.'

Jake said, sitting down, 'You mean a Turkish dog.'

'You have a point.'

Robins had one too: 'What made us shoot down and hit the bottom as we did?'

'We had to get deeper quickly, to avoid that Turk. At twenty feet the bridge and periscope standards aren't far under the surface, you see. But we must've been in or on a high-density layer of water – to break through it we had to take in ballast and speed up. It did the trick rather too well. And we were in shallower water than we'd thought.'

Robins rolled over on to his back. Question-time was over, apparently. Jake asked Burtenshaw, 'Don't you want any explanations of anything?'

'Since you mention it.' The Marine pointed to a brass flap in the deck amidships. 'That bearded chap sloshed two bucketfuls of what looked like dirty water down through the hole there. Is that a reasonable thing to do?'

'The battery tanks are down there. Two of them. The cells stand on wooden gratings, and if you get a crack in one of them you get acid spilling. To neutralise it we dump in a solution of common soda that washes through under the grating and gets pumped out at the other end. If you didn't, the acid would burn a hole, eventually – and there are ballast tanks further down, under the batteries. Also, if salt water mixed with the acid you'd get chlorine gas, which – well, you're hot on science, aren't you?'

'Oh, red-hot.' Burtenshaw quoted from some text-book, '"Yellowish-green gas of pungent and irritating odour and peculiar taste. Acts violently on the lungs and causes—"'

From outside the hull – for'ard somewhere – a harsh, rasping noise…

'Stop together – slow astern together!' Instantaneously, Wishart had taken over. Nick thought, trying to keep out of everybody's way, *Here we go again…*

Jake Cameron headed for his chart table. Moving away, he'd knocked Burtenshaw's book off the corner of the table. He turned back, and picked it up.

'Sorry.'

Burtenshaw nodded, and finished that quote: '"-causes death by choking".'

'What?'

'Chlorine gas. Causes—'

'Oh, yes.' He went to the chart table. The scraping noise was drawing for'ard as the boat gathered sternway to clear the mine wire. Jake saw that Wishart had recently put a new DR on the chart and that at about this time they should have been altering course to starboard, eastward, to round Nagara Point.

'Stop port. Starboard ten. How much water here, pilot?'

'On the DR there's thirty-one fathoms, sir.'

'Magnetic course to clear Nagara?' Wishart saw Dixon still working on the gyro. 'Leave that. I want you on main motors, Dixon.'

The scraping noise stopped. In the thick silence Jake told his captain, 'Course of north sixty-six east should take us down the middle.' Wishart nodded, giving the thing time. Crabb's and Morton's eyes were fixed on their gauges; Morton, as ever, streamed with sweat. McVeigh's mouth was slightly open, showing his yellow teeth. The other two ERAs, Knight and Bradshaw, stood motionless, staring at fixed points on the deckheads, their expressions perhaps deliberately preoccupied. Signalman Ellery squatted near Agnew, close to the after bulkhead; his brown eyes in the monkeyish face never seemed to look anywhere except at Wishart. Agnew looked tired. He was a growing lad and he needed regular sleep. Burtenshaw, in the chair opposite Nick's, was leafing without much apparent enthusiasm through the pages of his Tolstoy, while behind his shoulder Able Seaman Louis Lewis leant against the curved edge of the latched-back bulkhead door and picked his nose with a thumb and forefinger. Lewis was not, Nick thought, the ideal choice for a wardroom messman.

'Stop starboard. Midships. North sixty east did you say, pilot?'

'Sixty-six, sir.'

Wishart cut into the helm and telegraph acknowledgements. 'Port fifteen. Slow ahead together. One hundred and fifty feet.'

Roost's broad, countryman's face was placid, amiable as he spun the wheel. Port wheel, starboard rudder. 'Fifteen o' port wheel on, sir.' The motors' forward thrust allowed screws and 'planes to bite, and the 'planesmen had her edging downwards. Jake, staring at the chart, wondered whether the middle of the channel, the track he'd just pencilled on it, was really the best bet. One might alternatively have hugged the shoreline around the point or gone over to the northern side. But for that matter one might also have spun a coin. The mines might be anywhere. This might be the best track, or the worst. He saw again in his mind that line in his own erratic scrawl, *You needn't worry for two seconds about me, you know.* But thinking of her, of what might become of her if she were left alone, *that* brought worry. Real, and sharp. He told himself not to think about it: to remember that thing about the coward dying a thousand deaths. Of course, one could argue about whether it could really be considered 'brave' to be unimaginative; but that wasn't the point, it was a matter of control, of simply not allowing the imagination that much rope. Mental discipline, he told himself. He was leaning with his forearms on the chart, looking down at the shape of the Dardanelles and this zigzag bottleneck in the middle of them. He decided that even if it was not cowardly it was damn silly to allow oneself to think about the one and only aspect of one's situation that made this kind of ordeal difficult or frightening. (Begging a question slightly there: but never mind, the basic reasoning was sound enough.) The reason you did think about it, of course, was that it was there, real, and it was bad, so your mind dug away at it in order to flush it out, beat it somehow. But you couldn't: and you knew by now that you couldn't, so surely to God—

A *clang-* sharp, and then reverberating. On the other side, starboard side, amidships.

Several pairs of eyes – heads – had jerked in the direction of the sound. Jake had caught his breath; he let it seep away through clenched teeth. That clang had been the slap of a mine-wire against the submarine's side, and now it had begun its grinding passage aft along the saddle-tanks.

'Stop starboard. Port ten.'

Jake looked over at the passengers. Burtenshaw was facing the other way; he couldn't see if he was reading or just holding the book and listening. Robins, up on the bunk, had his eyes shut and he'd jerked his hands up to press their palms against his ears. Well, when you'd nothing to do except lie there and listen... Only Everard was watching what was happening in the control room. Jake wondered if he was scared, or as unruffled as he looked. That lack of expression could well be a mask: as one knew only too well oneself... He turned back to the chart. He heard CPO Crabb's report, 'Hundred an' fifty, sir', and the other two – young Agnew's and the helmsman's. He realised, studying the chart, that in fact there wasn't really any alternative to this track that Wishart had put them on. The straits ahead at Nagara were less than one mile wide from shore to shore, there was very little room on the northern side, and closer to the point itself there were several shallow spots. Also, there was a note on the chart in his own recent Indian-ink lettering about a reported inshore current on that side. It had put *Goeben* on the beach here – obviously she'd tried to cut it too fine, but a submarine certainly couldn't afford to monkey with it. If she got swept up on those shallows the Turks would get some easy target practice, they'd take their time about blowing her to pieces. What it came down to was brutally simple: that to get through this narrow stretch you had to take your chances with whatever mines or nets they'd planted in it.

Chapter 5

'Down periscope.' Wishart told Hobday, 'Still too murky for a fix. But we're more or less in the middle, and that's what matters.'

The clock on the for'ard bulkhead showed two thirty-five. By dead reckoning E.57 should have been more than two miles past Nagara Point. After another two-and-a-half miles they'd be out of this widening funnel of land and in a position where an eighteen-mile run on one course would take them through to the Marmara. Two-and-a-half miles, with the submerged tide added to the boat's slow grouped-down speed, would take half an hour; and barring accidents or interference the final run could be expected to take another three or four.

Wishart moved over the the chart table and leant on it beside Jake Cameron. A favourite attitude for them both, Nick thought, glancing that way. Characteristic. Seen from the rear like this, their posteriors, side by side, looked elephantine. Burtenshaw pointed: 'You could move that column over to this one.'

'Ah.' Nick rather wished the Marine would allow him to play this game of patience on his own. He nodded.

'So I can.' Burtenshaw was on the other side of the table, seeing the cards upside-down and trying to spot each opportunity before Nick did. He moved the file of cards. 'Thanks.' Patience, indeed; and a card out of Wishart's hand, the example of his dealings with Robins. Wishart's voice reached them quietly from the other side of the compartment: 'I think we can trust the DR all right. We'll turn here—' he poked with dividers at the next and last turning-point, an alteration of about thirty degrees to port into that long home stretch – 'say at five past three.'

Jake nodded. 'Puts us about halfway.'

'It's not the mere distance that counts, pilot, is it? In terms of the bally awkward bits we're the devil of a lot better off than halfway!'

The Narrows were behind them. A few hours ago the thought of being through and on this side of them had been a kind of mirage thought, a distant dream to long for. In fact the process of getting this far hadn't been nearly as tricky as it might have been.

'Plenty of water.' Wishart was checking the soundings on the chart, along the pencilled track. The nearest sounding to the DR position indicated a depth of fifty fathoms – three hundred feet. He muttered, thinking aloud, 'Might try it at a hundred. Get us the tide and—' following the soundings all along that track '—yes, safe enough all the way. H'm?' He nodded, and pushed himself off the table. 'Hundred feet, Number One.'

The farther out she got now, into the wider north-eastern reach, the less likely it was that there'd be mines or nets. The narrow sections were the obvious ones to block. A feeling of relief had begun to make itself felt as much as half an hour ago, when Nagara Point had been reckoned to be just abaft the beam. The preceding period had been unpleasant and getting more so, and it was about then that they'd begun to realise that intervals between mine-wire encounters had been lengthening. *Up to* that point, they'd been shortening. From there on until Wishart had ordered periscope depth for this last check on their position, the boat had been motoring quietly along without incident.

Now she was gliding down again. Hobday murmured, 'Easy with the angle, cox'n.' He was wary of the tricky densities, anxious to avoid another nose-dive or more bouncings on the seabed. If she tried one of those stunts here she'd hit nothing until she was three hundred feet down, and that was well below her tested depth.

After a period of tension, its lessening produced a sense of ease, even of exhilaration – at having come through, survived the hazards. You knew it could start again, but it never felt as if it would; it felt as if the strains were over, the testing process left behind for ever. There was a tendency to joke, and for the jokes to seem funnier than they were. Everyone was relaxing without anyone admitting to having been in a state of tension: and when you thought about it, even *that* seemed funny... A number of men requested permission to go aft to the heads; they'd been allowed to, one at a time. Not to the heads them-selves, except for two men in the last few minutes, because at depths below thirty feet you couldn't use them. Sea-pressure prevented them being blown, discharged, when the boat was deep. For use below thirty feet there were buckets behind the engines.

Twenty-six feet: twenty-seven... The 'planesmen were easing her down very gently.

Robins, in Hobday's bunk, propped himself up on one elbow as the needles crept down past the thirty-feet mark.

'Are we past the Narrows yet?'

Wishart had just propped his weight against the control-room ladder. He glanced round, towards that corner, and nodded.

'Yes. We're—'

A jarring thump: and then heavy slithering noises overhead.

'Stop both. Half astern both.'

'Both motors half astern, sir!'

It sounded like something weighty being dragged along the casing. It had started up forward near the bow, but – well, whatever it was it must be sliding up the jumping-wire and the wire would be pushing it upwards, right over the tops of the two periscope standards if the boat maintained her forward motion. But she wasn't; she was going astern now. She jerked: it was a sort of lurch, quite a powerful one. A fish would be like this when it had taken a hook and the line suddenly tightened so that the fish felt it for the first time and tried to wrench away.

'Stop together. Group up.'

Robins had flopped down, and shut his eyes. Burtenshaw rested his forehead on his clasped hands on the table top. Everard was rather slowly shuffling the cards.

Grouping up was going to shake the guts out of the battery. Jake Cameron read the log, noting the figure and the time in his navigator's notebook, then marked a new and corresponding DR position. Doing that, he broke the lead of his pencil. He had plenty of spares in the rack, already sharpened.

Unlikely to be a mine-wire. Net? But when it had got hold of her she'd been at about thirty feet, and now she seemed to be right *under* it. A net with a bottom edge at thirty feet would hardly seem worth laying, in fifty fathoms.

The submarine's motors were stopped, and yet she was rock-steady, still. Wishart looked from the gauges to Hobday.

'Trim can't be all *that* perfect.'

The needles were so static that the gauges might have been shut off. The for'ard one read thirty-six feet and the coxswain's a foot more than that. The bubble in the tube reflected the same bow-up angle.

Nick was shuffling the cards still. If it was a surface net, there might be mines below it. It was a combination that had been used for some while in the Dover Patrol's defences in the Channel. You forced the U-boats to dive in order to pass under the net, and they dived into a curtain of mines. It had seemed a good idea, as a device for catching *German* submarines, but from where he was sitting now his view of it was somewhat different.

Wishart said, 'My guess is we're not *in* a net, but just hanging on the bottom of it somehow.'

He looked quite calm, thoughtful, trying to work it out. Hobday suggested, 'Might be the gun hooked in it.' Wishart nodded. 'I thought of that, but what about the jumping-wire?' Other faces reflected his own puzzlement. He shrugged. 'Anyway, let's see if we can spare the battery and break loose by flooding alone. As last time, only static.' He told Hobday, 'Stand by the internal main ballasts.'

He didn't mean all of them: just the ones that had kingstons. Hobday ordered, 'Stand by "A", "B" and "Z" kingstons.' Hobday had switched over to his 'calm' tone. Lewis scuttled over to crouch in the wardroom corner with his hands on the wheel of 'B'. That internal was under the for'ard battery tank, and the shaft from the wheel ran down inside the chain-locker, which was immediately for'ard of it. About six feet further for'ard, in the torpedo stowage compartment, Able Seaman 'Close-'aul' Anderson folded his long body down so he could get a grip on the operating wheel of 'A'; and in the after ends Stoker Peel would be ready by this time to open the stern tank, 'Z'.

Wishart called for'ard, 'Open "A" kingston!'

There was a small lurch, as the sea rushed into the tank. The bow might have dropped about an inch. The needle in the for'ard gauge had quivered; now it was still again.

'Open "B" kingston!'

Lewis wrenched the wheel round. You could hear the movement of the gearing in the shaft and the slam of sudden pressure entering the tank below. From above, outside the boat, there was a creak, a sound of straining; then nothing more.

Crabb muttered, 'Somethin' gave, up top, sir. By the gun, I reckon.'

'Third time lucky, cox'n.' Wishart ordered, 'Open "Z" kingston!' Ellery, at the bulkhead doorway, passed it aft, and a second later the boat trembled very slightly. Not enough to make any difference on the gauges, but the bubble had shifted for'ard by about a quarter of one degree. And everything was silent now: warm, close air, nobody moving, smell of oil and sweat and the yellowish light glinting on brass and on the running condensation on the paintwork and on the shine of pale, sweat-damp, stubbly faces.

Wishart looked disappointed. Annoyed, perhaps – but not, Nick thought, particularly worried. It might be an act, he realised, or it might be that to the submariners this was less hair-raising than it seemed to an outsider.

'Pity. Have to use some juice after all.' Wishart rubbed his jaw. 'Never mind. Once we're past this lot we'll be home and dry. We're – what, grouped up?'

Agnew confirmed it.

Jake was thinking that dawn would be breaking soon, up there. Daylight would flush the surface of the straits and light the hills. This submarine was only ten yards below the surface, and she was suspended probably from large, brightly-coloured buoys which presently she'd start tugging to and fro. Ten minutes ago they'd been preparing to congratulate themselves, thinking they'd come through the worst of it. He told himself soberly, *That was the silly thing. This is the reality. We knew it was going to be difficult and here we are, it is, and we've some way to go yet, that's all.*

Robins lay like a dead man, flat on his back with his eyes shut. What did a man like Robins think about, Jake wondered, when he wanted to turn his mind elsewhere? Bob Burtenshaw had climbed up on to Wishart's bunk, after first offering it to Nick Everard. Everard was sitting with his shoulder against the drawers underneath the bunks, and still fiddling with those cards. Not looking at them: just fiddling with them, shuffling, cutting, shuffling again.

'Half ahead together.'

The boat trembled as her motors, with 220 volts on them, sent her surging forward. The depth-gauge needles swung sharply – but not far: one to thirty-four feet and the other to just under thirty-five. She'd only made that lunge, and been brought up hard, stopped dead.

'Stop together.'

'Stop together, sir.' Agnew's voice was higher, thinner than it had been.

'Half astern together!'

For a second, or two it felt as if she was going to pull clear. Then the rush astern stopped just as the other had. As if rubber bands of vast dimensions had been stretched to their limit and finally held instead of breaking.

'*Full* astern together!'

The note of the motors rose to a high, pulsating whine. From overhead they heard that same creaking noise. Straining metal. Wishart called, 'Stop both!'

If he'd let the motors go on racing he'd have burnt them out, as well as draining the batteries. Now all sounds died away again, gave place to new ones – the odd ticking of relaxing steel, easing of strain from rivets. Jake was thinking about rivets because of that creaking, which had sounded like metal bending, and because Wishart, moving as if for no special purpose, had just come to this end of the control room and stopped, quite casually, to examine the deckhead. He said to Hobday, still staring up at the lines of rivets, 'Better pump out those internals.'

'Shut "A", "B" and "Z" kingstons!'

Wishart was on his way back to his usual position by the for'ard periscope, midway between the steering pedestal and the 'planesmen. Jake asked himself, *Now what?* Around the stuffy, hot compartment he could see much the same question in other faces. Facial expressions, movements of the facial muscles, could very largely be controlled; but eyes, after a certain period of strain, tended to give the game away.

As navigator, of course, he was lucky in that respect. He could turn his back on the others while he studied the chart, and he could fiddle with the instruments while he rested his powers of resilience, recovered his mental breath. But there was only one answer he could find to the question he'd just asked himself, that *now what?* Simply that if you couldn't get out of a net when you were dived, you'd have to surface and cut it free as they'd done earlier in the night. But then two other questions came up at once. One: would it be possible for the boat to surface, with the enormous weight of the net on her? Two: if the answer to that question was 'yes' – which he rather doubted – could the job be done soon enough and quickly enough to take advantage of whatever period of darkness or semi-darkness was still left? Depending on how thoroughly enmeshed they might be, how long might they have to lie up there exposed to coastal batteries at point-blank range and illuminated by what would almost certainly, in these exotic parts, be a sensationally beautiful sunrise?

'Stop the port ballast pump. Shut "A" suction.' Hobday had already pumped out 'B' and shut it off, but the other pump was still sucking on 'Z'. He looked better now: during the burst of full-ahead grouped up his face had been stiff with agony – because his battery had been having its guts torn out and they might as well have been his own for the way he'd felt it. He told McVeigh now, 'Stop the starboard pump. Shut "Z" suction.' Shutting the inboard vents as well as the suctions would be automatic. Ellery was passing that last part of the order aft; Wishart looked across at Jake.

'Ready for another bathe, pilot?'

Oh, Christ... He nodded. 'Sir.'

'Second cox'n, you fit?'

'Aye, sir.'

'Get ready then.' Hobday told Morton, 'Ask the TI to come and look after the fore 'planes for you.'

'Signalman.' Wishart nodded towards the lower hatch. 'Open up.' He told Hobday. 'Might get a preview through the ports. See how we're snagged.'

Round the gun, Jake thought, that's where... He also guessed that the gun was being just about dragged off its mounting. During that surging to and fro it had felt as if the point of suspension was just about overhead, slightly for'ard of the conning tower – which was where the gun was, the twelve-pounder, on its gundeck a few feet higher than the casing. Wishart had climbed up into the tower and Ellery was at the bottom of the ladder, peering up through the open lower hatch. Jake tied the tapes of his swimming collar, and Burtenshaw, up on Wishart's bunk, lifted a couple of fingers and muttered, 'Once again, best of luck.'

'Thanks.' He liked Burtenshaw. It was pretty sporting of a Harrow boy, he thought, to join up in the ranks. But none of these people, once the war was over, would want to know anyone like Jake bloody Cameron. As for Everard – still clutching those cards, for God's sake – Everard, a baronet's son who'd eventually become a baronet himself, might as well have been a creature from some other world. He *was*, in fact. Jake thought, *It doesn't matter: when the war ends I'll be too busy earning a living to worry about keeping up with baronets.* But did he care, really? He didn't know: and this was no time for considering one's place in the class system. The *war* wasn't a time for it: that was the whole point, surely, the way the question arose in the first place! The torpedo gunner's mate – known as the TI, short for torpedo instructor – had come from his domain for'ard and was sliding on to the fore 'planesman's seat. CPO Rinkpole's bald head gleamed in its half-circle of greyish hair. Hobday murmured, 'Morning, TI.'

'Like old times, sir.' Rinkpole grinned sideways at the coxswain. 'All right there, Reggie?' Morton came for'ard in his net-cutting outfit, carrying tools for both of them. Jake relieved him of one set and told Hobday, 'We're ready.'

'Stand by to surface!' The routine reports began to come in, and Wishart climbed back down the ladder; he looked cheerful.

'We've got net – wire-rope mesh – all over the forepart of the boat, at right-angles to the fore-and-aft line. It's draped over the jumping-wire and the starboard side of the hanging edge has meshed itself over the twelve-pounder. All we've got to do – you and Morton, pilot – is get that clear and over the side. You may not even have to cut it, once it's slack all round – and I'm going to *try* to slip out of it as we surface.' He turned to Hobday. 'We need another trimmed-down surfacing, but it'll be stern-first and we'll have the weight of the net for'ard. We should be far enough up when there's ten feet on the gauges – so stop blowing at, say, twelve.'

Hobday nodded. He looked a bit doubtful, though. The big question was whether with the weight of the net on her she'd come up at all. It was quite possible, Jake thought, that even with all her tanks blown the thing would still hold her down. It was more than possible, it was *likely*, he thought. And in that case—

In that case she'd be stuck, in this outsize fish-trap. 'Now you two—' Wishart was addressing him and Morton – 'It's not as dark as it might be, now. We won't show more of ourselves than we have to, but we're certain to be spotted at once, this time, and obviously we'll be shot at. Consequently—' he smiled suddenly – 'don't loaf about, what?'

Morton had taken the point. 'Faster 'n that, sir.'

'Ready to surface, sir.'

Hobday meant, to *attempt* to surface.

'Number One – we'll go astern, slow grouped down, enough power just to pull us back from—' he jerked a thumb upwards and for'ard '—*that* damn thing, and get out from under at least some of its weight.' Hobday nodded. Wishart told him, 'Blow five, six, seven and eight to start with, then three and four if she isn't coming up. If you can get her up like that, leave one and two main ballast full. If the bow's awash it'll be easier to shove the net off or slide out from under it. Right?'

'Aye aye, sir.' Hobday looked happy enough with the programme. Wishart put one foot on the bottom rung of the ladder.

'Group down. Slow astern together.'

Jake and Morton, clanking with tools, moved up behind him. Agnew reported, 'Grouper down, sir, both motors slow—'

'Surface vessels closing from astern, sir!'

Weatherspoon: from the cabinet. Changing everything…

Ending everything?

'Stop both.' Wishart, wooden-faced, stepped off the ladder. Weatherspoon reported, 'HE is confused, sir. There's more than one. Might be the same pair comin' back, sir.'

With his eyes on the gleaming, dripping deckhead, Weatherspoon frowned – as if, Jake thought, watching him – as if something most unpleasant had just been whispered to him through the earphones. He'd closed his eyes now, concentrating. Opening them, blinking, he eased the headset backwards, freeing his ears; he told Wishart, 'Two littl'uns coming from right ahead, sir, and this new 'un, bigger 'n slower, closing astern.'

Wishart nodded slowly, digesting that, putting the scene together in his mind. For just a moment as he turned away, Jake glimpsed a flash of anger – despair? – in his captain's eyes. Then there was nothing but the habitual calm appraising of a new situation. That would have been anger, Jake told himself, not despair: he'd be sick by now of being messed about. Who wasn't, for God's sake? Wishart announced quietly, 'Unlikely we'll be surfacing. But you two hang on—' he'd glanced at Jake and the second coxswain – 'in case they're just passing.'

You didn't need earphones now to hear the Turks' propellors. Like the first sound of a distant oncoming train: once you heard it, it got louder quickly. Weatherspoon, in the doorway of his cabinet where he could see and be seen, said, 'This pair's launches, sir. Other's more like a gunboat, trawler, somethin'.'

Wishart folded his arms on a rung of the ladder and rested his chin on his forearms.

'One of 'em's stoppin', sir.' The leading tel added, 'One o' the launches. Big one still closin'.'

That one was stopping was enough to confirm what it was about. The Turks knew they had a submarine in this net.

'Shut watertight doors, sir?'

'Not yet, Number One… But you two—' he meant Jake and Morton – 'get dressed. No outing this time. Number One – pass the word for all hands to keep quiet and not move about.'

Hobday sent Ellery aft and Lewis for'ard with that order. The propeller noise rose to a peak as it passed overhead; it drew away, lessening, on the other side. The net, evidently, could be crossed by surface craft. Weatherspoon reported, 'Slowin', sir. Stoppin', shouldn't wonder.'

You could hear the decreasing revolutions – slowing and fading. But through that disappearing sound a deeper, stronger rhythm was developing: the newcomer from the south. This would be the gunboat. Out of Chanak, probably. Burtenshaw whispered from his bunk, 'What's happening now?'

He wasn't deaf: he must have known. Jake guessed he wanted to be told it wasn't as bad as he thought it was.

'Patrol boats. They may start dropping charges, presently.' Everard had said it. Jake nodded. 'It's possible.' He went to the chart table before the Marine could ask a question that he'd have to try to answer and might find difficult. Something like *How can we possibly get out of this?* He pulled his serge trousers up and began tucking shirt-tails into them while he listened to the rising note of the approaching screw. Much heavier-sounding and slower than the first pair. A trawler of some sort, and it would carry depth-charges as well as at least one gun, and with E.57 immobilised in this trap they wouldn't have to *waste* any charges either. In the days of the first Dardanelles patrols, one had heard, when they caught submarines in this kind of situation they lowered small charges on wires from boats and detonated them electrically. In those days there'd been no such things as depth-charges. Just little ones on wires. They wouldn't be little ones today. The drumbeat of the trawler's screw was slowing.

Stopping.

Robins had his eyes open. He was lying on his back still and he didn't appear to have moved a centimetre, but his eyes were open and staring at the deckhead, the rivulets of condensation – or trying to see *through* it… Jake told him in his mind, *You won't see them floating down, chummy. You 'll hear them, when they arrive.* Burtenshaw was looking at him: Jake winked. Everard was leaning forward in his chair and watching Wishart, who'd just told Hobday that he was going up into the tower to take another gander out through the ports.

Jake thought suddenly, *Surface, man the gun, chance our luck?*

If the trawler was really close to E.57, the coastal batteries would have their fire masked. Perhaps the submarine could pop up suddenly – if the net allowed her to – and loose off a few rounds from the twelve- pounder at point-blank range while he and Morton cut the net free: and the Lewis gun would come in handy too, spraying the Turks' decks to keep them away from *their* gun… A few seconds ago the idea had seemed crazy, a daydream – but wasn't it something more than that, when you thought about it? At least, a chance? Better than lying here like a salmon in a net, waiting to be gaffed? This way there was *no* chance, none at all. That was what he'd been anxious not to have to admit to Burtenshaw. He looked round now, a first move in what would be a hesitant, diffident approach to the skipper. Third hands weren't expected to advise their captains or propose tactics… One might also argue that if one had been anything other than a third hand one might not have allowed oneself to start thinking on such suicidal lines. And then again, which was suicide: trying that, or waiting to be blasted to the surface?

Wishart, returning from the tower, stopped halfway down the ladder.

'We might wangle ourselves out of it, if we're clever. Come up here, Number One. Pilot, take over the trim.'

Jake moved into Hobday's place behind the 'planesmen. 'All right, cox'n?'

'Never better, sir.' Jake thought, *Hell of a lad, old Crabb!* He added in that nut-cracking voice of his, 'Skipper'll soon 'ave us out o' this little lot, sir.'

'Of course he will!'

As if he'd never doubted it... And he could see more hopeful expressions all around the compartment. A swift and total change of mood. Ten minutes ago there hadn't seemed to be much anyone could do except wait for the bangs to start; now Wishart had his tail up again, and if whatever he was planning didn't work, Jake thought, he'd put forward his own scheme for a shooting-match.

Hobday came down the ladder. 'Cameron – you're wanted up there.'

He went up. No sound from the enemy over their heads. What might the Turks be so busy with – fitting detonators to the charges?

'Here, pilot. Take a look.'

He climbed a few rungs and joined Wishart in the tower. One would hear the trawler's screws again, of course, before any charges came, there'd be that much notice. 'Here.' Wishart moved aside, giving him access to the little conning-tower port with its thick glass window.

Between Jake and Wishart, there wasn't much room to spare.

Greenish-black water: but the shape of the submarine's forepart was clear to see. He saw the net too, a web overhanging everything. Only the half-light of very early morning made it hazy; the water itself was totally transparent. Wishart said, 'Look at the gun and the way it's caught up.'

Wiping the glass made it much clearer; condensation gathered quickly. The gun was a dozen feet for'ard and below the level of this observation port; its barrel pointed upwards at twenty degrees to the horizontal and was trained fore-and-aft, so that looking down from this angle you saw its whole length, breech-block to muzzle. The net was a pattern of loops and distorted rectangles shimmering in what looked like greenish jelly. He wiped the glass again, concentrated on the entanglement round the gun. Wishart said, 'The bights under the barrel can't be difficult to get rid of, once we dislodge the other bunch. We're double-hooked – that's why we couldn't clear it either ahead or astern. But I think if we lighten her and move ahead, with the angle right, that lot under the breech will swing clear – once the weight's off it, d'you see? Then I'll angle her the other way and come out stern-first. But the timing's got to be just right. What I can't have is any degree of time-lag between my orders and the motors doing what I tell 'em – and that's what *you're* for – there, in the hatch. Go on.'

He slid down the ladder and took up a position with his head in the rim of the hatch. He heard Weatherspoon report to Hobday, 'One launch on the move, sir – one o' the first lot.' Wishart called down, 'Blow three and four main ballast!'

No need to repeat it: those valves were already open on the tank inlets, and McVeigh had heard the order and wrenched open the high-pressure valve; there was a roar of expanding air as it ripped into the LP line and through it into the pair of midships saddle-tanks. Jake looked up, saw Wishart's face close to the glass port; he waited for the next order. With the noise of blowing, that roar of air, he'd be needed this next time.

'Stop blowing three and four!'

He yelled it almost instantaneously, and the noise cut off abruptly as McVeigh shut the blow.

'Slow ahead both!'

'Slow ahead—'

Ellery shouted the order aft. Quicker than using telegraphs.

'Stop together!'

Jake saved his breath: the signalman's shout had overlapped Wishart's order. But now a new sound was building up: fast screws closing, coming over. They were too fast-revving to be the gunboat's... Wishart shouted, 'Blow five and six!'

The rip of air again... And propellers passing over now: fast, loud, reaching a peak of sound and then – fading, into the blowing sound... 'Stop blowing! Slow ahead together!'

Jake yelled the orders down, and the noise cut off; he heard Ellery pass the slow-ahead order, and almost immediately after that the first charge exploded. A ringing crash: as if the submarine was a gong and they'd belted her with a hammer. The crash of the explosion reverberated away in jerky throbs as the boat flung over to starboard: lights flickered, went out, came on again. The launch, obviously, had dropped that charge, and Jake guessed that the larger ship had brought charges up, that the peaceful interval had been the time she'd taken to issue them to the launches.

'Stop together!'

Jake and Ellery in chorus…

'Open five and six main vents!'

McVeigh grabbed the levers and jerked them back, and Jake heard the thuds of the vents dropping open in the tank-tops.

'Blow one and two main ballast!'

Getting a bow-up angle now, so as to slide the gun's barrel out of its enclosing wires… The second launch – or the first one making a second run – passed overhead. Jake realised that Wishart must have got the breech-end of the gun clear in that first bit of joggling around; otherwise he wouldn't be angling her the other way now, he'd still be trying to shed the first lot. He had the shadowed, greenish picture of it in his mind, the net draped down over the jumping-wire, its starboard-side folds caught in and around the gun. She must have struck not quite at right-angles, for it to have swung in under the wire like that.

'Stop blowing!'

'Stop—'

The second charge was closer than the first. The boat rattled like an old tin can as the echoes of it boomed around her, through her. The lights went out: Wishart's voice called down into pitch darkness, 'Slow astern together!' Jake heard Ellery pass that aft. Looking upwards he saw greenish light glowing through the little oblong window and illuminating the top half of his captain's face. That was daylight filtered through thirty feet of Dardanelles. He felt movement: she was responding, coming astern, pulling herself out of the net's grasp. He told himself, *Easy – don't count your chickens…* Lights came on: the emergency ones, fewer and less bright than the main ones. He moved down one rung on the ladder; he'd gone up one at some point without being aware of doing so.

'Stop together!'

But there'd been a flat, angry tone in that order. And if she'd been clear of the net, he wouldn't have stopped her, he'd have gone on, got her right out away from it; the net, after all, had to be the Turks' point of aim with their depth-charges. So what *now*? Jake stared up at his captain's dark bulk half-filling the tower; and distantly, but rapidly getting louder, he heard one of the launches starting another attacking run. A moment ago he'd thought they were free, on the move… Wishart told him, 'There's still some net caught round the trainer's handwheel, the base of it.' The enemy's screws were pounding closer, louder. If the launch passed close over the submarine's forepart, Jake realised, Wishart might actually see it, see the dark hull rush past and the whirring silver of its screws. He shouted upwards. 'Mightn't it part with some weight on it, sir?' Then he understood, while Wishart still peered out through the port and didn't answer, what his objection would be. They'd heard the strain coming on the gundeck earlier, and much more of it might wrench rivets loose in the pressure-hull. The gun was bolted to its deck, but the gundeck in turn was riveted to the hull; if the bolts held, the strain would come on the actual plates. The enemy launch was about to pass right overhead: the peak of its propeller noise was coming – *now...*

'Half astern together!'

Ellery had shouted it aft: Jake felt, through the rungs of the ladder, the vibration from the boat's motors. He looked up towards Wishart in the tower, and at that moment the charge exploded. He saw Wishart blinded by its flash and thrown backwards against the far side of the tower. Signal flares cascaded from a locker, rained down on him: everything was coming down, including Wishart, and he grabbed the ladder tightly, braced himself just in time to receive his captain's not by any means puny weight. The boat meanwhile seemed to have shot astern with a steep and increasing stern-down angle and a sharpish list to port: she was righting herself from the list now. Wishart roared beside Jake's ear, 'Open one, two, three, four main vents! Fifty feet!' Main vents thudding open: Wishart had hauled himself off Jake: he was up there shutting the deadlight on the observation port. He shouted, 'Go on down, pilot!' Jake dropped through the hatch. The submarine was on an even keel athwartships but still had stern-down angle. He glimpsed the needles in the gauges passing forty-two, forty-four feet, then he was at the chart table and Wishart, tumbling through the hatch, panted, 'Stop together. Half ahead together. Signalman, shut the hatch. Pilot, what was our last course?'

'North sixty-east six east, sir.' It felt like a hundred years since they'd run into the net. Wishart told Roost, 'Steer that.' Gathering way forward, the boat was levelling and the 'planesmen weren't having to work so hard. Fifty-four feet on the gauges. Hobday saw Wishart looking at them

144

critically and said, 'Rather not change the trim until I have to, sir. I think she's settling down.'

'Sixty feet.'

'Sixty feet, sir...' Now he *would* have to pump some out. Jake was thinking that sixty feet was fine so far as passing under the net was concerned, but there was still the possibility of mines at lower levels. Wishart might have been considering the same point: he told Hobday, 'Three minutes, to make sure we're under, then we'll come up to forty.' These next few *seconds*, Jake thought, were surely the ones that counted. But you couldn't have it both ways: you either risked catching the bottom of the net in the periscope standards or you made sure of passing below it. They could have ripped it, too, and there might be pieces trailing.

'Slow ahead together.' Wishart had glanced at Agnew: Hobday told him, 'Telegraphs.' With the motors running, the surface craft could hear them anyway. If they stopped rushing about and listened; and not even Turks would be so daft as to have headphones on while they were dropping charges.

'Both motors slow ahead, sir.'

'Any damage, Number One?'

'Slight leaks under the gun-mounting, sir.'

Wishart went quickly to the for'ard end of the control room, and Jake turned from the chart table and stared up at the deckhead. At first he couldn't see anything at all; the softness of the emergency lighting didn't help. Then he spotted it: the smallest trickle, from one in a line of rivet-heads.

He reached up, touching it. 'Here, sir.'

'Couple here, too.' Wishart said as he walked away, 'We'll see to it in the Marmara. At least, our gallant engineers will.' McVeigh grinned at him wolfishly. Wishart asked, 'Dixon doing something about the lights?'

'Yessir.' Hobday turned and looked at him; he'd got the trim right, at last. He said, 'By the way, sir – congratulations.'

'Eh?'

CPO Crabb growled, with his eyes on the gauge in front of him, 'Lads 'd say the same, sir, I reckon.'

'Oh.' Wishart shook his head. 'That last charge did it. There was a double loop round the trainer's handwheel, and the charge snapped it like a bit of string... God knows what shape your gun'll be in, Roost.'

'We'll find out by an' by, sir.'

The lights came on. Seconds later, the emergency ones went out. A long way astern, a charge exploded. Laughter exploded too. It seemed hilariously funny, in that moment, that the Turks might be thinking they still had a submarine in their net.

'Forty feet.'

'Forty feet, sir!'

'How long on this course, pilot?'

'Two miles, sir – then north forty-one east.'

'We'll alter by log reading.' It would be full daylight up there now, and silly to shove up a periscope if you didn't have to. If they wanted to imagine they still had her trapped – well, that was fine! Wishart added, 'We'll go to a hundred feet when we alter, and catch the current. Meanwhile, Number One, let's spare the box. When you're happy with the trim, stop one motor.'

'Aye aye, sir.'

The battery would be just about at its last gasp, by this time. There was no point in taking readings, though; however flat it was, it would be flatter before they reached the Marmara.

The leaking deckhead, Jake thought, might not be quite so small a trickle when they went deeper. In about half an hour they'd find out.

'Forty feet, sir.' Hobday told Agnew, 'Stop starboard.'

'Stop starboard, sir.'

Wishart moved for'ard, in the direction of the chart table. 'All right, Stone?'

Leading Stoker Stone nodded. 'Thank you, sir.' He was a railwayman from Newhaven. His job at diving stations was looking after the starboard ballast pump – the pump itself, not the starter and motor, which McVeigh had charge of. A thin, worried-looking man. He'd told Jake – the night before they'd sailed, when Jake had been nosing around, trying to get to know the ship's company in a hurry – how he'd come to 'volunteer' for submarines. He'd had a cushy number in HMS *Vernon*, the Portsmouth torpedo and mine school, and the drafting PO had remarked to him one day, 'Time you made killick, Stone. Make a right good killick, you would.'

'Killick' meant, in this context, leading hand; a killick was the fouled-anchor badge that a leading seaman wore on his left arm. Stone, flattered, had listened; the PO had flannelled him along and told him, 'They're cryin' out for killick stokers, down the road.' He'd let his name go forward – and a few days later found himself in Fort Blockhouse, learning about submarines.

'*Dahn the road*, 'e says! If 'e meant *acrorss the bloody 'arbour* whyn't the bugger say so?'

Wishart asked him, pulling in his belly in order to squeeze by, 'Heard from that young lady of yours lately?'

'Writes reg'lar, sir.' He looked pleased about that. Wishart propped himself in the doorway of the wireless cabinet. 'Anything happening up there?'

'Confused HE astern, sir. Reckon they're chasin' their tails, sir.' Wishart nodded. He backed out of the cabinet and told Hobday, 'Fall out diving stations, Number One. Let's have a cup of tea.'

Chapter 6

'When you were briefing Cameron the other day, remember you mentioned the Flag Officer Aegean being sent home after *Goeben*'s breakout?'

Hobday was in the armchair, addressing Wishart, who was on his bunk. Robins was on the other bunk, Cameron was on watch, and Nick and Burtenshaw were across the table from Hobday. Wishart asked, 'What of it?'

'Were you joking when you said he dribbles?'

'By no means.' Wishart shuddered. 'It's no joking matter. He smokes a pipe continuously, and slobbers down his chin. Politeness demands that one should look at him when he's mumbling at you, and looking at him makes one feel sick. Anyway he's back in London now. Dribbling over the Board of Admiralty, no doubt.' He nodded. 'Some justice in that, too.'

'C-in-C sent him home?'

'Yes. First-class man, Calthorpe.' He was referring to the Honourable Sir Somerset A. Gough-Calthorpe, Vice-Admiral. He shut his eyes. 'Look here, I think I'll try for a bit of shut-eye now.'

'Right. Sorry.'

Robins spoke from the other bunk. 'Want to use this one, Hobday?'

Hobday glanced up, startled. Nick and Burtenshaw looked just as surprised. He chuckled. 'Most kind. But I'll wait until we're in the Marmara, thanks all the same. Not much good at cat-naps.'

'I'd've thought you'd have to be.' Burtenshaw asked him, 'D'you expect we'll be undisturbed, in the Marmara?'

'You lot won't be. That's when you start earning your pay, isn't it?'

Robins chipped in again. 'At what time *will* we get there?'

'Cameron?' Hobday twisted round in his armchair. 'What's ETA Marmara?'

Jake came over. Like a bear, Nick thought. It was that shambling walk of his. He told them, 'Can't be certain of the tide – but allowing three knots for it, plus the one or one-and-a-half we're getting from slow speed on one screw – well, eighteen miles from where we altered and went deep at four-twenty... Say eight-thirty, well clear?'

Robins observed that thirteen hours was a great deal longer than the passage had been expected to take. Nobody answered him. The assertion was undeniable, and his voicing it might have been intended as a criticism or might not. Nobody cared much, either way. Nick was conscious of a peculiar sensation of timelessness, of being shut off, of having left the world behind and no longer belonging to it. Even Sarah: he frowned, at the suggestion of disloyalty, desertion which came in with that thought. But in Sarah's case it wasn't only the cutoff feeling that the submarine and its situation gave him, it was also the lack of contact with her earlier, the sparsity and sterility of her letters.

'What?'

Jake Cameron had said something about having supper in the Marmara. He repeated it now. Nick thought, *If it's all plain sailing from here on*. He was beginning to get the shape of things – which included a certain unwisdom in taking anything for granted.

Supper in the Marmara… And then, as Hobday had just said, the business of the landing. It was an extremely vague briefing that Reaper had given him. What it amounted to was that Robins would introduce him and Burtenshaw to certain contacts ashore, and they – Turks, or at any rate local residents – would provide the information and guidance for an attack on *Goeben*. Nick was to take Burtenshaw and Burtenshaw's explosives under his command and see the thing through to the best possible conclusion, adjusting his plans according to the situation and developments ashore. Robins would be going his own devious, foreign-office way, politicking either with or in competition with the French. Reaper knew very little about that side of the business; his only instructions so far as Robins was concerned were that he was to be put ashore in company with the Frenchmen. But the outcome of the landing, of the political string-pulling or arm-twisting, and hopefully of the destruction of the *Goeben* – which was the *piece de resistance* – all this superimposed on the wider strategic developments, was expected to take the form of a Turkish surrender, and Reaper wanted to have Nick ashore in Constantinople when and if this came about. He'd be in communication with Reaper, and through Reaper with the C-in-C, by clandestine wireless links now operated by the people to whom Robins would be introducing him. These included an English woman to whom Reaper had referred as the Grey Lady. Nick would be expected to report on what was happening ashore, and might be required later to make arrangements of one sort or another for the arrival and safe reception of the Fleet.

Tall orders, Reaper had admitted. Tall, and vague. They could hardly, in the shifting circumstances, be more definite. And the situation might well be complicated by Robins, who had his own instructions from London and would almost certainly want to throw his weight about. But Robins wasn't truly a naval man – Reaper seemed to expect to have his cake and eat it too, on this point – he wasn't a professional, and Reaper didn't trust him. Nick was basically to confine himself to the naval aspects of the situation; it was in areas where naval considerations over-lapped political ones that he might find problems. He'd find problems anyway, and he was to act as he thought best in whatever circumstances arose.

'Whatever you do,' Reaper had told him, 'you'll have my support.' Nick had nodded, liking that assurance. The commander had added, 'But if you make a mess of it, we'll both be for the high-jump.'

–

Jake Cameron had gone back to the centre of the control room. He had Rowbottom at the wheel, Finn on the fore 'planes and Anderson on the after 'planes. Rowbottom stolid, slow of speech: Finn, stocky and curly-haired, a complete contrast, one of the boat's humorists. Anderson, the tall torpedoman, was a close friend and shore-going partner of Finn's; he was nicknamed 'Close-'aul' Anderson, which had something to do with the belief that he sailed close to the wind in his dealings with the fair sex. He was alleged, certainly, to have one fiancée in Liverpool and another, a Greek girl, in Corfu town. E.57 had left Corfu only three weeks ago; until this *Goeben* flap had started she'd been part of the flotilla employed in blockading the Adriatic, keeping the Austrian fleet bottled up.

Dull work; but the general view was that having Corfu as their base compensated for it. And they hadn't been out from England long enough to get bored by the uneventful patrols.

ERA Percy Bradshaw leant against the panel of vent and blow controls. 'Polecate' Bradshaw had worked for Cammell Laird at Birkenhead until early in the war. He could still have been there, if he'd wanted to be, earning big money in a 'reserved occupation'. Bradshaw's beard; Jake noticed, had grown during the night to a remarkable extent. He ran a hand over his own jaw; he was in a similar condition. Anderson was looking fairly rough too; but on Finn and Rowbottom, who were fairhaired, the stubble didn't show so much.

'Bit light for'ard, are we, Anderson?'

'TI went aft, sir, did'n 'e?'

'Close-'aul' glanced over his shoulder as he said it. Most of his length was legs; he had trouble finding room for them when he was on the 'planesman's stool.

Jake had forgotten about Rinkpole having gone aft. At this slow speed through the water – hopefully the boat was moving faster in relation to the land – the trim was easily upset. He glanced at the clock; ten minutes to five. About three-and-a-half more hours in the straits, that meant. He felt hungry. It would be marvellous to be out in open water, to sit down to a meal, relax, have a smoke… He crossed over to the chart table and leant on it, studying the Marmara, the entrance to it where the Gallipoli Strait widened out from this miserable crack between two land-masses. Quite a sizeable piece of water, the Marmara. About 120 miles long and 50 wide, with these straits at its western end and Constantinople and the Bosphorus at the other, and various islands in the middle. Fascinating to look at it and think how, in 1915, British submarines had forced their way in through these straits and virtually ruled the area, sunk everything warlike that had moved on the Marmara's surface, closed it as a waterway to the nation who owned the land all around it. In the process, lost some ships and lives and made some reputations. When you considered the achievements of those early submarines, what was being asked of this one didn't seem so much. It also made it imperative that she should score her own success.

'Permission to go for'ard, sir?'

'Carry on, TI.'

He leant against the polished steel ladder. Peace and quiet, except for the murmur of Burtenshaw's and Hobday's occasional spasms of conversation. A heavy, drugging peace. Half of it was the stuffiness, warmth generated by the motors, batteries, breath. The leaking rivets were no worse than they had been. At a hundred feet sea-pressure might have made them *much* worse. Perhaps the trickles ran a little faster; but even that could have been imagined. It was what you expected to see, so you saw it. And as Chief ERA Grumman had observed half an hour ago, greater outside pressure might actually reduce the leaks by forcing the loosened rivets home.

Jake didn't believe it. He didn't think Grumman had either... He heard Burtenshaw ask Everard, 'You were at Zeebrugge, weren't you?' Everard must have nodded. Burtenshaw said, 'I tried to go on that stunt. I did some work at Deal with Brock – well, what I mean is he was in charge of all that side – Brock, d'you know who I mean, the chap who organised all the flares and smoke, rockets and—'

'I knew him quite well. At Dover. We all did.' He'd heard Burtenshaw mention Brock before, in a conversation with Jake Cameron. Hobday asked him, 'Did you know any of the submariners, the chaps who blew up the viaduct?'

'Yes. Tim Rogerson.'

Hobday smiled. 'Same term, Tim and I. Well, well!'

'He's about a year, year and a half senior to me.' It was Everard who'd said that. Adding now, 'Quite a pal, actually. D'you know his sister Eleanor, by any chance?'

'Can't say I do.'

Burtenshaw put in, 'Wasn't C3's captain one of the VCs?'

'Sandford. Yes.' Hobday added, 'Known in the trade as Uncle Baldy. Marvellous chap.'

'Have to be, I suppose, to be picked for a job like that one.' The Marine sighed. 'Not *my* luck, I assure you.' Hobday chuckled. 'Not exactly long in the tooth yet, are you.'

'Perhaps not. But the war's likely to conk out soon, and all I've done has been loaf around such places as Deal!'

'Not loafing about Deal *now*, are you.'

'Thank heavens, no. But—' Burtenshaw hesitated: Jake murmured, 'Watch that depth, Finn.'

'Sorry, sir.' Jake thought, *Daydreaming about some Pompey tart…* Burtenshaw was saying, over in the corner, 'Compared to a chap like you, Everard – and if you'll forgive my mentioning it you're not such an awful lot older than I am—'

'Old enough to have been at sea before the war began, though.' Nick said, 'Over that period of time one could hardly *not* see a certain amount of action.'

'You've done damn well, by all accounts.' Hobday spoke without any sign of envy. 'And one needs no powers of second-sight to see you following in your uncle's tracks. Admiral Sir *Nicholas*—'

He'd pronounced it Nickle-arse.

'I don't think so.'

Jake turned, and looked across the compartment at Everard. He saw him shake his head.

'I'm not sure the peacetime Navy is quite my mark. I – er —' He was hesitant, looking at Hobday across the table. 'I don't know. I disliked Dartmouth, and Dartmouth wasn't frightfully keen on me. I've a feeling peacetime service might be rather like that: polishing the brightwork, minding one's p's and q's, being careful whom one knows and what one says to them, and – oh, I don't know…'

He'd heard himself saying it. He hadn't previously voiced such thoughts, except to really close friends like Rogerson, and quite privately. It was this shut-off feeling, he thought: as if this was another world – isolated from the real one.

Well, it *was.*

Hobday said, 'It'd be an awful lot to throw away. Being your uncle's nephew is a terrific card in your hand. And your record's fairly sensational. Those medals—'

'Chaps with a lot of ribbons were looked down on, before the war.' Nick's uncle had told him this. 'They used to call them glory–hunters. It wasn't at all a thing to—'

'Never mind about what happened *before* the war.' Hobday wagged a finger. 'If you wanted to make absolutely *certain* of reaching flag-rank yourself now, what you should do is marry an admiral's daughter.'

'Would you do that?'

'If I found one I could stand. Why not? You've got to fit in with things as they are, you know.'

'Well, that's not *my* meat.'

Jake Cameron, who'd spent several days in *Terrapin* as a fellow passenger with Nick Everard, saw it more clearly suddenly. It wouldn't have been *his* meat, either. Not that he, Jake, could have had any such opportunity; Lieutenant Nicholas Everard DSO DSC Royal Navy was a baronet's son and an admiral's nephew, and Hobday was right, the cards were ready to his hand if he chose to pick them up and play them. Jake's own options were the merchant navy or the alternative of some humdrum bread-and-butter work ashore. The two of them were miles apart. In spite of that, he felt instinctively that he and Nick Everard, if you cut through to the bone of it, were similar animals and might have more in common than – well, than Everard had with Hobday, say. Or Cameron with Hobday.

Not that he in any way disliked the little man. There was just that sudden picture of a peacetime Navy, all yes-sirs and no-sirs and admirals' daughters, and plenty of Hobdays willing to 'fit in' with it.

Might that make the Camerons and the Everards long-term losers?

He thought, *Thank God for the mercantile marine!*

Or for the tedious shoreside job? How would one react to a straight choice between that and Hobday's ceremonial sailoring?

'Sir.' Leading Telegraphist Weatherspoon saved him from having to resolve that less simple question. Weatherspoon had poked his head out of the silent cabinet; he had his headset pushed back off his ears. 'Reckon we're bein' follered, sir. That trawler.'

Hobday had gone over to him.

'Joined on astern, sir. Come up gradual – I was thinkin' I'd got some HE, then it'd stop, sort of before I was sure, an' I'd think *no, I'm wrong* – then—'

'Keep listening.' Hobday went back to the other side and shook Wishart's arm. 'Captain, sir...'

–

'Stop port.'

'Stop port!' Agnew passed the order verbally. In an effort to keep as quiet as possible they weren't using the telegraphs. This submarine was the mouse and there was a cat up there watching her every move.

'Port motor stopped, sir.'

That meant both motors were silent now. Wishart looked round at Weatherspoon, on his stool just inside the doorway of the silent cabinet. The leading tel nodded. 'Still closin', sir.' Then his eyebrows lifted. 'Enemy stoppin', sir!'

Which finally proved the point – that the trawler, or gunboat, was trailing them. Each time E.57 had stopped her motors, the enemy had stopped too. When the submarine's screws had stirred into life again, a few seconds would crawl by before the slower, more powerful screw would resume its leisurely beat. They'd checked it out several times now — hoping for a different explanation. It might, for instance, have been some patrol vessel making its way slowly up-straits and stopping now and then to listen through its hydrophones. Like a fly-fisherman working a stretch of river. But it wasn't so. Whatever E.57 did, the shadower kept his distance. His revs per minute increased when the submarine's did, lessened when she slowed. On the whole he was stopped more often than they were; he was obviously taking care to keep astern and at his chosen distance.

It was uncanny. Dislike for the Turk was mounting. You could see the anger in men's faces when they looked upwards.

McVeigh asked Wishart, 'Mak' a suggestion, sir?'

Wishart glanced at the wild-looking Glaswegian, and nodded.

'If we wen' up tae periscope depth, might we no gi'e the swine a bash oot the stern tube?'

'It's a nice idea.' Wishart shook his head. 'But we want all our fish for *Goeben*. Anyway he's a small target and he's watching us already – he wouldn't sit and wait for it.'

The ERA wiped the back of his wrist across his nostrils. He nodded angrily. 'Aye.' Wishart said soothingly, 'We'll shake him off, by and by. Once we get into the Marmara we'll lose him.'

'Losing trim, sir.'

'Slow ahead port.'

'Slow ahead port!' Finn passed it on aft from Agnew. Wishart joined Jake at the chart table. 'Where do we think we are?'

'Coming up to this point, sir.'

It was about an hour since they'd gone deep and turned on to the present course. If it was a three-knot tide as estimated they'd be roughly level with a place called Kodjuk Burnu. It was on the southern, Asiatic shore, and at this point the coastline bulged into the straits, narrowing them to about three thousand yards.

'Hadn't realised.' Wishart scowled at the chart. 'Narrowest since we cleared Nagara.'

'Yes.' Jake pointed with his dividers. 'And twenty-five fathoms is the shallowest mid-channel sounding we've come across.'

The same thought was in both their minds. A narrowing of the waterway with a rising seabed was a natural place to block with nets. Jake suggested quietly, 'That one may be following to see us get snagged up again.'

'Let us hope *not*.' The battery wouldn't stand for much more of the net games. Wishart stooped, peered more closely at the chart. 'Not a great deal we can do about it, old lad. Only way to locate a net, unfortunately, is bump into it... You know, I don't believe this Kodjuk is a place, as such. I reckon it means "headland" or "point". The *burnu* bit, I mean.'

There were quite a few other *burnus*, here and there, and they did all seem to be headlands. Jake remembered afterwards that he'd been looking for others along the coastlines, hoping to find one that might disprove that theory of Wishart's, and that Weatherspoon had just reported that the enemy had stopped his engine again – that word 'engine' was the last word, last moment – last *conscious* moment, before—

It must have been *in* that moment that the mine blew up.

As if all the sea they floated in had exploded. You had only one barely glimpsed flash of thought: *finished, over!* Your *mind* detonated... It was — total, so overwhelming that there was nothing else, nothing left or existing: the noise and impact and then the echoes and reactions all part of it, booming through hollow, shattered minds blanked-off from memory, will-power, consciousness. You were *in* it, part of it, you couldn't fight it or resist or — reason, comprehend... It was dark, absolutely black, and the universe was rolling over: the sound of shouting from all directions was far away, remote, although it might have had your own voice in it. A rush of water broke through then, roaring like thunder for a time before it stopped dead with an enormous jolt: and now trickling splashing sounds growing fainter, fading into silence in the darkness, stillness. A swaying motion, and water-sounds soft and whispery through steel plating. In the rush of water — that hard, loud rush — he'd thought yes, this was how death came, how in his heart of hearts he'd always known it would; it was surprising now that he was dry and still drawing breaths and letting them gush out again. More voices suddenly, rising all together as if they'd been there all the time and now the volume was being turned up to normal: it was possible, he thought, that something had happened to his ear-drums. Now that had been a *lucid* thought: he clutched it and got more, an argument in favour of his ears being undamaged because other-wise he wouldn't have heard the water-sounds, the small ones. Someone was shouting about lights, and immedi-ately there was a second crash of high-explosive: but that one had been farther away, enormous enough by normal standards and with a rocking effect that followed it, but compared to the first one – *nothing.*

'Dixon? Is Leading Seaman Dixon seeing about some lights?'

Wishart's voice. Insistent, but unexcited, rather as if this was another exercise, a practice evolution, one of his *out lights, main vents in hand* games. Jake struggled to his feet and began groping his way towards the auxiliary switchboard. Stumbling over someone who was crawling: cursing hard. A lot of cursing. Lights blazed suddenly: the main ones, not the emergencies. He found that he was facing the for'ard periscope, grasping its wires, his two hands slimy with its thick, grey grease. He thought he'd been unconscious, or semiconscious. The compartment seemed to be dry: and yet there'd been water forcing in – hadn't there?

'Check bulkhead voicepipes. Reports from all compartments, please. Are both motors stopped?'

You could see men trying to control their breathing, accept the surprise of being alive. Jake went to the chart table and found all his bits and pieces strewn around. Water was dripping much faster from the deckhead than it had been before. ERA Knight had come to this end of the compartment to have a look at it; he was muttering, 'Could be worse. Could be better but it could be worse, much worse.' Nodding, as if he liked the sound of that. He'd patted Stone's shoulder as he moved away: 'All right, Andy lad?'

Lewis had been lending his ear to a babble from the voicepipe in the for'ard bulkhead. He reported, 'Dry for'ard except a leak on the starboard torpedo tube, sir. TI says 'e 'as it in 'and, sir.'

'That's good, Lewis.'

Reality and normality returning as the elements of the machine recovered separately and began to mesh together. Hobday asked Wishart, 'Shall we keep watertight doors shut, sir?'

'For the moment, yes. Who shut them?'

Lewis admitted, 'I did this 'un, sir.'

'Well done you!'

'Polecat' Bradshaw kicked the after door. 'I got chucked ag'in it. Brought it to me mind, you might say.'

'Good man, Bradshaw.'

Burtenshaw put in diffidently, 'I think Lieutenant-Commander Robins is concussed, sir.'

Nick Everard said quickly, 'I'll see to it.' He looked fairly dazed himself. Wishart asked, 'Reports from aft?'

'Nowt from after ends yet, sir.' Stoker Adams was on that voicepipe. 'No leaks nor nothin' in engine-room an' motor-room. Some fuses an' that gone, LTO says. Waitin' for after end's report, sir.' Adams was from Rochdale. Tall, stooped, yellow-headed. Wishart asked Morton, 'That gauge shut off, is it?'

'Aye, sir, but it's bust, too.' Crabb put in, 'This one'll do for 'im an' all, sir.' His gauge, the after one, showed a hundred and forty-three feet, and that matched the charted soundings off Kodjuk Burnu all right.

'Pilot, go for'ard, see how the TI's getting on and what the trouble is, and pass the word around that we seem to be intact and not much damaged. Tell 'em we'll open bulkhead doors soon as we know a bit more about the state we're in.'

'Aye aye, sir.' Jake told Lewis, 'Warn 'em I'm coming through.' The door had to be unclipped before you could open it. At the other end of the control room Lofty Adams reported, 'After ends dry 'cept for leaking shaft gland port side an' a spot of floodin' back through the 'eads. They're lookin' after it, sir.'

Wishart looked at McVeigh. 'And the outside ERA will see to it more thoroughly in a few minutes, the lucky dog… Number One, don't use the port screw unless we're forced to.'

'Aye aye, sir.' Hobday called to Adams, 'Tell the Stoker PO to see what Peel's doing about the shaft gland, and to have all bilges checked and auxiliary tanks dipped… Lewis, I want Cole to come and check the battery tank.' He added quietly to Wishart, 'Seems we've been lucky, sir.'

'Let's hope so.' Wishart was peering at the bubble and the depth-gauge, and now at the other spirit-level, the curved one on the deckhead that showed any list to port or starboard. 'Since so far as we know nothing's been flooded, there's no reason we should be bottomed, is there?'

'We aren't necessarily all that heavy, sir. A bit of pumping should bring her up. If the explosion pushed us downwards…'

'I'd have sworn I heard a lot of…' Wishart shook his head. 'We've this list to port.' He looked puzzled. 'Anyway, pump some out aft, let's have her tail up and the screws clear. Pump on "Z". If she looks ready to move, put a drop in "A" to hold her down. Can't move before we know what's happening up there…' Glancing round for

Weatherspoon, he found the leading tel waiting to report to him.

'Can't 'ear nothin', sir. I don't *think* the gear's scuppered, but—'

'Your own ears, perhaps?'

'Not likely, sir. Didn't 'ave the 'eadset on when it went off. But there was that bloke up top there, and now I can't 'ear 'im, can't 'ear nothin', sir.'

'Let me have a listen.' Wishart took the headset from him, moving into the cabinet. Jake came back from the torpedo stowage compartment and tube space. Hobday had got the pump sucking on 'Z' internal main ballast now, and he beckoned him. 'Captain's using the hydrophone. Is it all right for'ard?'

Cole had come through behind Jake; he was clipping the door shut. Jake said, 'Sluice door on the starboard tube must have been jolted open and then banged shut again – enough to fill the tube under pressure and lift the relief-valve so hard it jammed open. Rinkpole belted it with a mallet and it's all right now. Anderson fell between the tubes and I think his wrist's broken... The fish in that tube – TI'll pull it back and do a routine on it as soon as there's a chance.' He nodded. 'That's all. Shall I take a look aft as well?' Hobday nodded, and Stoker Adams began to wrench the clips off the other door.

Wishart handed the headset back to Weatherspoon and backed out of the cabinet.

'I can hear water noises all round. Doubt if there's anything wrong with the gear. You'd better give yourself a break.' He looked round: 'Agnew – take over for a while. All right, leading tel?'

'Aye aye, sir.' Weatherspoon pressed his palms against his outsize ears, looking worried. But it was a relief to know the gear was working; without it they'd be deaf as well as blind. Wishart said, 'Our friend up there's waiting to see what floats up. Probably reckons we're a dead duck. Thanks to Messrs Vickers, we aren't, we're a *tough* one.' Men smiled, their faces glistening under films of sweat, eyes fighting not to show uncertainty. He told them, 'While he stays there, all we can do is sit tight... Adams – Lewis – pass the word to all compartments: no hammering, no spanners, no row at all.'

Adams had just clipped the door shut again behind Jake; now he passed that order through the voicepipe. Cole was shining a torch down one of the battery-tank sighting holes. Hobday had the port ballast pump working on 'Z' internal; he asked Bradshaw, 'Getting anything out?'

'Not much, sir.' He was crouched over the pump, which had pressure gauges on it. 'Relief-valve's gagged an' all.'

You had to gag the relief, which was set to lift at fifty pounds to the square inch. Hobday told McVeigh, 'Stand by to put some air in "Z".'

It was sea-pressure on the outlet valve that made the pump's work difficult. Increasing the pressure in the tank would balance it. McVeigh had his hands on the HP air-valve and his eyes on Hobday; Hobday said, 'Open... *Shut!*' The ERA had sent a burst of air thumping down the line. Bradshaw looked up from the pump. 'Lovely!' Jake came back, and reported to Wishart. 'Leech doesn't think the shaft gland'll get any worse, sir, and it's nothing much. The heads were in a foul state – still are – but there's no flooding now. The screw-down valve was shut, but not *tight* shut.'

The heads were McVeigh's bugbear. He growled, ginger beard wagging angrily, 'They dinna blow 'em richt, so it's solid muck they screw the valve doon on. Then ye get a *whumpf* like yon, an' it a' blows back an'—' He waved his hands, indicating that high-pressured shower of foulness. Jake nodded. 'I'm afraid it did.' McVeigh muttered to Bradshaw, his mate, 'Safer wi' a stack o' bedpans. It's the puir bluidy outside ERA has tae go an'—'

'Price you pay, McVeigh, for being a mechanical genius.' Wishart was looking at the depth-gauge. 'That tank must be about out by now.'

Emptying a tank that held five-and-a-half tons of water when it was full, and must have had at least half that much in it before they'd started pumping, seemed to have made no difference. And that made no sense. It was like two and two making three. Hobday said, 'I'll take some out amidships, sir… Although the bubble has shifted slightly, hasn't it, cox'n?'

'Less'n half a degree, sir.'

'Darn it.' Mysteries were irritating, as well as threatening future embarrassment. 'Stop the pump. Shut "Z" suction. Open "X" suction and inboard vent.'

Wishart was at the door of the silent cabinet. 'Hear anything, Agnew?'

The boy tel pushed the headset off his ears. 'Bit of a noise a minute ago, sir. Like – I dunno, sir, but I been thinkin' might it 'a been a ship lettin' 'er anchor go.'

'Why didn't you report it, for heaven's sake!'

'Did'n know what to call it, sir – I mean, I—'

'Report everything you hear. Even a lobster gargling – I don't care *what* you call it!'

'Aye aye, sir. Sorry, sir.'

Wishart leant with his back against the chart table. Hobday had just put some pressure into the midships tank, as he'd done for the other. Wishart began, thinking aloud, 'I'll accept it was the Turk anchoring. He'd have been following astern of us, with a good idea of where we were, and knowing – I'm guessing this – knowing they'd got a net ahead of us with controlled mines in it. Or not a net – just a line of mines wired to the shore. He'd have been signalling to his friends ashore – giving 'em lots of warning to be ready for us… Now he's dropped a hook and he'll sit up there until either he's sure we're done for or he hears us move.'

Jake had been checking soundings on the chart. He told Wishart, 'Shelves to eleven fathoms near the southern shore here, sir, and on the other side it varies between six and ten. He could be at anchor on either side and still be within a thousand yards of us.'

CPO Crabb reported, 'She's shiftin', sir!'

'Stop the pump. Shut "X" suction… Anchor her for'ard, sir?' Wishart nodded, and Hobday told Lewis, 'Open "A" inboard vent.' There was residual pressure still in 'A'; when the vent was opened, air hissed into the boat, and you had to swallow to clear your ears. But you couldn't flood water into a tank against pressure, and you couldn't vent it outboard without sending up a bubble to the surface.

A few seconds later Crabb reported that the spirit-level bubble was moving aft. Hobday stopped flooding the for'ard tank, and shut it off. Now the submarine's bow was weighted down heavily enough to hold her anchored to the seabed while her afterpart and screws floated clear of it.

Cole said – a mumble through his thick, black beard – 'No acid in the battery tanks, sir.'

'Good.' But there was still a sense of unreality. The uncertainty about what had happened – where all the extra weight had suddenly appeared from – added to the strangeness. It was like an aftermath of dying, of *having died*... As if they weren't intended to be alive, should not have been. But alive they were, and you couldn't lose track of several tons of ballast and just ignore it, pretend it didn't matter. You had to find out what had happened – before you found out the hard way, in an emergency, when it might be too late. It was like knowing there was a time-bomb somewhere, and searching and still not finding it. Wishart, of course, would be battling not only with that problem but with others too, the whole situation: the Turk sitting over them, and shore-controlled mines most likely covering the entire area – those were the *external* threats, and one had to consider them in conjunction with internal factors such as a battery that couldn't have much life left in it and air that was becoming thin and foul. He had to decide on *some* move. Eyes in tired, sweaty faces followed him, waiting for the decision. Robins was stretched out on Wishart's bunk, and Nick saw Wishart looking that way; he told him, 'He's all right now. Only had a bump.' Wishart turned as the stoker PO arrived from aft and asked Hobday out of that ventriloquist's mouth of his, 'You want *every* tank dipped, sir, that right?'

'Hang on, Leech.' Wishart ordered, 'Open watertight doors. Number One – we'll stay here. One officer and one hand on control-room watch. Everyone else turn in. Only one light's to be used in each compartment. No moving around at all.' He looked at Leech. 'Yes. Dip all the auxiliaries and check dry-stores, every space there is. And don't drop a pin while you're doing it, or I'll shoot you, d'you hear?'

'Can't kill a Yorkshireman wi' a bullet, sir.' Leech looked quite serious about it. Wishart said, 'All right, then, I'll hang you.' The stoker PO wagged his head, concurring. 'Ah. That's different.'

–

Robins, who'd admitted grudgingly that he'd sustained no lasting injury, asked Wishart what they'd do if the Turk sat tight – stayed up there, on top of them.

'Then we sit tight too. If necessary until it's dark again.'

Robins was in the bottom, pull-out bunk. Wishart and Hobday were in their own, and Burtenshaw was stretched out on a blanket on the deck. Nick had accepted a blanket for the same purpose but for the time being he was comfortable enough in the armchair; he'd be able to doze, he thought, by leaning forward across the table with the folded blanket as a pillow on it. Plenty of deck-space anyway, since there'd be no one moving around.

Wishart had explained to Robins that they couldn't move without making a periscope check of their position first. Which way or how far the boat had travelled between the explosion and bottoming was anybody's guess.

'You mean we'd lie here – what, *twelve hours*?'

'Nearer sixteen, if we have to wait for darkness… All the more reason to pipe down now and go to sleep.'

Jake Cameron had moved the telegraphists' stool to a spot just outside the cabinet. The headset's lead reached that far and the cabinet doorway served well as a backrest. He'd be on watch for two hours now, and every half-hour he and his fellow watchkeeper, Stoker Burrage, would take turns on the listening gear. There'd be nothing else to do except keep quiet, stay awake, ensure that no noise was made from elsewhere in the boat. There'd been a period of noise-making, certainly, since the explosion, and the Turk would probably have heard some of it, but with any luck he might convince himself that he'd been listening to the submarine's death throes.

Making everyone lie down and do nothing was also the best way to conserve oxygen. It was stuffy in the compartments now, with a thick, oily, heads-reeking, submarine humidity. It wasn't pleasant to breathe, and yet you needed to take deeper breaths than usual. By nightfall it might be fairly horrible, Jake thought. Six or seven hours ago they'd had that short spell on the surface, but unless the diesels were started up – which unfortunately they had not been – you didn't get much fresh air into the boat just by opening a hatch. Hobday hadn't run the fans, during that minute on the surface, either. Hindsight told one that he should have, but like everyone else he'd had his mind on the net that had fouled them and on the shore batteries and searchlights.

All through the boat men slept, now. Asleep, you used less air, and minimal lighting saved power. Both commodities would be crucial to survival.

Sixteen hours, Wishart had estimated. Add that to the fourteen since they'd dived. And then there were still fifteen more miles of the straits to get through, and nobody would be so rash as to count on it being a straight-forward, uninterrupted fifteen-mile run either. Count, Jake thought, on *nothing*... A couple of times in recent hours there had been a premature, illusory feeling that the worst was over... He glanced round the gloomy, deep-shadowed compartment. If one could have foreseen being in *this* situation... As well, perhaps, that the future hid itself, that one could only take things as they came. In any case – he told himself – they *were* winning: they'd got this far, and the rest of it couldn't be much rougher than some of the stages they'd already survived. Wishart was right to be cautious, to play for long-term safety rather than for a quicker breakthrough. The object was not to get into the Marmara in a hurry, it was to arrive there intact and fighting-fit.

Warmth, and silence. The Turk up there wasn't kicking any tin cans about either. Only soft water-sounds from outside the hull. Through the headphones the same sounds were greatly magnified. In many seas there'd be dead submarines lying much as this one was now, with dead men lying about, very much as E.57's crew were lying now and similar sea-sounds whispering on and on... If it hadn't been for the headphones one could easily have drifted into sleep. He could see that Burrage, blinking at the depth-gauges opposite him, was finding it hard to stay awake. Burrage was short, broadshouldered, curly-haired. If he'd been of lighter build you could have taken him for a jockey. He was sitting with his back against the HP compressor and he had his eyes open but switched off, as in a dream. Jake remembered ERA Geordie Knight telling him that Burrage's major enthusiasm was for motor-racing, his hero the great S.F. Edge. You could guess that at this moment Burrage wasn't here, trapped in silence at the bottom of the Dardanelles, but racketing along in a bedlam of roaring exhausts at Brooklands, risking his neck at speeds of up to sixty miles an hour.

Burrage hung around Knight a lot and talked to him about that sort of thing because he wanted a job in the motor business, after the war, and he knew Knight's father owned a garage.

The bulkhead clock showed six-twenty. By the original reckoning they'd have been in the Marmara hours ago. Eight hours from the Kum Kale minefield, the estimate had been. He wondered how long the passage might have taken *Louve*; even whether the French boat had got through at all. She might have been lucky and slipped through without much trouble. The Frenchmen were efficient enough, according to Wishart and Hobday; E.57 and *Louve* had exercised together on the way from Mudros to Imbros, and *Louve* had seemed to be well up to scratch.

When darkness came, the Turk might still be lying up there, like a cat over a mouse-hole. They'd have to be very canny, creep away from him. Not easy. Even less so if Wishart was right in his guess that the area might be sown with shore-controlled mines. If that was the case there'd be hydrophones ashore to pick up the sound of the boat's motors when she moved. Screws approaching their mine-barrage would be what they'd react to. You could imagine the Turks ashore there in headphones with their fingers on the firing keys…

Better not to.

He told himself, *It's all guesswork. Pointless. Wait and see what happens, no good trying to anticipate it.* He wished he could hit on some possible solution to the mystery of the trim. Leech had dipped all the auxiliaries – internal main ballasts, trim tanks, comps, buoyancy, WRTs, even the fresh water, oil-fuel, lub-oil and dirty-oil tanks. Bilges too, of course. Every other space – stores, magazine, every cubic foot of her – had been inspected. There was still no answer to that weight they'd had to shed. He remembered the flooding, rushing-water noise he'd heard. Or only imagined? He'd thought of himself as dead, or about to die, and one's mind might play odd tricks. He shifted his position cautiously. His damaged shoulder – the one the net had lacerated – still ached and smarted. The coxswain had painted the abrasions with iodine for him. He wanted to breathe deeply and at the same time not breathe at all. He looked at the clock again. The bulkhead behind it, an oval of white enamel lit by the glow of the single lamp, ran with condensation. Six-thirty. In Mudros, Imbros, and aboard *Terrapin* in the Gulf of Xeros, everyone would be counting on their being in the Marmara by this time.

–

Nick was thinking about Reaper, who'd be in the gulf now, in *Terrapin*. Reaper wouldn't hit it off with Truman, *Terrapin's* captain, he thought. Truman had a pompous manner, a way of making his pronouncements sound weighty even when they were quite trivial. It wasn't just his awful voice, it was his style in general. Reaper, on the other hand, was an unassuming, straight-thinking man with no time for blather and no sense whatever of his own importance. Those exchanges he'd had with Robins at the meeting aboard *Harwich* – Nick had thought about it, and he realised that Reaper hadn't been quick to slap the man down for the sole reason that he wouldn't have wanted to waste that much time and effort; he'd wanted only to get on with the briefing. In the same way, when Nick had let Reaper see, at Dover at the turn of this year, that he thought Reaper was letting him down, that he'd had the job done for him – the trawler sunk and its crew brought back as prisoners – and no longer cared what happened next to the man who'd done it for him, Reaper hadn't said a word, he'd let Nick go off in that surly, let-down frame of mind, and left it to him to discover what had been done for him. His first command – of *Bravo*.

(With air as foul as this already, Nick wondered, what would it be like by nightfall? But lacking submarine experience, he couldn't tell *how* bad it was, or how much worse it could get and still be breathable. He shifted on the chair, pulled the rolled blanket closer and rested the other side of his head on it.)

No sufferer of fools, was Reaper. He wouldn't enjoy being cooped up with Truman, any more than Nick had; and being a destroyer CO himself he'd been treated as the captain's guest, not the wardroom's. For Reaper it would be worse, though, because loitering in the Gulf of Xeros and listening out for wireless messages wouldn't involve Truman in much work; he'd have time to play host, entertain his guest. Reaper would be bored stiff, Nick thought.

He had a French wireless expert with him, for communications with *Louve*, and a leading telegraphist from the Mudros staff, as well as *Terrapin's* own operators. He wouldn't be expecting to hear anything from either of the submarines, but he'd have set a round-the-clock listening watch for shore transmissions – from the people the landing party were to tie-up with later – and after the landing he'd be expecting reports from Robins, and from Nick as well, through that same clandestine channel. Neither of the submarines was to break W/T silence except in a situation of drastic emergency; the hope was that the enemy in Constantinople wouldn't suspect the presence of submarines in the Marmara. But they'd be able to receive messages, and Reaper had drawn up a time-table of broadcast periods, alternating in English and in French, during which they were supposed to listen out. *Terrapin's* wireless would transmit orders or information, particularly if anything reached him from the shore contacts if it affected the submarine's or the landing party's plans.

Reaper would be under strain, Nick thought. To sit there in *Terrapin* with no word from E.57 or from *Louve*, and knowing the hazards of this passage of the straits, and with the whole enterprise depending on their getting through. Then he'd be waiting for news from shore – from this Grey Lady and her friends – on some unreliable home-made wireless set…

He had said *something* about the 'Grey Lady', before he'd gone on to some other subject. He'd asked Nick, half jokingly it had seemed, 'Would you believe in an English maiden lady of middle age and impeccable social background having charge of our espionage and insurrectionary operations in Constantinople?'

Thinking back on it, it was like a dream that came and went. Breathing *through* the blanket, face-downward, as if it might filter the foetid air. Might Sarah be lying awake now, thinking about him, thinking of him with his head in the fresh air – in sunshine even, because he'd told her he was heading for a warmer climate?

Might Sarah have told the old man about what had happened at Mullbergh?

He'd been dropping off to sleep. The question burst like a fire-cracker in his brain, woke him with a start. He'd moved sharply, dislodged the blanket and practically dislocated his neck.

'Why not lie down?'

A murmur from Jake Cameron – who'd swapped places with the young stoker, Nick saw. He must have dozed for longer than he'd thought. He rubbed his neck: he'd pulled a muscle in it. Nodding to Cameron, and feeling sick now from the oppressive atmosphere. He moved as quietly as he could, hearing a gentle snoring which he thought came from Hobday, and spreading the blanket with two folds in it so that it was long and narrow, bunk-shaped. Cameron was back in his own thoughts, gazing tiredly at the shadowed, moisture-running deckhead. The dripping from it was as frequent now as if one was on the fringe of a thundery rainstorm, and the corticene covering of the deck had big wet areas from it. Nick still had that question in his mind as he lay down on his blanket: *Out of guilt, remorse?*

No. She was a very moral, self-disciplined person, and she'd been shocked at her own behaviour; but however badly she'd come to feel about it she was also a sensible, very level-headed creature. As well as beautiful and sweet and – *good*. And it had happened: it was still incredible, marvellous as well as frightening—

Why on earth had she gone down to London, of her own volition, to join a husband whom she loathed?

Whatever the answer was, it was *not* that she could have told him. She knew only too well what sort of man she'd married. Sir John Everard would have shown no mercy: he'd have destroyed her. He'd have destroyed Nick too, if he could have found a way to do it. And Sarah would have realised that; for his sake alone she wouldn't have dreamt of – of trying to ease her conscience by confessing. And yet she had gone down to London and spent ten days with her husband in the house in Curzon Street. She must have heard that he was back from France about a week after Nick had left Mullbergh to take up his job on Bayly's staff at Queenstown; and rushed straight down as if she and her husband were lovebirds who couldn't wait to be reunited!

In the middle of July, that had been. She'd told him about it quite matter-of-factly in the letter that she wrote soon after her return to Mullbergh. It had included the news that his father was likely to be sent home soon, for good. Brigadier Sir John Everard had been commanding an equestrian establishment – remount depot and riding-school for newly-commissioned officers; it wasn't needed now, apparently, and the War Office had no other job for him. Well, the war was ending, anyway, and presumably they'd decided they had enough horses and enough officers to ride them. She'd written in that letter, *Whatever the reason, he should be home well before the end of the year, on what is called 'indefinite leave'. It was for discussions at the War Office that he had come back at such short notice. Have you written to him, in recent months? I think you should. There are matters that must now be forgotten, however we may feel about them...* Then there was a passage to the effect that the ending of the war would be a time for families to re-unite, and how much happiness was in store; the suggestion seemed to be that she, Sarah, looked forward to some new kind of happiness with his father. Reading it through again he'd decided that she'd phrased it badly, that she'd really been talking about the country in general and not about herself at all. It was the only interpretation he could put on it, because if she'd intended it to be read exactly as she'd written it then it was a sham, a gross pretence. He couldn't believe that she'd be capable of such dishonesty.

She'd always been open and straightforward with him. And he'd doubted her only once. It hadn't been an honest or justifiable doubt, only his own jealousy sharpened by the knowledge that he'd be leaving Mullbergh next morning. His appointment to Admiral Bayly's staff had arrived in that day's post: he was to report in London forthwith for his routing instructions. He and Sarah were in the small morning-room at Mullbergh; it had a french window opening to a south-facing terrace and she'd turned it into a sort of office. She'd mentioned Alastair Kinloch-Stuart, an old, close friend of hers and of her family's, who'd been killed in France in April. For a while Nick had suspected the relationship between Stuart and Sarah; he'd thought he had some reason to, although he knew now there'd been nothing in it. He was ashamed that he'd thought such a thing of her, now. When the news of his death had reached her she'd written to Nick – wanting his sympathy, and telling him everything there was to tell: and he'd accepted without question that she'd done nothing to encourage the man's feelings for her. She'd been fond of him, and lonely, and that was all. There'd been no need, even, for her to tell him that much. He'd wished that he'd never doubted her, and thanked God that she was quite unaware he ever had. But now, suddenly, because she'd mentioned the man's name and he, Nick, was having to leave her and hating it, he'd uttered some sneering, offensive comment almost before he'd known he was going to say it. Something about 'replacing' him quickly enough.

Well, there was an RFC captain in the recuperative wing with whom he'd thought Sarah had been spending too much time.

She'd spun round from the window, bright and hard with quick surprise and anger.

'*What* did you say?'

Stupidly, he'd felt he had to stand by what he'd blurted out. She'd left him to dine alone, and he had plenty of time to realise what a mess he'd made. He'd gone up to bed about midnight, feeling absolutely miserable. Sarah meant everything to him; she had done ever since he'd been a child. Of all the people he could have hurt, she'd be the last he'd dream of hurting: and he'd done it on his last night. He couldn't sleep. He kept thinking of his departure in the morning, and Sarah taking care to be busy with her patients, shut away from him. He'd leave without seeing her, without a word… In the small hours, desperate now, he went to her room and knocked. After several minutes and more knockings, she called, 'What is it?' He told her, 'Me – Nick. Sarah, *please*—'

'Wait a minute.'

Her tone had been impatient, snappy. Well, he didn't expect much else. But at least he'd see her and apologise. Better than to leave Mullbergh without even saying goodbye.

Her key turned in the lock, and he saw the door pull back. She was wearing a silk dressing-gown and her brown hair was a wild, loose mass; it made her look even younger and more beautiful than she did when it was tied up in its bun. She stared at him calmly, appraisingly: for a second he was remembering another occasion on which he'd come to her room in the night. He'd been woken by her scream: there'd been a door smashed in, and his father in a violent, drunken rage. *Years* ago...

'Well, Nick?'

'I want to say I'm sorry. Terribly, *frightfully* sorry, I—'

Smiling at him now. That gentle, vulnerable mouth... 'You *were* a bit silly, I think. But—'

'You'll forgive me?'

'*What* a silly question!'

'Oh, thank *God*—'

He'd put his arms round her and kissed her cheek, and he felt *her* arms slide up round his neck. Relief was overwhelming: he was happy enough, suddenly, to weep for joy. And without knowing it was going to happen, he'd started doing exactly that. She felt the wetness on her face.

'Nick, my darling, but you're crying! Oh, my precious—'

He couldn't remember which of them pushed the door shut.

Chapter 7

Jake clenched his teeth as the chain-sweep clanked, crashed its way across E.57's stern. This was the second time the thing had found her: last time – ten minutes ago, but it felt like an hour – it had dragged over just like this, and gone on, leaving the silence to grow as the beat of screws faded across the straits. The trawler – a new one, not the one still anchored up there – had made another pass without the sweep locating her; now it was here again, and on the end of the chain there'd be grapnel hooks designed to claw and hang on to what it found.

The air was poisonous. Bulkheads running wet. The chain, moving in a succession of crashes linked by the steady, rasping slither, was an instrument of torture in itself. All you could do was wait – and stifle the imagination, not let your mind see what was happening outside. He began to use a soft eraser to tidy the chart, rubbing off old position lines. He thought the Turks might be under the impression they'd made a kill. If they believed otherwise they'd—

A jolt, and a heavy thud from aft: the grapnel had caught and held and now the strain was coming on the chain, taking the bight out of it while its weight acted as a spring. The submarine jerked and began to slew, pivot on her anchored forepart. Sweat-sheened faces stared upwards: then, as men took hold of their own reactions, glanced at each other and away again. Some frowns: a shrugging grin, a man's eyebrows raised disdainfully; Jake saw Louis Lewis's lips move, and it occurred to him that behind those stubbled, pallid faces there'd be a variety of prayers forming. Even if you weren't exactly devout in normal times it was almost physically impossible in a moment like this not to surrender to the urge to ask for help. He began his own: *Please God, let—*

'Time we moved, I think.' Wishart spoke easily but he looked like something out of a grave. 'Don't know about the rest of you, but I'm—'

The noise — scraping, straining — was suddenly much louder. It had a penetrating quality like metal being gouged: and it gouged the mind, it—

Stopped!

Silence — except for that throbbing, high above them. The boat hung motionless, free again, while the slow beat of screws moved on like a churning pulse. Wishart finished the sentence that had been interrupted: 'I'm hungry.'

At noon, he'd had 'up spirits' piped — in a whisper — and as well as the issue of rum for all hands they'd had corned beef and pusser's biscuits. The extra rum would be written off in the books as spillage. For the brief period of the meal men had crept about barefooted and spoken only in whispers, and after it they'd all turned in again. Now it was just on ten o'clock. They'd been dived for nearly thirty hours.

CPO Crabb muttered, "'Ear, 'ear, sir.' His beginnings of a beard were jet-black, with none of the grey that patched his head. Wishart patted Hobday on his shoulder: 'Let's have her off the putty, Number One.'

'Open "A" suction and inboard vent. Pump from for'ard.'

Andy Stone had the suction valve open on the pump, and McVeigh pushed the starter-switch on its motor. Lewis had opened the main-line connection to the tank.

'Pumpin', sir.' Stone had gagged down the relief valve. Wishart murmured, 'Watch her like a hawk now.' He wiped his eyes; like everyone else's they were having fits of watering. It was the battery, the acid reek rising from near-spent cells into oxygen-starved air. Hobday nodded, acknowledging Wishart's caution. Nothing had turned up yet to account for the sudden heaviness, all the pumping they'd had to do after the mine had nearly finished them. These were hardly circumstances in which one would want to lose control and shoot up to the surface.

It all seemed to be happening in slow motion. And for the Turk with his sweep, third time might be lucky. *Don't worry for two seconds about me…*

'Bubble's shiftin', sir.' Crabb's voice was a rasp. Jake saw Burtenshaw watching from Wishart's bunk. When the chain-sweep thing had started half an hour ago and the hands had been sent quietly to their diving stations, he'd got up there out of the way. Nick Everard was in Hobday's, and Robins for once was bunk-less, chair-borne, and peevish-looking perhaps because of that. Or just being his usual self. Jake felt his own weight leaning more heavily than usual against the chart table, and he realised that as the boat had lifted herself clear of the seabed her list to port had increased. Just as he noticed it he heard Hobday say, 'Stop pumping. She's off, sir.' Anyone could have told him that. For nearly half a minute the feel of her had been quite different. Jake thought, *Come on, come on now*...

'Slow ahead starboard, full field. What's causing this list?'

'Slow ahead starboard full field, sir.'

'One hundred feet.'

'Hundred feet, sir.' Hobday's gingery stubble shone like pale gold around his sharp-edged jaw. The 'planes were tilting upward. Weatherspoon reported, 'Enemy surface vessel is turning, sir.' As she rose, the list was still increasing. Even two or three degrees could feel a lot, but this must be six or seven. Wishart said, 'Give me a course up-straits, pilot.'

'North forty-one east, sir, but—'

'Port five. Steer north forty-one east.'

'Port five, sir...'

Jake tried again: 'Sir, that course depends on—'

'I know, pilot, I know.' What he knew was that they didn't really know anything about their position, except so far as one might guess it.

'There's one shallow patch beyond the bulge – Kodjuk – and to starboard, sir. But if we clear the headland we should go wide of the shallows too.'

The gauge showed one-oh-seven feet. Hobday was adjusting her trim virtually by half-pints as she rose. Jake was trying to remember in fuller detail the confused minutes following the explosion of the mine, and in particular that noise – unless he'd dreamt it or imagined it when he was groggy-minded – of an inrush of water. Of *rushing* water. The recollection came to him because he was thinking about this list and whatever might have caused it: explosion, list, heaviness, all simultaneous and all therefore connected. There was a slant of about ten degrees on her now; you had to haul yourself up the incline or hold on to something so as not to slide down it. Wishart murmured to Hobday, 'Can't think why they didn't give us transverse trimming tanks.'

Some of the E-class had them, and some didn't. There wasn't normally much use for them; and even if they'd had them and been able to trim the list off her it wouldn't have answered the vital question – *why* was she listing?

'Course north forty-one east, sir.'

'Depth one hundred feet, sir.'

'Very good.'

'Stop the pump.' Apart from the list, he'd got her trimmed finely. Bubble a degree aft, 'planes amidships, needle static at the ordered depth and only one motor slow ahead. The lopsidedness spoilt the effect considerably. Hobday asked Wishart, 'Spare hands to the high side, sir?' He meant, use crew-weight to balance her. Wishart, instead of answering, pointed upwards. Jake heard it at once: it was the trawler coming back, the one towing its grapnel sweep.

He wondered if the Turks would have any way of knowing they'd hooked her once and that she'd spat out the hook.

'Slow ahead port, full field.'

'Slow ahead port, full field, sir... Both motors slow ahead, sir.'

'Seventy feet.'

The 'planes swung over again. Enemy propeller noise was louder and closer, but it was likely to pass astern, Jake thought. And Wishart was taking advantage of the Turk's own noise to speed up a little, hoping it would drown the sounds the submarine made and deafen the shore hydrophones. Jake thought, *Perhaps now we'll fool him, slip away...* But he checked that quick spark of hope, reminded himself that there could very likely be more nets ahead, or mines, or both, and that at this end of the straits, coming up towards the town and harbour of Gallipoli, there would as likely as not be a shoaling of patrol craft. One had also to bear in mind that there were still a dozen miles to cover before they reached the Marmara, and that plenty could happen in twelve miles of Dardanelles.

Condensation dripped like slow rain. Everywhere it glistened, trickled over sweating steel. The leaky rivets added their quota of wetness: the broad streak of it had a different shine from the wet enamelling over which it ran en route downwards to the bilge. He wondered about the shaft gland: that port screw was being used now. And using both motors meant using twice as much battery juice as running on only one had done. Theoretically the box should be flat already... Twelve miles: with the deep tide, say four knots. Not less than three hours – uninterrupted. He wiped his eyes: it would be wrong to rub them, rub the acid into them. McVeigh, who should have known better – he looked like some sort of hobgoblin over there, or a beast at bay crouching in its cave – had been rubbing his, and they were bright red, streaming. Breathing open-mouthed – one tended to, when the air was as poor as this, it made you feel as if you were jogging uphill all the time – McVeigh was displaying his narrow, ratty-looking teeth. He'd have looked at home gnawing the bark off trees, Jake thought; the image that came into his mind amused him and he must have smiled, because Wishart, glancing his way just then, looked surprised and asked him, 'Happy in your work, pilot?'

'It's a grand life, sir.'

'Ah. You'll *all* think so presently, when we're having our breakfast in the Marmara.'

CPO Crabb growled, ''Ell of a big breakfas' it'll need to be.'

Wishart looked just about played out. It must have come on suddenly; this afternoon, when Jake had been on watch and the skipper had sat chatting with him and the other watchkeeper for an hour or more, he hadn't looked tired at all. He asked Crabb now, 'Did they give us plenty of fresh eggs, cox'n, this trip?'

'Not so dusty, sir... But there's bacon an' beef sausage and fried bread – bread's 'ard, but *fried* it won't—'

'What'll we eat the rest of the patrol, for heaven's sake?'

'We're victualled for a month, sir. An' there's chickens in them Turk dhows, an'—'

Hobday reported, 'Seventy feet, sir.' He repeated his earlier suggestion: 'Try sending spare hands to the high side, sir?'

'If you like.'

'Or a puff of air in number four?'

'Not that.'

Weatherspoon said. 'Enemy passin' astern left to right, sir.'

Wishart nodded. 'We've slipped our chain, I think.'

'Not the one was sweepin', sir – the one what anchored. She's turnin' towards, sir.' Jake thought, *Damn them...* The leading tel said, 'Revs decreasin' – slowin', sir.'

'Stop port'

'Stop port, sir... Port motor stopped.'

Wishart ordered, 'Everyone who's free to move, get over to the starboard side. Pass that for'ard and aft.' Lewis sent the message into the torpedo stowage compartment. Ellery, sweat gleaming through the fuzz of brown beard around his mouth and running down the deep channels in the skin of his neck, passed it aft. Wishart stood watching the bubble in the small curved spirit-level on the deckhead.

'It's moving already, damn it!'

'Enemy's stopped, sir.'

Wishart nodded, still watching the bubble. Only a few men had had time to move, and the angle was already coming off her. Jake could feel her swinging over. Now a dozen or twenty men would have moved an average of, say, five feet; surely it oughtn't to make *this* much difference. She was on an even keel, already. Wishart's attention still on the bubble, which was the size and shape of a small broad-bean in the green-tinted tube. *She was going on over, listing the other way...*

'Back to your stations!'

But she was still swinging over – as if having once started she couldn't be stopped. Wishart muttered, 'She's gone cranky. Doesn't make sense, damn it. She's—' He pulled out a handkerchief to mop his streaming eyes with. Everard looked as if he more or less understood what was puzzling everyone; the Marine just as plainly did not. 'She's – stopped again...' Wishart, frowning at the bubble. 'Just gone over and *hanging*...' He sounded relieved, Jake thought, that she hadn't gone right over – or at any rate far enough over to slop acid out of the battery cells. Weatherspoon reported, 'Enemy still layin' stopped, sir.'

Enemy listening to them, in fact. Just as he had before when he'd followed them along, starting and stopping and holding his distance astern of them. It struck Jake that if the Turk was out to drive them mad he was going about it in a very shrewd way. Also that the last time he'd trailed behind them like this there'd been a mine barrage ahead and he'd more or less herded them into it.

Wishart suddenly slapped his forehead.

'I'll be *damned*!'

Hobday glanced round at him. Wishart told the outside ERA, 'Get a wheelspanner on the conning-tower drain, McVeigh. Stand by to just crack it and then bang it shut again double-quick.'

'Aye, sir...'

Hobday muttered, staring at the hatch, 'Of course... I must be cuckoo!' Wishart told him, 'Get a pump working on the bilge. Account for everything, eh? The weight – and after the bang I heard a flooding sound – and now the list, and everywhere else normal. Top-hamper pulling her over... Be ready to run both pumps together if we have to.'

He watched McVeigh clamp a wheelspanner on the valve-wheel of the conning-tower drain. The pipe led from the bottom of the tower to the bilge; if there was water up there – if the boat had dived with her top hatch open, for instance and you opened that valve, seawater from the tower would flood down into the bilge at full sea-pressure.

Wishart must have been thinking about that, too, and decided to check his theory where the pressure wasn't quite so great.

'Belay all that. Wait, McVeigh.' He told Hobday, 'Come up to forty feet.'

Hanging over to starboard like this she felt like a duck with one leg shorter than the other. Clumsy: and in any emergency she'd be clumsy to handle too. But she was lumbering upwards now as the 'planesmen coaxed her towards the surface – a surface that would be dark now. It felt better – Jake thought – to be going up. Admittedly they could be rising into nets or mines; but by this time they'd be getting past that Kodjuk bulge of land, the rounded headland pressing in like a corset and giving the straits the inward curve of a belly-dancer's waist, and once the boat got out to where they widened again – *let's not*, he thought, *follow that simile too far* – her chances of running into lethal obstructions should become less with every yard she covered. His hands were resting palms-down on the chart, and he watched forefingers and middle fingers crossing. He didn't want to be caught off-guard again; too often, as one had begun to relax, something damnable had happened… Hobday was making adjustments to the trim as the boat came up; Wishart ordered, 'Thirty feet.'

'Thirty, sir.' Weatherspoon called out, 'Enemy movin', sir!'

'Which way?'

'Can't say yet, sir.'

Thirty-six feet. Thirty-five. Hobday glanced round at Wishart, obviously wondering whether he should still take her right up, with an enemy up there on the prowl. Thirty-four feet – thirty-three…

'Comin' towards, sir. Follerin' astern, like before.'

'Closing?'

'Very slow revs, sir.'

Following, then. *Exactly* as he'd done before.

Waiting for them to suffocate, or for the battery to die?

There was only one place where the straits narrowed again significantly, and that was off Gallipoli, roughly eight miles further on. But in any case this stretch was only two miles wide. There could be minefields, or mined nets anywhere.

'Thirty feet, sir.'

Wishart looked at Weatherspoon. The leading tel nodded. 'Still comin', sir.'

'Closing?'

A shake of the head: 'Not *loud*, sir.'

'Right.' Wishart told Hobday, 'Pump on the bilge.' He looked at McVeigh: 'Ready?' The spanner was hanging from the brass wheel; McVeigh reached for it. 'Aye, sir.' Hobday reported, 'Pump's running on the bilge.' You could hear it, from down there out of sight, making a noise like some monster child sucking on an already empty mug. Wishart told the ERA, 'Crack it, and shut it again immediately.'

The Glaswegian took a grip with both hands on the shaft of the spanner, and swung his whole weight on to it. The noise of water jetting through the pipe had the suddenness of a gunshot: its roar stopped dead as McVeigh jammed the valve shut again. There was a slopping sound from the bilge; but the pump would be returning that gushing intake to the sea now.

'There's our answer, then.' Wishart reached up and banged his fist against the hatch. 'Tower's full. The one space we didn't think of checking. That's where the extra weight's come from and that's what's heeling us over.'

'Enemy closin', sir!'

'Seventy feet.'

Crabb and Morton flung their wheels around, and the 'planes slanted to drag her down. Morton hissed, 'Give us some angle, 'swain?' Crabb told Hobday, 'She's awkward, sir. Slow answerin'.'

'Bound to be.' Wishart didn't seem to have been made unhappy by his discovery. It would present certain immediate problems – surfacing would be a slow and rather dangerous procedure – but at least the mystery had been cleared up, and depending on precisely what the damage was it could probably be repaired, later on. He told Crabb, 'Have to manage as best we can, cox'n. Engine-room department'll have their hands full, though, once we get into the Marmara.'

He'd glanced round at the ERAs as he said it: at McVeigh, Knight, Bradshaw. Bradshaw looked as if he'd just climbed out of a bath, except that there was nothing clean about him; he'd tied a rag around his head to keep the sweat out of his eyes. Knight looked as if he'd been crying. Come to think of it, everyone looked pretty frightful. Eyes particularly. Holes in skulls with water running out of them. Little Agnew, propped against the after bulkhead under the telegraphs' brassy gleam, could have been the ghost of some lost child. Roost, square and upright at the wheel, blinked continuously and regularly, as if a motor moved his eyelids while he watched the lubber's line against the image of the compass card. It was just as well that the master compass, above their heads in the flooded tower, lived in its own watertight binnacle. The long and stringy frame of Stoker Adams, in the starboard after corner, was drooped into a sort of S-bend: knees forward, head and shoulders slumped, the eyes red-rimmed and glaring murderously from under matted brows. None of us, Jake thought, can look much like the portraits in our parents' living-rooms. Even the passengers… Adams, though, looked particularly fiendish, possibly nastier even than McVeigh; he was yellow-skinned and the gloss of dirty sweat made him seem almost orange.

Wishart cocked an eyebrow at Weatherspoon. The leading tel told him, 'Close now, sir.'

The needle in the gauge was approaching the 55-foot mark, and Crabb, anticipating a sluggish response, was already easing the downward angle of the dive.

'Agnew – I shan't be using telegraphs. Go and sit in the doorway and pass orders by word of mouth.'

'Sir.' The boy looked grateful as he edged over past Ellery. Wishart said, 'Anyone who doesn't have to stand, sit down. Pass that through the boat.'

'Seventy feet, sir.'

'Very good… Here comes Willie.'

They could hear him suddenly – the thump-thump-thump of that churning screw. Trawler – gunboat, whatever Willie was… Almost over the top: but not quite, the volume of sound was still rising. Overhead just about – *now*. Jake wondered if the Turk might be dropping depth-charges.

If he was, they'd be on their way down now, floating down, turning end over end as they sank through still black water towards the submarine… The – *no*… He'd seen this point rather late, and he recognised an unusual slowness in his mental processes: if the trawler had been dropping charges she wouldn't have been moving at such slow speed. The Turk would blow his own stern off, that way. And one's brain was, undoubtedly, working at a similarly low speed. Oxygen starvation? He heard the enemy go over and the sound of him begin to fade, saw Wishart staring upwards at the deckhead as he listened too. Poor lookout if *his* brain had brakes on... Everyone was sitting, squatting on the deck, leaning against whatever came handy, and Jake let himself slide down too. Use less oxygen: skipper should've thought of it before. Hell of a good man, though. This afternoon – after the noon snack and tot of rum – Jake had taken over again in the control room, and Wishart had come and sat down too; they'd chatted for quite a while. At first Wishart had talked to Smith, the tattoo'd torpedoman who'd been sharing the watch with Jake; he'd talked about Smith's harmonica and how he'd learnt to play it, and from that to the Smith family in Hampshire. The torpedoman's father was a water-bailiff on some rich stretch of the Test, and Smith was full of stories about fish and fishing and poachers' ways. Wishart had had some fishing stories of his own to tell. When that conversation ran dry, he'd turned to Jake.

'Go back to the Mercantile Marine, will you, when their Lordships release you?'

He'd shaken his head. 'I don't know. It's a bit – difficult, in some ways.'

Eventually Wishart had got the whole thing out of him. About Jake's mother alone and panicky, and no one but him to care for her, take his father's place.

'Your father must have been away a lot, surely?'

'Then she had me with her.'

'My dear old lad—' Wishart had seemed genuinely concerned – 'parents do lose their children. Not *lose*, in any final sense, but—'

'Then most of them have each other to fall back on?'

'Listen.' Wishart waved a hand, wiping out Jake's arguments. 'Your mama isn't the only widow in the British Isles, not by a very long chalk. Thousands and thousands of 'em, *millions* of 'em, old lad. And some of 'em have lost sons as well as husbands, poor things.'

'Yes, yes, I know. But – well, some people take things harder than others do. And in this particular case…' It had been hard to explain. His mother wasn't at all worldly, she wasn't equipped for living on her own. She was child-like; at an early age he'd discovered that she needed him more than he needed her, and that she worried needlessly and constantly about any decision she had to make for herself. Like a child struggling to cope with an adult world. Jake's father would come home after a few months' absence, unravel her self-made problems and put everything straight for her, settle this and that and ask X and Y to keep an eye on her, and go off to sea again. Sighing, Jake suspected now, with relief? As *he* had done, after that terrible 'compassionate' leave?

'Enemy's stopped again, sir. Couldn't only just 'ear 'im – if 'e'd gone another minute I wouldn't 'a 'eard 'im stop.'

The pattern was not the same as it had been before. Before, the Turk had stayed back, kept his distance astern of them.

'Either he's changed his tactics, or he's lost us. Or he thinks we're sunk, left the other one trawling for us and he's gone on about his own business.' Wishart was talking to Hobday. Leaning on the ladder, mopping at his face with an already sodden handkerchief. He swivelled, leant on it frontwards, one foot on its bottom rung and his arms extended upwards, hands grasping a higher one. 'Number One.'

'Sir?'

Hobday's skin looked as white as paper; the lower half of his small face was gilded with ginger stubble. Wishart told him, 'I think we'll go up and have a look. Dark now – and we're doing no good as it is.' He pushed himself off the ladder. Jake thought he was working hard in the effort to think straight, act straight. 'Thirty feet.'

'Thirty feet, sir.' Hobday asked him, 'Use the port shaft, sir?'

'No.'

'Thirty, sir...' Crabb and Morton worked like machines, coping skilfully with the awkwardness of handling her with the list on. By 'going up', Jake realised, Wishart couldn't be talking about surfacing. It would be a dangerous thing to risk here even if she was in good shape and undamaged. With the tower flooded, they'd have to wallow up there while it drained down to the bilges and the pump shifted the water overboard; until the tower was empty you couldn't open the lower hatch, and until you were on the surface you couldn't start the draining process. So for several minutes the submarine would lie blind and helpless. But if only – he shut his eyes – if *only* it could be possible... To surface, get moving on the gas engines, with fresh air flooding through the boat!

Something to dream about...

He forced his eyes open, pulled himself together. They *would* be surfacing. Not yet, but a time would come – a little while yet, some way to go, just a matter of hanging on, and then there *would* be a moment when the engines would roar into life and you'd feel the sweet, cold air, drink it, wallow in it: the thought was enough to make you cry with longing for it...

You needn't worry for two seconds about me, you know.

Wishart had said to him this afternoon, 'Look here, old lad. You say you might take some job or other, anything to stay near her... Have you considered how that would be? Thousands and thousands of men have awful, humdrum jobs – jobs they loathe and just have to struggle on with, year in and year out – near killing 'emselves in the process. Would you contemplate that – when you don't have to, when you're a seaman, a first-class one, highly trained and experienced and a very, *very* useful man?'

There'd been a pause then: close to them, on his blanket on the deck, Everard had muttered something in his sleep. Wishart asked Jake, 'What advice d'you think your father would give, if he was here to give it?'

Jake had pointed out that if his father had been alive to give advice, the question wouldn't be arising in the first place. Wishart brushed that aside; and Jake had only been stalling, trying to stave off an argument that was entirely right and logical as Wishart saw it but which didn't take into account the deep, emotional feelings running counter to it.

'D'you think in the long run it'd do your mother most good for you to be in some frightful job, coming home each night done-up and dispirited – needing to get drunk to forget it, and turning green with envy when you run into some old shipmate who *hasn't* thrown up the life he was born for – that, or having a son who's happy, getting on, commanding his own ship soon enough – *that* fellow, coming home a few times each year, a son she'd be really proud of?'

'Well, it's more than—'

'Listen to me, old lad. *That* would be taking your father's place. *That's* what he'd like to hear about when she joins him!'

'Thirty feet, sir.'

Wishart checked the gauge and the bubble. He looked over towards Jake.

'May get a fix in a minute, pilot… Number One, bring her up slowly and carefully to twenty feet.'

'Twenty feet, sir. Handsomely now, cox'n.'

McVeigh hoisted his scraggy, scarecrow-like frame to its feet. He looked like something that had been run over by a horse-tram in Sauchihall Street, but he was alert enough to realise he'd be needed now to operate the periscopes. Ellery got up too; Wishart was waiting near the after periscope, and on that small one it was necessary for relative bearings to be read off a bearing-ring on the deckhead.

'Twenty-two feet, sir.'

'Up periscope.'

'Twenty-one…' The brass tube was hissing upwards, drops of greasy moisture glinting on its bronze, grey grease clinging wetly to the wires. The bulky eyepiece end came up clear of the well; Wishart grabbed the handles at knee-height, and before the single lens jerked to a stop at eye-level he'd jerked them down and settled to the search.

'Twenty feet, sir.'

'Black as pitch…' Muttering to himself as he circled, right eye pressed against the lens, left eye shut. He stopped only halfway round, snapped the handles up. 'Down!' McVeigh depressed the lever, sending the periscope slithering back into its hole in the deck; Wishart murmured, squeezing for'ard between Roost's position and the ladder, 'Can't see a damn thing with that one.' Looking at McVeigh again he raised his hands and twitched the fingers, and McVeigh sent the big 'scope sliding up. A necklet of drops of water glistened like diamonds around the gland where the big tube passed through the deck-head.

'Depth?' He'd clicked the magnification in. Hobday answered, 'Twenty feet, sir.' Wishart circled slowly, his toes against the raised sill around the well... 'God almighty!'

He'd trained back the other way: his throat bulged as he swallowed.

'Port ten.'

'Port ten, sir.' Roost, rock-like, moved his wheel around.

'Ship's head?'

'North forty-five east, sir. Forty-six. Forty—'

'Midships. Steer north fifty east. Pilot – before I altered course there was a headland with a sort of beacon or sawn-off lighthouse on it about one hundred yards on our port beam.'

'*One hundred*—'

'Now – high bulk of land bearing... red 132 degrees.'

'Ship's head north forty-eight east, sir!'

Jake scribbled the figures down. On the big Grubb periscope a relative-bearing ring was etched on glass inside. Applying relative bearing to ship's head at the same moment gave you compass bearings.

'Hear anything, leading tel?'

'Nothin', sir.'

Circling... That was the *world*, up there, that he was staring into. Open, dark, clean, with a wind to ripple the surface and drive the clouds: up there, you could fill your lungs, let it all out, fill them again… Difficult to imagine! 'Pilot – other coast now – the highest bit of a longish line of ground, and the right-hand edge of it: bearing – green 93.'

'North fifty east, sir!'

And one more? No, he'd finished. Two position lines, plus what he'd said about being almost ashore on some headland. Compass variation of two degrees west. Lots of hills, mountains, edges on the chart: it was a matter of fitting those three items together so they'd make sense. He heard the periscope hissing down, and Wishart joined him.

'Point here, sir – *Karakova Burnu*. Then we'd have this height here called *Sarair Tepe* – for the first bearing…' He ran the parallel ruler across the chart from the compass rose. 'And then – this?' A longish ridge of high ground on the Asiatic coast, with an altitude of a thousand feet at its western end. It all fitted and there were no sensible alternatives; Jake ringed the point of intersection as a fix. They were close to the European shore and they'd come about two miles from where they'd lain bottomed all day. He laid off the present course of north fifty east.

'Three quarters of an hour, then back ten degrees to port?'

Wishart turned away.

'Have to get past that Turk, if he's still hanging about.'

Jake was suffering quite badly from the thin air and the stink in it; he was conscious of the shortness of his breath and a sort of fuddle growing in his brain. When you had something positive to do you could push the discomfort to the back of your mind, but as soon as you stopped it closed in on you again. Wishart had just ordered, some way off, 'Up periscope'. Jake told himself, *Stay awake…* Wishart asked Weatherspoon, 'Anything?' The leading telegraphist guessed what he was being asked, and shook his head. Drooping eyelids gave him a haughty look as he peered out from the cabinet. The periscope had thumped to a stop, Wishart had grabbed its handles and clicked it into low power, and he was making a rapid all-round search. In high power you had to sweep around more slowly, rather like using a telescope instead of binoculars; you saw further, in high power, with a narrower field of vision.

'Down.' He stepped back. 'Can't see much.' He'd shut his eyes, screwing his whole face up and shaking his head as if to clear his ears of something. He'd be having to work hard, too, to think straight. The mind had a tendency to go dim, drift away. Jake wondered, *We might surface, chance it? Better than playing safe and suffocating?*

'Seventy feet.'

'Seventy, sir.'

Wanting to get back into the lower tidal stream. Nick Everard, Jake saw, was lying on his back and reading Burtenshaw's Tolstoy book. Or just holding it up over his face as an umbrella against the dripping deckhead. Burtenshaw was at the table, making card-houses that never got to be more than two storeys high. He'd offered Robins the bunk he'd been on for a short while, not long ago, and Robins had accepted with a grunt that might have been taken as some form of thanks. He was asleep now. Burtenshaw had admitted during their snack lunch, his tongue perhaps loosened by that tot of rum, that he wasn't really getting much out of the Tolstoy. Jake had commented, 'Conan Doyle's *my* mark. Limit, just about.'

They'd all agreed on the fascination of Sherlock Holmes. The ship's expert on the great detective, apparently, was Chief ERA Grumman; Hobday had said you couldn't trip Grumman up, he knew every detail of every case. Burtenshaw had opened Tolstoy, read a line of it, sighed, shut it again; he'd asked them, 'Anyone read the Guy Thorn book, *When It Was Dark?*' Hobday, who'd had the watch and had been keeping an eye on things at the same time as he munched his corned beef and biscuit, said he'd read some of it. He hadn't thought it worth his while to continue with it. 'I don't want some other fellow's quirky notions about religion. A man who tries to push those kind of views on other people – well, the *conceit* of it, the sheer—'

'Oh, I don't know.' Nick took up the argument on Burtenshaw's behalf, since the Marine was looking embarrassed by Hobday's vehemence. He seemed rather prone to this kind of awkwardness. Nick suggested to Hobday, 'You're objecting to it because you're seeing it from the standpoint he's proposing to reject. If your mind could allow the possibility that much of the stuff we've been taught to believe is up the pole—'

'I don't want it to, thanks!'

Jake grinning at them both. Like many large-built men he was easygoing, and it amused him to see others stung to argument. Burtenshaw licking corned-beef fat off his fingers. The rum had flushed his boyish cheeks; nobody guessed what a kick there was in navy–issue rum until they tried it.

'Seventy feet, sir.'

Jake looked up with a start: jerkily, as if he'd been woken out of a dream. He was sitting on the deck, leaning against the chart table. He couldn't recall the act of sitting down. Across on the other side Burtenshaw was dozing over the scattered cards. Nick Everard was still holding the book but it was resting pages-downwards on his chest, and his eyes were shut. His jaw was dark with stubble. Robins's embryo beard was blueish, and it gave him a Middle-Eastern look. Armenian, he could have been. Better be careful, Jake thought, when he landed; the Turks had nailed horseshoes to Armenians' feet, amongst other pleasantries. Everard had told him so, and Everard had had it from that chap Reaper. Robins, at the noon meal, had questioned Wishart about the rum issue. How officers could have been allowed it: and weren't the sailors supposed to have it diluted in water, in the form known as 'grog'?

Wishart had told him, poker-faced, 'Fresh water's one of our biggest problems, on patrol.'

'Hear anything, leading tel?'

Weatherspoon must have shaken his head. He was in the door-way of the cabinet, where he could see and be seen. Anyway, there'd been no answer, and Wishart seemed to have been satisfied. The ticking of the log was extraordinarily loud: like a heartbeat in the silent, airless, greenhouse heat and acid, lifeless air. If the submarine had a heart it was down below this deck, the battery. A miracle that it still beat at all. When it ceased to do so they'd have no option but to blow themselves to the surface and face the Turkish guns: and for a lungful of clean air might not the price be too exorbitant? He heard a rasping noise that pulled him out of the fringes of a daydream; the retch had come from his own throat, and he tried to turn it into a cough. Wishart said, 'Thirty feet.'

Jake *thought* he'd said it. Wishart was clinging to the ladder with his arms up and spread. He *must* have ordered that change in depth: leaning forward and rising slightly, one could see up-angle on the 'planes, and the needle in the depth-gauge beginning to circle slowly. Was he thinking of surfacing? Morton, at the fore 'planes, was rocking to and fro, his torso shifting rhythmically from side to side, about an inch in each direction. Keeping himself awake. Hobday, standing behind Morton and the coxswain, kept jolting up and down on his toes – heels – toes… He could have sat down and still done his job all right, and used less air, Jake thought.

Adjusting trim now as she rose, he'd stopped those irritating, jerky motions. Extraordinary to think of all that sea inside the tower. Observation ports blown in, probably. Perhaps Wishart hadn't clamped the deadlight shut over the middle one after the struggle in the net. But – it was getting harder all the time to concentrate one's thoughts – Jake *thought* he'd seen him doing it…

'Thirty feet, sir.'

Hobday had more or less whispered it.

'Leading tel?'

Weatherspoon's ears were blocked off by his head-phones, but he didn't need to hear the question. He saw it, as Wishart glanced at him, and he shook his head. 'Nothin', sir.'

'Twenty feet.'

'Twenty feet, sir. Easy with her, now.'

'Aye, sir.' No change in Crabb's deep growling tone. Jake saw McVeigh drag himself upright, using the steel guard over the main vent levers as a handhold. Jake realised he might be wanted too, to take down some bearings.

He had no idea, absolutely none, of how much time had passed since the last fix. When he was up on his feet he looked round to check the time by the bulkhead clock, but the clock was a whitish haze without hands or figures, more like a hazy full moon than – one lost track of one's own thinking. He was shaking his head, blinking, using his fingertips to clear his fogged-up eyes.

'Twenty-two feet, sir. Twenty—'

'Up.'

Hss – ss – ss… *Thump.*

Clack of the handles banging down. Hobday's report: 'Twenty feet, sir.'

'Well done, well done…' Calm, easy-mannered, friendly. Marvellous chap, Aubrey Wishart. 'Keep her up now though, don't for Pete's sake—'

Muttering as he swung around, his arms hooked gorilla-fashion over the handles, his weight hanging there so that his legs and feet hardly seemed to be supporting him at all, just sort of shoving around the circumference of the well as he trained the big periscope around. 'Better light now, I can—'

He'd gasped: and he was still for a moment, frozen… 'Down!'

The handles clashed up, McVeigh pushed the steel lever over and the gleaming brass barrel jerked, flowed downwards. All eyes were on the captain: mouths open, sweat running, breaths short like the panting of men running uphill under load.

'Seventy feet.'

'Seventy, sir…'

'Planes turning, digging into the sea to pull her nosing into its depths. Wishart told them, 'The Turk's about fifty yards – thirty, perhaps – on our port bow. I think he's anchored. It's a gunboat, like a big yacht with one tall funnel. He's showing a few lights through scuttles in his superstructure.'

He and Hobday exchanged glances. Now Hobday had turned back to the gauge, the 'planesmen. Wishart muttered, 'I could sink him, easily. One torpedo at close range – sitting duck.' Hobday whipped round eagerly; CPO Crabb growled, 'That's the ticket, sir!' Men were getting to their feet, wiping their eyes and blinking, happy. Jake quite suddenly felt better, really more or less back to normal. He slid open the chart-table drawer where he kept his navigational instruments, and took the attack stop-watch out of its box, so he'd be ready for the attack procedure when Wishart ordered it.

But why go deep, he wondered vaguely, if you were about to start an attack?

Wishart murmured, 'Can't do it, unfortunately, cox'n. Have to save all our fish for *Goeben*.'

Light of excitement fading. Like so many children robbed suddenly of a treat. Hobday said dully, 'Seventy feet, sir.' Wishart glanced round the disappointed faces. 'Not a squeak, now. Agnew, go aft very quietly, tell 'em I don't want to hear a sound. Lewis – tell 'em that for'ard.'

Object: sneak past Turk. Turk sitting up there in comfort, breathing fresh air. Jake had eased himself down to sit on the deck again. Condensation raining down everywhere. If you tasted it, it has a sweet, sickly rankness like human sweat. He found he had a stopwatch in his hand, for some reason. Must have picked it up without thinking. In the dream he reasoned carefully that not going for the Turk made sense, because if they could get past him and if he thought they'd been finished by that bloody mine, then they'd be creeping into the Marmara presently and the enemy wouldn't know they'd got through. He heard Wishart order, 'Twenty feet.'

'Twenty feet, sir.'

'*Certain* there's been no sound from him?'

Time had passed. He didn't know how much. Time was mixed up with the reek of the gassing battery and men's breath and sweat and the other stink wafting from the engine-room, from the row of covered sanitary buckets. The gas, of course, was hydrogen – described in the battery-maintenance manual as 'not actually poisonous, but will not support respiration'. Another way of saying 'It won't kill you, but it won't let you live.' But it was all one stench: indivisible, disgusting. Wishart's voice broke through: 'Up periscope.' It was part of the dream, it didn't concern reality. Then he heard the *thump* as McVeigh replaced the lever in its 'stop' position and the ram stopped sliding because oil at high pressure blocked its motion. When the ram extended, it increased the distance between sheaves around which the wires ran; that was what pulled them and hauled the periscope up or down. You could exercise your mind on visualising a thing like that, and it was better than thinking about fresh air or a cool night breeze dimpling the surface of the straits. He was in the process of getting to his feet: a big man, heavy, lurching upwards. Stop-watch: he pulled the drawer open, and put the watch carefully in its box. Shutting the drawer again, he glanced up and focused on the bulkhead clock. Twenty-five past twelve. Morning of day three, for God's sake! They'd been dived for – he made himself work it out – thirty-two hours... Submarine regulations still in force stipulated various impractical air-freshening routines after *fourteen* hours dived. They weren't out of the straits yet.

'We've passed him.' Wishart had his eyes at the lenses and he was facing aft. 'If it wasn't for his cabin-lights I wouldn't be able to see him. We're past and clear.' He began to swing himself slowly round, pausing now and then to study features of the shoreline. With only stars for illumination, you wouldn't see much else. Jake told himself, wanting to believe in it but still needing to be convinced, *We can go through now. Nothing left to stop us!* Except – well, there could be more mine barrages, and nets. The fact they'd got past one Turkish gunboat didn't mean it would be all plain sailing from here on. Wishart turned up the periscope's handles and stepped back, and McVeigh sent it down.

'We're nicely out in the middle, pilot. What was that course you had us on?'

'North forty-one east, sir.'

'Ah, yes.' He turned, and rested a hand on the helmsman's shoulder. 'Starboard five, old Roost.'

'Starboard five, sir… Five o' starboard wheel on, sir.'

Roost was grinning, tickled by that prefix 'old'. There were glimmers of happiness in other faces too: in Stone's, Agnew's, Adams's, Knight's… Premature, perhaps; but Wishart's brighter tone and manner were infectious, and even a momentary lifting of spirits had its value. Wishart said, 'Steer north forty-one east, old Roost.'

'North forty-one east, sir.'

'Seventy feet, Number One.'

'Seventy feet, sir.'

Wishart joined Jake at the chart table. Leaning on it beside him, he lurched heavily against him. Jake glanced at him in surprise; Wishart said, 'Shove up, pilot. You're getting too damn fat, d'you know that?' He looked round over his shoulder: his face was bloodless, middle-aged. 'Lewis. You'd better reduce the navigating officer's rations.'

Crabb said, 'That's an extra breakfas' comes *my* way, Lewis.' Jake told him, 'You'll need to be damn quick on your feet, cox'n!'

Laughter...

Wishart eased over, allowing him some room.

'Now then. Let's see where we think we are.'

–

Two-seventeen...

There'd been the orders, routine actions and reports of preparing to surface. It was a dream, of course. You went along with it because there was always the hope it might come true.

There had been other preparations too. Both ballast pumps were ready to start sucking on the control-room bilges, to pump out the water that would flood down from the tower. Wishart had said, 'Stop her at six feet', and Hobday had pointed out that she'd be unstable with the tower's weight out of water. Jake had thought, *Can't drain it any other way, you stupid clown*, but Wishart's answer had been more practical; he'd said, 'Blow port and starboard tanks separately if you need to. Just keep her upright till it's empty. Won't take many minutes.' Around them, men did their jobs mechanically, listened to the orders, made their reports, waited for whatever might come next. They didn't believe in it either, but he could see that like him they were ready to pretend they did. They were the faces of sick men who for some hours now had been breathing poison.

'Blow three, four, five and six main ballast!'

McVeigh snarling, panting like some wild beast as he sent air roaring to the saddle-tanks. Hydroplanes hard a-rise.

Going *up*!

Eighteen – fifteen – thirteen...

Watching the needle circle round the gauge: and the bubbles, particularly the transverse one, as the list increased and she began to sway over as she rose – ten feet...

'Stop blowing four and six!'

Those were the port-side tanks. The list was to starboard.

Eight feet. Seven. List coming off her now.

'Start the pumps!'

Deafening noise of expanding air: it filled the mind, allowed you to believe the dream was coming true while all the time you knew that at any second the whole procedure could be reversed by an order, 'Seventy feet: get her *down*!'

'Stop blowing one and three! Open the conning-tower drain!' The noise of blowing was shut off suddenly with the air, and Geordie Knight jerked the drain-valve open, starting it with the wheel spanner and then wrenching the thing around by hand. Water pounding in the pipe. 'Pumps are sucking, sir!'

There hadn't been anything sure about that, either. Battery readings taken just now by Blackie Cole had shown density readings that were horrifying, well below the safe-discharge limit of 1.180.

'Pilot – behind me on the ladder, on my legs.'

Jake shambled over. There was always pressure in the boat when she'd been down for a long time. You could see it on the aneroid. When it was really bad, a captain opening the hatch without extra weight to hold him down could be blown out and killed.

'Chief ERA in the control room!'

Lofty Adams called through for him. Grumman came in: vast, lumbering, nodding to the other ERAs, stopping with a hand like an oily leg of mutton on the edge of the bulkhead door.

'Sir?'

'The minute the top hatch is open, Chief, I want the gas engines started. Half ahead – three hundred revs starboard and a standing charge port. But no delay, not one second's.'

In case they met a patrol boat or other trouble, and had to dive again; at least the engines would have sucked the foul air out of her and drawn some of the fresh kind in.

Hobday had sent another blast of air into number three; and the list was no longer evident, as the tower emptied and she regained stability. Two hours, Wishart had said – so Jake remembered. If they were lucky enough to be left to themselves, they'd have two hours on the surface now, before dawn and daylight forced them down again.

Then what? For a full charge in normal circumstances the battery needed eight hours. Jake wasn't up to thinking that one out. His mind pleaded, *Let's just get up there – please?* Hobday told Wishart, 'The tower's empty, sir.'

Ellery jumped up on the ladder, pulled the pins out of the clips and then jerked the clips free. He grabbed the hinged bar and pushed upwards on it, climbing another rung on the ladder in order to force the hatch up and back, clanging heavily into the tower. A splashing of water, about a bucketful, rained down into the control room. The signalman jumped clear, and Wishart went quickly up the ladder. Jake followed him, into an odour of seawater and wet metal. Rush of air, a violent hissing, whistling: the port-side scuttle and deadlight had been stove in, leaving a jagged hole, and the boat's pressurised stink was gusting out of it. Higher up, he grabbed hold of Wishart's legs, wrapping his arms round him above the knees and holding tight. He heard him working at the clips on the top hatch, and suddenly the hiss of escaping pressure thickened to a roar as Wishart eased the last clip off and held the hatch's opening force on it. Foul air rushed up round them: a fog came with it, an evil-smelling mist pouring out of the boat's sewer-like compartments. Wishart flung the hatch open and yelled downward, 'Start the engines!' Jake bawled it down and climbed after him, heaving himself up out of the hatch's rim and into the wet bridge and the incredibly clean night air. In the pause before the diesels coughed and spluttered into life he heard, from not far away in the darkness on the beam, a dog's high, mournful howl.

A *Marmaran* dog!

Chapter 8

'Let us pray.'

Fifth day: Sunday morning... Wishart glanced around the control room at the bowed heads of his ship's company. CPO Crabb's grey-streaked one was immediately in front of him, and Rinkpole's dome gleamed beside it. Leech, the stoker PO, had cut himself shaving, and a twist of blood-soaked cotton-waste clung to the side of his thick neck. Wishart's eyes rested for a moment on the depth-gauges with their needles static at seventy-five feet; E.57 was bottomed, off the west coast of Kalolimno Island, and there wasn't a hint of movement on her. Satisfied, he opened his prayer-book at one of the strips of signal-pad he'd put in as markers, and began to read into the warm underwater quiet, *O most blessed and glorious Lord God: we thy poor creatures whom thou hast made and preserved, holding our souls in life and now rescuing us out of the jaws of death, humbly present ourselves again before thy Divine Majesty to offer a sacrifice of praise and thanksgiving, for that thou heardest us when we called in our trouble, and didst not cast out our prayer...*

There'd have been some prayers all right, Jake thought. Most likely every single member of the ship's company had asked the Almighty for assistance at least once during the passage of the straits. Wishart had whisked some pages over, switching adroitly from one prayer to another: that first one, if he'd gone on with it, would have let him in for asserting that at some point they 'gave all for lost, our ship, our goods, our lives', and this would have presented an unjustifiably defeatist attitude. He continued instead, *Thou has showed us terrible things and wonders in the deep, that we might see how powerful and gracious a God thou art, how able and ready to help them that trust in thee...*

Jake had been looking at ERA McVeigh when Wishart had spoken of 'terrible things and wonders in the deep', and he'd almost burst out laughing, thinking that Angus McVeigh might be about the most terrible and wondrous of the lot... It was astonishing to think that only five days ago he'd had his work cut out just to remember these men's names; he felt now as if he'd known them all for years.

It had been about two-thirty on the morning of the third day when they'd surfaced at the Marmara's western end. There'd been two hours of darkness left; they'd spent them travelling eastward at six knots with one engine pumping the beginnings of new life into the tortured battery. Before dawn Wishart had dived her and taken her in close to the northern shore, to lie bottomed all day in twelve fathoms near a headland called Injeh Burnu. A day's rest, proper meals, clean air to breathe... During the day, Rinkpole and his torpedomen had drawn back the torpedo from the starboard tube, the one that had been flooded when the mine went off, done a full maintenance routine on it and then reloaded it. And Leading Seaman Dixon, the LTO, had got the gyro compass back into commission. The bigger repairs – to the conning tower and the leaky control-room deckhead – had had to wait.

That evening they'd got away from the coast and surfaced well out in the deep water. Heading north-east on the gas engines and charging all the time, they'd met no surface craft at all, and they'd taken this as evidence that the Turks had no idea they'd got through. Otherwise they'd have been hunting for them. Wishart, on the bridge with Jake that night, had murmured, 'Probably imagine they've made their straits impassable. Silly asses!'

'Wonder how *Louve*'s come through it.'

'Oh, those froggies'll be all right.'

There'd been hammering and filing noises from the tower under their feet, and for some time Grumman and Knight were down inside the casing, under the gundeck, using a shaded torch to examine the rivets that fixed it to the pressure hull. Those were the loosened ones – from the strain of pulling against that net – and Grumman's view was that the flooding of the tower had loosened them still further.

'Tower made 'er list; an' when she lists over you got the weight o' the gun pullin' sideways.' He'd moved one ham-like hand at an angle to the other. 'So there's all that movement actin' on the rivets, twistin' at 'em. I reckon we oughter take the gun an' the gun-mountin' right off 'er, sir.'

They'd done it yesterday, in daylight, right out in the middle with no land or ships in sight. ERA Knight had taken care of technical problems while Roost and his gun's crew did the donkey-work. Barrel and breech had been manhandled into the fore hatch – which had been opened for the bare minimum of time needed to get the loads struck down into the submarine – and were now stowed up for'ard in the tube space. The heavy circular mounting had then been unbolted from the gundeck, manoeuvred along the casing to the bow in order not to risk damage to the saddle-tanks, and there eased overboard to sink into four hundred fathoms of water. Leaving a slight trim adjustment for Hobday to attend to. And while that had been going on, Grumman with McVeigh and Bradshaw had bolted a steel patch on a rubber seating to the outside of the hole in the tower, and welded a back-up patch to the inside of it, with packing between the two to guarantee its watertightness. Hobday meanwhile had had both engines pounding away to bring his battery up to scratch; it hadn't been quite up, although the repair jobs had been completed, when the lookout on the bridge had sighted a wisp of funnel-smoke and they'd had to dive. Mid-morning, that had been; Hobday had grumbled at having had to cut the battery charge.

'Another half-hour, she'd have been right up.'

'We can't risk being spotted, Number One. The most vital thing now is not to let 'em suspect we're here.'

During the day, paddling eastward at periscope depth, they saw two freighters, one gunboat and about a dozen sailing craft, most of them dhows. The gunboat hadn't been patrolling, and her behaviour had reinforced their belief that the enemy were quite unaware of a submarine having gate-crashed their private sea. She'd been making about eight knots on a straight course, heading towards Rodosto; she hadn't been zigzagging, there'd been men lounging on her upper deck, and both her guns had canvas covers on.

E.57 had surfaced at five in the evening; there'd been nothing at all in sight, and Wishart had ordered 'hands to bathe'. They came up in groups of four men at a time; the procedure was to dive in, climb out, work up an all-over lather with salt-water soap and then go in again to wash it off. Nick had jumped at the chance of a swim, and so had Burtenshaw, but Robins had passed his up. And last night when all nominally clean-shaven men had shaved, preparing themselves for the Sunday morning service, Robins had abstained and advised the other two to do likewise. Nick had seen the point; it would be better to look scruffy and un-British when the time came to land. They were to be provided with some kind of local garb – whatever Turks or other denizens of Constantinople wore – and clean-shaven faces would have looked out of place. So now the three passengers were the only men in E.57's control room who weren't spruced up.

The rendezvous with *Louve* was scheduled to take place at dawn. Nick was more than ready for the move. Being a passenger had been bad enough in *Terrapin* but in this submarine it was worse still. One felt not only useless and idle but actually an encumbrance, an unnecessary body getting in the way of men with work to do. It would be a relief to move under one's own power, make one's own decisions. Not that he'd much idea *what* decisions, what sort of problems he'd be faced with. It was no good even trying to guess what opposition or what help there'd be. Robins was certainly *no* help: Nick had tried to get some background information out of him, about the situation ashore and so on, but the man was either as ignorant as he was himself or jealous of his special knowledge. It was just as well, Nick thought, that he wasn't going to have to rely on Robins later, that they'd be splitting up as soon as they'd got ashore and met Reaper's people – whoever, for God's sake, *they* might be… Robins had said once, answering a probe of Nick's, 'The Grey Lady's the king pin. You'll get everything from her, or she'll see you get it from some other quarter.' Then, realising he'd actually given a fairly straight answer to a question, he'd turned testy, asking, 'Did Commander Reaper not brief you fully?'

'Well, yes. As far as he could.'

'Ah.' Smirk. 'Quite!'

Robins, of course, loathed Reaper. Nick didn't bother to stand up for him, though. A sneer as nebulous as that wasn't easy to take issue with; and Reaper was capable of fighting his own battles.

What *had* Reaper told him? Anything else that he ought to have in mind and hadn't? He didn't think so. Only the times and positions for the two rendezvous appointments. Beyond that, one had a free hand to act as circumstances dictated. It had been Reaper's personal decision to bring Nick into it. As the operation had been conceived originally, he'd said, Burtenshaw had been no more than a ferret to flush *Goeben* out of her hole. He'd been a throwaway: no great difficulty in putting him ashore with Robins, and while he wasn't expected to achieve anything directly with his bag of explosives the hope was that his having been put ashore at all would alert and alarm the Germans to the possibility of sabotage attempts; so they'd move her out of the Horn, to where E.57 or *Louve* could get at her. Reaper's intention was that with Nick to steer him along, the Marine might make a real job of it. Implicit in the London plan – the one Reaper had been saddled with and which he'd now amended – was that Burtenshaw was likely to be caught, soon after he'd landed. It was the kind of White-hall cynicism that Reaper said he'd met before and never put into action in any of the stunts he'd handled. Nick had wondered whether his own participation was likely to make all that much difference. Reaper, he was aware, had a high opinion of his abilities, but that opinion was based on a performance – the Flanders coast raid – which Nick felt owed a great deal to sheer luck.

Mightn't Reaper be only throwing away two amateurs instead of one?

Remembering that talk with him, pacing *Harwichs* quarterdeck as night closed down on Imbros... Reaper had gone on to discuss what was expected to happen after Turkey capitulated. He'd said it was virtually certain that a British naval force would be sent through the Bosphorus into the Black Sea to support the White Russians in the Caucasus and Crimea.

'Not that your poor old *Leveret* is likely to be part of that.'

'I suppose not.'

And damn *that*, too. To have had a prospect of action – surface, destroyer action – instead of just the fizzling-out of the war and the onset of peacetime formality, would have brightened things considerably. It might even have made this submarine trip tolerable. He'd have been able to look forward to getting back to a world he knew and understood and could handle, felt at home and happy in. As it was, he faced a dogsbody job with little prospect of excitement in it. But he didn't want to show Reaper how low his spirits were; he said, 'At least it *is* a command, sir.'

Reaper had laughed. 'You've learnt not to look gift-horses in the mouth then, Everard!'

Bravo, he'd been referring to. And what *that* appointment had led to.

Wishart had read out a prayer for the King's Majesty. Now he turned the pages to another of his markers, and started on the 'Prayer to be said before a fight at Sea'.

O most powerful and glorious Lord God, Lord of Hosts, that rulest and commandest all things: Thou sittest in the throne judging right, and therefore we make our address to thy Divine Majesty in this our necessity, that thou wouldest take the cause into thine own hand, and judge between us and our enemies. Stir up thy strength, o Lord, and come and help us, for thou givest not always the battle to the strong but canst save by many or by few... And how often in past centuries, Nick mused, must Christian invaders of these territories have asked their God to 'judge between them and their enemies'. A nicely preconceived judgement they'd have been expecting too, seeing that the enemy in those days had been Islam. It wasn't now: despite what the Turks were up to at the moment, the real enemy was as Christian as they were themselves, and would probably be requesting much the same degree of assistance. Only Christian pressure from one side and Christian bungling on the other had brought Islam into *this* war: plus the fact that a small group of thugs in Constantinople had all the power in their hands... McVeigh was staring at the deckhead, and Lewis was counting something on his fingers. Eggs? Potatoes? Wishart had shut his prayer book; he glanced at the depth-gauge and then said, 'The Grace of the Lord Jesus Christ, and the love of God, and the fellowship of the Holy Ghost, be with us all evermore.' A general growling of 'Amen' finished it. Heads that had been bowed turned upwards as he cleared his throat, looking round at them.

'It wasn't any joy-ride, was it? But you came through it splendidly. I knew you would, and you proved me right. Thank you, and well done.'

He met Weatherspoon's eyes, small-looking behind those thick glasses. The telegraphist's head shook briefly, answering the unspoken question. Wishart told his ship's company, 'About dawn tomorrow we'll be meeting the French boat and transferring our passengers to her. After that we'll settle down to patrol across the exit from Constantinople. *Louve* is watching it at the moment. We'll be there all ready for *Goeben* if she obliges us by coming out and providing a home for Chief Petty Officer Rinkpole's torpedoes.'

The TI smiled faintly, ran a hand over his bald head. Wishart went on, 'It's vital that if *Goeben* does come out we should sink or cripple her. That's what we've come this far for. Don't imagine that getting through the straits was the tricky bit and now it's all routine. It won't be. We're in the enemy's back-yard and the game's only about to start. So – on your toes every minute, eh?' He turned to Hobday. 'All right, Number One. Fall out, please. Get her off the putty when you're settled.'

'White watch, watch diving!'

As the compartment emptied, leaving only watch-keepers at the controls, Wishart invited Nick and Robins to join him at the chart table. He used dividers to measure the run to the dawn rendezvous.

'Eighteen miles. We'll potter up that way all day, surface when it's dark in order to charge the battery, and we'll be there on the spot in plenty of time. *Louve* at the moment is *here*: so she has hardly any distance to come to meet us.'

222

He'd pointed at a pencilled rectangle a mile wide and eight miles long straddling all the likely courses out of Constantinople. He told Robins, 'After we put you in *Louve*, we take that area ourselves, and after she's dumped you off she'll be going to a long-stop patrol line at the western end.'

In case *Goeben* got past E.57. She'd have to get by the Frenchmen as well before she reached the Dardanelles. Wishart asked Robins, 'Where's your landing spot, d'you know?'

Robins stared at him for a moment, then glanced at Nick. There'd been a policy of not letting the left hand know what the right hand was planning. E.57 might have been sunk, in the straits, and there had been no reason for the submariners to know the details of the shoreside operation. But now, there didn't seem much reason why they should wot know. Nick told Wishart, 'Constantinople.'

'What?'

'We shan't be landing from *Louve* at all. Twenty-four hours after we join her, she has a rendezvous with a dhow.' Robins pulled a notebook from his pocket and flipped some pages over. 'Ten miles north-west of Ag.Etias Point.'

'I see...' Ag.Etias was the top-left corner of Kalolimno Island. Wishart ran the parallel ruler over and marked off the distance. 'There, then.' He looked at Nick. 'The dhow takes you right into Constantinople?'

'Where she's from. And we'll be got up to look like her crew – they're to have clothes for us on board. With the whole coast watched and guarded, it's really the safest way in, I suppose.'

–

'*Oh Eternal Lord God, who alone spreadest out the heavens and rulest the raging of the sea...*' Terrapin was as steady as dry land, slicing through a sea like marble, marble that veined white astern and then gradually reverted to unbroken blue. Truman, her captain, had no need to look down at the book in his hand: this was the everyday naval prayer and by the time he'd reached his fifteenth birthday he could have recited it in his sleep. He was on the gundeck of his destroyer's stern four-inch, while below him on her quarterdeck and up both sides of the iron deck as far as her foremost funnel the ship's company had assembled for Divine Service, their heads bared to the Aegean sun. *Terrapin* steamed slowly but in erratic zigzags across the wide entrance of the Gulf of Xeros. Astern and at this moment on her quarter was the brownish mass of the Gallipoli Peninsula, while ahead and much further off was the lower and less distinct outline of the European mainland. A single higher point of land on the port bow was Mount Chat; the rest was an uneven blur shimmering in warm, still air. Summer was lingering into autumn, autumn refusing to be squeezed out by winter; any day now it would change abruptly to grey skies, cold winds, heaving sea.

Nights had to be spent at the gulf's eastern end, the end nearest to the Marmara. Each day Truman brought his ship out twenty-five miles westward, and during that passage westward watched the sun rise, flooding the barren hills with colour. Reaper slept at those times. He had to be awake all night, or most of it, the hours set for wireless contact with the submarines and for messages from shore. It was because of the weakness of the shore transmitters that it was necessary for a communication link this far east; the submarines' sets had the range for Mudros easily. Or *should* have had. But any enemy observers ashore, or in the recce 'planes which from time to time came dithering like nervous moths along the coastline, were supposed to believe that *Terrapin* was just another patrolling destroyer. They weren't intended to know that she slipped back into the gulf at nightfall.

'...*that we may be a safeguard unto our most gracious Sovereign Lord, King George, and his Dominions, and a security for such as pass on the seas upon their lawful occasions...*'

Reaper was a difficult man to entertain, Truman had found. He was prone to long silences: he seemed to switch off, often in the middle of some interesting discussion, and then not to hear any more of what was being said to him. Of course, he had a great deal on his mind; but it was still exasperating. And it would be a great relief to have this business done with, join the flotilla at Mudros and resume normal destroyer duties. He shut the prayer book as he finished, '—*and the love of God and the fellowship of the Holy Ghost be with us all evermore—*'

He let them have the last word. Then heads lifted; there was a general stirring, straightening. Even *Terrapin* moved, heeling as she altered course to a new leg of the zigzag. Funnel-smoke was acrid, drifting downward in the windless air; it swept across the raised gundeck where he stood, curled lazily and dirtily across the wake. Harriman, with his cap pushed under his left arm and his bald patch strikingly evident from this gull's-eye view, was looking up at him expectantly. Truman nodded. 'Carry on, please.' He went down to the quarterdeck to join Reaper, and told him in case Harriman hadn't, 'We're invited to luncheon in the wardroom, sir.'

'Yes. Very kind of them.' Reaper added, 'I'll take the opportunity to give them the latest news.'

'Eh?'

Truman blinking owlishly... A cold fish, Reaper thought. At this moment history was being made, the shape of the world was changing, and all he could talk about was nuts and bolts, problems of engineering, fuel consumptions, changes in the signal code... It would be a pleasant change not to lunch alone with him today. Reaper was aware that his own nerves were on edge. Trying to be patient while the days passed and others did the work and faced the danger... Not a word from either submarine – well, that was good – and not a peep from inside Turkey either. No sudden flurry of Turk wireless activity, for that matter. It was probably what one dreaded most, at this stage of the operation: so thank God for all the silence. But – he shook his head, staring out astern over the pile of white that rose under the destroyer's counter – as a staff man, a planner and organiser, he should have been used to the waiting, guessing. He wasn't, though, and he doubted if he ever would be.

He turned, strolled for'ard – making himself stroll and not walk briskly. There were a few minutes to pass before it would be time to go down to the wardroom, and a circuit or two of *Terrapin*s upper deck might save him from being trapped again by Truman. Walking for'ard now, past the after set of torpedo tubes, hearing the pipe, 'Hands to dinner!' So the rum issue had been completed; time *did* pass, if you made yourself relax, forget it. Strolling on... There'd be no work done this afternoon by the two off-duty watches; it would be a traditional Sunday afternoon of letter-writing, sleeping, patching clothes, haircuts on the foc's'l during the dog watches while the killicks' mess gramophone churned out *Dixie* or *Alexander's Ragtime Band*.

Remarkable, how cheerful and enthusiastic the men kept, considering how little entertainment or shoregoing came their way. From the regulars you could understand it, because this was the life they'd chosen for themselves; but even the Hostilities Only ratings seemed content enough. One tended to look carefully, listen hard, these days, when there was so much talk about discontent in the Fleet. It was about pay, mostly. Their Lordships at the Admiralty were aware of the grouses, and in sympathy; Beatty had written from his Grand Fleet flagship urging an overhaul of all rates of pay, and the First Lord, Geddes, had been pressing the Treasury hard. The Treasury, used to pressure and to ignoring it, hadn't so far responded. It was not a case of discontent between the men and their officers – in that respect the situation was excellent, generally speaking, and officers' pay was as badly in need of reform as the lower deck's. Flag Officers, for instance, drew the same money they'd had in 1816 – 102 years without a rise. But sailors on leave in England had seen civilian earnings soaring while their own families couldn't make ends meet; they'd also seen how civilian rates had been pushed up by strikes. There'd been talk in Fleet canteens of a naval strike: but in naval terms 'strike' and 'mutiny' were synonymous; mutiny was mutiny, and there was only one face that any commissioned officer could show to it.

There was certainly no sign of unrest here in *Terrapin*. Truman seemed to take that for granted: when he and Reaper had discussed it, the suggestion that there could *ever* be such disturbances had shocked him. Not a very long-sighted man, Reaper thought. To put it more plainly, Truman was rather a damn fool. Because if the Navy was to be sent into the Black Sea after the Turks surrendered, and sailors came under the influence of Russian Bolsheviks, and if the war against Germany ended and the HO ratings, burning to get home to their families, were kept out here in some kind of policing job, while back in England men who hadn't fought at all were getting home to their wives every night and drawing four times the pay...

The Treasury would have to wake up, and quickly. And, please God, let any intervention in South Russia be a very temporary affair. There were British troops in Archangel, of course – but that was primarily to stop the Hun drive through Finland, since the Bolshies had declined to stand up for themselves. Reaper found himself walking, still deep in thought, into *Terrapin's* wardroom. Harriman asked him, 'Gin, sir?'

'How very kind. I'm afraid I've warmed the bell somewhat—'

'You're precisely on time, sir.' Harriman had beckoned to Link, the steward, and Link was bringing a glass of gin and the bitters shaker on a silver salver from the side-board. It was lower deck pay that had to be seen to most urgently, Reaper thought. Never mind the fact that he as a commander drew the same money as a Scottish dockyard matey whose only responsibilities were a hammer in one hand and a cold chisel in the other. Mr Shriver, the gunner (T), came over. Grey-haired, long-nosed, close-together eyes... 'A pleasure to 'ave your company, sir.' Granger, the tall young sublieutenant, asked him, 'Any good buzzes,

sir?' Granger was sipping Tio Pepe. *Terrapin's* wardroom
had stocked up with it at Gibraltar, on the way through.

Reaper nodded. 'I've quite a bit of news for you, as it
happens... Thank you, Link.' He accepted a cigarette from
the wardroom's silver box. Gough-Calthorpe's staff in
Mudros kept him informed of everything that mattered, in
their daily ciphered signals. In an operation like this one,
with so much politics involved and at least one nation's
surrender imminent, it was vital to have a broad and up-
to-date picture of the developing strategic situation. He
added, expelling smoke, 'But we'll wait for—'

'Oh. You're here already.'

Truman's surprise at finding him down here was *almost*
a criticism. Link had Truman's sherry ready-poured for
him, and Granger was offering him a light for his cigarette.
Harriman asked Reaper, 'May we hear your news, sir?'

'Quite a few bits and pieces.' He sat down on the
padded fender. 'For a start, we sent some 'planes over
Constantinople yesterday, calling on the Turkish people
to kick the Huns out. In view of what I've to tell you in a
minute, that *might* have been rather a waste of effort...
Second point, though, is the Aegean squadron's being
reinforced with two dreadnoughts from home waters –
Superb and *Temeraire*.'

Truman had raised his eyebrows: 'Suggesting that a
sortie by *Goeben* is considered likely, eh?'

Explaining the obvious to his officers. There'd been no
need for him to comment; Reaper had given him all this
news earlier on.

'There's certainly no other enemy unit in these waters
worth two dreadnoughts. Four, counting the pair we have
already.' He thought it was possible that London was

taking a longer view than just the *Goeben* threat; the Black
Sea was very much in mind now, and the Russian ships
there, the possibility of their falling into German hands.
He nodded. 'But here's the more important news. The
Turks are sending a delegation to talk about an armistice,
and London has authorised Admiral Gough-Calthorpe to
receive them on board *Agamemnon* – any day now, in
Mudros. How's *that*?'

'Calls for another drink.' Harriman looked round for
the steward. Truman said in his fruity voice, 'Armistice
talks do not inevitably result in a cessation of hostilities.
One may *hope for*—'

'Yes. Let's hope.' Reaper put his glass down on Link's
salver and took another in its place. 'But one warning I
must give you – mum's the word.' He glanced up. 'Hear
that, steward?' Link nodded. Wardroom stewards were the
eyes and ears of the ship's company. Harriman raised a
forefinger at him warningly: Link grinned, moved with
his tray to Truman's elbow. Reaper explained, 'As you
know, we've this French wireless chap Rostaud on board.
And for the time being we aren't letting the French in on
our negotiations with the Turks. London's view is that *we*
are the naval power here. We've taken the brunt of the
action and it's become our show. So to that extent…' He
shrugged. 'I don't *feel* perfidious. But you see, the fact that
Turkey wants to make peace does make a raid by *Goeben*
rather probable. If the Huns see the ground being, so to
speak, cut from under their feet – eh?'

The rest of his news came from farther afield. The
German lines in France were disintegrating. The enemy
had evacuated Zeebrugge and Ostend. Scheer had recalled
his U-boats from patrol; it was believed in London that his

intention was to redeploy them in support of some offensive action by the High Seas Fleet. It made sense, Reaper explained. With defeat in sight, Scheer would be bound to come out. He'd attack the Channel ports, perhaps, and have submarines patrolling outside fleet-bases to catch Beatty's ships when they emerged to counter the assault. But not just to counter: this might be the battle for which, ever since Jutland, the whole of the Royal Navy had longed. One could imagine the excitement and high spirits prevailing now in Rosyth, Invergordon, Dover, Harwich, Immingham...

Reaper read the expressions on the faces round him, and understood them. Any one of these men would have swapped a year's seniority to be back in home waters now.

–

By nightfall, he could feel the tension in his nerves again. In a few hours the cogs he'd set in motion would be meshing. He stared into the darkness, towards the Marmara. 'Not long now...' It was a mutter, and more to himself than to Truman, but as he said it he realised he'd used exactly the same words not more than ten minutes ago. A give-away: as good as an announcement of the state of anxiety he was in. He could have kicked himself, for exposing that degree of weakness, particularly to a man like Truman. He was with him on the destroyer's bridge now as she nosed into the rounded cul-de-sac that had Cape Xeros to the south and Saros Adalari Island in the middle. The nearest piece of the Marmara was only eight miles away, across the narrow Gallipoli peninsula; and eighty miles east was the rendezvous position where at dawn the two submarines would surface, link briefly in that alien and secret world, then separate again to perform their respective tasks. If one of them failed to keep the appointment, the other was authorised to break wireless silence.

So the best news, from Reaper's point of view, would be none at all. But even that wouldn't be positive evidence that all was well. Conceivably, and knowing how hazardous the passage of the Dardanelles must be, *neither* submarine might keep the rendezvous.

He heard Cruickshank, *Terrapin's* navigator, order quietly, 'Port fifteen.'

'Port fifteen, sir.' That was PO Hart, Chief Buffer, at the wheel in the centre of the bridge. *Terrapin* was moving at slow speed but with frequent applications of rudder. The odds were that she could have anchored and lain in peace all through the wireless broadcast hours, but there was just a chance that the enemy could have got wind of something and sent a U-boat prowling after her. Even at long odds you couldn't accept that risk.

'Midships.'

'Midships, sir.' Quiet voices broke the silence like stones falling into a still surface. The land was a dark hump in the south and a vaguer, more distant one to nor'ard; you saw the land's shape where it blotted out the lower stars. Eastward one could see nothing. Reaper said, 'I'm going down. Be in the W/T office or the chartroom.'

'Very well, sir.' Truman had a canvas bed up here on the bridge. The black shape that was Reaper melted towards the ladder. He'd only been on the bridge for half an hour, a breather from the stuffiness below. Now he'd be returning to the wireless room because it was about one o'clock and the change-over time from a French language broadcast hour to the second English language one. One of the two sets was used for listening all through the dark hours for any transmissions from shore, while on the other the two submarines had been allocated alternate hours.

Reaper went down the starboard ladder to the foc's'l deck, and in at a steel door abaft the ladder's foot. This was the W/T room, under the rear half of the bridge; a hatch in its for'ard bulkhead connected it to the chartroom.

The Frenchman, Rostaud, had just handed over the Type 15 to Telegraphist Michaelson. Leading Tel Stewart was on the Type 4. Reaper leant sideways to let the tall Frenchman edge past. The compartment was only eight feet square and half its depth was taken by the operators' bench, under the sets along the after bulkhead. Rostaud muttered, '*A deux heures, alors.*' His droopy moustache gave him a downcast, apologetic air. Reaper pulled the door shut behind him. The little space was fuggy with cigarette smoke and the peculiar hot-metal smell of electrical equipment.

'All quiet, I suppose.'

'Graveyards get jumpier, sir.' Stewart sniffed. This wasn't the most exciting job a man could have. He was young, studious-looking. Michaelson, on his right, looked older than the leading hand. Reaper said, 'This is our last English transmission period before they join up at the rendezvous.'

'Don't worry, sir.' They seemed to read his thoughts. 'Anything comes up, you'll get it.'

Michaelson had the easier job. Stewart on the Type 4, which was tuned to short-wave shore transmission, had to be sharp-eared and sharp in more general terms, too, to recognise what might concern them and what didn't.

Reaper said, 'I'll be next door.' He went outside and into the chartroom, where he'd be near enough if anything developed and where he had a bunk-settee to relax on. He sat down on it, and swung his legs up.

Quarter past one. Lying back, he stared sightlessly at the deck-head with its heavy steel I-section beams. It was one thing to make plans, another to have to live with them. He allowed his eyes to close. When it was a plan on paper, ships and men were symbols; now the ships had names and the men were people he'd come to know. He thought he'd only just shut his eyes when the door banged open, waking him with a jolt.

Mayne, the leading signalman.

'Sorry, sir. Didn't know you was kippin'. Come to ask would you like a cup o' tea, sir.'

He'd never intended to let himself fall asleep.

'Thank you. Nothing I'd like better.' Except, he thought, powers of telepathy.

Half an hour later Mayne pushed into the wireless office and shut the door. You could hardly see the operators for the cloud of cigarette smoke. He jerked his thumb at the chartroom hatch and told the leading tel, 'Out like a light again.' Stewart nodded. Mayne said, 'Been like a scared cat all day.'

Stewart adjusted the position of the headphones on his ears and leant forward again across the bench, his weight resting on his forearms. There was an anchor tattoo'd on the left one and a heart with initials in it on the other. *Terrapin* heeled as she swung to a new course. Mayne was leaning against the for'ard bulkhead and he'd begun to roll himself a cigarette; he did it without looking down at his fingers, and the cigarette seemed to form itself as if by magic. He saw Stewart jerk upright, grab a pencil in his right hand while his left flew to a tuning knob on the Type 4. Mayne began slowly stowing the tobacco tin inside his jumper; the cigarette was in his mouth, unlit. Stewart had begun to scrawl on the pad in front of him. Plain language, not code.

Control from Kitten – French subma
'Bloody 'ell!'
Fiddling at the set's adjustment... Mayne pulled back the hatch to the chartroom. 'Signal comin' in, sir!'

> Submarine captured intact and brought Constantinople where papers given commander German U-boat which now sailed intention ambush E57 at rendezvous – ends...

Reaper snatched up the pad. The door swung open behind him, banging to and fro. Mayne reached past him and shut it. Reaper drew a sharp, hard breath, as if something had kicked him in the stomach. Then, just as quickly, he'd recovered and reacted.

'Start calling E.57.'
Michaelson's hand began rattling the key like some kind of machine. Reaper leant between the two men and began to write on a fresh sheet of pad, *Control to Wishart. German U-boat waiting at rendezvous in place of Louve. Keep clear of R/V position. Louve intact in enemy hands. Will transmit new orders midnight tomorrow Monday.*

'Code that up.'
Mayne edged over to the pile of code-books at the end of the bench. Michaelson was still tapping out E.57's call-sign. Smoke wreathed away from the stub which

Stewart had spat into a shellcase ashtray. The other two were setting the message up in five-letter code groups. Reaper asked Michaelson, 'Are you sure it's going out?' The telegraphist pointed with his spare hand at a quivering needle in a dial. 'Full power, sir.' Reaper looked at the clock again: he was almost as white as the enamel on the bulkhead it was fixed to. In two minutes the submarine would be closing down her listening watch, and in about ninety she'd be expecting to meet *Louve*.

Chapter 9

E.57's diesels rumbled steadily into the empty, pitch-black night. It wasn't going to be pitch-black for long, though: eastward, a glimmer of brightness pushing up from an invisible horizon showed where presently the first-quarter moon would come sliding up. Wishart had lowered his binoculars and he was staring in that direction, over the submarine's quarter as she forged slowly north-westward. Trimmed right down, she was showing very little of herself above the flat plane of the sea.

Stoker Burrage, on watch as lookout, had moved up to the for'ard side of the hatch to make way for the two telegraphists, Weatherspoon and Agnew, who'd been sent for to strike the W/T mast and aerial. They'd just about done it now; they were manoeuvring the coiled aerial and its insulators, and the dismantled mast, to the hatch; Agnew had slipped down inside, on the ladder, and Weatherspoon was passing the gear down to him. Burrage went back down the other side to the after end of the bridge; Weatherspoon reported to Wishart, 'Mast and aerial's struck, sir. Goin' down now.'

'Very good.'

They were in position, near enough, and the battery was just about fully charged. There was no point in waiting for that moon to rise and floodlight them. Wishart said quietly, matching his tone to the surrounding silence, 'We'll sit on the seventy-foot layer while we wait.'

Submariners in 1915 had discovered a high-density barrier at seventy feet, in this and some other areas of the Marmara, on which a boat could lie as securely as she could on a seabed. As the seabed hereabouts was two or three thousand feet below her safe diving limit, it was a useful phenomenon.

'Stop together. Out both engine clutches. In port tail clutch. Shut off for diving.' Wishart straightened from the voicepipe and glanced towards a vague shape in the after end of the bridge. 'Down you go, lookout.' Burrage vanished into the hatch like a genie returning to its bottle. The engines' grumble died; you heard the sea now, loud because it was so close, the hiss of it along the tanks and under this platform where it swept across the pressure-hull and washed around the tower's base.

'You can dive her, pilot.' The submarine wallowed sluggishly, losing way. Wishart called down, 'Group down, half ahead together.' Straightening from the pipe again he told Jake, 'Give 'em a minute, then pull the plug.'

'Aye aye, sir.' This was doing it gently, diving in slow time, being kind to men off watch who could sleep on and only discover when they woke later that she'd submerged. They'd be shaken in an hour or so anyway, in preparation for the meeting with *Louve*. Wishart had gone down, and Jake was alone on the bridge, thinking what luxury it was going to be – to have no passengers and all that space. He bent to the voicepipe: 'Open main vents!' As he was shutting the voicepipe cock the vents crashed open, air roared up out of the tanks; then the sea slid over the tanks' tops and spray plumed up in the escaping air, salt water raining on him as he reached up to grab the hatch by its brass handle and drag it down over his head. When he stepped off the ladder into the control room the depth-gauge needles were swinging past the twenty-foot mark.

'Seventy feet.'

'Seventy, sir.' Hobday was at the trim. 'Slow together.'

'Slow ahead together, sir.' That was Burrage at the tele-graphs. Smith's tattoo'd hands caressed the wheel. Morton and Rowbottom were on the 'planes. ERA Knight had just slammed in the main vent levers. Passing forty feet: forty-five now... Wishart sloped over to the wardroom corner, and tossed his old reefer-jacket on to his bunk. Jake ambled that way too as he peeled off a sweater. Burtenshaw was stooped over a letter he was writing, Robins was reading, and so was Nick Everard. Everard had borrowed a Sherlock Holmes story from Chief ERA Grumman and he was trying to finish it before the rendezvous with *Louve*. Jake rested his bulk against the edge of the chart table and waited for Hobday to be ready to hand back the watch to him. He'd be due to relieve him of it again at half-past: hardly worth changing over, really. Hobday said like a mind-reader, 'I'll hang on now, Cameron.'

'Thanks.' Decent of the little man, he thought. He was about to retire to the wardroom corner, that living-area which in an hour and a half would seem so palatial, when Burtenshaw came over to him.

'Where are we now?'

Jake began to point out positions and future move-ments on the chart; then he realised the Marine wasn't really listening. He'd brought the letter with him – the one he'd been writing – and he pushed it towards Jake. It was addressed to Colonel J.H. Burtenshaw RAMC, with a War Office address. He asked quietly, 'D'you mind? Only – oh, you know, if one came to grief?'

Blushing with embarrassment... It wasn't easy to imagine this schoolboy character performing usefully in a place like Constantinople. One could see him as a hero on some cricket field, but that was about the limit of it. He had Everard to hold his hand, of course; but even Everard, for all his medals and his reputation, was a destroyer man, not a cloak-and-dagger merchant. Burtenshaw murmured, even pinker now, 'Only if things went smash, you know?'

Three-fifteen: the hands had closed up at diving stations. And only just in time, because Weatherspoon had picked up distant HE, propeller noise. He was listening to it now, and for a change all eyes were on him instead of on Wishart.

Roost had opened the twelve-pounder magazine and brought up Burtenshaw's rucksack of demolition charges. It was under the chair that he was now sitting on, and it was all that any of the passengers would be taking with them. They had some personal kit in *Louve* already, and in the dhow tomorrow there'd be the Turkish gear for them to change into.

'Starboard beam, sir. Faint, still.'

Wishart checked the ship's head by gyro. Starboard beam: it meant that *Louve* was approaching from the east-ward, and that was as anyone would expect. He glanced at Hobday, '*Punctual* frogs.' Weatherspoon's eyes rested on Wishart for a moment; he shook his head slightly, as if something was puzzling him. Now he'd looked down again, concentrating on whatever he was hearing. He was on his stool, in the doorway of the cabinet. Wishart said quietly, 'Let's have her up, Number One.'

'Aye aye, sir.' Hobday set the pump to work on 'A', which an hour ago he'd weighted to hold her on the high-density layer. Weatherspoon blurted suddenly, 'It's a submarine, sir – not the Frog boat, though.'

Everyone looked at him. One or two men smiled. 'Professor' Weatherspoon was a bit of a joke, for'ard. Wishart moved towards him, squeezing behind Hobday. 'Think you may have forgotten what she sounds like?' The two boats had spent a day exercising together between Lemnos and Imbros, and Weatherspoon should have had plenty of time to familiarise himself with the characteristics of *Louve's* HE. But this was precisely the time for her to show up, and exactly the right place, and so far as anyone knew there were no other submarines in the Marmara. Jake looked across at the passengers: Robins was staring impatiently at Weatherspoon, and Everard looked puzzled. Wishart said, going back to his usual position, 'See how she sounds when we're closer. Know her then, I dare say.' Hobday ordered, 'Stop the pump. Shut "A" suction and inboard vent.' He asked Wishart, 'Twenty feet, sir?'

'Yes, please.'

'Slow ahead together. Twenty feet.'

Agnew pushed the telegraphs around: *Louve's* hydrophone would hear that noise echoing through the sea between them, and now she'd be listening to E.57's screws as they stirred into motion. Jake thought of that little tough-nut skipper, Lemarie, the glint in his hard brown eyes as the French operator picked up the HE and reported it. One couldn't envy Lemarie *his* passengers; and now he'd be very crowded indeed, for the next twenty-four hours. Jake looked over at the wardroom corner again: he'd never appreciated before how generous the designers had been, with all that space for only three officers. A bunk *each*, for heaven's sake! Sixty feet on the gauges: fifty-eight… Hobday muttered, 'Easy does it, cox'n.' Crabb grunted; he'd already started to bring the bubble back a bit, and Hobday must have seen it, so all he'd been doing had been anticipating a similar instruction from Wishart. Fifty feet. Jake saw Weatherspoon staring fixedly at Wishart, and an urgent gleam behind the spectacles.

'Definitely not 'er, sir.'

Jake felt a first twinge of doubt. It came from Weatherspoon's tone of certainty. He wasn't a very self-confident or self-assertive man. Wishart seemed to have been pushed into a moment's doubt, too. He was looking at Weatherspoon and frowning, hesitating. Now he'd turned away. It couldn't, he knew, possibly be anyone but the Frenchman.

Jake wondered if *Louve* might have damaged a propeller – caught it against a net and chipped a blade, for instance. Anything like that would dramatically change her signature-tune.

'Captain, sir?'

Wishart's head jerked round towards the telegraphist. The gauges showed thirty-five feet: thirty-three. E.57 was approaching a surface that by now would be streaked with silver. Weatherspoon said doggedly, 'Boat I'm listenin' to ain't *Louve*, sir. Certain pos'tive it ain't. Nothin' *like* 'er, sir.'

Wishart stood silent, staring at him.

'What's she bear now?'

Weatherspoon was right: this was not the Frenchman. Jake *knew* it, suddenly. Other thoughts followed quickly: the Turks had no submarines, so that left only one thing it could be. But the sheer coincidence of time and place… *Coincidence? If she'd been sunk, and a survivor hadn't stood up to interrogation?*

Weatherspoon, jaw set hard, looked simultaneously determined and scared.

'Up periscope.'

The big for'ard one. Depth-gauge needles moving more slowly as the 'planesmen levelled her towards the ordered depth. Twenty-five feet. Twenty-four. The glistening tube rose, a bronze pillar with McVeigh watching it and his hand on the lever ready to bring it to a stop. Hobday reporting quietly, 'Twenty-two feet, sir… twenty-one…' Wishart snatched the handles down, rose with the periscope, training it round as he straightened up. His eyes were at the lenses and McVeigh had stopped it.

'Twenty feet, sir.'

Weatherspoon's voice cracked across the silence: 'Torpedo fired, starboard bow!'

'Hard a-port, down periscope, forty feet, group up, full ahead together!'

'Torpedo approaching starboard!'

Weatherspoon was rising from his stool – eyes dilated, finger pointing out towards the oncoming missile that only he could hear. Crouched, gesturing, gargoyle-ish as the boat swung over and angled downwards and the grouped-up full-ahead power began to drive her down. Then they all heard it: a rushing, churning noise with a steeply rising note, sound surging up, expanding: Nick sat frozen, brain-bound and muscle-bound: then it had passed, whooshing by overhead, and he found that the Conan Doyle novel in his hands was bent hard back along the spine, that he'd practically torn it in half.

'Midships. Starboard fifteen. Group down, half ahead together. Bearing of the submarine's HE now?'

'Right a'ead, sir.' Weatherspoon corrected, as the boat swung on, 'Five to port – broadenin'—'

'Ease to five. Twenty feet.'

'Dead a'ead, sir.'

'Twenty, sir.' All calm, laconic now. Roost, mild as a church-warden, reported he had five degrees of starboard helm on. That meant five degrees of port rudder. Weatherspoon had settled back on his stool again. His breathing was short and jerky and he was still chalk-white. Gauges showed twenty-six feet: twenty-four... 'Up.'

Periscope shimmering greasy, wet-running as it rose. 'Twenty-two, sir—'

'Midships. Bearing now?'

'Ten on the starboard bow, sir, movin' left.'

'Twenty feet, sir.'

Training the periscope slowly left... Then he stopped, and they heard him gasp. Weatherspoon didn't hear it: he was on his own, reporting, 'Very close, sir – revs increasing – *very*—'

'Shut watertight doors! Group up, full ahead together, starboard five!'

Lewis and Ellery dragged the doors shut at each end of the compartment and began slamming the clips over. Jake saw Weatherspoon pull the headphones off his ears. Wishart ordered, 'Midships... Steady!'

'Steady, sir – oh-eight-four—'

'Stand by to ram!'

Hunched at the periscope, not training it at all. Steady bearing meant collision course. Now he pulled his head back and snapped the handles up, grabbed elsewhere for support, clutching the ladder just as she hit the U-boat. It felt more like steaming full-tilt into a cliff-face. An enormous jolt, and from for'ard the noise of tearing metal. Some who hadn't caught hold of solid fittings had been sent flying. Wishart shouted, 'Stop both!' The impact had flung her bow upwards: she'd be on top of her victim but her own foreparts might easily have been holed. There could be *two* victims. Bow sinking now; and still that noise of metal being wrenched apart. She *felt* heavy for'ard. Morton reported, 'Fore 'planes won't budge, sir.'

If her for'ard half was flooded—

Jake Cameron heard himself whisper, *Christ, now here we go!* He was sweating suddenly: he begged himself, *Oh, steady now...* On the other side of the compartment Nick thought, *Well, here it is after all.* During the passage of the straits, even in the bad moments when they'd seemed trapped and done for, the calmness of the submariners had made him doubt whether matters could be as touch-and-go as they'd seemed. Then when the torpedo had been coming straight for them he'd felt numb with hopelessness: there'd been an unexpected thought of Sarah knowing nothing of all this, living her own life and guarding her own secrets, Sarah in a world he couldn't share with her now because he'd already left it. Now as the submarine began to plunge downward, angling steeply towards the seabed three thousand feet below, he understood suddenly that it was inevitable, that he might have known it was, if he'd let himself face it squarely. The landing business – all that – well, at least he wouldn't have to play *that* game now…

But he'd glimpsed the truth, similar awareness, in several other faces. Masks had slipped, just momentarily. Even Cameron's: and Cameron was in control of himself again now, glancing round in that mild, rather deadpan way of his… 'Report from for'ard!' Urgency in Wishart's tone: even Wishart had forgotten his customary drawl. Lewis jumped to the bulkhead voicepipe and began to unscrew the cock on it. With so much bow-down angle and such a rate of descent it seemed quite likely her forepart might be flooded. If the TSC was full there'd be a jet of water through that voice-tube. And there *wasn't*. But that still left the tube space, the bow compartment. Hobday asked Wishart, 'Blow one and two main ballast, sir?' Wishart shook his head: 'No.' But the needles were rushing round the gauges, the angle steepening. Jake Cameron thought – hoped – *The seventy-foot layer'll stop us.* He'd crossed his fingers. Burtenshaw was staring at him wildly with his mouth open: Jake winked at him. Everard saw that, looked round at the Marine, smiled and said something to him. Burtenshaw seemed to have snapped out of it. E.57's stem would be embedded in the enemy's side, and whether or not she herself had any flooding for'ard the other boat's weight would be dragging her down; the German would have at least one compartment torn open to the sea. Out there, just a few yards away, there'd be men dead, drowning, struggling to live. If they shouted, might Weatherspoon hear them through his earphones? Jake saw the needles passing sixty feet as Lewis reported that the tube space and TSC were dry and had sustained no damage.

'Open bulkhead doors.' Less than forty-five seconds had passed since the ramming. Lewis and Ellery working at the doors' clips. And a different kind of noise from for'ard suddenly; Weatherspoon looked up and swallowed, agitating his adam's apple.

'Blowin' 'is tanks, sir.'

Wishart nodded as if he'd been expecting it. It was a loud, harsh noise, like sandpaper rubbing on a drum. Jake leant across the chart, resting on his elbows, hearing it and guessing what was happening in the other boat. Men trapped, frantically trying to break free by blowing themselves to the surface. Their submarine was speared on E.57's bow, held by her deadweight, like a swimmer being pulled down by a shark.

Seventy feet. Seventy-one...

The angle was lessening and she was settling very slowly. The racket for'ard suddenly shut off. Seventy-three feet on one gauge and seventy-four on the other. Bulkhead doors open now. Close-'aul Anderson, one arm in a dirty sling, had stuck his head through the doorway to mutter something of Louis Lewis. Blowing noises again: at this rate it wouldn't be long before the Germans ran out of bottled air. You built up reserves of it by running a compressor that filled the groups of air-bottles in various places in the boat. If you emptied all the groups you'd have nothing left to blow with; and you could only run the compressor on the surface with a hatch open. A lot of this Hun's air might be just bubbling up through holes in his ripped hull.

E.57 lurched, resettled with a bow-up angle.

'Open "A" and "B" kingstons!'

Lewis dived for the wheel that opened 'B'. Beyond the bulkhead Close-'aul would be working one-handed on 'A'. The enemy was trying to lighten himself and for that moment his efforts had looked as if they might be about to succeed, but now Wishart was adding ballast to E.57's for'ard section to counter that lightness and hold her down.

'Bubble's coming back, sir.'

Hobday had said it as detachedly as if this was some ordinary trimming problem they were dealing with. Jake remembered sparrows that he'd drowned: in a sparrow-trap, made of wire netting, which his father used to set in the vegetable patch. Often there'd be a dozen or twenty birds in it; his father had shown him how to take the whole cage and hold it under the surface of the pond while they died. It was the kindest way, he'd explained, of doing it. Jake thought, leaning on the chart table, *We're being kind to Germans, now...* Well, if the Huns had been luckier with that shot, E.57 would be a tangle of metal on the seabed by this time. Two thousand feet down: and in a drawer here in the middle of the wreckage would be a letter which until it disintegrated would still read, *You needn't worry for two seconds about me...* He heard the blowing start again: it had stopped for about half a minute and now they'd opened up again: and vibration suddenly, a terrific shaking: he realised what it was just as Weatherspoon reported, 'Using 'is motors, sir. Full group up, sound like.'

'Shut "A" and "B" kingstons.'

Precaution. Might want to pump out or blow those tanks in a minute, and you couldn't when they were still open to the sea. Wishart had moved in beside Hobday where he could see what was happening to the bubble.

He'd want to make sure the German didn't get any up-angle on her through his blowing; if he managed that he might be able to slip off.

'Group down, slow ahead together.'

'Slow ahead together, sir!' Agnew whirled the telegraphs. By putting the motors ahead Wishart was maintaining a pressure that would keep his stem dug into her.

The vibration stopped suddenly: Weatherspoon met Wishart's enquiring stare as he looked round over Hobday's head: Weatherspoon opened his mouth to say something, and the shaking began again. He told Wishart, 'Tryin' it astern now. Or it was astern before an'—'

'Yes.' Wishart looked at Agnew. '*Half* ahead together.'

He turned to Hobday. 'Number One – if he's blowing bubbles under our bow, we could be getting some of his air into our for'ard tanks.'

He meant, through the open kingstons in the bottoms of them.

'Could be, sir.' Hobday sounded doubtful. Wishart glanced over at McVeigh. 'Open and shut one and two main vents.' McVeigh grabbed the levers and wrenched them back; the noise from for'ard muffled the sound of the vents opening, but the bow dropped suddenly in a downward lurch: eyes flew to the depth-gauges as McVeigh shut the vents again. Seventy-five feet: seventy-six…

'Through the barrier, sir.' There was alarm in Hobday's voice. And some reason for it: with the deadweight of the part-flooded submarine on her stem to drag her down, fore 'planes jammed and four hundred fathoms under them… They'd passed eighty feet and the needles were circling faster now – eighty-five – ninety—

'Stop together.'

'Stop together, sir!'

One hundred feet. Wishart muttered, to nobody in particular, 'It's worse for him than it is for us.' Jake guessed at what might be in his mind: the U-boat would have leaks, strained plates and rivets: as depth and sea-pressure increased she'd suffer more and more. And in his state the German couldn't do much to help himself: he was being dragged down, drowned, getting heavier all the time. If as they went deeper the two submarines broke apart, the damaged one would almost certainly go on down – and down... Until the sea crushed him, burst him like a nutshell. But there was still that rather colossal 'if' – *if* they broke apart: it was possible, conceivable, that they might not. If when Wishart tried to separate he found he couldn't, the German would still go on down but he'd be taking E.57 with him.

One hundred and twenty feet. Wishart was watching the depth-gauge intently. Hobday had just muttered something to him; he'd frowned, shaken his head, glanced at his first lieutenant as if he was surprised at him: and just at that moment, everything went quiet. It was the enemy's motors that had stopped, and the vibration they'd been causing. The difference – silence – was uncanny... The two submarines were locked together, sinking towards the seabed quite fast, gathering downward momentum... Hundred and forty feet. Hundred and fifty. Roost said, 'Lost steerage way, sir. Turnin' all the time an' I can't stop 'er, sir.'

Like something dead, spiralling down. Visualising it as it would look from the outside, the sea out there, one couldn't help seeing it as a wreck on its way to the bottom.

Two locked into one. Jake heard Hobday ask Wishart very quietly, almost whispering, 'Permission to blow "A" and "B", sir?'

Wishart shook his head, without taking his eyes off the depth-gauge. There was a grim, shut look on his face: as if he had pressures in himself too, and was holding them back, forcing himself to see the thing through to its end, not to let go now as perhaps he'd have rather done. Everyone's eyes were on him: he'd be used to that by now, but this time they weren't just standing by for orders or clues to his intentions, they seemed to be trying to hypnotise him into some action they all passionately wanted. Such as blowing main ballast before—

'Blowin' again, sir!'

Half a second later you didn't need hydrophones to hear it. It was the same sound as before, a rip of high-pressure air racketing out: then, within seconds of it starting, it was weakening, fizzling out.

Stopped.

Hobday said, 'His air's done.'

'Yes.' Wishart turned quickly, decisively. Jake guessed this was the climax he'd set himself to wait for. 'Blow "A" and "B" main ballast. Half astern together.'

'Open "A" and "B" kingstons! Stand by to blow—'

'Both motors half astern, sir!'

Blowing the extra ballast out, and pulling astern to clear the German. If there was anyone alive in that boat now, there wouldn't be much longer. The two internals' kingstons were open: McVeigh sent air booming into the tanks to force the sea out through them.

Passing two hundred feet: and no change to the bow-down angle.

'Stop together. Group up.'

Hobday pitched his voice up over the air noise: 'Stop blowing! Shut "A" and "B" kingstons!'

'Grouper up, sir!'

'Half astern together.'

Agnew flung the telegraph handles round. 'Both motors half astern, sir.' Hobday asked Wishart, 'Shall I put a puff in one and two main ballast, sir?' He wanted her bow up, the angle reversed. Wishart shook his head: *he* wanted to get her unlinked from the German first, not waste E.57's air on slowing the wreck's descent as well as his own.

Two hundred and twenty-five feet on the gauges now. Twenty-five feet below tested diving depth.

Two hundred and thirty...

'*Full* astern together!'

The motors' note rose as the screws speeded... Jake saw the needles circling on. Loss of ballast and all that power astern wasn't stopping her. He wondered if Wishart wasn't going to have to change his mind: whether they weren't close to a point of no return.

Wishart must have come to the same conclusion... 'Blow one, two, three, four, five six, seven and eight main ballast!'

The whole lot: too late for half-measures. McVeigh had flung himself like a mad dervish at the panel and he was wrenching the valves open. Even now there was no certainty – and if it failed: well, the German had been forced to use every ounce of air he'd had: now it could be a taste of one's own medicine that was coming. Blowing: and motors grouped up: nothing in reserve if this failed... Air at three thousand pounds to the square inch smashing through reducers into the LP line and through it to the tanks: depth two hundred and forty-five feet. Two-fifty...

'Stop blowing seven and eight!'

Keeping the bubble from going mad: and shouting to beat the din of air – which dropped slightly as McVeigh shut off the after pair of tanks. Two hundred and sixty feet: and suddenly alarming noise from for'ard: creaking, straining... Jake leant over the chart table, listening to it and at the same time not wanting to hear it. It sounded like the bow being torn off.

'Stop blowing one, two, five and six! *Half* astern both!' Like a section of hull-plates being ripped away. Jake told himself, *Always sounds worse than it is...* Under water every sound was magnified, distorted. But *something was* being wrenched apart... 'Stop blowing three and four!'

The boat jerked, tilted as her bow hauled free and began to swing upwards – much too fast... 'Open one and two main vents! Stop together – group down!'

It was going to be a tussle now to get her back into control and trim: but she was already rising fast towards depths that she was tested for. The quiet, after all that noise, was startling. There was no sound at all from outside: nothing out there that anyone could have heard. Only wreckage sinking into a half-mile depth of sea. It would be a long way down by now and it would only stop when it hit the bottom. He felt sick and shaky, as if his own hands had been locked on someone's throat.

The sparrows, he remembered, had always fluttered, for a little while.

Chapter 10

'Not *cold*, is it?'

Nick had only this moment woken from a heavy sleep: and he was warm, in the bunk. Wishart's bunk. He'd opened his eyes to see Jake Cameron pulling on an extra sweater, on top of a sweater he had on already. Obviously he was going up to take over the watch from Hobday. He'd sat down now, to lace his canvas shoes, and he was looking up quite angrily at that question.

'No. It's like a greenhouse. If you're swathed in layers of bloody blankets.'

Nick grinned. The more he saw of Cameron the more he liked him. 'Sorry.' Turning out for night watches wasn't most people's idea of happiness. He looked across at the clock and saw that it was two twenty-five – in the morning of day seven, Tuesday. And – almost fully awake now – he realised that it *was* cold. The diesels were sucking a torrent of night air down through the conning tower, and the boat had quite a bit of movement on her as she rumbled eastward with a southerly breeze and a choppy sea on the beam.

Eastward, because the rendezvous had been changed.

Reaper had moved fast after he'd had E.57's wirelessed report last night. Within minutes he'd replied with confirmation that *Louve* had been captured intact and that the submarine they'd sunk had been German, and he'd told them to keep listening-watch for further orders. Then he must have been in contact with his friends ashore, and half an hour after midnight he'd come on the air again, switching the R/V position eastward, twenty miles nearer Constantinople, and telling Wishart it would be a caïque, not a dhow, he'd meet.

Robins had been quietly jubilant. He was in command now. And Reaper's orders had said he was to represent French as well as British interests. But an hour ago he'd complained of 'slight indisposition' – he'd meant seasickness. He was on the bridge now with Wishart and Hobday. But Burtenshaw, Nick thought, was much the sicker of the two. Pale and sweating, corpse-like on Hobday's bunk. Kinder not to speak to him.

It had been a trying day. After they'd sunk the U-boat Robins had wanted Wishart to surface and send off a report immediately; even if *Terrapin* hadn't been listening at that time, Mudros would have got it. But Wishart, much to Robins's indignation, had preferred to lie low until nightfall – and Nick had agreed with him. If they'd broken wireless silence at once, the Germans and Turks at the Horn would have had notice of their survival and therefore of the U-boat's destruction; whereas if they kept quiet, the enemy might believe his U-boat was keeping silence in order not to alert the Aegean end of the British operation. If nobody went on the air until dark, the enemy would have only a few hours between hearing the transmissions and the time arranged for rendezvous with the dhow, and hopefully that might not give them time to interfere.

The German had known the time and position of the E.57/*Louve* link-up, so perhaps they'd know about the next appointment too. But if all *Louve*'s papers had been given to the U-boat commander and he hadn't shared his knowledge with the authorities ashore before he sailed, then only the fishes had it now. The considerations had been: one, Reaper had stressed how vital it was to push this business through to a successful conclusion; his phrase had been 'any effort, any risk', and if that meant anything at all it meant exactly what it said. Two, at this time – when they'd been discussing it – the rendezvous with the dhow had seemed the only way they could get the landing party ashore. So the appointment had to be kept. If the enemy did have that much information, it could be highly dangerous, even suicidal. On the other hand, a lack of sound alternatives put it into the 'any risk' category. The alternatives were first to make a landing elsewhere, using the submarine's Berthon collapsible boat; but this would be even more chancy, since no information was available about landing places, patrols, shore-guards or observation posts. Second – Nick's suggestion – was to capture some small sailing craft, keep its crew prisoners in the submarine, and let him sail into Constantinople. He'd proposed loading it with Burtenshaw's guncotton and a torpedo warhead as well, laying it alongside *Goeben* and detonating it. Robins had opposed this plan strongly, on the grounds that it wouldn't get him ashore. Nick had seen a snag or two in his idea, but he still thought it would have been the best way to carry out Reaper's orders – *his* part of them – and it would have been a straightforward, basically *naval* plan of assault, the sort of thing he'd have felt at home with. Wishart had been in sympathy, but had felt bound to accept Robins's veto. Robins was the man in charge, and Nick was a latecomer to the operation. Wishart's decision had been to reconnoitre the R/V area thoroughly in the hours before dawn, and then to make a very cautious approach to the dhow, making certain there were no other ships about and that the dhow wasn't armed, and so on. After he'd transferred the passengers to it he'd accompany it at periscope depth as far as he safely could, on its passage to Constantinople.

One other area of danger couldn't be insured against. This was the possibility of the dhow's identity being known ashore, so that they'd be met on arrival. This was their personal risk, not the submarine's, and Wishart left that decision to Robins, who said he'd make up his mind after he'd been aboard the dhow and questioned the Turks in it.

Then Reaper's latest signal had arrived and cleared away all the question-marks.

Nick heard Burtenshaw groan that sea-sickness was a pretty rotten thing. Jake Cameron looked up at the bunk. 'Not your first experience of it?' The Marine must have nodded, or something; Cameron told him, 'It'll be worse in a caïque, my lad. Much worse.' He added, when Burtenshaw didn't answer, 'Never mind. You'll have Robins to hold your hand. Or you can hold his. Take it in turns, perhaps.' He stood up, ready for the bridge; Burtenshaw stopped him.

'Won't forget that letter?'

'I'll hang on to it. Give it back to you later.'

'Thanks.' Nick guessed at what sort of letter it must be, and he wondered if he should have written one for Sarah. But saying what? And if his father should be at Mullbergh, released from the Army, and *he* opened it? A fine legacy to Sarah that would be… He slid down off the bunk; he'd slept enough and he was wide awake, and one of the others would be wanting to turn in presently. It truly *was* cold… Burtenshaw asked plaintively, 'Is there anything one can do, for sea-sickness?'

'Yes.' Cameron answered over his shoulder, 'Be sick.' He went over to the helmsman. Nick told Burtenshaw, 'Wear a tight belt, eat dry biscuit, don't drink anything at all.' Cameron had told the helmsman, Finn, 'Relief OOW.' He glanced back to the wardroom corner: 'It'll be much, *much* worse in the caïque.' He winked at Nick. Finn was yelling up the voicepipe, 'Permission to relieve officer of the watch sir, please?'

Wishart called down, 'Ask Lieutenant Cameron to wait until I get down.'

There was good reason not to let the bridge get over-crowded on patrol, when the boat might have to be dived quickly in emergency. Jake sloped over to his chart table, pausing halfway to let CPO Rinkpole get by. Rinkpole, heading aft, had a gloomy look about him.

'Still having bad dreams, TI?'

Earlier in the day he'd told Jake that he'd had a night-mare about the torpedo in the starboard bow tube, the one that had been flooded under pressure of the mine's explosion. He'd completed a maintenance routine on it since. In the dream it had done something-or-other that had greatly upset him.

He shook his head. 'Not sleepin', sir.' With his torpe-does he was like a hen with chickens. Jake picked up the dividers to measure the run to the caïque rendezvous; they'd be diving in an hour or less, so as to be out of sight before daylight came. The same routine as yesterday: except this time Wishart would believe anything Weatherspoon told him.

'All right, pilot.' Wishart came off the ladder. 'Room up top for you now.' He eyed Jake's solid frame meaningfully as he said it. Jake stared back at him: he didn't think there could be more than a few pounds between their weights.

'D'you mean you'll be staying below now, sir?' Wishart jerked his head. 'Get up there.'

'Is Lieutenant-Commander Robins staying on the bridge?'

'He's under the weather. Has to be fit for when we meet our caïque.' Wishart shrugged. 'Not for long.' The bridge seemed to be full of very little men. One of the pair abaft the hatch would be Robins, of course. Jake asked Hobday, 'Who's the lookout?'

'Stone.'

Andy Stone, Leading Stoker, Hostilities Only, railwayman from Newhaven. In the dark, he and Robins, lieutenant-commander from the Foreign Office, were identical black gnomes. Hobday said, 'That's ten minutes watchkeeping you owe me.'

'If you'll agree it's ten minutes hanging around the control room you owe *me*.'

'Damn sea lawyer...'

He wasn't a bad fellow. A bit pompous sometimes, but quite a decent sort. Jake's eyes were adjusting to the dark; it took a few minutes to tune them in, which was partly why OOWs and lookouts didn't change watches at the same time. Hobday told him, 'Course oh-seven-six, three-two-oh revolutions, running charge port side.'

'Any special orders?'

'None except we'll be diving on the watch before long, and I'd like a shake before we do.'

'Why?'

'What d'you mean, *why*?'

That was the area of pomposity. Thinking the boat couldn't be dived unless he was there to catch a trim. Jake shrugged in the dark. 'No skin off my nose... Anyway, I've got her.'

Alone — except for the two silent figures further aft — with the throaty grumble of the diesels and the wash of the sea, a little spray occasionally flashing over from the starboard side. There was more motion on her up here, of course, since the bridge's fifteen feet of height made for an upright pendulum effect, swaying to and fro while waves broke regularly against her sides, swept aft, frothed over the saddle-tanks and surged across the trimmed-down hull. If she hadn't been as trimmed down as she was, low and weighted in the sea by full or half-full tanks, there'd have been a lot more roll on her. He'd jammed himself against the for'ard periscope standard; there was a bracket at just the right height for his elbow to hook over. In worse weather than this, bridge watch-keepers would lash themselves to the standards with ropes' ends, and now it was just a matter of steadying oneself well enough to be able to concentrate on a careful looking-out with binoculars. The other two were propped against the after standard. Like twins, book-ends, one each side. Astern, beyond their silhouettes, white froth alternately heaped up or spread, disintegrating, as the submarine's afterpart swung up and down; at one moment you'd glimpse the shiny black whaleback of her, then it would be all churned sea humping, bursting upwards as the two sides met and merged. There was only a faint whiff of exhaust fumes; the wind was taking it away to port. Leading Stoker Stone, with glasses at his eyes, was like a small statue slowly turning, the binoculars' length foreshortening as he swung, pivoting on his heels. A serious, very reliable man, was Andy Stone. His 'young lady' in Newhaven – Lewis had said her name was Florence – would be getting a very steady, sound provider, when she took him on.

When the war ended… That phrase, that idea, was everywhere. Jake was sweeping down the port side. He didn't know what the answer was going to be to his own post-war problem. See what *she* thought about it, perhaps. Wishart had been right, but Wishart didn't know it all, didn't know *her*, for instance. In the sense that Stone was a railwayman and took it for granted he'd be a railwayman again, he – Cameron – was a seaman, and could see a similar sense in continuing to be one. If he found that she could take it in the same way – for granted, something she wouldn't question unless he questioned it himself? The problem had come close to solving itself more than once in the last few days. Once or twice in the straits, and yesterday's Hun… Spin of a coin. But a certain amount of skill and watchfulness came into it, it wasn't *only* luck. Lowering the glasses, resting his eyes for a moment as he turned back to start on the port bow and sweep across and down the starboard side, he saw Robins standing hunched, inactive, useless. If he was so determined to stay up here, couldn't he at least add a pair of eyes to the looking-out?

Beneath his dignity, perhaps. What a creature to send on a jaunt like this one! Only kind of chap they could get for it, perhaps. Others all fighting, and plenty of them dying, dead. When you thought of the horrors of the trench-lines... He'd paused, sweeping back now, over a place where he thought there'd been a flash of broken water. Nothing, though. Easy to imagine things. He thought, starting a search on the bow again, that he – all of them – were lucky, truly *very* lucky, with this job. Nothing could be as awful as that sort of fighting. *Nothing.* But the static war had ended now, by all accounts; armies were moving forward, sweeping across Europe. Swinging down past the beam now: he'd thought suddenly that the diesels' note had changed, risen and thickened: then the truth hit him in two stages, the first a suspicion of what it was and the second a jolting awareness of danger and the need to act. In the next fragment of the same split second he'd thought it might be more distant – *not* dangerous, only sound carried in the wind; then it was loud again, louder, beating down out of the night sky astern, everything at once and no time to think, he'd shouted, 'Down below!' and the other two were a blur in the dark as he yelled into the voicepipe, 'Dive, dive, dive!' Flashes – fire-stabs and cutting streaks and an explosive hammering, a black bat angling over – seaplane, he glimpsed its cigar-shaped floats and its gun-muzzle flaming, engine-noise deafening as it crashed over. Stone yelled then, 'This orfficer's 'it, e's—' *Something...* Pieces of metal flying from the after standard: but noise receding, black as pitch, main vents crashing open: he'd got hold of Robins and Stone screamed at him, 'Done for – no *use*, sir—'

'Get below!'

Dragging Robins, hearing the engines cut out and the dwindling racket of the seaplane, the pounding of the sea as the submarine wallowed down. His hands were wet, sticky: Robins had been hit and badly hit, but that didn't necessarily make him dead. Inside now on the ladder, trying to get Robins down inside too: it was incredibly difficult and the sea was loud all around him, gurgling and thumping, crashing against the plating as she dipped under, angling down. He had one hand on the grip under the hatch's rim, the other wrenching to free a leg that was still in the way. Sea would be flooding over at any moment. A hand from below grabbed his own leg, let go and struck at him, and Wishart bellowed, 'Get down and shut the hatch!' He'd accepted Stone's belief, obviously, that Robins was dead. But the hatch still had that leg in it – or something; water spouted, leapt over. There'd been spray and splashing but this was solid, lopping over, green sea beginning to pour in and no chance whatsoever of getting the hatch shut. So – *lower* hatch... He let go of everything, and dropped. One foot hit the rim of the lower hatch, twisted, and pain shot through his ankle: then his shoulder had struck in about the same place and he'd cracked his face hard on some fitting in the tower; the sea was a flood now, drenching down. He heard a shout of 'Shut main vents!' and thought of the seaplane up there quite likely circling for another run: if Wishart took her up this soon they'd – Jake had fallen through the lower hatch and on his way through he'd grabbed its handle so as to drag it down and shut the sea out. Robins's body must have been carried through the top one by the rush of water, and now it came thumping down like something falling off a butcher's hook. The hatch was swinging down with Jake's weight on it and the sea on its other side to add to that: he saw Robins's face in sharp, clear close-up, a death-mask sheeted in blood and with one eye open and entirely white, and then the hatch had crunched down like a nutcracker crushing bone and brain and flesh. Nightmare: beyond it, the scene in the control room was a reality in which he, part of the nightmare, was an intruder. Above him the hatch was ringed with pink and scarlet, a dripping stain…

'Cameron!'

He focused on someone who turned out to be Aubrey Wishart. 'Seaplane, Stone said?'

Take nodded. 'By the time I heard it, its gun was—'

'All right.'

Wishart wasn't looking at him now, and Jake was aware, mostly from expressions on other faces, of the state he was in. He wasn't seeing only the horror of Robins's death, he was looking beyond it too, wondering whether the operation, the landing part of it, had been knocked out in that burst of machine-gun fire. And shock at the danger he'd put the boat and all her ship's company in, by messing about up there: although what else he could have done – not knowing whether he was dead or—

'Go and wash, pilot. Signalman – get a bucket and swab, clean this up.'

'Aye, sir.'

'Thirty feet, sir.'

'Bring her up to twenty. But don't rush it.' He glanced round, frowned at seeing Jake still standing there. 'For God's sake, man—'

'Sorry, sir, I—'

'Everard, you'll go ahead with Burtenshaw, the two of you, I take it?'

Hobday suggested, 'Doesn't the seaplane's attack on us suggest they're wide awake, know we're here and know we've sunk their U-boat?'

'They'll know we're somewhere about, I'm sure.' Wishart's tone was patient. This was a council of war. They'd surfaced, drained the tower, buried Robins's remains. Dawn had given him a colourful send-off, theatrical lighting effects in silver, bronze and crimson while Wishart had read the burial-at-sea prayer and they'd put the body over, weighted with twelve-pounder shells. McVeigh meanwhile had examined the periscope standards and found that apart from chipping and scoring by machine-gun bullets there'd been no damage done. Six minutes later they'd dived again. Jake had the watch now and the meeting with the caïque was to be at five a.m.

Wishart answered Hobday, 'They'll have heard our wireless transmissions, for one thing. But the seaplane attack was nearer the old rendezvous position than the new one, and I'd say it was unlikely that Reaper's friends ashore would have set up a new plan that wasn't secure. Their necks are just as much at risk as ours, one might suppose. But we won't just charge up to the caïque without taking a damn good look around first – if that's what's worrying you.' He turned to Nick. 'You haven't said much, Everard.'

Nick glanced up. 'Isn't much to say, is there?'

'Well, you were expecting some sort of help from Robins—'

'Only that he was going to pass us on to someone or other when we got ashore. Now the caïque's crew'll have to do it. Or there may be a reception committee in the caïque, for all we know. Alternatively—' he looked at Burtenshaw – 'we have the name of a hotel or hotel bar in Pera – place called the Maritza – and the code-name of a – er – lady-friend of Commander Reaper's.'

'And you're happy with that?'

'*Happy?*'

Hobday chuckled at his surprise at such a question. But Wishart was waiting, apparently expecting some sort of answer. Burtenshaw did look quite happy, now he'd got over the shock of Robins's death. At least he was under the orders of someone who'd talk to him occasionally. Nick saw Jake Cameron hovering close by, listening to the discussion; he asked him, 'Are *you* happy?' Cameron shrugged. He looked tired and withdrawn. Nick offered, 'Come along with us, if your skipper'll spare you.'

'Not a chance.' Cameron's eyes met Wishart's for a moment. Wishart said, 'Best navigator I ever had. I'm hanging on to him.' Cameron felt himself colour slightly, and turned away. He'd been thinking, in the last grim hour or two, wondering if he hadn't been taught something, given a lesson in priorities and clear thinking. Robins hadn't been helped, and the boat might easily have been lost. Now if when he left the Service he took a shore job, would it do the old woman the slightest good, long-term?

The parallel was a loose one, but it was there all right. It told him that he needed to acquire a capacity for ruth-lessness: not just for his own sake, but for everyone else's too. As he moved back towards the 'planesmen he heard Wishart explain to Everard, 'What I meant was, are you worried at going ahead with this now?'

There wasn't time to be worried. There wasn't time to *think* about being worried. Nick told Wishart, 'I'd be far more worried *not* to be going ahead with it.'

Burtenshaw, still pale although the boat was steady now, nodded faint agreement. Wishart looked thoughtful. 'Not a bad answer, that.'

Not bad: but *mad*?

Nick was reacting to events as if they were real – as if he'd seen Robins dead, Robins's skull crushed in the hatch, Robins's blood and brains all over Cameron: and as if he, Nick Everard, was actually going to make this attempt to blow up one of the most powerful fighting ships afloat; but he didn't believe in it, any more than someone tossing about in a half-waking nightmare believes in what he's dreaming.

'Good God, look at this!'

He focused on Hobday, who'd come up from somewhere below the table. There *was* a dream-like element… But it was a canvas parcel – bag – that Hobday had thumped down on to the table.

'Gold sovereigns, by golly!'

Wishart murmured, as if he didn't believe it either, 'I'll be damned.'

Hobday had found it in a drawer that Robins had used. Burtenshaw said he knew about it. He'd forgotten: but Robins had mentioned that he'd be taking five hundred pounds in gold for someone ashore.

Burtenshaw didn't know *who* for. They counted it: there were twenty rolls and twenty-five sovereigns in each roll.

'Better take it with you, Everard. Dare say someone'll pop up and ask for it.' Wishart glanced round at the hovering messman. 'What d'you want, Lewis?'

'Spot o' breakfast, sir?'

'Well – if you're quick with it...'

Pilchards, washed down with what Lewis thought of as coffee. Burtenshaw closed his eyes and turned away from it, although Nick warned him there was no telling when they'd next get a meal or what it might consist of. There were some jokes then, about Turk menus, which didn't make the Marine feel any better. Nick ate rapidly and hungrily, with a pistol already strapped to his side in a webbing holster, while E.57 closed in towards her appointment with the caïque.

Chapter 11

The caïque's crew certainly weren't feeding them. No food, no drink. No sign of anything like friendship either. They were sailing them into Constantinople all right, but whether they'd cut their throats before they got there or sell them to the authorities on arrival was anybody's guess.

At first Nick had hoped it was only a strangeness that would wear off, mutual suspicions that should dissipate as they all got to know each other. Now, the best part of a day later, he'd no wish at all to know them any better than he did already. There were four of them: wolf-like men with cunning, vicious faces, and all four were armed with knives. When Nick had asked for water to drink there'd been whines and finger-twisting gestures: *money...* Then unmistakable threats.

No money, no drink...

The money was in Burtenshaw's rucksack with the demolition stores. It would obviously be far too dangerous to let these people get a sniff of it.

A day of dirt, discomfort, hunger and – above all – thirst. But now Constantinople, which for hours had been a shimmer of white and green in a distant, bluish haze, was enclosing them as the caïque's sails drove her in on the southerly breeze. Three cities in one, glowing in the light of the dying sun. The mosques and minarets of Scutari to

269

starboard and Stambul to port burned like the embers of a fire; ahead lay the entrance to the Bosphorus, the gateway to the Black Sea – to Odessa, the Crimea, Batum; and on the caïque's port bow, beyond Serai Point and on the far side of another half-mile of blue water, Pera's white buildings gleamed among the dark slim cypresses. Blue water, white stone, green foliage, white sails everywhere, and the sun setting it all alight. Here to port Stambul's sea-walls showed double, reflected upside-down in the water at their feet. It was startlingly beautiful, making you believe in the most highly-coloured travellers' tales; with more immediacy one was aware that beyond this point of land – Serai – where presently the caïque would swing round on to the port tack, Galata Bridge straddled the entrance to the Golden Horn, where *Goeben* lay. A kind of Holy Grail built of grey steel, armed with eleven-inch guns, scheduled for destruction.

By two men in a sailing-boat with pistols and a bag of bombs?

It could be a mistake, Nick realised, to let the mind dwell on the sheer unlikeliness of such a hare-brained scheme succeeding. Just press on, he told himself. Like bringing a ship into a tricky, windswept anchorage in the dark: no good dithering, taking her in too slowly, or you'd just drift into *worse* danger. You had to grit your teeth, get on with it.

Burtenshaw, happy to be leaving the responsibility to Nick, was suffering now from nothing except thirst. He waved a hand in the direction of Stambul.

'Santa Sophia.'

'What?'

'That big dome with the four minarets round it. Built by the Emperor Justinian in about five hundred AD as a symbol of Byzantine Christianity. Gone Mohammedan now, of course. Hence the added minarets.'

'Where d'you get all this from?'

'Well, it's famous.' He shrugged. 'And one learnt a certain amount about the ancient world – at school, you know?'

'I didn't. Except which way Rodney turned in some battle or another… Talking about learning, though, how do you happen to talk German?'

'Ah. Well, to start with, I had an Austrian governess. And my mother's half French, so I wasn't too bad at that, and when one had reached a certain standard – at school, I mean – there was the option of doing German instead. So—'

'Are you fluent?'

'Oh, not by a *very* long chalk!'

'No…' Nick stared at the slowly passing scenery. The whole thing was hopeless. If one could have put the clock back, been back in Wishart's submarine, would one still agree to go ahead, elect to be here now?

Lunacy… And yet, how could one have backed out – having got this far, having been brought through the straits, and with Reaper back there expecting miracles?

He sighed. The thing was, to shut one's mind: move from moment to moment, not think about what was happening in any general way… He unfolded his hand-drawn map – traced from the chart of the Bosphorus – and studied it. It was enough to show the rough layout of the three cities: this entrance, with Stambul on the left and the Horn like a wide river behind it, separating Stambul

271

from Pera but with two bridges – the Galata and the Old Bridge – spanning it. Scutari was the city on the Asiatic side, over there to starboard and linked only by ferry-boats to the European shore. Simplified, the waterway could be thought of as having the shape of a capital Y. The lower part of it, the stem, was the entrance from the Marmara, the channel they were sailing up now. On the right was Scutari, and the right-hand branch of the 'Y' was the beginning of the Bosphorus. The left-hand branch was the Golden Horn, a cul-de-sac of protected anchorage dividing Stambul from Pera. That was about the sum of it.

Nick folded the map and pushed it into a pocket of the jacket they'd given him, a loose garment of stained and threadbare linen. Under it he had a sort of vest, and his trousers were sailcloth. He didn't know what he might pass for in this get-up: an Armenian horse-trader, an off-duty kitchen porter? The fez made him clearly a Mohammedan – Burtenshaw had one too, with *his* jumble-sale outfit. The caïque's captain had invited them to select garments of their choice from a heap on the cabin deck, and it had been a matter of picking out what came closest to fitting. They weren't the only living creatures in this gear, and they'd stood the greasy fezes upside down in the sun in the hope of baking out whatever forms of insect life resided in them. After the clothing issue and a parade in the open for the amusement of Aubrey Wishart at his periscope, the Turk captain had made his first demand for payment: Nick had refused it, and initial fawning had changed immediately to animosity.

He'd been thinking about the money. He told Burten-shaw, 'See if you can get a couple of the sovereigns out of the bag without our friends seeing what you're doing. And slip them to me. I'll pay them when we land.'

'Just two?'

'Someone ashore may well be expecting to get the whole five hundred, intact. And I doubt if these chaps see gold very often, anyway.'

Near Oxia Island, eight miles and several hours back, Wishart had raised and lowered his periscope three times, the prearranged signal that he was leaving them to go on alone. They'd been careful not to wave, since the crew were watching them and they hadn't wanted to advertise the fact that the escort was deserting them. Nick had pictured mentally the other end of that bronze tube, the now familiar control-room scene. It had felt like leaving home: and he'd never expected to have such feelings for a submarine! He'd heard in memory Wishart's final words: 'Best of luck, old lad. You'll make a job of it, I'm sure.'

He might have been sure!

Grey Lady: Maritza Hotel: it wasn't much to go on. Nick had counted on finding some reasonably helpful character aboard the caïque.

Coming up close to Serai Point now. On the other bow the entrance to the Bosphorus seemed to be widening as the caïque moved into the wide joint of the 'Y'. Sails flapping as the wind faltered and then returned: gear creaking. Slap of wavelets against the timber hull… Wishart had observed, not long before he'd surfaced this morning, that however hazardous the landing operation might seem, it was a fact that submariners in this Marmara had done things just as crazy, in the earlier Dardanelles campaign. Two submarines' first lieutenants, for instance, had swum ashore pushing explosives along with them on homemade rafts, and blown up railway lines under the noses of Turk soldiers. There'd been all sorts of improbable adventures. He'd added, 'Truly, you're in the best of company.'

Some of which, Nick recalled, was dead. Wishart hadn't mentioned this point, of course.

Burtenshaw pointed suddenly, and announced, 'Galata Bridge!' At the same time his other hand nudged at Nick's side. 'Here. The money.'

They'd rounded Serai Point. To their left a narrowing sheet of blue water was the approach to the Golden Horn; the Galata Bridge, straddling the 200-yard wide waterway, had its central span pulled aside. The bridge was of masonry resting on floating iron pontoons, and to open it they towed the middle ones outwards, like opening double doors. The caïque was swinging round now under rudder, and one of the crew had padded for'ard to tend its foresail as the craft turned close in around the point, almost in the shadows thrown by the walls of some kind of fort or castle. About four hundred yards to go, to that gap in the bridge: and then they'd be actually inside the Horn – with *Goeben* practically within spitting distance!

They'd have some sort of guard, surveillance of the traffic entering, surely. He turned to Burtenshaw as he pocketed the two sovereigns.

'If we get any problems like police boarding us, keep your mouth shut and give the crew a chance to talk us out of it. And do what I do.'

'What will that be?'

Of all the damn-fool questions... 'If we have to split up, rendezvous in the Maritza bar. Right?'

Burtenshaw licked his dry lips. 'Right.'

'Whatever happens, don't lose that rucksack. And don't let your pistol show.'

The Marine pulled his rubbish-heap jacket together, to hide the webbing belt. The sun was a blinding golden halo around a mosque near the south end of the bridge. Two other caïques had emerged from the opening in the bridge's centre: black silhouettes, dramatic on silver water, creeping up the northern shore towards the Bosphorus. Some steam-driven craft – tug or launch – was fussing about near the gap. The low sun was dazzling: but the tug, if that was what it was, seemed to have gone through, into the Horn… His nerves were a bit taut: they were close to the target now, the prize that had drawn them through so many obstacles, for which *Louve* had been lost, E.14 sunk – and a lot more, more distantly, an enormous lot more besides. She was *there*, somewhere beyond that bridge… He leant forward, shielding his eyes against the yellow searchlight of the sun: his throat felt as if it was lined with brick-dust. Burtenshaw, also peering towards the bridge, was humming a tune he must have picked up from Leading Seaman Morton, E.57's second coxswain. Morton was always humming it – an old sailors' ditty about a seafarer who spends a night with a girl, and, leaving her bed in the morning, gives her certain advice. The song was familiar enough to Nick, and he sang the words of the chorus now for the education of the ignorant leatherneck.

> 'Saying "Take this my darling for the damage
> I have done,
> If it be a daughter, or if it be a son;
> If it be a daughter dandle her upon your knee,
> If it be a son send the bastard off to sea—"'

He'd caught his breath: and his thoughts had flown a couple of thousand miles: to Sarah's precipitate visit to his father and to the lack of any sort of reason or explanation... He, Nick, had been with her at Mullbergh: they'd spent that night together on some other planet and in the morning he'd left – because he'd had to – and within a very few days she'd—

If it be a daughter or if it be a son...

Sarah? As ruthless as that – as decisive and guileful?

Just like that, seizing a chance so that if he, Nick, had fathered a child by his own stepmother, Sir John Everard would accept it as his own?

Burtenshaw said, 'I think they're about to shut the bridge. They would do, I suppose, at sundown. But we'll get through, all right – so long as the wind doesn't die on us, or—'

Babbling about wind... Nick told himself to think about something else: about *now*, for instance, and what the hell they were going to do when they got ashore. Maritza Hotel. Grey Lady. Find the first, ask for the second. It was all one *could* do. What had Reaper told him about the situation ashore, the general background? Reaper's calm tones drawling as they trod the oak planks in step, their hands behind their backs, turning at precisely the same moment at each end of the cruiser's quarterdeck: 'Remarkable place, Constantinople. Beautiful and sophisticated, and under the surface it's a snake-pit. Now more than ever. The Turks are – well, unpredictable. "Changeable" might be a better adjective. At the moment, luckily for Robins, they're in a flat spin.'

'Having to surrender – and the Germans there to stop them doing so, you mean?'

'They're split. Only the Young Turks are pro-German and pro-War. The Young Turks, I suppose you know, are the ruling faction. The new Sultan – old one's drunk himself to death, one hears – this young one, Vahid-ed-din Effendi – hates them like poison. Which is what they are, of course. The three top ones are Enver Pasha, Talaat Bey and Djemal Pasha. They'll do a bunk, I'm advised, once they find their German friends aren't there to protect them any longer. Enver's a small, vain man, with curly ends to his moustaches. Ruthless as a snake. Talaat's a vast brute, like a gorilla only more vicious. Djemal's the Minister of Marine – sports a heavy black beard. Enver got himself and Talaat into office by shooting their C-in-C, old Nazim, back in '13. *And* it's pretty clear he's the chap who murdered the Heir Apparent. The story they put around was that he'd killed himself – opened the arteries inside his arms – here and here, in the crooks of the elbows. But both arms at once really needs a contortionist – specially as he was lashed to a chair at the time. Those three'll have to disappear, I'd guess, or swing.'

'Will Robins – will we – find a welcome, d'you expect?'

'From the underground, yes. All the Christians, and what's left of the Armenians. The Turks have massacred most of the Armenians, or transported them. Not that there's much difference – they sent one caravan of eighteen thousand men, women and children away to Aleppo in '15, and exactly one hundred and fifty got there... But yes. I'd say we'll find plenty of co-operation when the balloon goes up.'

The caïque was inside: the bridge had been towering up, and in the last seconds it had swallowed them. Now the Turks could shut it for the night. But there were no big ships in here: certainly no *Goeben*... The crewman who'd let down the foresail sprang ashore with a rotten piece of frayed rope, passed it round a bollard and leapt back on board again: he was walking aft along the top of the gunwhale, balancing effortlessly on wide, bare feet whose thick skin must have been splinter-proof. His eyes were on the Englishmen and one hand hovered near the hilt of his knife. Two other crewmen were between them and the jetty; and the skipper was coming for'ard too now. Nick murmured, 'Strap the rucksack on, Bob.'

'Shall we ask for directions to the Maritza?'

'What, tell these thugs where we're going?'

'Oh. No – I suppose not...'

Ashore, lights were being turned on. This was Galata, and they were berthed on a stone quay not far beyond the bridge. There were other small craft about, but very little movement anywhere; it was as if with their arrival everything had suddenly closed down for the night. But against a corner of a warehouse sixty yards away, two policemen lounged, smoking and spitting: it was the sound of expectoration that had drawn his attention to them, and the gleam of light on brass buttons that revealed police-type uniforms.

Goeben was not between the two bridges, so she could only be in the larger anchorage above the second one, the Old Bridge. The distance between the two was about half a mile. Nick thought it might be their good luck that she wasn't in a Galata berth, because if she had been there'd surely have been German sentries and boat patrols all over the place. As it was, with both bridges shutting off the waterway, they probably didn't think much more protection could be necessary.

Nearer to the higher bridge, just this side of it, he could see a yacht moored alongside. She was about a hundred and fifty yards away and the flag over her stern was the Stars and Stripes. Puzzling over this, he remembered that America was not at war with Turkey.

From shorewards came the familiar sounds of urban life. Voices, hooves and iron wheels on cobbles, snatches of music, tram bells clanging, a general background hubbub with individual sounds rising from it. The caïque's skipper shuffled closer and stuck his hand out.

It wasn't a request. His three crewmen were barring the way to the jetty. Nick looked over their heads, towards the corner where the policemen had been leaning. They'd gone.

He said, holding out one sovereign towards the malevolent-looking skipper, 'You ought to be paying *us*. Here, take it.' The last words had been hardly necessary: the man had snatched the coin, examined it, and now he was testing it with his teeth. The crewmen were crowding closer and there was a mutter of what appeared to be dissatisfaction; now one dirty hand was out again and the other was gesturing, pointing at the men behind. The swift, unintelligible gabble might have been to the effect that one coin was all right for him, but what about the staff?

Nick made a show of conferring with Burtenshaw. He said, 'He can have the other one, but he's got to believe it's all we've got. Argue with me – tell me I mustn't give it to him.'

'You mustn't give it to him.'

'Damn it, can't you put some *feeling* into it?'

The Marine bawled, 'You must not give it to him, I say!'

'Well, you can go to blazes!'

Staring at each other: Nick apparently angry, and Burtenshaw bewildered. Nick glanced back at the caïque's captain, and produced the other sovereign; he also turned the pocket of his jacket inside out, as proof that there wasn't any more.

'Here. And may you break a tooth on it.' The hand clawed out; Nick muttered, 'Come on, Bob, while the going's good.' He pushed past the rabble and vaulted over to the jetty. Cobbles. 'This way. Let's not look as if we're *running away.*' All very well to *talk* like that, but as he said it he was sharply aware of his own exposed back and the knives in the crewmen's sashes. Burtenshaw, at his side, marched as if he was on parade – Beating the Retreat, perhaps – with his jaw out-thrust and eyes glaring straight ahead, arms swinging stiffly from the shoulders. He was going to need quite a lot of jollying along, Nick suspected; he told him, 'There's no one on the saluting base today, Bob.'

'What's that?'

'Relax. We aren't on a parade ground.'

'Perhaps not. But I think they're following us.'

'Oh, rubbish!'

'Just listen, then…'

Three women – dark shapes, veiled and shawled – appeared out of one of the alleys that joined the quay, and watched them as they passed. An old man popped out of an arched doorway, stared at them, shot back inside and slammed the door. Nick heard a sudden twitter from those women, and an answering growl in a man's voice: he glanced over his shoulder and caught a glimpse of the three figures huddled close together and another skulking past them, yet another showing very briefly and nearer, ten yards further this way: then there was nothing, only the women walking back the other way along the cobbled quayside and a long area of darkness in the cover of the wall, pools of it blacker still in the angles of buildings shielding alley-ways. Burtenshaw said, 'Two of them at least. I heard one call the other, or swear at him. Actually I heard them when they were coming ashore from the caïque and I thought you must have too.'

'You've got damn good ears.'

'They're closer than they were.'

The Turks, he meant, not his ears. But what to do now, Nick wondered. Stop and face them? But they'd have knives, and it would hardly be wise to use revolvers on them. Those two policemen couldn't be far off, and shots would bring them running – plus any other guards there might be in the vicinity. The crewmen following must either suspect that there'd be more gold where that sample came from or be wanting to know, for their own ulterior purposes, where their former passengers were going. They might easily draw *baksheesh* from both sides, from the Turk authorities as well as from Commander Reaper's contacts.

Make a break for it – run, hope to lose them?

No. Daft. They'd know these alleys thoroughly, and to try anything of the sort would be playing right into their hands. As well as attracting the attention of any policemen or German sentries who might be about. It was a fairly weighty problem and there wasn't much time, he felt, for dithering; then, suddenly and not far ahead, he saw the Stars and Stripes.

It was floodlit, on the yacht's ensign-staff, and her name – *Scorpion* – was painted in gold letters across her transom. In all the circumstances, he decided instantly, to pass her by would be looking a gift-horse in the mouth.

'We'll go aboard that Yank.'

'Could be a trap. How *can* there be an American—'

'They aren't at war with Turkey. And anyway, it's our only hope.' He heard the footfalls behind them, very much closer than they had been, and he grabbed the Marine's arm: 'Now – run for it!'

As he rushed to the gangway where it slanted down abreast a tall, slim funnel, his eye recorded a clean sweep of deck and a high clipper bow and twin raked-back masts. A pretty ship: and if American hospitality was what it was cracked up to be she was in the right place at the right time. He swung himself on to the lit gangway between polished brass stanchions, and Burtenshaw came pounding up the planks close behind him. As they reached the top, a large individual in the uniform of a petty officer in the US Navy stepped forward into the light.

'Far enough, till I know who you might be!'

'Friends! Allies!'

Burtenshaw had yelled it. Nick amplified, 'There are some Turks with knives chasing us. I think they intend to rob us.' But now another man had materialised from a shaded deckhouse doorway. He was tall, slim, about Nick's age, with shiny swept-back hair and spectacles that flashed in the radiance of the gangway lamps. He was dressed in immaculate evening clothes. The other man, after a word from this newcomer, had gone down to the shore end of the gangway, and could be heard now talking to one of their pursuers. It was one of the caïque's crew, all right, and he'd stopped on the edge of the pool of light down there.

The well-dressed American turned to Nick.

'That is no Turk, sir. That is a Lazz – else I'm a Dutchman.'

'A Lazz?'

'Scum of the earth. Smugglers, thieves, murderers. They'll smuggle gold out and kidnapped virgins in. Whatever you may have a hankering for, a Lazz will quote you a price for it: or if someone else pays him more, he'll cut your throat.' He listened for a while, cupping a hand to one ear; then he turned back to them, satisfied that the other man was handling the shoreside situation well enough. 'If I were to make what you might think was a somewhat personal comment, gentlemen – I wouldn't say you were dressed quite like you sound?'

Nick admitted, 'By and large I suppose we're dressed Lazz-style.'

'Allies, you did say?'

'Well, most certainly—'

'Counsellor.' The petty officer stepped off the gangway. 'We have a coupla dog-collar men headin' this way.'

'Might have known there would be.' The tall man told Nick, speaking more quickly now, 'I'm Benjamin Mortimer. This yacht is the ambassador's *stationaire*. Ambassador Morgenthau is in the States at this time, the embassy's closed during his absence and I'm sort of looking after what still has to be done... Might I assume you two are British, perhaps escaped prisoners of war, something like that?'

Nick agreed. 'Something like that.'

'Well, as you are probably aware, the United States and Turkey are not at war, and it so happens we represent British interests here when we're called upon to do so. Regrettably, that does not permit me to – ah – harbour you, as it were... They still coming, Parker?'

'Sure are.' The petty officer stepped on to the gangway and headed down towards the jetty. Benjamin Mortimer murmured, 'He'll stall 'em, but I'm the one talks their lingo... We might say you were Bulgarian soldiers – fought in Turk formations and gotten wounded, now you're fresh out of hospital, and in the goodness of my heart I'm contemplating employing you as maintenance hands aboard this yacht?'

Nick smiled gratefully. 'Your heart's good, all right.'

'Blood's thicker 'n water, I guess. Now look, though – aren't that number of Bulgarians walking around talking your kind of English. Stay dumb, eh?'

He turned away towards the quayside. Parker was coming back up the gangway. At its foot, two swarthy, fattish men in dark uniforms like the pair they'd seen earlier but with brass crescents slung across their chests were blinking upwards at the lights. Mortimer went on down, and Turkish compliments flew to and fro. Parker said, getting off the gangway, 'Special police. They have this ship under surveillance most days an' nights. Anyone comes or goes, they show up.'

'Dog-collar men, you said?'

'Says *Quanum* on them brass tags. Means "Law". They're worse'n the regular ones. Mr Mortimer pays 'em plenty not to bother us more'n they have to.'

The conversation down there still sounded polite enough. Nick commented, 'Very pretty ship, this. Do you take her to sea at all?'

'Not so often.' Parker stared at their clothes as if he'd only just noticed them. Now he noticed Nick noticing the inspection, and he politely glanced away. He nodded. 'Time o' the Spanish-American war, this little lady was a blockade-runner. Had steel armour fixed all down her sides.'

'She's used to troubled waters then.'

'You could say that.' He looked round as Mortimer, smoking a black cigar now, came back up the gangway. 'All serene, sir?'

'Well.' Mortimer waved the strong-smelling weed. 'Let's say they found it difficult not to accept the facts as I described them.'

Parker rubbed his heavy jaw. 'Ain't much they don't find it difficult not to accept.'

'They are indeed − receptive.' Mortimer smiled drily as he reached for his cigar-case. 'Care to smoke?'

They both declined. Nick said, 'What we *would* care for − if it's not overpresuming on your kindness − is something to drink.'

'Brandy? I've only a Greek variety, but—'

'Water − please?'

Hard to think about it... Burtenshaw ran a dry tongue over dry lips. 'Yes − if—' Mortimer had suddenly understood. 'Parker, whistle up that steward. Gentlemen − please, if you'd step inside...'

'Inside' turned out to be a warmly-lit saloon, all mahogany, soft carpet, oil paintings and the gleam of crystal glass and silver: and within minutes, cool fresh water trickling down one's throat. Burtenshaw sighed, 'Oh, delicious!' and poured himself another glass. Nick said, 'Can't tell you how grateful we are to you for taking such a chance on us.'

'Coupla months back, don't know I would have.' Mortimer wagged his head. 'Now – well...' He'd a tumbler of brandy and water in his fist. 'There's a rumour around suggesting your British fleet won't be long coming.'

'Let's hope rumour's right for once.' Nick asked him, 'Any rumours about a French submarine called *Louve*?'

'Sure is.' The American put his glass down. 'Towed her in right past us here, coupla days back. She's higher up – beyond where they have *Yavuz* now.'

'*Yavuz* – that's—'

Nick cut across Burtenshaw's quick excitement. 'Crew still on board *Louve*, d'you know?'

'They have them in the Military Prison. That's in the Ministry of War compound in Stambul.' He'd jerked a thumb south-eastward. 'Seems she got beached under the guns of one of their Dardanelles forts. Don't know how. Some place near this Marmara end. Her captain wasn't able to blow her up on account he had certain civilians on board and when he passed the word "abandon ship" they wouldn't budge. Too scared, I guess. And she got taken in one piece.'

Nick glanced at Burtenshaw. They'd been an odd-looking bunch, that French cloak-and-dagger party. Mortimer added, 'The civilians did 'emselves no damn good, by all accounts. Bedri Bey had 'em tortured and the word is they're dead. Bedri's old Talaat's right-hand man – and he's one mean Turk.' He looked from one of them to the other. 'Care for some'n stronger, before you leave us?'

Nick declined, but he also took the hint. 'Before we do leave you – one more bit of information? You mentioned *Yavuz* – the battle-cruiser we still call *Goeben*—'

'Well, I have to call her *Yavuz Sultan Selim*. She flies the crescent and star, and her crew wear fezes. Not my business what language they converse in. I can fly *my* country's flag here because we don't happen to be at war with Turkey. But if I had to say that ship was a goddam Fritz, well...'

Nick saw the point. 'But – is she anchored or moored out in the stream, or is she alongside?'

'The latter. They had her between buoys, but she berthed on the quayside yesterday. Last evening. Looks like she could be going someplace. Been loading stores all day, taking in fresh water, had a collier alongside top. Parker here reckons she's raising steam.'

Nick was up on his feet, trying to look as if he wasn't in a hurry. Burtenshaw, half up, was reaching for the ruck-sack which he'd kept beside him. Mortimer sank lower in his chair. Smoke drifted from his lips as he smiled gently, watching them.

'Boy, you're subtle. I'd *never* guess what brought you here. Never in a billion years.'

'One more favour.' Nick was thinking about the two dog-collar men. Somehow they'd have to get past them without being stopped and questioned. 'Tell us how we can find the Maritza Hotel?'

The American stared at him, as if he'd asked for something difficult this time. He shook his head slowly. 'I guess I better not.'

'Why—'

Mortimer took the cigar out of his mouth, and sighed. 'They raided the Maritza, last evening. Tell you the truth I wouldn't know what delayed 'em this long. *Bakhsheesh*, no doubt… Dog-collar men took off a whole load of the regular clientele, so I heard. If I were you, I'd stay clear.'

Nick stared at him while it sank in. He was thinking of *Goeben* raising steam, sailing at dawn, taking everyone by surprise again. The least he'd be expected to do was get a signal out. But without contacts, *how*?

Benjamin Mortimer had risen to his feet.

'Your intention had been to meet a friend or friends there, I might suppose.'

'Never know your luck.'

'Quite so.' The Counsellor nodded seriously. 'But it's not impossible I might be able to point you the right way – if you'd tell me the identity of the person you're hoping to locate.'

Nick wondered if he'd already said too much. You could take risks when it was just your own neck at risk – but other people's? The Grey Lady's?

Mortimer frowned.

'My credentials – if that might be what's causing you to hesitate – are flying over this ship's stern, sir.'

'I'm sorry.' He was embarrassed. 'I'm not for a moment questioning your—'

'Then permit me to make it simpler for you. Would your contact happen to be of the female sex and your own nationality?' Nick nodded. The American crossed the saloon and stooped to a bureau drawer: cigar in mouth, groping in the drawer… 'Street map here, some place…'

E.57's diesels growled steadily into the darkness, a white-flecked blackness that felt so thick with danger that you could imagine something there every time you put your glasses up; this close to Constantinople there'd *have* to be destroyer or gunboat patrols. Particularly with a flap on – the Germans knowing that at least one hostile submarine was patrolling in the Marmara – and even more so if there was any likelihood of *Goeben* breaking out to sea... The boat was trimmed down so low in the water that there was no more than her bridge to be seen; but standing on it, in these circumstances, it felt as big as a haystack and illuminated by the white foam flooding over the hull and tanks below it. One felt – in a word – conspicuous... Wishart, Jake and Ellery were on the bridge, and all three pairs of binoculars were busy all the time, lowered only for the few seconds it took occasionally to wipe lenses fogged by the sea-dew. They'd been on the surface for about half an hour now, straining their eyes to probe the night, breathing the faint reek of oil exhaust, and conscious of the closeness of the Turkish coast. The voicepipe squawked, and Jake answered it.

'Bridge.'

'Permission to rig W/T mast, sir?'

Wishart muttered an affirmative, and Jake passed it down.

But they wouldn't be transmitting. It wasn't only the breaking of wireless silence that would be bound to alert the enemy: there would also be the customary display of blue sparks from the aerial connections – a frightening piece of self-advertisement when one was as close inshore as this. Jake, sweeping with his glasses across the bow and trying to keep track of the dividing line between sea and sky, heard Weatherspoon and Agnew clattering about and muttering to themselves as they rigged the mast and aerial at the back of the bridge. Wishart called, 'Quick as you can, leading tel.'

Five men on the bridge were about three too many, in this situation.

'Aerial's rigged, sir!'

'Well done.'

Familiarity with the job made for speed. The telegraphists practised in harbour with blindfolds on and stop-watches timing them. They'd left the bridge, now.

'I'm going below, pilot.'

'Aye aye, sir.'

Now it was only himself and the signalman; both of them circling slowly, continuously. No good staring at any one point for more than a second: the eye was best at picking up a 'foreign body' as it passed over them. It wasn't the object that you saw, it was the difference between it and its dark surroundings. Over the bow, and down the starboard side; the voicepipe yelped, 'Bridge!'

'Bridge.'

'Time for the next leg to port, sir.'

'Starboard ten.' They were carrying out a programmed zigzag, and the helmsman down below watched the times for each alteration. Jake called down, 'Ease to five and steady on one-two-oh.' He straightened, raised his binoculars again, leaving Anderson to get on with it; he'd covered about ten degrees of black horizon before something glimmered white. Back on it now: it looked like a small, dim light, but he knew it was a fast ship's bow-wave.

'Dive – dive – dive!'

Racket of the klaxon – vents thudding open… Ellery was down inside and Jake followed down on top of him, dragging the lid shut and jerking its clips over, shouting to Ellery to tell Wishart, 'Bow-wave – destroyer or patrol-boat – northerly bearing about five cables, coming towards!'

Bearing and range were rough, just guesswork… He heard Wishart order forty feet, felt the angle as she tilted downwards, nosing deep; then he was off the ladder and Ellery had climbed up to shut the lower hatch; Weatherspoon reported, 'HE – true bearing oh-one-four – fast, reciprocating, closing, sir!'

'Group down, stop starboard.' Agnew repeated the orders as he clanged the telegraphs around; Hobday was getting the trim adjusted for the forty-foot depth. Glances drifted upwards as the Turk patrol craft, whatever it was, thrashed overhead. Wishart asked Jake, 'Any chance he could have seen us?'

'Doubt it, sir.'

'Fadin', sir.' Weatherspoon added, 'Bearing just west of south now, sir.'

Holding a straight course, then. Which meant he had *not* seen them.

'Twenty feet.' Wishart looked over towards the silent cabinet. 'Still on to him?'

'Just about gone, sir.'

Hobday was having to work on the buoyancy tank now, as she came up again. Jake wondered how far Nick Everard and the Marine had got. He heard Hobday order, 'Stop flooding.'

Twenty-four feet: twenty-two…

'Stand by to surface.' Wishart told Weatherspoon, 'Be ready to come up when I pass the word. You'll have to bring the aerial down and dry out the contacts, then rerig it, and I want it set up and working before we have to dive again.'

So he thought it was to be *that* sort of a night. And it would be, probably. You couldn't expect to be left undisturbed this close to an enemy port. Weatherspoon stared commandingly across the compartment at his assistant. Agnew, who'd be doing all the donkey-work with the aerial, looked fed-up and sucked his teeth. ERA Bradshaw muttered reprovingly, 'It ain't *all* beer an' baggy trousers, lad.'

'Ready to surface, sir.'

Ellery pushed the hatch open and got down off the ladder; Wishart started up it.

'Surface!'

Hobday snapped, 'Blow three, four, five and six main ballast!' He'd only blow them half out. She'd lie like a hippo with her nostrils just clear of water, practically invisible and ready to slip under again in seconds. Nobody was going to get much sleep tonight.

–

Nick and Burtenshaw had been ready to leave the yacht, but Mortimer had stopped them.

'You want to meet Bedri Bey? The dog-collar men'll be on you before you're round that corner!'

Burtenshaw looked glumly at Nick. 'Not to mention the caïque's crew. Be out there somewhere, won't they?'

'We'll have to run for it, dodge 'em somehow.'

'Wait.' Mortimer had sent for Parker, the PO. Waiting for him, he'd explained, 'He can send some of the boys ashore on a punishment fatigue. With you two in among 'em. Once you're at the bridge in the traffic, your own mothers wouldn't find you.'

Parker had rounded up a dozen volunteers. *Scorpion* had a crew of seventy men, Mortimer had told them, and twisting Turks' tails had become their favourite sport. Within minutes they were all moving off at the double, Nick and Burtenshaw in the centre of the squad. Long before they reached the north end of Galata Bridge they could see the dense tangle of carts, cabs, motors honking impatiently, and moving like glue all around and through it, a mob of pedestrians. The sailor doubling on Nick's right told him as they jogged along, 'We'll wheel left and left again on the first block up from the bridge, sir. At the second turn you go straight on up the hill. You'll be like part of the crowd there got caught up with us.'

'Very much obliged.'

'Our pleasure, sir.'

Twenty minutes later they were entering the exclusive European district of Pera. The Galata Tower had been the first landmark; then the Tokatlian Hotel, where behind plate-glass windows facing the street fat Turkish officials and pompous-looking German officers were entertaining richly-dressed, jewelled women at supper tables. Glimpses of champagne bottles in silver ice-buckets, obsequious waiters scurrying around. A bored-looking girl stared straight at Nick with an expression of disdain: he smiled at her, and saw her companion half turn in his chair and glower: he was a scrawny, beak-nosed German, something in the region of a colonel, and his anger was directed at this low-class street-lounger who'd insulted the girl with his grin... Hurrying on – and getting into smaller, confusing streets now, ten minutes later. Still quite a sprinkling of pedestrians: but all hurrying, not looking at each other, each minding his own business.

'Which?'

Burtenshaw pointed.

'How d'you know?'

'See trees through that other gap. And we had to pass between two areas of park?'

'Right.' He muttered as they started off again, 'You'd make a navigator.'

Young cypresses now, and old houses; little courtyards roofed with vines. A smell of dusty flowers: lights glimmering, passers-by fewer and flitting quickly through the quiet, near-deserted alleys.

'Left here... I think.' Burtenshaw whispered it as they paused; it wouldn't do to be heard talking English. 'The curved street, he mentioned – and the side-road across the hill behind it?'

'Right.' They were getting close now. 'Look for a courtyard entrance and trees at the back of it before the house.'

And the house would stand well back and have blue shutters and vines over a long veranda. The American had sounded as if he knew it well. The narrow curve of street was silent except for their own thudding footfalls. They stopped at an archway, tall and narrow with a curved top coming to a point. High, grey wall – and ten yards farther down, heavy wooden gates, shut. Nick slipped in through the archway with Burtenshaw close behind, looking back down the street to be sure no one had followed. Sweet-scented bushes: ahead, a cluster of feathery-looking trees stood out against the sky. The gleam of light from behind them must be coming from the house, and in the house – please God – they'd find the Grey Lady. The American had professed not to know any other name for her. He moved to the left; from the locked gates there was a carriageway to the house, and to walk along the side of it would be easier than groping through this perfumed jungle. Burtenshaw had stopped to change the rucksack from one shoulder to the other for about the sixth time; after the runs and the long uphill trek he was evidently feeling its weight. Well, *he* was the explosives expert. Approaching the trees and the house, Nick saw light pouring from an unshuttered window; he also saw what looked like an exceptionally large motor standing in front of the house. At closer quarters it turned out to be an open tourer – but a huge, swagger-looking contraption. This was the back end of it. Its long, silvery bonnet was bright and gleaming in the pool of light flooding from the window.

Burtenshaw had grabbed his arm, hissed something in his ear. Nick stopped. 'What?'

'Mercedes Benz. German!'

He thought, *Oh God, what next*... Then he rose over the quick reflex of despair: the mere presence of a Hun-made motor-car meant really nothing. Burtenshaw, he thought, tended to become alarmed too easily... There was an emblem of some kind on the motor's near-side door; Nick stooped to examine it. Beside him Burtenshaw whispered, 'That's the German eagle! Must be some official—'

'Oh, shut up!'

Think, now…

They'd raided the Maritza. And discovered there what might have led them here? In that case, the Grey Lady herself might be under arrest. But – not Germans, the raid had been made by the police, the dog-collar men, Mortimer had said. This was all guesswork: and Mortimer's account, for that matter, had been only hearsay. The thing was, Nick realised, to get a look inside the house and see who might be in occupation. If this was the Grey Lady's house and it was full of Germans, then he and Burtenshaw were on their own entirely. He began to creep quietly towards the window. His aim was to get to the side of it, keeping out of the light, and stand up slowly and look in. He was stooped like a baboon, passing between the motor and the house; he heard a sharp *click* and the headlamps sprang up like great floodlights. A man's voice shouted some sort of command.

The language matched the eagle crest. German.

Nick had frozen, with one hand covering his eyes against that blinding glare. He thought, *Finished*… Burtenshaw, right behind him, had yelped like a kicked dog and now stood facing the lights, blinking, with his hands up at shoulder-height. That shout had come from the driving-seat of the Mercedes Benz. Ten to one the Hun would have a pistol or rifle aimed at them from behind that dazzle of brilliance. He'd shouted again: and this time another German answered – from the house, behind them. But – ten to one? One chance in ten would be better than none at all, and he *might* not be armed.

'We'll have to make a dash for it.' Nick spoke out of the side of his mouth to the Marine. 'When I say *Go*, shoot at the lights and run. Out through the arch and turn left.

Make for the nearer park. I'll go right and join you later.'

You had to *move*, that was the thing. The Germans were exchanging shouts as if in disagreement over something; or they were shouting at the Englishmen and getting angry at the lack of response. Of course, Nick realised, neither he nor Burtenshaw could easily be taken for English. He asked the Marine, 'What are they saying?'

'Well – it's – it's a bit difficult to—'

A woman's voice: a stream of – Turkish?

From the house. *Grey Lady?* If so, free or captive?

'We're English! British officers!'

Clutching at straws: and giving the game away. Why had he done it? He didn't know. Except the urge to do *something...* The echoes of his shout rang through the darkness. Nobody answered: then the silence was broken by the snap of a rifle-bolt being jerked back. It convinced him that he'd blundered. He took a breath, *knowing* suddenly that this was as far as they were going to get. Then a new thought – that anything, even a bullet in the back, would be better than an interview with Bedri Bey. He murmured, 'Stand by again and be ready to run like blazes. If I don't meet you at the park try to get back to the Yanks.'

The woman's voice called again, but this time in very clear, educated English and from only a few yards away: 'English, indeed... You certainly don't *look* it.'

Chapter 12

The Grey Lady was tall, angular, authoritative. No beauty, but she had a certain charm that was entirely feminine. Forty, forty-five? About that, he thought. She wore a serge suite, and brogues; she could have been some country squire's unmarried sister, organising a village out of its mind.

She'd already had reports on the battlecruiser *Yavuz's* preparations for sea, but the raid on the Maritza had disrupted her communications system and she hadn't been able to signal Reaper.

'Not that it matters now, since your submarine is waiting to torpedo her and you've arrived to play *your* part.'

She seemed unaffected by the knowledge that she was talking to two amateurs. Nick had told her about Robins being killed, and he'd been quite open about his own and Burtenshaw's lack of experience of this kind of clandestine operation. She'd shrugged it off: *nobody* had such experience, she said, until they found themselves involved in such work. And the business before them now, of sabotaging *Goeben* alias *Yavuz*, had nothing to do with the late Lieutenant Commander Robins. She was to have put Robins in touch with a certain individual in the Sublime Porte – Turkey's 'Whitehall' – but otherwise she'd have had no dealings with him. *Goeben* was what mattered here and now.

Nick gestured towards Burtenshaw. 'Really *his* pigeon.'

'Pigeon?'

'Burtenshaw here is the explosives wizard.'

'But you are in command of the operation?'

He had to admit it. But had anyone, he wondered, ever been less qualified or trained for such command? He hadn't the least idea what he was going to do. He didn't say so now: there was a brisk impatience in her manner, a touch of steel in the large, really rather captivating eyes. Her contempt for cold feet would, he felt, be blistering. In any case, she proceeded now to solve the problem for him — casually, as if this sort of thing was only part of an ordinary day's work.

'I've sent the other two Germans — on foot, of course — to fetch uniforms for you from their barracks. You—' she looked at Nick — 'would do well to shave. You'll find a razor in the bathroom upstairs. Shaving may be less important in your case, Mr Burtenshaw, since you are not so dark and it shows less. Besides, many of the German troops are quite shabbily turned out these days. *Quite* going to the dogs.' She smiled, pleased about it. 'But you must board *Yavuz* before sunrise, which I understand is the likely hour for her sailing. You'll have little time for sleep, I'm afraid.' Another smile. 'Never mind. We all have our small discomforts, do we not.'

It was rather like sitting in some country parson's study and being briefed on a plan to rob the Bank of England. You could listen and nod agreement from time to time, but if you really thought about it — about, for instance, the intention that they should actually walk on

board a German battlecruiser within the next few hours…
Better *not* to think. The only dividends from it were cold
shivers and a sense of madness. Just listening to her was
bad enough. The Mercedes Benz outside, for instance,
belonged to the German C-in-C, General Liman von
Sanders. She'd bought it from the general's driver. The
driver and another German soldier – one who spoke some
English and acted as interpreter – were the pair who'd now
gone to steal uniforms. The third Hun, a partner of the
driver's, was outside on guard, but the Grey Lady had the
ignition-key on the table in front of her. She did not, she
said, trust Germans.

She had arranged several days ago to buy the huge
motor, not for the purposes of the present operation but
because arms dumps had been established in various parts
of the city, ready for an uprising by Christians and other
anti-German elements, which would take place before the
arrival of the British fleet. A large, fast vehicle had been
needed to tour the dumps and collect the weapons quickly
when the time came for action. She'd fixed it through
a Greek henchman of hers named Themistoclé, and her
plan now was that the motor should be used to take Nick
and Burtenshaw, dressed as German soldiers and carrying
baggage belonging to von Sanders, to *Goeben/Yavuz* just
before she sailed.

It was a very simple plan, and there was virtually
nothing that could go wrong with it, she said. Nick asked
her soberly, 'Do you really believe that?'

'Why, most certainly!' She looked genuinely surprised.
'Don't *you*?'

'Well…'

'In more normal circumstances, I agree, it might seem – perhaps reckless. But this country is in a state of near collapse, and the Germans are nearly as demoralised as the Turks. They know we have the upper hand in Europe now, and they also know their Turkish allies will round on them as soon as they can do so with impunity. As for the Young Turks – our lords and masters – well, they're said to be preparing to abandon the sinking—'

The lights went out. In here, and outside too. No gleam through the trees, no glow above the distant roofs. In pitch darkness, the Grey Lady laughed delightedly. Nick wondered if she might be off her dot.

'What a perfectly *splendid* coincidence!' She laughed again. 'I was on the point of mentioning that the Young Turks are rumoured to be getting ready to make a bolt for it – and in fact only this afternoon I was told that a plan had been laid for the fuses at the power-station to be drawn for an hour or two tonight, in order to facilitate the departure of those frightful rogues Enver, Talaat and Djemal. And – lo and behold!'

Nick murmured, 'Not beholding much, myself.' Burtenshaw asked, 'Doesn't this mean it's good as ended? The war – at least Turkey's—'

'Hardly *that*. I should say it marks the *beginning* of the end, and that it should gready help the progress of the armistice negotiations… Did you know that discussions were in progress?'

They'd heard nothing of that sort, Nick told her. He explained to Burtenshaw, 'We still have to dish *Goeben*. Long as she's in fighting trim she could stop the Turks signing any armistice. She could keep us out, too – stop our minesweepers getting in, to start with.'

'Very true.' A match flared: they saw her face close to it, its harsh light darkening her deepset eyes, deepening the lines in face and neck. Then the gentler glow of candle-light spread through the room and she'd blown out the match, lost ten years of age and become softer, feminine again. Leaning towards the candle, peering at a little watch on a loop of chain: 'High time those wretches were back here… Lieutenant Everard, you did not by any chance bring with you a parcel of sovereigns?'

'Why yes, we did.' Burtenshaw stooped to grope in his rucksack. Nick told her, 'We didn't know what it was for. But if it's intended for you…'

'Only too glad.' Burtenshaw put the canvas bag on the table. 'Weighs a ton.'

'Heavier the better!' She whisked it away, to a cupboard. Nick apologised, 'Two sovereigns short, I'm afraid. We had to pay the caïque's skipper something or they'd have cut our throats.' She frowned at that; then she explained, 'I was forced to pay three hundred for the motor. Exorbitant, of course; but they wanted *five* hundred to start with, and of course Themistoclé takes his commission. I could only scrape up a hundred, and I promised them the rest of it would be here within a day or so. So when you told me of Commander Robins's death…' She sighed, and smiled; you could see she'd been worrying about it. Nick was impressed by her not having mentioned the money until now. He told her, 'We'd have lost it very quickly if the caïque's crew had had a sight of it.'

She had already apologised for the Lazz fishermen. Faced with the sudden emergency when she'd had Reaper's distress call, she'd had to give Themistoclé his head, and that had been his easy answer to the problem. She said, 'They're all *so* mercenary. And once a German decides to sell out – well...' She sighed. 'There'll be a price on the uniforms, of course, too.' She'd glanced up at them, smiling suddenly: 'I have a bottle of Kirsch here, if you'd care for some. *Also* from the Germans, I might say. Shall we have a glass now, while supper's cooking?'

Supper was a mutton *pilaff*, followed by bread with a kind of raisin jam called *pekmes*. She apologised for so strange a meal; food-rationing and shortages were a curse, and a cause of unrest particularly in the poorer quarters of the town. She introduced Celeste, the young girl who'd cooked the *pilaff*, as one of about sixty convent girls, mainly of French parentage, whom she'd rescued from Bedri Bey's intention of turning them out into the streets. It would have meant the brothels. She'd found safe homes for all of them. Nick gathered, from as much as she told them, that by standing up to such moves as this openly and fearlessly she'd won the authorities' respect, or at least their tolerance, while her charitable work among the poor had not only made her well liked in the city but had also cloaked her more clandestine activities.

He'd dozed off. He came-to once, to hear argument or hard bargaining in progress between their hostess and the Germans. Then – only minutes later, it seemed – she was waking him and the electric lights were burning.

So it *hadn't* been a dream?

'Time to put on these dreadful uniforms. They won't fit at all well, but we can't expect miracles.' Dressing, he'd still been muzzy with sleep and a kind of horrified disbelief, but returning to the living-room he'd found more of Celeste's thick, aromatic coffee ready, and it had brought him back to life – in no kind of comfort, but more or less clear-headed.

The Grey Lady showed them two heavy leather suitcases. Her manner was brisk but entirely calm, and the effect of it, Nick found, was steadying.

'These belong to von Sanders. Quite a *nice* man, really. No business at all being German. See – his name on them. One each to carry – otherwise they might wonder why there should be two of you. How fortunate that you should speak German, Mr Burtenshaw.'

Nick was wondering how much German the Marine *did* speak.

They were to go on board as the general's personal servants. Ostensibly coming from so high an authority, they'd almost surely be let by without question. Germans were like that, she said. As a matter of fact, we English were like that too. Herman, the driver, who was a familiar figure behind the wheel of the easily-recognised official motor-car, would declare at the gangway that he was delivering the Herr General's baggage as previously arranged. Nick and Burtenshaw would haul it up the gangway, and once inside the ship they – presumably – would know what to do. Herman would wait on the quay until nobody much was looking at him, and then drive away, and when anyone noticed that he'd gone they might assume the baggage porters had gone too.

Burtenshaw was speechless: numb – Nick thought – with fright.

As a target area for the explosive charge Nick had first thought of the midships torpedo flat. If a biggish amount of guncotton could be detonated close against a torpedo warhead, or better still in the warhead store, the results might be rewarding. But access would not be easy. It would be four or five decks down and through armoured hatches, well below the waterline. Modern German warships were honeycombs of small compartments all subdivided from each other: this was why they tended to remain afloat even after substantial damage... On reflection, he'd decided it might be best to go for the steering compartment, right aft and in the bottom of the ship. To set the charge off there probably wouldn't sink her, but with smashed steering gear she'd be immobilised, which would be enough for Reaper's purposes. It would also make her a sitting duck for Wishart.

He asked the Grey Lady how she could be sure Herman wouldn't blow the gaff once she'd paid him.

'He has at least as much to lose as you have, Lieutenant. He'd be shot out of hand.' She was looking them both over, as that triggered another thought; she murmured, 'Such a pity you haven't your own uniforms to wear under those dreadful suits.'

Nick caught the reference: the possibility of being shot. To be caught dressed as German soldiers would qualify him and Burtenshaw for 'out of hand' treatment, too... But they were starting now, actually walking out of the house. The guncotton, divided between the two cases, weighed very little. Climbing into the back of the car... If ever there'd been a truly madcap scheme, it was this one: and he, Nick Everard, was in command of it! Panic flared: but there was no *time* for panic... He told Burtenshaw as the Mercedes Benz backed out into the road with one of the Germans yelling advice to Herman, 'Once we're up the gangway, turn aft as if we're heading for the admiral's quarters where the luggage is supposed to go. Then duck inside and out of sight. We'll need to get right aft and down as many decks as she's got – that'll be the deuce of a long way down.'

They were out in the road and the other Hun was shutting the gates. Herman sent the big motor trundling along the narrow curve of street. Nick added more advice: 'And keep well closed up. If anyone questions us, say we're looking for the store for General Liman von Sanders's baggage. Naturally *you'll* do all the talking, if any has to be done.'

Burtenshaw, white-faced, turned and looked at him. 'You don't honestly think we can get away with this, do you?'

'Not get away with it?' Nick hoped his astonishment looked real. 'But why shouldn't we?'

The Marine shrugged. He looked away again, keeping his mouth shut tight as if he couldn't have trusted himself to speak again. At the end of the street they'd turned downhill across the intersection, and now the driver eased his wheel over to slant away north-westward, switching to the road that led down to the quayside on that higher reach of the Golden Horn. Motoring down to the Horn, for heaven's sake – to *Goeben* herself… No daydream either, the action had started and there was no way of stopping it. High above them, somewhere off to the right, a *muezzin* greeted the dawn, bearing witness in a raucous chant to Allah's greatness, calling the Faithful to their daybreak devotions. Visualising the robed figure aloft on some minaret that he couldn't see from the rumbling motor, Nick was reminded of a diving platform high above the Dart, a plank protruding from a hulk's side, and himself aged thirteen on the end of it. It was a very high board and until he'd got out on it he hadn't appreciated how far below the water would be. Looking down at it had brought a chill of fear: an instructor's bellow had floated up to him – 'What are ye waitin' for, the tide?' The only way off that platform had been over its edge, into the gulf: and it was just like that now. *Oh Sarah, my darling...* What had sent her image into his mind? What about her anyway – suddenly even his own feelings were uncertain, whether he regretted, would have put the clock back if that had been possible, undone what had been done... *Would* one? There'd been no moment of decision, no conscious act: it had happened, as something natural and inevitable: for both of them, he thought, it had been like that. And no, he did *not* regret it, because if it had not happened there'd have been an ingredient missing, something that was important now. Might she feel the same? And if the reason for her rushing to join his father in London was the one he'd guessed at, how would it seem to her – if it had all happened, and she'd buried the truth so well – as time passed, how would it be for her?

The possibility that she'd keep the secret even to the extent of never discussing it with *him* was a new and startling concept. It had sprung, of course, as an answer to the puzzle about those letters she'd written – the attitude of detachment, mild stepmotherly affection... If it turned out that he was guessing correctly now, receiving finally the message that she'd been trying to impart to him, would he be able to play that game, act as if nothing had ever happened between them? Could so large a lie be so firmly established that to all intents and purposes it would become the truth?

Burtenshaw's voice croaked beside him, 'It's – God, it's *hopeless*!'

'What is?'

He wouldn't have to tell any lies, or live one. He couldn't, he knew, possibly survive this – Burtenshaw was right, this *hopeless* operation. Gleam of water ahead: dawn's silver on the Golden Horn. That dark mass rising against godown rooftops was smoke – a big ship's funnel-smoke. Burtenshaw answered him: 'This stunt, this attempt to blow up a—'

'God's sake, man, who'd have thought this time yesterday that we'd get *this* far?' He wished at once that he hadn't said that. One shouldn't admit to *any* doubt. He added, 'You'll feel better when the action starts.'

The motor's tyres thrummed as Herman turned without slackening speed around the corner of an ugly red-stone building. Port offices of some kind. Now the tyres sang on cobbles. Quayside: a wide area like a square in a small market town. The water was right ahead, its black sheen broken by the silhouette of a waiting tug. There was a graving dock between the waterfront and the building on their left. But they'd swung right, behind a long cargo shed with chains on its doors and a stink of wet hides in the air around it. Near the farther end of it, Herman turned his head and shouted, pointing a gloved hand towards the left; then he had both hands back on the wheel and he was leaning sideways in the effort of turning the Mercedes around the end of the warehouse and towards the quay.

At the same moment, almost like a fanfare greeting their appearance, Nick heard a bugle-call. The Prussian equivalent of a *muezzin*, he realised, a Hun sun-up ceremony. Shades of a dreary youth-time spent in Scapa Flow! On *Goeben*'s stern the black cross with the eagle in its centre would be mounting the ensign-staff. Guard and band to welcome them, now? By God, there was! A double rank of guard with rifles at the 'present', right aft on the great expanse of quarterdeck; and the band was striking up now, brass instruments cocked up under the looming barrels of the after eleven-inch turret. All the Germans were wearing fezes. The band had thumped out its short ditty and the bugles blared what must have been their form of 'carry on'; rifles were thudding to the 'slope', a rippling flash as the ranks of bayonets swayed over and the dawn light caught them, silvery-pink light glittering across the *Halic*, the Golden Horn. Looking upwards, he saw that at the main *Goeben* was flying a broad-pendant with a black cross on it, a commodore's flag.

No vice-admiral then, on this trip?

They were rumbling straight towards the after gangway, which led up to the quarterdeck near the stern turret. A point he'd over-looked in his thoughts of where to place the charge struck him as he stared up at the ship's impressive twenty-three thousand tons of fighting power: since there'd be a bow torpedo room and a stern one in addition to the torpedo flat amidships, it might be possible to get close enough to the after one to blow the whole back-end off her. Drums were beating a tattoo now, boots crashing on oak planking as the quarterdeck was cleared, guard and band marched for'ard. All horribly familiar from one's own big-ship days: a slightly different, foreign flavour to it, but otherwise much the same. He leant forward and tapped Herman's shoulder, pointed at the other gangway, up near the first funnel.

'That one. Stop *there.*'

Herman was used to driving his general and other senior officers, who invariably would be received on quarterdecks. He was chauffeuring private soldiers now. Lights still burned somewhat unnecessarily at the tops of both gangways. Officers on *Goeben's* quarterdeck stared down at them; the quay was shadowed here by the ship's bulk. As they passed the bottom of the after gangway Nick saw a one-stripe officer in front of a single rank of men with bayonets on their rifles. He looked ahead, at the gangway they'd be stopping at: there was a similar guard at the foot of that one too. Mustering sentries, perhaps, men recalled from posts elsewhere on the quayside. He saw Burtenshaw staring at the bayonets as if he was mesmerised by them: he looked sick. The motor stopped, and Nick muttered, 'Come on.' He pushed the door open, grabbed one suitcase, and stepped out on to the running-board and down on to the cobbles, wet from the sea-dew of dawn. Glancing back, he saw the Marine standing, holding the other case and staring up nervously towards the ship. Turning, Nick saw a two-striper coming down the gangway with his eyes fixed on them and far from friendly.

'*Was is das?*'

One didn't have to be a linguist to get the drift. He was pointing at the suitcases and he wanted to see inside them. Nick was thinking, *Caught. Already. Well, it was a pretty hopeless thing to have tried.* He grinned, as a dim-witted soldier might, and turned the case so that the German could see von Sanders's name on it; then Burtenshaw, joining him quite suddenly as if he'd that moment snapped out of a trance, stared rather haughtily at the

Kapitan-leutnant and let rip with a string of German. Nick swung round, astonished; afterwards he realised that his open-mouthed surprise must have been goofy enough to have matched the earlier grin. The *leutnant* shrugged, and pushed past them on his way to muster the squad of sentries: and the gangway was unguarded, reaching up into the great grey ship above them.

It felt about as long as Piccadilly: and as exposed as a high-wire in a circus. Burtenshaw was leading: he'd taken the initiative on the quayside and it looked more natural for him to go up first. Halfway up Nick told him, 'At the top, slant right, go in the screen door and take the first ladder downward.' Burtenshaw nodded. The head of the gangway rested a few yards for'ard of the foremost of the battlecruiser's secondary armament of six-inch guns on this starboard side, and the screen door led into the ship at the lowest level of her bridge superstructure. Stumbling up the ribbed slope behind the Marine, Nick was trying to work out the probable location of the beam submerged torpedo flat. It had to stretch clear across the ship, in order to have one tube on either beam, so it had to be somewhere where there was no gun-turret, since the lower parts of each turret, ammunition hoists and so on, extended right down to the bottom of the ship. And with the layout of *Goeben's* main armament that really left only the area below the bridge – roughly, therefore, this point of entry. Which would be excellent, because the sooner the charge was placed, the better; and the torpedo flat, with its own explosive content and its location below the waterline, would be a splendid place for guncotton.

Burtenshaw was off the gangway, crossing the ten feet of steel deck towards the open screen door. Now he'd paused, glancing back over his shoulder; Nick passed him and led the way inside.

There was a ladderway leading upward, another downward, and a transverse passageway over to the port side. Guessing there'd be the same up-and-down ladder system duplicated over there and that on the outboard side there might be less coming and going, Nick went straight ahead. And he'd guessed right: there was a matching down-ladder leading through an open rectangular hatch and with a taut chain for a handrail. He went down it quickly, with Burtenshaw's German boots close above him clumping on the steel treads. At the bottom they were in a fore-and-aft passageway with various doors leading off it and dim lights glowing on the painted bulkheads; and they were still well above the waterline. A group of sailors came by, hurrying, glancing at the soldiers curiously as they passed. One of them shouted something that made others laugh, and Burtenshaw waved his free hand, grunted in a friendly way. Five minutes ago he'd seemed to be a dead loss; now, he was worth his weight in diamonds. Nick clapped him on the shoulder: 'Marvellous… We need to get down a couple more decks. Perhaps three.' The head of the next ladderway was a dozen feet aft: they clattered down it, clutching their cases of explosive. Ladders and passages were narrower than in large British ships and deckheads were much lower: had one been a claustrophobiac, Nick thought, one might well feel uncomfortable, down here. More so, oddly, than in the submarine. Burtenshaw panted, close behind him, 'This is absolutely – *impossible*, it's—' and Nick cut him short: 'Don't think about it. Too late for thinking.' He thought it might be the key to Burtenshaw: keep him moving, doing. Well, it might be the key to anyone. Down another ladder, and he thought they'd be roughly at the water-level now. He was stepping off the ladder when a hand grasped his arm.

A petty officer: the insignia suggested some engine-room rate. He'd barked a question – loudly but in quite a friendly, semi-amused manner, something like *Where the hell d'you think you're going?* Nick let his lower jaw sag, assuming a baffled expression which was less a matter of acting than of having no other way to react, and Burtenshaw came up trumps again, saying they were searching for the officers' baggage store. He showed the PO the name on the cases: the man's eyebrows rose and fell, and he looked vaguely contemptuous – perhaps to make up for the fact that for the moment he'd been impressed – as he jerked a thumb, told them to get back up three levels and then right aft; and get a move on, or they'd find themselves at sea… He'd pushed them towards the ladder, one hand on each. By the time they were halfway up it, though, he'd moved away for'ard and swung a bulkhead door shut behind him, and they started down again. They were below the waterline now, and the lower they went in the ship the hotter, clammier it got. Inside the coarse uniform, Nick was already streaming wet. He muttered to Burtenshaw, 'Your German gets by, all right'; the Marine made a face, as if he wasn't all that sure of it.

Where this ladder ended – it took them into the centreline of the ship, port and starboard ladder-systems combining – was an entrance for'ard to a messdeck, and a transverse passage with humming machinery behind steel-mesh cages, and over on the port side another passage of some sort led aft; but at this point there was no way on down. The messdeck, however, was deserted, and a short way inside it was a closed hatch.

'See what's down here.'

Better than dithering about: and the sooner they got this stuff planted, the better.

Only two clips held the hatch shut. Nick loosened them by kicking the butterfly nuts round with his heel, and Burtenshaw knocked them off; then they pulled the hatch up, and Nick slid through on to the ladder. Dim lighting, and a peculiar smell that was in a way familiar and yet out of place, seemed not to belong. Thrum of machinery: not down here, but aft, trembling through the ship. Moving off the quay? There'd be help from tugs until she was out clear of the floating bridge. Here was a wet-smelling, odd-smelling, cramped steel flat, and on his left at the ladder's foot was a hammock-netting – a railed enclosure like a stall in a cattle-market – full of hammocks and kitbags. Near it a door, which he opened, and found himself looking into a bathroom flat, or washplace. Steel basins, lavatories, lagged pipes, and a grating overhead with the whirr of fans sounding from it. Burtenshaw mutterered, 'No torpedoes. Just—'

'What's that say?'

Outside, and on the far side of the ladder, a small, elliptical door was set high in the after bulkhead, and there were German words stencilled in red beside it. Burtenshaw translated, 'Entry forbidden except to authorised personnel on duty'. There was a padlock on one of the retaining clips, and it was about two inches thick. Nick thought this might well be a way into the torpedo flat. Almost certainly there'd be something in there worth damaging, and the odds were that it would be explosive.

It might, he thought, be the torpedo warhead store, connecting to the flat itself on the other side. In any case it was as good a bet as any. Then, looking round, he saw the concrete.

This was what he'd smelt. It was the bulkhead nearest to the ship's side, beyond the hammock netting. They'd painted it grey, which was why he hadn't noticed it at first, particularly in this rotten light. It was a concrete lining to the real bulkhead, and the only possible explanation was that this was how, with the extremely limited repair facilities here at the Golden Horn, they'd repaired the ship's action damage – quite possibly mine-damage sustained during her last sortie, when she'd sunk the monitors in Kusu Bay.

It was a perfect spot for the explosion. Smash through that concrete, and you'd be blasting into previous – existing – damage.

'Set your charge up.' He put his case down. 'I'll make a space for it.' He began to drag hammocks out of the netting, dumping them temporarily against the ladder. They'd be useful, to tamp down the charge as well as to hide it... Working fast, before someone might come down and catch them at it. 'Quick as you can, Bob.' Burtenshaw had the cases open and he was piling all the guncotton into one, lashing the whole lot together with tape, in the shape it had been in before they'd divided it. Nick pulled out one more hammock, leaving a hole deep enough to drop the charge right down into the angle between deck and bulkhead – the concrete one. He looked round again: Burtenshaw had taken a detonator out of a little tin that held half a dozen of them, and he was fixing one end of the white coil of fuse into it, squeezing it tight with pliers and then sliding the detonator into the middle of the charge, with a loop of tape around the fuse to hold it in place. He looked up.

'Ready.'

'Light it, then.'

'Right.' His hands were shaking as he set it going. For a moment nothing happened, then the end of the fuse glowed red and began to fizz. He shut the case: then hesitated, opened it again. 'Best not have it airtight. Might put it out.' Nick helped him lower the suitcase with its lid slightly open into the nest among the hammocks and other gear, and then they piled the rest back in on top of it.

Done. And if they could get well away from this part of the ship, it would be a thousand to one against the thing being found before it went off. Burtenshaw murmured, as if struck suddenly by the enormity of what they'd been doing, 'It's a *huge* charge.'

'Good.' Nick turned to the ladder, and picked up the other case. 'Back up now, up at least two decks, then aft. Far away from here as possible.'

'I'm – with you there.' He'd actually smiled. Nick told him, 'You lead. If we're stopped again, ask to be directed to the admiral's quarters.'

'Couldn't we get right up on the upper deck?'

'Not yet, anyway… Up you go.'

How would one explain an empty suitcase with two men to carry it? Not easily, he thought. But the general's name might pull a certain amount of wool over Teutonic eyes. They'd reached the top of the second ladder; he answered Burtenshaw's backward glance with a nod. 'Up one more, then turn right.' Climbing again: and the ship was definitely under way, the machinery noise a steady, throbbing hum. He wished they *could* have gone up top, into fresh air and where they could see what was happening; it occurred to him that while they'd been down in that empty messdeck they should have borrowed some sailors' gear instead of the field-grey they were wearing so conspicuously. *Damn…* Worth going back, he wondered? Dressed as sailors, in a ship with a complement of about a thousand men, you could hide for ever, with any decent ration of luck… But he decided against it: now, leaving harbour, all the hands not working would be fallen in, lined up on the upper deck and fully fezed, no doubt; but at any moment *Goeben* would be out clear of the Galata bridge and the hands would be dismissed and go pouring down the ladders. The possibility of being caught down there where they'd placed the charge wasn't one that could be taken. Tramping aft now, boots ringing on the steel deck. The ship had a sparse, stripped-down look: when you looked closely you saw that there was nothing inflammable anywhere, only bare steel, not a stick of wood in sight. A ship intended for fighting, not for living in. Bulkhead doors on either side at intervals, with high sills: machinery noise getting louder as they went towards the stern. Now and then a sailor glanced at them, muttered something as they squeezed past, or stared through an open doorway: all right so far, but luck had some limit to it: and God, Nick recalled suddenly, helped those who helped themselves. Helped themselves to sailors' uniforms – from some other messdeck? Now, quickly, while there was still a chance and before the hands were sent below?

'Hey, Bob.' Burtenshaw looked round. Nick beckoned him: 'Down here.'

Back into the great ship's guts. There'd be messdecks pretty well all through her, for'ard of the machinery spaces. So the route had to be downward and certainly no further aft. He explained, 'We must find another messdeck and swap this gear for sailor-suits.' One could see that the idea didn't much appeal to the Marine. And he himself was aware of two obvious dangers in it. One: being caught in the act of stealing the uniforms and shifting into them; the answer to it was to be very quick, get it done before the ship relaxed into watchkeeping routines. Two: there was a risk that the theft might be discovered and the soldiers' uniforms found, and an alarm raised. But it was still a better chance, he thought, than continuing to parade around in these clowns' outfits. He led the way down: into a wider passageway with a row of doors with German labels on them. Officers' cabins? Not far enough aft for that, surely. Offices, perhaps. Not wanting to waste time in asking Burtenshaw to tell him, he'd turned for'ard, looking for another down-ladder: and a voice barked, '*Halt!*'

Burtenshaw, behind him, gasped.

It was the *Kapitan-leutnant* who'd come strutting down the gangway and looked like stopping them and then, at the sight of Liman von Sanders's name on the cases, thought better of it. There was a one-striper – *Oberleutnant?* – and also an older man, some kind of senior rating, with him.

'*Ziegen Sie hier! Aufmachen!*'

Burtenshaw was stuttering uselessly: his nerve had gone, and so apparently had his linguistic powers. It seemed to be the suitcase again that the German was interested in. Burtenshaw looked round despairing at Nick, then back at the trio advancing on them. Nick snapped, 'Here, quick…' He turned back towards the ladder they'd just come down; but the CPO, whatever he was, barred his way, while behind him the other two had grabbed Burtenshaw and the empty case.

Chapter 13

'Smoke, all right. Lots of it.'

Wishart, hunched at the for'ard periscope, muttered it to himself. Hobday, who'd been keeping the periscope watch ever since they'd dived before first light, and who'd spotted the smoke and shaken Wishart, was terrier-like with excitement.

Goeben?

'Port ten.'

'Port ten, sir… Ten o' port wheel on, sir.'

That was Louis Lewis at the wheel. Finn was on the fore 'planes and Morton, stripped to his bulging waist and as usual shiny with sweat, was on the after ones. Depth-gauges showing twenty feet. Wishart told Lewis, 'Steer oh-three-nine.'

'Oh-three-nine, sir.'

It was the bearing of the Horn, according to a fix Hobday had taken a few minutes ago. Jake, disturbed by the flurry of activity, had rolled out of his bunk and sloped over to the chart. Distance to the Horn nine point five miles. If *Goeben* was coming out she could be passing over this spot in half an hour.

Wishart was taking a careful all-round look. No good getting excited about a target and letting some patrol boat jump on you from the other direction. No good getting

320

excited anyway – not even if it did turn out to be *Goeben*; and the odds were heavily against that dream coming true so fast. The smoke might be from a factory or a fire or from a freighter of some sort. Jake, slumped across the chart table, begged silently *Please God, let it be Goeben.*

Wishart was motionless again, with the periscope trained on that north-easterly bearing. All their eyes on him – on as much of his facial expression as was visible. Faces ready for disappointment, but with hope in them too. Wishart glanced sideways, at Hobday's sharp alertness.

'Close the hands up, Number One.'

'Diving stations!'

A swift, quiet rush of men… They'd gone to diving stations a thousand times, and quite often there'd been some degree of tension or expectancy. This was different: if you hadn't known it, Jake thought, watching them as they settled to their jobs, you'd have read it in their faces.

Goeben: the big one, the one they'd come for, through steel nets and minefields.

'I want a word with Rinkpole.'

'Pass the word for the TI!'

CPO Rinkpole came aft looking interested but calm. He was too old a hand to get excited all that quickly. Wishart stepped back from the periscope and McVeigh sent it hissing down.

'TI – presently we'll stand by all five tubes. That means your chaps'll have to slap it about a bit.'

Rinkpole ran a horny hand over the dome of his head. 'Aye aye, sir.'

'She's worth everything we've got. If we get the chance to use it. But we certainly shan't get *two* chances.'

'One'll do us, sir.'

'Yes.' Wishart nodded. 'All right, TI.' He looked towards McVeigh and moved his hands slightly, and the periscope came rushing up. Rinkpole went aft to lecture his beam- and stern-tubes' operators – Finn with stokers Lindsay and Burrage amidships, and Smith assisted by Peel in the after ends. Hobday was using the trim-line to get her back in balance after the move to diving stations. Trim would be vital now: if you lost control during an attack you could lose your target: and the effort of the entire operation felt cumulative now – minefields, nets, near-suffocation, *everything*, building towards this coming moment in which you'd hit or miss. To miss was in fact unthinkable, and Hobday wanted his trim right to the nearest half-point. From that point of view, Rinkpole's meanderings through the boat were a nuisance. Wishart was circling quickly; he paused to check the bearing of the smoke and then began another circle much more slowly in high power. Back on the smoke: a long, careful study of it, while the low eastern sun blazed down the tube and threw discs of fire into his eyes.

'Down periscope. Half ahead both.' He looked fleetingly at Jake and told him, 'The bearing's steady.' Jake had the stop-watch ready on his plotting diagram, instruments and sharpened pencils at hand. It was extraordinary how brittle pencil-leads became in times of stress. The fact of the target's bearing being steady could mean that E.57 was in the right place; alternatively, and if this *was* their target, that she hadn't cleared Seraglio Point yet. In which case she might alter course sharply as soon as she was clear, and then the submarine might be in very much the *wrong* place.

It would, anyway, be quite a while before they knew for certain what sort of a hand they were being dealt: and slightly longer than that, even, before they'd be in a position to attack.

–

Burtenshaw had finally regained the power of speech, and asked to be directed to the admiral's quarters. The request had seemed to annoy the *kapitan-leutnant*, who'd had them frogmarched to the lower bridge instead. There he and the ship's captain had questioned them. The captain was a tall, angular man with hooded, birdlike eyes; he wanted to know where was the other suitcase and what had been inside the empty one. He spoke reasonably good English, and Burtenshaw didn't have to translate as he'd been doing for the other man, the two-striper.

Two sailors with bayonets on their rifles guarded them from the rear while the questioning continued. Burtenshaw had said he didn't know *what* had happened to the other case; the captain swung round to fix his sharp stare on Nick.

'You; *you* will tell me. *Kapitan-leutnant* Heusinger has reported that you came with two cases from the shore. Now we see only one case. Where is the other one?' Nick looked surprised. 'Other one?'

The expression turned colder.

'You know that I can order you to be shot, since you are not wearing your own uniform?'

'Well…' He was about to say something about the end of the war being imminent, and how pointless it would be – which seemed rather a weak argument unless he could frame it better – when he saw the commodore arriving.

A medium-sized, intelligent-looking man in his middle or late forties; he had a face that could easily have been English. The captain saw Nick's glance shift, and looked round; then he drew aside, making way for the senior man.

'Which of them is Everard?'

The question had been put in German, but Nick heard his own name. He was taking a quick check on the surroundings as the land fell away astern; the ship was under helm, altering from a course of south-southwest to about west-south-west. A course which would take her, he hoped, to where Aubrey Wishart should at this moment be waiting for her. And if the Germans could be stalled for that length of time, he thought, if they could be dissuaded from ordering up the firing squad until E.57 got her attack in, the execution might with any luck be postponed indefinitely. They'd be within their rights to do it, certainly, and he thought bird's-eyes quite likely would have; but this commodore had rather a gentle-manly, civilised look about him.

Goeben's captain had returned to his bridge. The commodore, flanked now by the *kapitan-leutnant* and a young commander — rather, *corvetten-kapitan* — was staring at him interestedly.

'Your father is Admiral Sir Hugh Everard, perhaps?'

'No, sir. That's my uncle.'

'Indeed.' The commodore nodded. 'You should be proud of such an uncle.'

'Yes.' Nick nodded. 'I am.'

'I should regret very much to be forced to deprive him of a nephew. Or to deprive you, of the possibility of following in his footsteps in your Royal Navy.'

His English was almost perfect, with only the slightest trace of accent. Coupled with his appearance and pleasantly affable manner, it felt as if one was having a friendly chat with a fellow countryman.

But the affability was fading.

'As I have heard Captain Steinhoff remind you, you *are* in a position to be shot, you know. And since we are not particularly stupid we must believe that your other portmanteau contained some kind of explosive charge. It would spare me the discomfort of ordering your execution if you were to tell me where it had been placed. The ship is being searched, of course, and it is probable that we will find it quite soon in any case; I am simply giving you this opportunity to save yourself...' Glancing at Burtenshaw: '*Yourselves*, I should say. How do you decide?'

'There's nothing I can tell you, sir.'

The German looked at Burtenshaw.

'You, sir?'

Burtenshaw shook his head. The commodore sighed, and asked the *kapitan-leutnant*, 'I am told you have an idea of the approximate location?'

'That is correct, Herr Commodore. The point of entry was at the for'ard gangway with two cases, and taking that into consideration with the place where they were apprehended with only *one* case I believe the other must be somewhere amidships, roughly.'

'And below the waterline, of course.'

The *kapitan-leutnant* agreed. The commodore added, 'The explosion, moreover, might occur at any time.' He looked thoughtful, not at all worried. In spite of what he'd just said – which was true, the charge *could* explode at any moment... Nick wondered how long that fuse was: it was a point which, in the tension and rush of getting aboard and placing the charge, he hadn't raised. Meanwhile, the commodore was a man in full control of himself as well as of his surroundings, he'd know the fuse would be burning and that getting excited wouldn't slow it. But there was anger in him too – and – as he turned his head and stared at Nick – menace, suddenly. Quiet menace, much more frightening – if one gave way to fright – than rage or threats would have been. He was a quiet man who worked logically: and cold logic wasn't noisy, any more than a snake was before it struck – well, *most* snakes... He'd nodded slightly as he reached a conclusion, and now he'd swung to face the man with three stripes.

'My compliments to Captain Steinhoff, and I suggest that all men not essential to the working of the ship below decks should be brought up. These two—' one hand gestured towards Nick and Burtenshaw – 'are to be confined below, amidships, in the bottom of the ship. You—' glancing sideways at the *kapitan-leutnant* – 'will go with them. Should they attempt to escape, you will shoot them dead. If on the other hand they should decide to disarm or remove their bomb from wherever it may be, you will permit them to do so and then bring them back here. Is that understood?'

–

Jake Cameron had fingers crossed on both hands. He heard the soft thump as McVeigh pushed the telemotor lever to 'raise' and the tube began its upward slither; then the sound of the handles clicking down as Wishart grabbed them. Glancing back over his shoulder he saw the skipper circling, checking the surroundings before he settled on the crucial bearing. Rinkpole passed through the control room on his way for'ard.

'Ah…'

The men whose jobs allowed them to watch Wishart brightened suddenly as they caught the sudden gleam of pleasure in his face. He said, 'I can see her foretop. It's *Goeben*. Stand by all tubes. Down periscope.'

McVeigh sent it down like a shiver of yellow light. Everyone taut with excitement now. Anyone of them would have said that in all their lives they'd hardly expect anything to matter quite so much: that was how it felt – like a moment you'd lived for and would live *on* afterwards. Glancing round, Wishart saw them feeling it, and murmured, 'Easy does it, now. This'll be an attack like any other… Slow together. Up periscope.'

'HE right ahead, sir.' Weatherspoon added, 'About three hundred revolutions, sir.'

'*Goeben's* maximum is about three-twenty.' Jake said it for Wishart's information. He'd done his homework. Wishart had finished a precautionary all-round search and he was rock-still again, watching his target.

'Stand by to start the attack.'

'Standing by, sir.' Jake's finger on the button of the stop-watch.

'Starboard ten.'

'Starboard ten, sir.' Roost span his wheel. Even Roost, behind those flashing spokes, was under tension. Muscles at each side of his square jaw bulged in and out like pulses, and for Roost this was about the equivalent of a fit of hysterics. 'Ten 'o starboard wheel on, sir.' 'Start the attack. She bears – *that*. Range—' Jake noted range and bearing and began to lay it off on the plotting sheet. 'Masts are in line bearing—' He checked it, and it hadn't changed. So enemy course was two-two-oh, Jake noted. Wishart said, 'I'm opening off-track on her starboard bow. Midships.'

'Midships, sir.'

'Down periscope. Steer oh-one-oh.'

'Steer oh-one-oh, sir.'

The time of starting the attack was zero minutes. Jake marked *Goeben*'s position on the diagram accordingly. When Wishart gave him a second fix on her he'd measure the distance between the two points and estimate her speed. Meanwhile he had to keep the submarine's own track, her courses and speed, up to date, extending the pencil record of it every few seconds, because the second enemy range-and-bearing wouldn't be taken from the same place as the first had been.

'Course oh-one-oh, sir.'

'Half ahead together.'

Agnew pushed the telegraphs around. Wishart would be visualising the oncoming battlecruiser – her course, speed, range, her bearing from the submarine, the boat's own movements and the two ships' shifting positions relative to each other. You needed a kind of insight and a sportsman's eye and a touch of gambler's instinct too. Hobday, intently watching the trim, was ready to correct the smallest imbalance if one showed up. The greatest hazard was the possibility of varying densities, hitting a freshwater patch or an area of increased salinity. Such a phenomenon could hit them at any second, and if he or his 'planesmen were too slow to react and counter the change, the result could be disaster. You stuck to your own job and at the same time there was a moving picture in your brain of the shape of the developing attack. Wishart was taking the submarine out clear of *Goeben's* track so as to get into position to fire from her starboard bow. The torpedoes would be sent out ahead of her so that they'd strike her finally at an angle of ninety degrees, on her beam. If they were aimed right and she held her course, they and *Goeben* would converge and meet.

'Slow together. Up.' The periscope was already rising. McVeigh watched him all the time and acted on periscope orders before they could be uttered. McVeigh was like a fighter poised for the bell to start the fight: on his toes, crouched a bit, beard bristling. As if he had springs inside him. Wishart, with his eyes at the lenses, asked Jake, 'Masthead height's what, a hundred and sixty?'

'Hundred and eighty, sir.'

You needed that height, for periscope ranging. You took the angle subtended by waterline and masthead; the periscope's graticulated glass was marked off in one degree spaces. (In high power you had to remember to divide the angle by four.) With that angle, and knowing the vertical height, you had a range that was the baseline of a right-angled triangle. Wishart gave Jake his second range-and-bearing, and pushed the handles up. 'Down. Half ahead together. Starboard ten.'

Circling round to port, increasing the off-track range slightly as he brought her right around to end up on a firing course. Joining Jake now at the chart table.

'Two-two-oh's dead right if she hasn't altered. And twenty knots won't be far out. Give you another set of figures in a minute.' He'd absorbed the plot's information and now he was going back to the periscope. 'Ease to five.'

'Ease to five, sir... Five o' starboard wheel on, sir.'

'Tell the TI I'll be firing both bow tubes, to start with. Midships.'

'Midships, sir. Wheel's—'

'Steer one-three-oh.'

'One-three-oh, sir!'

'Slow ahead together.'

Roost was easing the helm as she approached her firing course. Wishart was reducing speed each time he pushed the periscope up, because at lower speeds there'd be less feather where it cut through the calm surface. Calm-ish, anyway. But there was enough white flecking for reasonable security, thank God. The closer E.57 came to her target, the briefer would be her periscope's appearances.

'Twenty-two feet.'

'Twenty-two, sir.'

To show less periscope. The less that stuck out, the less there was to catch an enemy eye. The alternative to holding the boat a couple of feet deeper would be to lie or crouch low, not have the stick hoisted right up. The best answer was a bit of both. Wishart muttered, 'May they all be cross-eyed with schnapps. Up periscope.'

'Course one-three-oh, sir!'

'Twenty-two feet, sir.'

'Very good.' He jerked down the handles. 'Stand by for enemy range-and-bearing.'

Up for'ard in the tube space CPO Rinkpole, with Blackie Cole and Close-'aul Anderson, was going through the routine of bringing his bow tubes to the stand-by position. Firing reservoirs had been charged, shutter doors opened and the clutch reported clear. Now they were blowing water up from the WRT tanks to surround the fish inside the tubes and at the same time equalise the pressure inside with that beyond the sluice doors, the front caps of the tubes, so that those doors could be opened.

'Starboard tube full!'

Rinkpole shut off the air to the starboard WRT. Cole reported the port tube full as well. You knew when they were full because water shot out of the vents. So much machinery, pipes, pumps, wheels, air-bottles and so on in this cramped, cave-like space that the torpedomen had to worm about like reptiles.

'Open sluice doors!'

There was a wheel with geared shafts on each tube. The shutter doors, beyond the sluice doors, were opened or shut by one larger, central wheel, between the tubes. Stinking hot... Anderson was using both his hands now; his messmates had got tired of his famous broken wrist and he'd been shamed into declaring it fit for use again.

'Clutch up side-stops to firing bars!'

When the firing mechanism was activated, the side-stops that held the fish from sliding about inside the tubes were automatically withdrawn. Rinkpole saw those connections made. He ordered, 'Open screw-down outboard vents', and reported back via Lewis to the control room that bow tubes were standing by. Wishart had already received a similar report on the stern tube from AB Smith, and Finn had the beam tubes standing by as well. Wishart sent the big periscope down and moved to the smaller, after one, the attack periscope. He ordered, 'Bow tubes to the ready.'

'Open stand-by valves.' Rinkpole snapped it, and Cole and Anderson moved like lightning: 'Tube ready, tripper down, vent closed!'

Rinkpole eased the two safety-pins out of the firing gear. He called back to the control room, 'Bow tubes ready.' Wishart could fire electrically from the periscope now; alternatively, Rinkpole could do it in the tube-space by hand, triggering the shots from his wooden seat between the white-enamelled tubes. In his mind the TI was whispering to his torpedoes, his babies whom he'd nursed and cosseted for so long against just such a moment and purpose as this one; he was asking them, *Now don't you go and let me down, my dears…*

—

Deep in the ship's belly, as far below the waterline as E.57 would be at periscope depth and with half a dozen vertical ladders and solid hatches between this point and the nearest exit to fresh air, the messdeck was identical to the one they'd come to before. And there was a hatch in it and a ladder leading down, just as there had been from that other one. The *kapitan-leutnant* sent them down it; he had a revolver in his fist and, behind him, a sailor with a rifle and bayonet.

Nick went down – into a flat with a hammock-netting and a door through to a bathroom flat. And in this space at the foot of the ladder where the hammock stowage was, one bulkhead was faced with concrete…

It was like a dream with elements of reality distorted, lopsided, a nightmare in which you'd come to a place you'd been in before, and yet hadn't. The effect was muddling, disorientating, and when you set it into the background knowledge that somewhere quite close by there was a burning fuse and enough explosive to split the ship's side open… He got it, suddenly. The mess-deck above them now had to be immediately aft of 'their' messdeck. This bathroom flat would share plumbing with that other one – adjoining it, and with only a thin sheet of steel dividing the two. The two access flats connected with the washplaces in an athwartships direction and must be similarly close. That concrete-strengthened ship's side bulkhead ran along the outside of both. It meant that the guncotton and the smouldering fuse could be no more than ten feet from where he stood now as Burtenshaw, white-faced, came down the ladder to join him.

The *kapitan-leutnant* sat in the hatchway above them, pistol held loosely in one hand with its barrel pointing downwards, towards them. He was looking up into the messdeck, passing some order to the attendant rifleman.

'What's that he's saying?'

'Telling him to report that we're in 4C messdeck's washplace. There's a telephone just up there, apparently.'

'How long a fuse did you set?'

They were both whispering, with their backs to the man on the ladder up above them.

'The whole lot. I don't know how much there was. I should have cut it to a set time but I didn't think of it. I don't *know* how long.'

'Half an hour? An hour?'

'I tell you I don't *know*...'

Or he wasn't capable of putting his mind to it. He looked terrible. Not only sheet-white, but sweaty, wet-faced. He'd muttered on the way down, 'We can't just stay there – to be blown up or drowned, like rats in a trap—' The *kapitan-leutnant* had shut him up, then, while Nick had thought about rats in traps, and that German U-boat they'd drowned here in the Marmara, and thoughts like

tit for tat… Burtenshaw said it again now: 'We can't just –
stay here, and—'

'We can't do anything else, Bob.'

It was what they'd come for. What a submarine and
her whole crew had risked their necks for. And Reaper
had said, 'Any effort – or cost.'

–

Wishart had accepted Jake's estimated enemy course and
speed of two-one-eight, nineteen knots. He threw a
glance at McVeigh, and the attack periscope slid up.
'Watch your depth!'

She'd slipped downwards by six inches. Coming back
up now. Wishart was crouched at the periscope with his
knees bent and his arms draped gorilla-fashion over the
spread handles. McVeigh's pink-rimmed eyes never left
him. Young Agnew was twitching with excitement and
trying not to show it. ERA Geordie Knight, usually calm
and placid, was flushed, aggressive-looking. Stoker Adams
was stooped like a mantis, breathing jerkily, eyes glaring
under jutting brows. Ellery quick-eyed, hovering behind
Wishart. Wishart had the periscope set at the firing-angle
he'd worked out; he trained left now though, checking
on how far his target had to come before her stem would
cross the hairline in the glass. Resetting it before he sent it
downward: and now he'd stopped it, brought it whizzing
up again. Bit of a periscope artist, Aubrey Wishart. He was
making one more quick check: and snapping the handle
up. 'Down.' On his knees: counting seconds like a man
praying. He moved his fingers, curling their tips upward
about an inch, and McVeigh caught the signal, pulled the
lever: the bronze tube was a pillar of greasy yellowish metal

skimming up. He grabbed the handles and stopped it three feet off the deck.

'Stand by.'

'Stand by, sir!'

Seconds crawling past. Jake, leaning over the chart table, shut his eyes and thought *Please, God…*

'Fire one!'

Triggering the starboard tube, he'd also given the order verbally in case the electrical firing system might have failed. A thud, long hiss of venting air, rising pressure in the boat: Wishart shouted, '*Damn* the bloody thing!' His eyes stayed at the lenses. Hobday had whipped round, and Wishart snapped, 'Fire two!' Another thud and hiss; that was the tube venting after the discharge and then filling from the compensating tank. Wishart ordered, in a state of fury, 'Port fifteen, port beam tube to the ready!' He snapped at McVeigh, 'Dip!' He meant him to lower the periscope and raise it again immediately: a periscope kept up for longish periods of time was far more likely to be spotted. Wishart told Hobday, 'First one broke surface and ran wild.' Pointing suddenly over Hobday's shoulder – 'Keep her *down*!'

Nineteen feet – eighteen – and bow-up angle increasing. Sixteen…

'Open "A" kingston!'

For'ard, Rinkpole felt the upward lurch and heard the order to flood that for'ard tank. He guessed there'd been some hang-up in the timing of the inflow of water compensating for the loss of the torpedoes' weight, and that Hobday couldn't have seen the upset quickly enough to have dealt with it before she started tilting up. Now the bow dipped from the extra weight in 'A': she was bow-down, diving. He ordered, 'Shut sluice doors!' One of his fish – the one he'd done a routine on and then dreamt about – had run amok, and he was shamed, mortified. Climbing off his seat he rasped at Anderson, 'Goin' aft to the beam tubes.' But Wishart's warning echoed in his memory: *We certainly shan't get* two *chances...*

On *Goeben's* bridge they'd seen the first torpedo leap almost right out of the water and then topple in a great splash and vanish. Steinhoff had barked a helm order and twenty-three thousand tons of German steel had heeled hard as she swung away to starboard, turning her bows towards any torpedo that might *not have* gone crazy. The battlecruiser had been about halfway through her turn when E.57's periscope standards, and then the top of her conning tower, had come foaming up into sight; another sharp command had increased the angle of rudders, tightening the turn in some hope of catching the submarine, ramming her. But she'd dipped under long before there was any chance of it, and a few seconds later the second fish had streaked past, leaving its effervescent trail fifty feet clear to port.

Helm was now reversed, to bring her back on course. There was a lot of shouting into voicepipes and telephones, and turrets were training back to where they'd started from. The English submariners had certainly got their boat down again quickly: but in terms of an attack they'd really made a mess of it.

Below, they'd felt the lurch and heel of the big ship's full-rudder turn, and heard the whirr of machinery as the turrets near them trained around; then they heard the *kapitan-leutnant* ordering the rifle-toting sailor to find out what was going on. He'd gone to the telephone on the messdeck up there, and Burtenshaw told Nick what he was doing. The man was coming back now, and reporting to his officer.

Burtenshaw said, 'There's been a torpedo attack. Missed. The submarine's well astern now.'

He was panting, needing a breath between each two or three words. Nick stared at the sick-looking face; he thought, *That only leaves us, then*... He felt ill himself: until now, he realised, there'd been some hope that they might not have had to see it right through to its highly unpleasant end. He told Burtenshaw – as much as anything to keep his spirits from rock-bottom – 'If or when the charge goes off, go straight up that ladder. Well, I'll lead, if you like – but don't think about his revolver, because for one thing he'll probably miss and for another he'll more likely be running like a rigger for the upper deck.'

Burtenshaw shook his head. 'When it goes off – I told you, it's *big*, there'll be no hope of—'

'Bob, there's always hope!'

Cock-and-bull, he thought. *And never know now, about Sarah*... But in the same mental breath he realised that he *did* know: as clearly as if she was speaking to him inside his head he knew for certain that he'd guessed the truth. And nobody else now would ever know it. Only Sarah herself. Would she ever tell the child, he wondered? She might: honesty, her forthrightness, might make her do it. But on the other hand – Burtenshaw's eyes on him, all fear as they shifted to the bulkhead, visualising (Nick guessed) the explosion, the steel splitting and the concrete cracking open, the inrush of sea and the hatch up there slamming shut on them: Nick shut his mind to it, tried to shut it also to the sense of suffocation, claustrophobia much stronger

337

than anything he'd felt in Wishart's submarine. He told himself that Sarah would *not* tell her – *his* – child the truth, because she'd realise that to do so would be to shift the guilt, lump a burden on the child which it had done nothing to deserve. Not its fault, and not Sarah's: only his, Nick Everard's, and he'd be gone, leaving her to carry it alone. Burtenshaw whispered hoarsely, his eyes frantic, 'Don't you feel *anything*?'

Difficult to know, for a moment, what he'd meant. Nick had closed his eyes: like a long, slow blink. Now he'd opened them and nodded. Burtenshaw was glistening: all sweat. Nick was too: thinking about it, he could feel it.

'Yes. As much as you do, probably.'

Or more. Like a suppressed scream in the mind, a scream you needed to let out and couldn't. Not *shouldn't*, but *could not*. Like the man up top who knew your uncle and coldly, politely, sentenced you to this. Expressionless, to all intents and purposes mute – as Sarah would have to be about the most important, vital thing in all her life. She'd have the urge to scream it, too. If one could have grovelled, sobbed or—

Please God, let us out of this?

–

Wishart had spun her fast to starboard, using one screw full ahead and the other full astern, risking the trim they'd only just recovered and weren't too sure of yet – risking *anything* for the unexpected second chance. A very long-shot chance – if it existed at all. Long range, and with the submarine badly placed; she was just about on the German's beam, which meant the fish would approach him from abaft it, actually having to chase after him to some extent instead of going in to meet him at something like right-angles to his course.

They'd been deep, struggling with a haywire trim. When Hobday had regained control and they'd got back up to periscope depth Wishart had expected to see nothing more than *Goeben's* smoke as she steamed away towards the Dardanelles.

Rinkpole reported from the beam tube space, 'Starboard beam tube ready!'

'Up periscope.' He'd only briefly dipped it. 'Stand by. Ship's head?'

'Two-six-oh, sir.'

'Twenty-one feet, sir—'

'Fire!'

He'd slammed the handles up. 'Thirty feet. Full ahead port. Port fifteen. Port beam tube to the ready.'

Another shot – at even longer range and a still worse angle?

'Thirty feet, sir.' Hobday wasn't taking his eyes off the trim for a second, this time. He'd no idea what had gone wrong before. Agnew had swung the telegraphs around and Roost had spun his wheel; Rinkpole called, 'Port beam tube ready, sir!' Firing from this other beam would mean sending the fish off to chase *Goeben* from her quarter. The rate of closing, Jake realised, subtracting *Goeben's* speed from the torpedo's, wouldn't be much more than twenty knots.

'Slow ahead both.' Wishart watched her head as she swung. If that last fish had been going to hit, Jake thought, they'd have heard the bang by this time. Range, torpedo speed and stop-watch time told him so quite clearly.

Wishart said, 'Midships. Steer oh-six-five. Twenty-two feet.'

'Twenty-two, sir.'

The 'planes angled to bring her closer to the surface. Twenty-five feet. Twenty-four.

'Up periscope.'

The small, low-powered one again. Even at this range he wasn't taking chances of being spotted.

The *boom* of the torpedo exploding was a smaller sound than they'd have expected. The long range, of course – and the much louder bangs they'd been subjected to in the straits. It was such a small sound that Jake hadn't thought of it as a hit at all. But now shockwaves following the explosion came like a double echo to confirm success: unless, of course, the fish had only dived and exploded on the bottom... Wishart grabbed the periscope's handles, jerked them down and put his eye to the single lens. They heard him gasp, saw the flash of incredulity and then joy. He'd swallowed, found his voice.

'Right aft. God, what a *fluke*!'

He whooped, suddenly, flung his arms up, did a little dance. Men were cheering, slapping each other on the back. CPO Crabb muttered, glowering at his depth-gauge, 'Bloody mad'ouse...'

–

As the crash of the torpedo-hit boomed and shuddered through the ship, for a second Nick's taut nerves reacted as if it had been the much closer, louder bang which he'd been expecting, trying to be ready for. In that second he thought his heart had stopped: and beside him Burten-shaw had jerked rigid as if he'd had an electric shock...

Then there was a stillness, a sensation of the surroundings dying: and *that*, Nick realised as reality and sense came back, was the machinery slowing, stopping. Lights began to flicker and weaken as power failed. Somewhere in the distance there was muffled shouting and an alarm–bell ringing: and immediately above their heads the *kapitan-leutnant* was sending his man to the telephone again, to find out what was happening. Burtenshaw croaked, 'Make a dash for it?'

The man on the ladder was watching them. In the half-light his face was indistinct but Nick had an impression that he was smiling, *hoping* they'd try to rush him. Imagination, perhaps: but he could see the pistol, light gleaming on its barrel. Also, they could hear the sailor bawling into the telephone: and now it sounded as if he'd got an answer, that he was in conversation with someone up there.

Nick muttered, 'Must have taken a second crack at it, out of his stern tube or a beam one.'

He *hoped* that was it. And that the hit had been in some vital spot, not something they'd be able to deal with and get the ship moving again. If she was stopped permanently she'd be a sitting duck, at Wishart's mercy.

Burtenshaw suggested in a hoarse, pleading whisper, 'If she's done for couldn't we give up now?'

'Wait.' Overhead, the sailor was back and reporting to the *leutnant*. 'What's he telling him?'

'I missed the start of it, but—'

The *kapitan-leutnant* was shouting down to them in German. Nick caught one word – a German version of 'torpedo'. He could have cheered – for Wishart, and with personal relief; but relief was premature, because the guncotton could blast them at any moment. Burtenshaw translated in a fast, excited gabble, 'It was a torpedo-hit aft and she's stopped because the steering's smashed and they think one shaft as well. He says they're finished anyway so why don't we—'

'Yes.' Nick cut him short. 'Tell him we'll disarm the charge.'

Or rather, he thought, as the Marine began shouting up towards the hatch, *You'll* disarm it... But he'd go with him, to see he didn't bungle it. It was a matter of getting to that other messdeck and down to its bathroom flat, digging the case out from the hammocks and yanking the detonator out of the explosive. It would serve no purpose to have it go off; if *Goeben* was immobilised, the job – Reaper's job – was done.

Chapter 14

'What we knocked off was her main rudder. She had two, you know, one behind the other. Stern's so narrow they couldn't fit 'em side by side, and they needed a certain rudder area and that's how they achieved it. The little one on its own is quite useless. But we'd bent the port shaft too, and made quite a decent hole in her quarter, with surprisingly extensive flooding.'

Wishart was filling in some details of the story, in Truman's cabin aboard *Terrapin*, at anchor in the entrance to the Bosphorus. Truman wasn't present; he'd been summoned to an interview with the Chief of Staff, aboard the flagship. Wishart was telling the story mainly for the benefit of Johnny Treat, his navigator who'd been stricken with appendicitis back in Mudros. Treat had come through as a passenger in one of the other destroyers; he was still pale, convalescent-looking, and fed up at having missed this Dardanelles trip which looked sure to have been the last offensive submarine patrol of the war.

His CO went on, 'I had the other beam tube ready, and the stern tube as well. After that hit she'd stopped, so of course we were able to catch up with her quickly enough, and I was about to make a real job of it at close range when damn me if I didn't see her ensign being struck. By courtesy of Everard here. He'd had the gall to point out to the German commodore that they'd no hope of getting anywhere – except to the bottom when we put some more fish into her – and that it'd be Turkish colours, not German, that he'd be hauling down, and that even if by some miracle he managed to get her back into Constantinople it'd be about as humiliating for him as anything could be… Not bad, on the spur of the moment, and after spending half an hour or more sitting on a bomb. Eh?'

Reaper nodded. 'Not at all bad.'

'They weren't far off shooting us as spies.' Nick explained, 'The mind does tend to concentrate.'

'Whatever the circumstances—' Reaper stubbed out a cigarette – 'the fact remains, it worked. And the Commander-in-Chief is by no means displeased. As you'll be discovering for yourselves presently.' He looked from Nick to Wishart. 'Both of you. What's impressed him most, apart from the achievement of the desired result, is the way you pushed ahead with the operation in the face of numerous setbacks. *Louve* – Robins – the lack of a reception committee for the landing party…' He glanced up. 'Oh, one thing I'd best mention – the Admiral has had champagne put on ice for us.'

Wishart licked his lips. 'Crikey.'

'His flag lieutenant was kind enough to warn me. In case any of us had thought of taking a stiffener before we went.'

Great days were upon them suddenly…

The war wasn't *quite* dead. But the German fleet had mutinied. Admiral Scheer had been preparing a fleet sortie, offensive action that would have led to a showdown such as the Royal Navy had been praying for ever since

344

the inconclusive results of Jutland. But the men of the High Seas Fleet had refused to take the Kaiser's ships to sea. They'd seen enough of British guns at Jutland: their propagandists might claim they'd won that battle, but it was significant that they weren't ready to come to the test again. Significant, and also bitterly disappointing for the Royal Navy.

The news had come yesterday by signal. So in the letter that Nick had just had from his uncle, in the first mail to be brought through to Constantinople, there'd been mention of the battle that was expected. By now, Vice-Admiral Sir Hugh Everard would be as disappointed as any other of Beatty's officers. As Beatty himself must be... But Hugh Everard had had no other news. He'd not seen or heard from Sarah. So the sense of vacuum persisted: and Nick realised, after he'd read quickly through the letter, that he'd been *expecting* news – of Sarah, and of the kind he'd guessed at. Because Sarah might have arranged for him to hear of it through his uncle. Because she couldn't send it to him herself, directly, and also because – well, if he'd been right with that other piece of guesswork, the idea that he and she were never to discuss it or even to admit that there could be anything *to* discuss... Family news, reaching him by a roundabout route of her own devising – implying nothing, compromising no one...

Well, it *could* have been like that.

Nick had never appreciated how deeply his uncle felt for Sarah until a few months ago when Hugh had come to visit him in hospital, after the Zeebrugge raid. He'd said quietly, privately, 'Look after her, Nick, if she should ever need it. *I* should, if I were ever in a position to be of service – but none of us can tell what's in store... I know

345

you're fond of her, and that she is of you; and we both know she's drawn a wrong card, eh? She'll not complain of anything – she's too brave, by half – I mean she'd never *ask* for help. That's my point – without asking, she may need it. Be ready, Nick, and a weather eye open?'

If he had any sense of shame or guilt, it was from knowing how shocked Hugh Everard would be if *he* knew. Nick had a greater respect and affection for his uncle than he had for any other man on earth.

Coming out of his thoughts, he focused on Reaper, who'd just lit another cigarette and was regarding him steadily through its smoke.

'Well, Everard? Now this is over, what's *your* future?'

In the long run – unpredictable. In the more immediate sense it was cut-and-dried and dull as ditchwater. He told Reaper, 'Suppose I'll beg a passage to Mudros, to take up my appointment to *Leveret.*'

'Ah.' Reaper blinked. '*Leveret.* Quite.'

Something odd in his expression, though. Some private knowledge or speculation?

As if he was holding back a laugh… And Nick was back in memory in a room in a requisitioned boardinghouse overlooking the destroyer anchorage in Dover harbour; he'd faced Reaper across a work-littered table and tried to mask his disappointment at the news that he was to join *Bravo* – a shaky old relic, outdated and outworn. Nobody had mentioned that he was being appointed *in command.*

Reaper was wearing that same secretive, tricky look that he'd worn then. He murmured, watching smoke drift towards the deck-head, 'Yes. Of course.' Johnny Treat, Wishart's navigator, asked, 'What happened to the Marine?'

Reaper turned to answer him. 'Burtenshaw is busy demolishing gun-emplacements and other fortifications in the Dardanelles. It's what he knows about, d'you see.'

There'd been some demolition and gun-spiking by landing-parties from destroyers moving up-straits behind the mine-sweepers, but only a preliminary clearance, enough to ensure the safe passage of the fleet. It had been a biggish fleet that had come through, a procession of warships sixteen miles long. Most of them had been British, but there'd been some French and Greek flags among the White Ensigns. The Greek battleships *Kilkis* and *Lemnos*, for instance, which, before they'd been presented to the Greeks, had been the USS *Idaho* and *Mississippi*.

Nothing German floated here now. *Goeben* lay in the shallows of the Gulf of Izmid, where if her bulkheads collapsed from the weight of water inside her she'd have a soft bottom to sit down on. She'd struggled into the gulf on one screw and well down by the stern, and lain for nearly a fortnight with E.57's reloaded bow tubes trained on her while her own men removed the breechblocks from her guns and the warheads from her torpedoes. Nick, as prize master, had supervised this drawing of her teeth.

A fair part of the British force that was anchored here now would be going through the Bosphorus in a day or two, into the Black Sea. Reaper, who was abreast of all the Intelligence reports, had said they'd probably see action soon enough. If not against Bolshevik-manned warships, at least in support of shore operations. General Denikin's drive into the Caucasus, for instance: he had 30,000 White Russians in his force, and the Cabinet in London had decided that he should be supplied and supported through Novorossisk, which he'd captured from the Reds at the end of August. And there was another White army in the Crimea: and the new Republic of Georgia, which had declared its independence from the Bolsheviks, was most likely going to need help in defending its littoral and the oil port of Batum against invasion from the north.

Action soon, then: and *Terrapin*, this destroyer in which he was sitting so comfortably now, was to be part of the squadron that was going in. While he, Nick, would be back in the Aegean, his enemies boredom, officialdom, envy of *these* people... Reaper was looking at his watch. The motorboat had just been called away, and presently it would be lying at the gangway waiting to carry the three of them to the flagship. Reaper nodded: 'Five minutes. Are we all chamfered up?'

Spit and polish for the C-in-C. Admiral Sir Somerset A. Gough-Calthorpe had scored his own huge success: his armistice negotiations had been brilliantly conducted, entirely off his own bat, and the extent of his command and responsibilities was enormous now: he was High Commissioner of Turkey, Commander-in-Chief of the Mediterranean and of the Atlantic as far as Cape St Vincent: the Black Sea, Caspian, Red Sea and the Danube were all in his command. General Allenby was his subordinate: Gough-Calthorpe, in fact, was God, so far as the Middle East was concerned. Wishart suggested to Nick, 'If you want passage westward, wait two days and you can come back with us. That'll make *two* passengers – you and Jake Cameron.'

'Well, that's very kind, and—'

Reaper interrupted. 'He may *not* be requiring passage westward.'

'Sir?'

'Would you be terribly chagrined, Everard, if someone else took over *Leveret*?'

So he'd been right about that hooded, secretive look. He sat watching Reaper, waiting for whatever this new thing was. Not allowing himself to hope *too* strongly...

'Well?'

'No, sir. I'd presume there was some – some interesting alternative.'

Reaper laid his half-cigarette down in the silver ashtray.

'Following the mutiny in the High Seas Fleet, a German naval surrender has to be prepared for. Amongst other needs is that for officers in certain categories of seniority and command experience who speak good German. Chaps of that sort are wanted back home immediately. And—' he paused, just fractionally – 'Lieutenant Commander Truman is one of them. Consequently—'

'*Terrapin!*'

'Damn it, if you'd allow me—'

'I'm sorry, sir.'

'As you say – *Terrapin*. I've suggested to the Chief-of-Staff that you might be considered suitable to relieve Truman in command. Should he agree, and should the Admiral concur, a signal will have been exchanged by now, I imagine, with Captain (D) in Mudros. On the other hand—'

On the other hand...

At odds of ten to one on, it would have been agreed by now. If Truman was to be relieved, he'd have to be relieved at once, since *Terrapin* had been earmarked for the Black Sea expedition. What other destroyer captain would they find available here at Constantinople? Reaper knew it too:

if he hadn't been sure of it he wouldn't have raised the subject, not until he'd had an answer to his proposal. Nor, probably – come to think of it – would he have expanded as he had earlier on the subject of what awaited a Royal Navy squadron on the other side of the Bosphorus.

He wouldn't be grinning at him like that, either.

Wishart was smiling too. Benign, big-brotherly: fresh from the deep minefields and the nets.

Nick found himself on his feet. 'Sir – I really don't know what to say, I—'

'Let it wait, then.' Reaper stood up too. 'Over the champagne, I dare say you'll think of something.'

Author's Note

The Englishwoman who appears here as the Grey Lady was in fact known — according to Francis Yeats-Brown in his book *Golden Horn* — as the White Lady of Pera. In using her as a fictional character it seemed best to change her shade. But she did (Yeats-Brown records) buy General Liman von Sanders's Mercedes Benz tourer, for the purposes stated and from his soldier driver, and for a while she had it guarded by a performing bear.

Enver, Talaat and Djemal escaped that night while the fuses were drawn, but all three came to sticky ends soon after. And *Goeben*, when Admiral Gough-Calthorpe reached Constantinople, was indeed in the Gulf of Izmid and, with extensive flooding aft, was moored in shallow water in case she foundered.

For readers to whom technicalities are of interest I would mention that details of E.57 were obtained from builders' plans in the National Maritime Museum at Greenwich, and from *General Orders for Submarines 1913, Notes for Officers under Instruction November 1918* and an E-class crew-list and watchbill, all in the RN Submarine Museum at Fort Blockhouse, Gosport.

The submarine-ambush episode is factually based. It happened in 1915. The French submarine captured intact by the Turks was the *Turquoise*, and operation orders found in her led to the German submarine UB 15 keeping a prearranged rendezvous with the British E.20. E.20, a sitting duck, was torpedoed and lost with all hands.

E.57 is of course a fictional creation; only 56 E.'s entered service. But Saxton White's attempt to reach *Goeben* in E.14, after the German sortie in which the monitors were sunk, did take place and did result in the loss of E.14 and the death and posthumous VC of her captain. White's was in fact E.14's second VC: the first had been awarded to Lt.-Cdr. E.C. Boyle, who commanded her in 1915.

A.F.